The Last of Days

The Last of Days

PAUL DOHERTY

headline

First published in 2013 by
HEADLINE PUBLISHING GROUP

1

Cataloguing in Publication Data is available from the British Library

ISBN 978 0 7553 9784 6 (Hardback)
ISBN 978 0 7553 9785 3 (Trade paperback)

Typeset in Sabon LT Std by Palimpsest Book Production Limited,
Falkirk, Stirlingshire

Printed and bound in Great Britain by
Clays Ltd, St Ives plc

Headline's policy is to use papers that are natural,
renewable and recyclable products and made from wood grown
in sustainable forests. The logging and manufacturing processes
are expected to conform to the environmental regulations
of the country of origin.

HEADLINE PUBLISHING GROUP
An Hachette UK Company
338 Euston Road
London NW1 3BH

www.headline.co.uk
www.hachette.co.uk

As always, to my beloved wife Carla.

Historical Characters

The House of Tudor

Henry VII (1485–1509): victor of Bosworth, founder of the Tudor dynasty

Henry VIII: King of England (1491–47)

Henry Fitzroy: Duke of Richmond (1519–36): bastard son of Henry VIII by his mistress Bessie Blunt

Edward VI (1537–53): Henry VIII's sole male heir by Jane Seymour

Mary (1516–58): daughter of Henry VIII and Catherine of Aragon

Elizabeth (1533–1603): daughter of Henry VIII and Anne Boleyn

Henry VIII's wives

Catherine of Aragon (died 1536)

Anne Boleyn (executed 1536)

Jane Seymour (died 1537)

Anne of Cleves (divorced 1539)

Katherine Howard (executed 1542)
Katherine Parr (died 1548)

The House of York
Edward IV: king 1471–83
Edward and Richard: sons of Edward IV, both mysteri-
ously disappeared whilst lodged in the Tower of London
Elizabeth of York: daughter of Edward IV, wife of Henry
VII, mother of Henry VIII
Richard III: king 1483–85, brother of Edward IV

Henry VIII's ministers
Thomas Wolsey (1473–1530): Cardinal Archbishop of
York, Henry's principal minister before falling into
disgrace
Thomas Cromwell (1485–1540): chief minister to Henry
VIII, executed 1540
Thomas More (1478–1535): humanist, scholar and
statesman, executed 1535

Henry VIII's Council 1546–47
Edward Seymour: first Earl of Hertford, courtier and
general
Thomas Seymour: brother of the above, courtier and
admiral
John Dudley: son of Edmund Dudley (executed by
Henry VIII), courtier and soldier
Sir William Paget: self-made courtier and secretary to
the Council

Thomas Wriothesley: chancellor under Henry VIII

Thomas Cranmer: scholar, Henry VIII's confessor and Archbishop of Canterbury; presided over Henry VIII's divorce and his break with Rome

Stephen Gardiner: scholar, Bishop of Winchester; a conservative, secretly a Romanist who wanted England to return to the Church of Rome

Thomas Howard: third Duke of Norfolk; one of Henry's principal ministers

Henry Howard: Earl of Surrey, son of the above, executed 1547

Foreign rulers

Charles V: Holy Roman Emperor, nephew of Catherine of Aragon

Francis I: King of France, contemporary and rival of Henry VIII

Prologue

In the wilds of Lincolnshire, at the very heart of the Fens, there once stood a sprawling gloomy tavern called the Hoop of Hades. God knows why, but this place had acquired a fearsome reputation as the gathering hall for devils. The tavern once served local villages totally annihilated during the Great Pestilence. Now, according to legend, on St Walpurgis Eve, the vigil of All Saints, a local necromancer could summon in all the demons and ghosts who roamed the surrounding wastelands. I freely admit, demons from Hell do not frighten me. I have met so many in the flesh, I would hardly turn a hair if an evil sprite popped up to confront me in a Cheapside alleyway. Nevertheless, this legend fascinates me, because in order to achieve this great summoning the necromancer had to use a chamber at the heart of the tavern called Haceldema – 'the Place of Blood'. An interesting conceit which I can only report, as both tavern and chamber were burnt to the ground during the Great Revolt against His Malignant Majesty King Henry VIII in that unholy Year of Our Lord 1536.

This journal, by my good self, Will Somers, is my gathering place. I was born in the year of terror 1485, when the present king's father toppled Richard III at Bosworth. To be sure, I have travelled far since then, in body as well as soul. I first glimpsed the light of day at Much Wenlock, in Shropshire. In my tenth year, my family moved to Easton Neston in Northamptonshire, where I entered the service of a local lord, Sir Richard Fermor. I graduated as his minstrel, fool, jester, innocent; whatever men wish to call me. In 1525, the year Rome was savagely sacked, I met our present King Henry at Greenwich. My master, Sir Richard, allowed me to perform at a royal banquet and there I pitched my standard. In brief, I made Henry laugh until the tears poured down those smooth, round royal cheeks and those light blue eyes, which later froze into icicles of pure terror, brimmed with merriment. Henry threw coins at me, bribed my master and cosseted me like a woman with her babe until I entered his service.

Oh, those were the golden days when the royal lion was magnificent in size, spirit and strength. A prince amongst princes who would stride out, one hand on my scrawny shoulder, the other looped around the arm of More, Wolsey or Cromwell. Of course he eventually sent all of these to the scaffold; as the skies clouded black, Henry's heart turned hard and the laughter finally ended.

All men talk to themselves, either directly or in

private. Henry talks to me. I have become his listening post, his whipping boy; a ready, always attentive audience for the royal tantrums, temper, tears and troubles. So, with Henry's knowledge, now, in these last of days, November 1546, I have begun this journal. Some twenty years have passed since I met the Merry Monarch of Greenwich, who has now shape-shifted to become the Malevolent Monster of Westminster. This journal will be my Haceldema, my place of blood, my gathering place, like that long-vanished tavern chamber. (I trust my own heart. Henry is plotting, and when that comes to full flower, blood will flow.) Here I will summon all the demons, and God knows their name is legion. First comes harsh-faced John Dudley, Viscount Lisle, son of a traitor, who has climbed through the tangled branches of politics' thorny tree. A dog of a man, a brutal but brave soldier, Dudley has pitched his standard alongside that of two other soldiers, Edward Seymour, Earl of Warwick, sly and subtle, and his proud-faced, womanising brother Thomas. These two have gained access to the Council because their sister, Henry's queen Jane Seymour, died giving birth to Henry's only male heir, the puny nine-year-old Edward. Others appear. Whey-faced Thomas Cranmer, Archbishop of Canterbury and, very rarely now, the King's conscience. Sir William Paget, vixen-eyed and sharp-featured; a self-made man, Paget has risen to be secretary to the Council and strives to maintain harmony amongst the wolf pack. Last, and certainly the worst of the wolves, Sir Thomas Wriothesley, the constant coat-turner and time-server who likes nothing more than to see a man (or, more deliciously, a woman), writhe in agony.

This league of self-serving, bloodthirsty opportunists are the reformists, dedicated to making the break with the Church of Rome deep and permanent. Confronting them are the Howards of Norfolk, led by Thomas Howard, third duke, a man steeped in years and guile. Norfolk is a heavy-eyed, long-faced hypocrite. At court he drapes rosaries and relics around his neck, but in his bed at Kenninghall he keeps his blowsy mistress, Bess Holland. Norfolk, like Paget, is secretive; both observe the rule 'Never tell a secret to more than one person'. He is always accompanied by his son, who is a far better man. Henry Howard, Earl of Surrey, is a roaring boy, a soldier, a courtier, and above all, something more lasting: a brilliant poet, whose verses dazzle the mind and catch the heart. With his wayward eye and foppish ways, he has one vice: an overweening arrogance. Perhaps Surrey has not forgotten, as Henry certainly has not, that the Howards fought against the Tudors at Bosworth, and that his grandfather won England's greatest victory of the age, the destruction of James IV and all the flower of Scottish chivalry at Flodden Field. While the Seymours crouch close to the throne through poor dead Jane, the Howards crawl more slowly. Norfolk's daughter was married to the King's only bastard son, Henry Fitzroy, Duke of Richmond, but poor Fitzroy, of weak stock, died young, and his widow, if gossip is correct, has certainly caught our king's lecherous eye. In politics, the Norfolks are like the others: self, self and self again. In religion, they hark back to the Church of Rome. They are guided in this by the jug-eared, proud-hearted Stephen Gardiner, Bishop of Winchester.

In the antechamber beyond, to continue the metaphor, others wait. Princess Mary, sallow-featured but kindly-eyed, constantly mourns her dead mother, Catherine of Aragon. Henry's sixth wife, the prim, pure Katherine Parr, also mourns, or so I think. She grieves at being locked and chained to her royal husband, whilst secretly cherishing, perhaps, the unmasked admiration of the lecherous Thomas Seymour. Somewhere too, but deep, deep in the shadows, stands Balaam, son of Beor, the man with the far-seeing gaze. Oh yes, Balaam the spy, the scurrier, the twilight man, always cloaked in the dappled shadow of secrecy. He is Princess Mary's link with those abroad who watch like hawks the maze of treacherous politics that has become the English court, and those rash or brave enough to thread that maze. All these assemble here in this journal, my Haceldema. They wait to dance attendance on their dread lord, the Master of Menace, the leader of the swirling, dangerous masque, Henry the King. No longer is Henry the golden-haired, fair-bonneted chevalier, resplendent in face and form. No, he has grown gross and heavy, eyes black slits in his podgy, moon-like face. A slow-moving mass of murderous deceit. '*Hola!*' as the Spanish say; the King has arrived and the swirling dance takes another sinister turn.

2 December 1546

I s our king dying? This constant question opened the doors of darkness and agitated my heart even as I returned to Westminster today. Henry, once the proudest monarch and the most glorious prince, is certainly declining, his sun setting in tawdry splendour. I was still pondering upon this when I disembarked at King's Steps to be met on the quayside by Sir Anthony Wingfield, Captain of the Spears, His Majesty's personal bodyguard of halberdiers. Scarlet-faced Wingfield, moustache and beard all bristly, questioned me closely about my journey along the river. He listened to my replies, nodded sagely and led me deep into Westminster Palace towards the King's secret chambers. It was late afternoon and the light was dying. Squares of pure wax glowed in their silver dishes. Torches flared beneath their caps in the cobbled yards, lamps glittered along the galleries. We passed empty chambers and rooms, the dwelling place of ghosts, though the palace kitchens

we went through seemed merry enough, their fleshing
tables heaped with slaughtered larks, storks, gannets,
capons and pheasants. Master Bricket, master chef and
a very valiant trencher-man, explained how he was
preparing a stew of sparrows, gelatines, and game pie
with a mess of cucumber lettuce and succulent herb
purslane, all favourites of the King.

Deeper into the palace we went, where the floors of
the chambers were strewn with fresh rushes, moist
and piquant to the smell. The royal presence chamber
I passed lay empty. The royal table on the dais was
unattended, though steaming dishes were still served
for the King by bare-headed courtiers who scuttled and
bowed as if they really were in the presence of His
Dread Majesty. In the antechamber councillors clustered
in their dark-furred robes, only the white of their
cambric shirts and the glitter of jewellery catching the
light. And yet, a true hall of shadows! A contagion, a
miasma seems to infect Westminster Palace, a place
crammed with the forfeited chattels of those caught up
in the furious thunder around the throne. Henry's court
remains steeped in dark deceits and false favours, a
shadow court paying service to a shadow king.

The King's sickness seems to infect the elegant
galleries, their ceilings marvellously wrought in stonework and gold. The news of his weakness creeps like
a ghost past the wainscoting of carved wood and a
thousand resplendent figurines in their countless niches.
Everything appears tarnished. The heavy gold- and

silver-thread tapestries are moth-nibbled. The thick glass in the mullion windows is stained and dirty. The courtyards, herb plots and gardens overlooked by these same windows remain weed-choked. The gilded butterflies of the court whisper how the King is past caring; oh, how wrong they are! He cares very much. He reminds me of a boar, heavy and shaggy-coated, hunted and wounded, so even more ferocious and dangerous for that. Memories of the past throng the dark chambers of Henry's marble heart. Is he trying to exorcise them? Is that why he wants me, Will Somers, hollow eyes in a lean face, shoulders hunched, in constant attendance upon him, as I have been for the last twenty years? I know Henry. He may be failing, but he is still plotting furiously, and that is why I keep this journal. I wish to chronicle these times, as well as record any coming storm.

This King is never more dangerous than when he broods. He worries about the ghosts of executed traitors that throng Westminster, unwilling to leave the goods seized from their estates: the purple-embroidered velvet bed coverings trimmed with gold that once belonged to Buckingham; the chamber furnishings of Edward Neville; the robes of the de la Poles, not to mention the fourteen thousand pounds of gold and silver, crosses and chalices looted from Cromwell's house at Austin Friars. Memories of those who served and failed him haunt my master. He mumbles how the ghosts of all the Thomases ring his bed at night: Wolsey, More and

Cromwell. They are brought by Thomas Becket, whose sanctity and relics the King so resolutely destroyed, blowing Becket's blissful bones from a cannon. Henry wakes in the dead of night and complains of these creatures of the mist, who cast no shadow in the moonlight, noiseless in their tread, fresh from the wastelands of the dead where no bird sings. All this rests heavily on our king, though not on his Council, that pack of ravenous wolves, greedy for power, those pernicious bloodsuckers of fallen men. As I passed through the chambers, I glimpsed my lords Dudley, Seymour, Wriothesley and others, Achitophels incarnate, all seemingly busy on this or that. In other rooms scurriers, couriers and messengers lounged booted and spurred, their horses ready in the freezing courtyards below to take messages across Henry's ice-bound kingdom.

A place of shifting murky light is how Goodman Balaam describes the palace. Long deserted galleries, fitfully lit; antechambers where those who move do so like the slippery shades of shape-shifters. The King's own inner chamber was closely guarded, its door half open. Inside, my lord Paget, that master of Hell, fur cloak still gleaming with river wet, as were his bonnet, beard and moustache. Paget's eyes glowed with cunning. Had he also been busy in the city and just returned? As always, I acted the humble commoner overcome by his surroundings. I kept my eyes down, shuffling my feet. In truth, the royal chamber is luxurious, hung with tapestries, chairs covered with cloth of gold, stools capped and cushioned with silk and taffeta. The purest candles glow and pots of smouldering dry herbs scent the air. Nevertheless, none of these can stifle the rank odour from the straw-covered urine flasks in their holdings or the stench of the close stools, their potted cisterns covered in black velvet fringed with silver. One of the King's trams, or moving chairs, stood half covered with tawny silk in a corner beneath a crucifix. His Satanic Majesty himself, clothed in a white bed shirt, his head towelled, sprawled on the great bed with its tester of scarlet, curtains of crimson and taffeta and counterpane of silk serge with golden-fringed pillows of the softest down. He lay back against the bolsters, a writing tray before him. On a table to his right were his rings and bracelets, placed there because the King's hands and joints are mightily swollen. These precious items, as always, caught my eye: rings set with diamonds, rubies and emeralds, all looted from ransacked monasteries. Precious stones of all kinds, including the Great Sapphire of Glastonbury, hacked from golden crosses. I suspect such plunder plays on our king's conscience.

Oh, how the mighty have fallen! His Majesty of England is no great prince now but a mass of bloated flesh and dry broken skin. I try to recall him in his prime. A painting by Master Holbein hanging in one of the royal palaces boasts of a time when this king was haughty and regal, fearing neither God nor man. All has changed. Gone are the gowns of scarlet and gold brocade, the crimson cloak and jewelled daggers.

No more the skirts slashed and puffed with white satin and clasped with jewelled brooches. No magnificent collars of twisted pearls and ruby medallions, no velvet cap jewelled and plumed with red and white feathers. The King is much declined, his eyes mere slits, black and gleaming. He uses glasses or spectacles, which he removes as he lifts his head; his lips are flaking, his cheeks and jowls sag and the skin of his face and hands has turned a puffy grey, dried and cracked, its bleeding dirtying the sheets and counter-pane. The stench from his body is offensive, and now, as he moved, fresh gusts of putridity wafted towards me. His Majesty was studying a document; he pushed this away and lay back as Physician Huicke, with Paget, Seymour and Dudley fawning behind him, made the most humble obeisance.

'Good Dr Huicke, good sweet Will.' The King's voice was piping and laboured, like that of a marsh bird, as if his very breath had to squeeze itself out. 'Good sirs, I am indisposed with fever again.' His Majesty glanced swiftly at me standing there in my green hooded jacket fringed with white craul, my red stockings pushed into dirty boots. For a few heartbeats he seemed to drop his mask of suffering, as if he was relishing playing the patient, those sunken slit eyes bright with malice. God be my witness, the chamber itself harboured a menace, as if foul spirits curled like vipers behind the tapestries, ready to lunge. Henry is the proudest of men and the self-styled most glorious prince, but he is a better

mummer than I. I recalled the legends about him. How
he had been likened to the Mouldwarp of ancient
prophecy, a hairy man, a royal devil with a hide like
goatskin who would first be praised before being cast
down by sin and pride. His Majesty has certainly lived
his life in war and strife, and in these, the last of days,
danger still presses in from every side. Those who
approach Westminster are terrified. They hang rue
around their necks as an amulet against witchcraft and
put sprigs of mountain ash and honeysuckle in the
harness of their horses against the evil that allegedly
seeps from the King's decaying flesh.

His Majesty is certainly sick in both mind and body.
He can no longer hunt, mount a horse or even climb
a step. He has, according to himself, the worst legs in
the world, and has to be carried up and down stairs
and move in a travelling chair from chamber to chamber.
He has two of these chairs, one upholstered in gold
velvet and silk, the other in russet, each of them complete
with brocaded footstools, for the royal legs are grossly
bloated and bruised. The physicians, in their long, fur-
sleeved gowns and black velvet caps, hover like carrion
birds. They wave their urine flasks and, like the fools
they are, constantly examine the King's water and close
stools. Balaam's spy in the Bucklebury Place spice
market, a man who moves easily among the apothecaries
and herbalists, has devised a list of the potions, plasters,
poultices, medications and elixirs being served to His
Majesty: capathol water and rhubarb pills, tablets of

rasis to fend off the plague, onions for his belly and greasy fomentations for his piles. Herbal mixtures and soft poultices are laid against His Majesty's head, feet, neck, spleen and anus. The King's face is swollen like a pig's bladder, his back is humped, whilst his legs, ever since a fall some years ago, throb like pangs of fire from open ulcers. He has concocted his own pulses made from marsh mallows, linseed, silver, red coral and dragon's blood, mixed with oil of roses and white wine. Yet despite all this, he is much fallen away, so unwell, considering his age and corpulence, he may not survive the winter. Sin, death and Hell have pressed their seals on this king, and all their retainers flock to attend on him.

I do not rejoice in such ruin. Henry reminds me of one of his tawny-coated lions kept in a cage at the Tower; Princeps was its name, a veritable prince amongst beasts, but it grew mangy, weak and wounded, though still dangerous. Henry the Magnificent, the striker-down of popes and princes, surveys his past and, believe me, mourns for what could have been. If only he'd begotten sons; not just sickly baby Edward or young Fitzroy, his bastard, now buried deep, but a pride of young lions to seal this kingdom as Tudor's fief once and for all. If a scribbler poet wrote a tragedy about this king, this is what he should describe: what might have been. How Henry strove for this dream yet, in the end, failed so disastrously. A tyrant, yes, but if I sift amongst the years, I detect a true greatness and majesty, though deeply flawed and heavily tainted by so much blood.

'I am ill.' The King's voice grew more strident, like the spoilt child he is. Eyes pleading desperately, he beat his fists against the bloodstained counterpane, demanding Physician Huicke attend him at once. Paget and the others withdrew, leaving only Huicke and myself. I helped the good doctor pull back the sheets and lifted the royal nightshirt to reveal the gruesome condition beneath. In truth, our king is a bolting hutch of beastliness. Ulcers perforate his legs, open fissures that Huicke tries to treat with horse hair and silk filament, tightening the skin around each ulcer so as to make it weep. The stench from the festering wounds is offensive. His Majesty lay cursing quietly, though now and again he would cry out for this person or that, some of whom are dead.

Next Huicke treated the King's bowels and belly, the latter so swollen and extended the stomach alone is fifty-five inches in circumference. His Majesty, laughing weakly at some comment made by me, complained bitterly how his bowels were so tight all journeys to the close stool had proved futile. He was then turned on his stomach, legs apart, his body sprawled like that of a huge sow on a fleshing table, much extended like a corpse left for days on a battlefield. No more than a great flabby sack of flesh, horrid to see, foulsome in smell, bruised and marked a purplish-blue.

'I am suffering,' His Majesty cried out, 'because of my sins against the innocents.'

'What innocents?' I retorted, thinking he was referring to Stafford, Duke of Buckingham, or the other great lords and ladies executed during his reign. The King, however, did not reply. He stretched out a puffy hand, picked up a set of coral Ave beads and began to thread these carefully through his fingers. I recognised them; they once belonged to the King's mother, Elizabeth of York.

'Your Majesty?' I insisted, hoping to distract him. 'What innocents have you sinned against?'

Henry beckoned me on to the bed, pulling me down beside him. 'The princes,' he murmured. 'You know, Edward and Richard, the sons of my grandfather, Edward IV of York, the nephews of the usurper Richard.'

'But we have the truth of that,' I replied hoarsely. 'Thomas More?'

The King's eyes did not flicker; they remained cold, hard black stones in that hideously white puffy face.

'More claims that Richard the Usurper killed the princes in the Tower.'

'Not so, not so,' murmured the King. 'More was wrong on that, as he was about so many things.' He stretched out, ignoring Huicke, who was working on his ulcerated legs again, a mass of dirty red blotches and festering scabs. 'Those two boys died of a fever. They were walled up in a chamber in the royal lodgings; the room is still there. It contains two skeletons.

I swear to God,' Henry continued, 'once I recover, I will remove those corpses and give them honourable burial.'

'Why hasn't someone done that before, Your Majesty? They were your mother's brothers.'

'Both princes died of the sweating sickness during the brief bloody reign of their usurping uncle. Richard was trapped. No one would believe their deaths were the result of a plague.' Henry heaved a great sigh. 'After all, they had been in his care. They shouldn't have been in the Tower to begin with. In the summer heat, that fortress is a midden mess with evil vapours from its stinking moat.'

'And your own father?' I asked.

Henry forced a laugh. 'Trapped also, Will. After his victory at Bosworth, my father entered London. He became affianced to Elizabeth of York, the princes' sister. For her sake, he made careful search for her brothers. The secret chamber in the royal lodgings at the Tower was opened and the remains of the two boys found. My father could not publish what he had discovered without raising the suspicion that he may have been party to their murder. Yorkist sympathisers still thrived in London. It would be only a matter of days before common report would claim how both princes were hale and healthy until my father arrived. In the end, the hidden death chamber was walled up again and kept secret, its whereabouts known only to my father and his closest councillors. The secret was bequeathed to me. I swore on my mother's soul that one day I would give her brothers honourable burial.' His Majesty, beating his fists against the bed, continued to bemoan the problems bequeathed to him by his father. At last, growing tearful, he recollected himself, asking what hour of the day it was.

In truth, His Majesty does not bemoan the deaths of two Yorkist princes. Oh no! What he truly fears is that once he dies, his own three children, Edward, Mary and Elizabeth, young and vulnerable, will themselves be spirited away to that sinister fortress to be walled up or secretly murdered. And where will Tudor then be? What reward for all of Henry's dalliances, alliances, wars and the great tumult he's caused in his own kingdom and beyond?

The King grew agitated. Huicke begged him to be at peace. The physician then had His Majesty's body anointed with oil, and delivered an infusion through the anus by means of a pig's bladder to which a greased metal tube was fixed. Despite the King's moaning and retching, a pint of lightly salted water mingled with herbs was also given, followed by a mixture of soothing honey and pap to lessen the soreness of his angry red piles.

After a while the King pronounced himself better, comfortable enough to sit in one of the moving chairs whilst Huicke brought in servants to change the bed sheets. His Majesty waited, a furred cape about his shoulders. He demanded his spectacles and had me bring in his tray of numerous clocks and timepieces, fashioned like miniature books or set in crystals and adorned with rubies and diamonds. He studied these carefully, as if fascinated by the time, before waving his hands for me to take them away. Only once did he stare long and hard at me, eyes as glassy and empty as those of a dead pig on a butcher's stall. He seemed lost in thought, gazing dully around, smiling briefly when I told him some crude jest about a cardinal and a lady of Rome. Dr Huicke mentioned how he intended to visit the Queen at Greenwich. The King simply grunted. Huicke then gave me the ingredients for a poultice for the ulcers on the King's legs before he was curtly dismissed. I was aware of others clustering around the door outside, impatient to present themselves. I felt the pot of court intrigue was bubbling merrily, though with what I could not say, except that the King instructed me to tell all the others to stay withdrawn.

For a while he waited, listening to the sounds fade in the gallery outside. Then he turned to me, that large moon-like face, those bloodshot piggy eyes, the pursed lips all petulant with unspoken grievances.

'How long have you been with me, Will?'

'Twenty-one years, nine months, two weeks, three days and six and a half hours.'

The King gestured at me to sit on the stool beside him.

'Is that candle straight?' he asked.

I turned, and as I did, he grasped the slender white cane close to him and brought it down time and again across my back. Despite his weakness, and my quilted jacket stuffed with flock, the blows hurt. As always, the King made sure he never cut my skin, though this time he missed and scored my neck. I felt the welt rise even as Henry, coughing and spluttering, threw the cane down. He breathed noisily, his fat-jowelled face quivering.

'You were busy,' he rasped. 'Now you are insolent.'

'I am always busy, sire. I am your conscience, your eyes, your ears. I listen to conversations that would never be uttered in your presence or that of your loyal councillors or spies. Terrible things they say about you.' I was thoroughly enjoying myself. Do I hate my master? Yes. Do I love my master? Yes. I might be his whipping boy, but I am also his friend, sometimes his enemy and always his father confessor. My stool is his mercy pew. I shrive the King of his worries and his anxieties. For over twenty years it has always been so. He regards me as the world turned topsy-turvy. I reply that we have a great deal in common because he has done the same. He rejected Rome, but he also poured scorn on Master Luther and Master Zwingli. I chide him. I grieve him and he beats me. I give him good counsel and he provides me with robes every quarter, a bulging purse of coins and, above all, his protection. He likes to bestow upon me some of the goods of those he executes. He even gave me Thomas Cromwell's fine purse, snatched from the great man's corpse when it lay spouting blood on Tower Hill scaffold. Henry demanded that the executioner hand it over or face the same axe he wielded. I always wear it on my belt, the purse once filled by the great despoiler.

'I remember Cromwell.' The King clapped his hands like a child and grinned, showing his yellow and black teeth in bloody sore gums. 'I can read your mind, Will.'

'Thank God you cannot,' I retorted, 'otherwise you'd know how I truly feel about you.'

The King's hand dropped to the white wand on the floor beside him.

'If you try and beat me, I will run away like any apprentice boy from his master.' I jabbed my finger at him. 'You cannot read my mind. You watch me. You saw me touch my purse; it's empty because of the bribes I've paid to collect the gossip you want.'

Henry's shoulders sagged. He made a sound as if sucking on a sweetmeat.

'I remember my good Thomas.' His lower lip quivered like a child's; tears filled his eyes. 'I could do with Cromwell now, Will.'

'He gave you wise advice.'

'Howard,' Henry spat the name out, 'Thomas Howard, Duke of Norfolk, advised me to turn Cromwell out. He hated him. He blamed him for my marriage to that ugly cow Anne of Cleves.'

'Hypocrite, hypocrite, you now call her your sweet sister!'

Henry snatched up the cane more swiftly than I'd anticipated. I tried to dodge, but he still lashed my shoulders. Then he tapped me on the top of the head as if I was some kind of performing dog.

'Stay here,' he murmured. 'Do you know, Will, what Surrey said when Cromwell lost his head? Surrey, Norfolk's proud brat?'

'"Now that foul sow is dead",' I retorted, rubbing my shoulder. '"So ambitious of other men's blood, now he is stricken with his own staff." That's what he said. You almost did the same with your own sword to your most hated enemy, Cardinal Pole. You would have had him executed along with the rest.'

'Friend of the Howards!' Henry took up the story. Oh, how my monstrous master loves to reminisce! 'Pole called Cromwell the messenger of Satan.' He sniffed. 'The day will come, Pole once declared, when Cromwell will feel the same pains of all those he has sent to die. On that day Londoners shall witness one of the most joyous entertainments.' Henry turned to the table beside him. He picked up a silver necklace and threw it at me. I caught it deftly. 'You can't keep it,' he pouted, 'it's mine.'

'No it isn't,' I replied, admiring the insignia on the central pendant. 'It belonged to Margaret, Countess of Salisbury, daughter of George of Clarence, niece to both Edward IV and the usurper Richard III.' I do love taunting His Majesty. 'She claimed to have better rights than you to the throne. She was also the mother of Cardinal Reginald Pole.'

'I know, I know,' the King moaned. 'Why do you remind me of that? Pole still refuses to return to England;

he moves from university to university. Do you know, Will, when I divorced Catherine of Aragon, he at first supported me?'

'He then changed his mind,' I interrupted, 'like so many did. He condemned your execution of More, Fisher and the Carthusians. He likened you to the tyrants Nero and Domitian of Ancient Rome. Little wonder he will not come home!'

The King did not stretch down for his cane, so I moved a little closer. 'He said you did not deserve your title of Defender of the Faith. How you had torn to pieces and slaughtered all true defenders of the Faith. How you had been led away, like Solomon of old, by your passion for Anne Boleyn, whose head you must sever if you were to rid yourself of all your offences against God.'

'Well I did cut her head off.' The King forced a smile, more of a grimace in that fat face. I recalled a line from a song about someone who can smile and smile again and still mean murder. Henry closed his eyes, head drooping; he may have been nodding off, or he may have been brooding about Cardinal Reginald Pole, one of the few men he really fears.

His Majesty certainly did not forget Pole's insults. The cardinal's younger brother Geoffrey was arrested, and after two months of strict confinement and brutal interrogation in the Tower, he accused his own family of treason. Geoffrey later tried to commit suicide, but was released to live terror-stricken for all his days.

Reginald's other brother Henry was executed on Tower Hill. Their mother Margaret, the aged Countess of Salisbury, was also confined so closely in the Tower, she greatly protested that she lacked the necessary apparel to change and keep herself warm. The countess refused to confess to any treason, and was so strong in her denunciation that her interrogators complained they had not dealt with her like before, proving to be more strong and constant than any man. She did not face trial, but was dragged out of prison to the scaffold on Tower Green, where she refused to lay her head upon the block, saying that it was for traitors, and she was no traitor. She kept twisting her head, screaming at the executioner that if he would have it, he must get it as best he could. He did so, hacking and cutting the old woman's head, neck and body.

Before her execution the good countess had taunted His Majesty about the faith of his own family. His parents had devoted themselves to relics and pilgrimages, so why had he rejected such cherished beliefs? She reminded him that his father had treasured a piece of the True Cross brought from Greece, as well as the leg bone of St George, to whose memory the old king had been most devoted. That his mother, Queen Elizabeth, had sent purses of silver to Our Lady of Walsingham, the Rood of Grace at Northampton and Becket's shrine, not to mention Our Lady of Eton, the Child of Grace at Reading and the Holy Blood at Hailes Abbey. His Majesty never replied to such tauntings. Now, in his last days, he fears Reginald Pole, a cardinal living in Venice. Reginald has sworn great vengeance and has taken a blood oath that if Fortune ever turns her wheel and he returns to England after His Majesty's death, he will have the King's corpse dug up and his bones blown from a cannon as His Majesty has done to so many of this kingdom's sacred relics. In truth, Reginald is a man after my own heart; I keep him close in my secret thoughts, one of the few men to truly frighten our nightmare king.

According to reports, His Majesty has, out of fear of what Cardinal Pole intends, issued strict instructions in his will about his own secure interment in a pure marble sarcophagus, once the property of Wolsey, that now resides in St George's Chapel, Windsor. He also, according to Princess Mary's spy Master Balaam, hired a professional assassin, one Ludovico dall'Armi, a Venetian, to kill the cardinal. However, Ludovico murdered two other men in a vendetta and His Majesty had to use all his good offices with the Doge and council to save the assassin from being garrotted.

'Cromwell!' Henry roused himself, voice powerful like it used to be. 'Cromwell swore to make Cardinal Pole eat his own heart.' The King moved to grip the arms of his chair, hands sticky with blood. He picked up a goblet of water and sipped noisily at it. I wondered if Dudley and the other wolves would come snuffling at the door. They had been warned often enough to stay away. If the King wanted them to whisper and to plot, to play hazard or chess, he would ring that damn little bell, which, like the cane, is never far from his reach. 'Norfolk destroyed Cromwell.' Henry's voice was now nothing but a whisper, a trick of his whenever he recalls the past and wishes to be absolved of all blame. 'I can't bring Cromwell back,' he turned, grinning at me out of the corner of his eye, 'but I will avenge his ghost.' He wiped his nose on the back of his hand and fell silent.

I knew the story well enough. Whatever he claimed, the King had agreed to his minister's destruction, so Norfolk had spoken privately to the captain of the guard and instructed him to arrest Cromwell after dinner on the appointed day and take him to the Tower. The captain wondered very much at this, but the duke insisted he need not be surprised, for the King had so ordered it. On the chosen day, as was the custom, the Council went to Parliament at Westminster. When they came out and were about to cross the yard to the palace for dinner, the wind blew Secretary Cromwell's bonnet to the ground. Now the courtly convention is that when a gentleman loses his bonnet, all those with him must doff theirs, but on this occasion the other gentlemen did not. Cromwell noticed this and exclaimed: 'A high wind indeed, which blows my bonnet off but keeps all yours on.'

They pretended not to hear, and Cromwell took this as a bad omen. They went to the palace and dined, and all the while they were eating, the other councillors did not converse with Secretary Cromwell as was customary.

Once they had finished, the rest of the gentlemen went to the Council chamber. Now it was Cromwell's habit after dinner to go close to a window to hear petitioners once the others had left. As usual he remained at his window for about an hour, then joined his colleagues to find them already seated.

'You were in a great hurry to get seated, gentlemen,' he declared. The other councillors made no reply, but just as Cromwell was about to sit down, the Duke of Norfolk exclaimed, 'Cromwell, do not sit there. There is no place for you, a traitor, to sit amongst gentlemen.'

'I am no traitor,' Cromwell retorted.

With that the captain of the guard came in.

'I arrest you!' he declared.

'What for?' cried Cromwell.

'That you will learn soon enough,' Norfolk jibed. Then the duke rose and said, 'Wait, Captain, traitors must not wear the Garter.' He ripped this from him, pushed Cromwell to the door and the guards took him to the Tower.

I know the story by rote. I should do. The King has recited it often enough.

'Why?' I asked abruptly. 'Why did you really destroy Cromwell?'

'He failed me, Will. Melted like wax in the heat of my temper. He roused the beast in me. He should have known better. What did Thomas More say to that courtier who said I was as playful as a bear? To be careful lest the fun prove fatal and turn to—'

'Murder?'

Henry leaned across and snatched away Salisbury's silver necklace.

'Cromwell begged for your mercy,' I added, eager to distract him.

'And he got it.' Henry pulled a face. 'For seven weeks he languished in the Tower, wondering if he'd be dispatched to Hell by the headman's axe or burnt to a cinder as a heretic at Smithfield. Norfolk wanted that. He said he'd arrange for the faggots to be green and supple so they would burn slowly. He was insistent that Cromwell should have no gunpowder tied around his neck nor, when the smoke billowed, be quietly strangled by the executioner.' He raised his hand. 'Will,' his voice was almost pleading, 'I showed Cromwell great mercy.'

'No you did not.' I pushed back my stool. 'You gave him the sweeter, swifter way to judgement by making him confess to certain secret conversations he'd had with you which proved you never consummated your marriage to the German, Anne of Cleves. You could then separate from her without offending her brother and the other German princelings.' Henry was now quietly sobbing to himself. He likes to reminisce, then to justify. He is fearful of Cromwell and the rest of the ghosts; he complains persistently of how they haunt him day and night. He has even made careful search on reports about strange events and sightings at the Tower, where, according to the testimony of members of the garrison, the earth-bound souls of the King's victims cluster about while their headless bodies lie crammed and rotting in arrow chests beneath the flag-stones of St Peter ad Vincula. Even more disturbing are stories from Blickling in Norfolk, once the home of Anne Boleyn. The ghost of the executed queen has often been glimpsed there, walking close to the great lake. She has even spoken to some local villagers, claiming she is searching for something she will never find.

'So, you went into the City.' Henry's blood-streaked fingers curled in the light of a square of burning beeswax.

'I went to St Paul's, that house of news, the mill of chatter and rumour which provides grist and grain for all those who take it.'

'And?'

'The lawyers and merchants parade arm in arm, faces close together along Duke Humphrey's Walk.'

'But what do they say?'

'Oh, how silent you have fallen . . . they wonder about the succession.' There, I had said it, a word that bubbles the fires of fear in our dread king's heart. I decided not to wait for his questions.

'They talk about the Princess Mary, daughter of your first wife, the Spanish Catherine. She is still popular because of her mother. Some people claim she has already been removed. Others chatter how imperial war cogs lie off the coast ready to whisk her away, of conspirators milling in houses close by where she lives, waiting for the sign to move.'

'I would like to see Mary soon.' Henry's voice was all sweet and cloying. 'I did her wrong, but there again, her proud Spanish blood wouldn't make her bend. What else do they say? Come on, Will, you must have heard the chatter?'

'You have only got yourself to blame for there being so little!'

Indeed he has. The recent Treasons Act has declared that 'If any person or persons do maliciously wish, will or desire by words or writing, or by craft imagined, invent, practice or attempt any bodily harm to His Majesty, he is guilty of high treason and shall suffer the full penalty of hanging and disembowelling.' Speculating about the King's death could provoke this. Those who are prudent heed such grisly warnings posted the length and breadth of both this city and the kingdom. It is now no novelty to see men slain, hanged, quartered and beheaded for trifling expressions later interpreted to have been spoken against the King. Indeed, when a man is a prisoner in the Tower, none dare meddle with his affairs unless to curse him, for fear of being suspected of the same crime. At court a man can neither speak nor be silent without danger. It is certainly perilous when the truth can be twisted into error by the altering of one syllable, either penned or spoken.

'What, Will?' bleated the King, clapping his hands. 'What else?'

'How your courtiers turn on each other. How my lords Seymour and Dudley play cards with you, but in the antechambers beyond they circle like wolves and search for the least sign of weakness in their rivals. A true carnival of blood! How your lords hide their naked villainy with scraps from Holy Writ. They seem the saint when in truth they play the devil.' I sighed to disguise my grin. 'People do not know what will come of it except that it is wise to plan for the worst because the best will provide for itself. How at court reformers and Romanists clash; even the bible, on which your councillors swear their oath of loyalty, has become a battleground. They say new men compete against the old, and some of the latter will never rest until they have done as much evil as they can to all who supported Cromwell. Yet even if this is settled, there are others, fresher yet, who will begin the bloody carnival again.' I paused. 'Do you really want to hear this, sire?'

'Nothing but divisions.' Henry grunted. 'Nothing new, it's safer that way. Continue, do not spare yourself.' He smirked. 'Or me!'

'Allegations of treason and treason yet again are thrown and hurled back, and if this does not suffice, the mere suspicion of treason can bring a man down. How the Lord Mayor of London has been commissioned to enquire secretly into all who speak ill against you or your Council. They say you are out of your wits yet you remain dangerous. What may be made today can be unmade tomorrow. Old men, new men, commoners or nobles. Have you not said there is no head, be it ever so fine, you could not make fly?'

Henry chuckled, clapping his hands. 'Remember, Will,' he hissed, 'it's best to lead men with love, but it is a sad reflection on human wickedness that most must be led by fear. Go on! I see you enjoy yourself!'

'In truth, never have you made a man but you later destroyed him with either displeasure or the sword. Brutal death has shattered anyone noble, whilst fear has shrunk up the rest.'

'And the succession?' Henry picked up the white wand and tapped it on the floor, pushing at the Turkey rugs like a shepherd would lambs with his crook.

'They say Princess Mary is illegitimate; that you made her so.'

'And I have changed that.' Henry glared at me. 'You know that. She is second in line if Heaven's own imp,' his voice trembled, 'my beautiful Edward dies without issue.'

'But you made her so.' I couldn't keep the anger out of my voice. Henry knows I am partial to Princess Mary and even more so to Lady Jane Bold, Mary's pretty fool. 'You see, Your Majesty,' I continued remorsefully, 'what can be undone then redone can be undone again.'

Henry lifted the cane and sighed. 'And the Princess Elizabeth?'

'What do you think? Little red-haired Elizabeth.' I emphasised every word. 'The gossipers call her the Great Whore's Daughter.'

Henry covered the side of his face with his hand. 'So the graveyard yawns,' he murmured. 'All the old ghosts are coming back. Ride on, Will,' he said wearily, 'tell me what the common tongue wags.'

'All the ghosts.' I felt the anger drain from me; the Princess Elizabeth was a sweet child, but one haunted by her mother's ghost. 'I plucked down a handbill posted at St Paul's Cross stirring up all the old insults spat out eleven years ago. How the Abbess of Whitby called Anne Boleyn a common stud, a goggle-eyed harlot. How she should have been burned as a common strumpet, how she was intimate with Henry Norris, the red-haired,' I emphasised the description, 'knight of your secret chamber. Indeed, how when Archbishop Cranmer ruled that your marriage was null and void, he made a slip of the tongue, claiming Elizabeth to be Norris's child. How Boleyn rendered you impotent, a witch with a spare teat. How when Anne was arrested, the ladies of her chamber were put to the torture. One of them was called Margaret—'

'I know this, I know this.' Henry's voice was all a-tremble, and for a moment he dropped his hand to show the tears glistening on his pasty skin. In truth, I am never too sure about our king's tears. He can cry at a blink, then act all marble-hearted. He worries about his daughters, yet this is a father who, on hearing how prim and proper the Princess Mary was, encouraged his old drinking partner, the one-eyed Francis Bryant, to approach her and say something salacious to discover her response. Princess Mary herself told me about this, as well as about her years of exile from both her mother and her father. How Boleyn had threatened to kill her secretly by poison, or, if the King left England and Anne was regent, to have her head taken on Tower Hill. Strange, strange, strange! Sometimes I think Henry likes to be reminded that if his wives failed, it was not his fault but theirs.

'One of these ladies,' I continued remorselessly, 'called Margaret, described how Anne searched London for the best-looking singer and dancer and found him in young Mark Seaton. How she fell in love with him and begged this old woman to bring him to her every night.'

'Enough, enough, I know this tale well enough.'

'Except, Your Majesty, the gossipers say that the only difference between Mary and Elizabeth is that although both were made illegitimate by statute, only one of them really is.'

'If I caught such a gossiper . . .' The King, eyes closed, rubbed his hands as if he was secretly watching the most grisly disembowelling at Tyburn. As he sat slouched in his chair, now and again a wince of pain would crease his puffy face. He looked mice-eyed. I also noticed that he grasped an insignia of the Garter, its ribbon besmirched and torn. I moved and glanced round at a book lying on the floor between the King's chair and his great four-poster bed. I recognised 'The Book of the Knights of the Garter', those who gather every year in St George's Chapel, Windsor. Henry had been busy. The tattered, stained insignia certainly belonged to Cromwell, the one Norfolk had ripped from him. The King had been reminiscing. I rose, picked up the heavy calf-skin book, turning the thick stiffened pages to the list of knights inscribed since his own coronation. Many of those names were now scratched out. Beside each of them Henry had scrawled in his own hand, 'Oh traitor!' I wondered how much I really dared tell him. Henry was weakening, his body failing, but that cunning mind was as sharp as ever. If I flattered him, he'd sense that and flail out with his cane, or, even worse, banish me. Despite being a mountain of lies himself, he had a nose for dissimulation.

'Any more news from St Paul's?' He leaned over and snatched the book from my hands. 'You went into the markets, the taverns. Tell me, Will, what did you find? What are you keeping in that journal I told you to begin?'

'You may read it yourself, Your Majesty.' I had already secretly determined he would not.

'I don't bark when I have my own dog. Moreover, Will, you use the shorthand Master Cromwell taught you; he claimed you were one of his most able pupils. I could never understand it. So, cut to the chase, what is happening amongst the common herd?'

'Unrest seethes like a fire bubbling beneath a pot,' I replied slowly. 'Rumours quicken. A Buckinghamshire man in open court claimed you were no better than a knave whose crown was only fit to play football with.' Henry started at the relish in my voice. I lowered my head. 'In Warwick, at the market cross, a travelling

35

tinker proclaimed Your Majesty a worse tyrant than Nero. When ordered to keep the King's peace, he retorted, before he fled, that he did not give a turd for the King. Strange prophecies are circulating: how the white hare shall drive the fox to the castle of care and the swift greyhound shall run under the root of the oak and there'll be such a gap in the west that all the forces of England shall have enough work to stop it.'

'What does such nonsense mean?' Henry snapped.

'Chatter from Somerset says this riddle predicts a war of religious fervour. A trader in Buckinghamshire muttered to a merchant who is sweet on one of the maids at the Lamb of God how dreadful dragons will land on the coast with a host of bare-legged chickens, a reference perhaps to a rebellion in Ireland. Marvels have also been reported, omens for the future.' I hid my grin. 'A dead fish, the like of which has never been seen before, a veritable monster thirty yards long, lies beached on the northern coast beneath the soaring battlements of Bamburgh Castle. Recently the Severn flowed in continuously for nine hours so water flooded the Guildhall at Bristol, whilst above it a ball of fire the size of a human head streaked the sky. A comet with a trail of flame as long as a Munster man's beard was also glimpsed in the skies over Norwich, or so they tell me.'

'And Monsieur Odet de Selve and my lord van der Delft, you mixed with their men? What did they babble? Did they allude to comets and stars, beached whales or a baby born with two heads? Is it true that Monsieur de Selve still complains about the cold? What does his master say, the noble Francis? Come on now, Will, tell me!' Henry beat the arm of his chair with his wrist.

'Sire, according to the French ambassador, the noble King Francis finds you the hardest friend to bear, at one time unstable, at another time obstinate and proud. You think you are wise but he considers you a fool. He judges you to be the strangest man in the world. But there again,' I grinned, 'he would say that, wouldn't he? We hold Calais and Boulogne.'

'And I'll go back there,' Henry whispered. 'I am designing new ships, Will. I have told my smiths to cast bigger guns and mortars to hurl pots of wild fire against the French. Is there any news about the Genoese?'

I decided not to reply to that: far too dangerous! Henry can be shrewd but at the same time so easily duped. Quite recently a Genoese, slippery as a Lincolnshire eel, proposed to construct a monstrous mirror on the top of the keep at Dover Castle. The machine would reflect whatever was happening along the French coast, so any hostile craft leaving the ports of France would be seen long before it ever reached the English shore. The King, and even Heaven must wonder why, believed the charlatan and sent him south with purses bulging with gold, but after that, no more: no man, no mirror.

'And my lord van der Delft, the Imperial ambassador? What do his men say?'

'That you set your lords at each other's throats like a pack of fighting dogs straining on their leashes. How you allow them to turn on each other so you can berate them all.'

Henry covered his mouth with his hand and giggled like a girl.

'How you pull back one pack and let the other take the lead. How you stir the pot, one day this way, the other that. The envoys complain bitterly about the huge bribes paid for spying on you. How there is no certainty which path you will follow. How you are King Janus looking this way, then that. How you condemn Rome and support the reformers on Monday, but on Tuesday persecute the reformers and secretly weep for Rome. How you are ever-changing, ever fickle.'

'That is not true.' Henry pulled at the rug covering his legs.

'You know it is,' I retorted. 'Didn't you receive the papal envoy recently and talk about a general council? Then you met the French. I was there! You secretly discussed a plan whereby France and the Empire would join you in a general denunciation and refutation of the power of the Pope.'

Henry thought this was amusing; he sat chuckling to himself. Huicke must have given him some opiate to dull the nerves and numb the pain. Nevertheless, I was curious. Henry was leading somewhere, but there again so was I: an opportunity to discover what was being plotted.

'What else did they say? I mean about my councillors?'

'Oh, how they plot against each other. And worse.' My voice sank to a whisper.

'What, Will?'

'Your Majesty, what if they unite to plot against you?'

Henry searched beneath the gold-encrusted rug and brought out a jingling purse. He tossed this at me; a fleck of blood from his fingers splashed my hand. As I grasped the purse, the King abruptly seized my arm, nipping the skin. 'There you have said it,' he murmured, 'the heart of the darkness.' He let go of me. 'Will, I meet the Council later this evening. You must be there in your accustomed place. First let me sleep for a while; bring me some white wine.' I rose and filled a brimming goblet, which the King supped, talking to himself in a chattering whisper I couldn't follow, although I caught the names 'Boleyn' and 'Cromwell'. He put the wine down and dozed for a while. Now and again he would mutter, at one time crying out for his mother and then calling for Tom, but whether this was Wolsey, Cromwell or More I couldn't say. I sat back and studied him, his mouth slightly open, saliva dribbling down. I was mindful that I was watching a snake that had been lying dormant but was now ready to strike. Henry was about to give the wheel of fortune another viciously swift turn. He talks about the past, but he does not concern himself too much about that. He often informs me how he and God are on the best of terms and he

39

has no problem with his conscience. Others would definitely disagree.

A darkness certainly broods over this kingdom. On my travels I do not recall having ever seen its people so morose as they are at present. They do not know whom to trust, and Henry himself, having offended so many, mistrusts everyone. He is still inclined to his amours, despite his age and ailments, at least in the eyes of his subjects. A porter at Syon was recently hauled before the Council for saying that the King kept a bevy of mistresses for his own amusement at a secret manor close by. A broadsheet published privately by 'a Sanctuary Man at Westminster' claims how a William Webbe, whilst riding out near Eltham, his pretty wench behind him, met the King coursing his hounds. His Majesty, according to Webbe, plucked down her muffler and kissed the wench. Indeed, the King, liking her so much and being puffed up with lechery, vainglory and pride, took the doxy for himself. On account of this Master Webbe has sworn bloody vengeance against the King, as have others. He certainly has his enemies. Little wonder Westminster and Whitehall are closely guarded by engines of war, gentlemen pensioners with their pole-axes and archers by the score. More dangerous, Balaam's spy in Bucklebury claims, there may be a plot to murder the King by slipping a poison into the potions and powders given to him, yet I've seen no proof for this.

The ubiquitous, all-seeing, far-gazing Balaam maintains that the cause and the root of the King's growing malignancy is not so much his amorousness; indeed, so Balaam reports, that is catered for most delicately by Her Grace the Queen, Henry's sixth wife, formerly the Lady Katherine Parr. According to Balaam, who can snout scandal as a hog would a truffle, the lovely Katherine conforms perfectly to the mirror of womanly excellence. She proves to be an ape in bed, a shrew in the kitchen, a saint in the church and an angel at the board. No, Balaam argues, the King's true malignancy is his insufferable pride. He will not be checked. Henry recently roared at his Council that he has the right of everything not because so many agree with him but because he, being learned, knows the matter to be right. His Demonic Majesty rejoices in wearing a gold bracelet studded with jewels and inscribed: '*Plus tot mourir que changer ma pensée*' – 'I would rather die than change my mind'. My Satanic master is, in his own view, the One Supreme Head and King, having the dignity and royal estate of the Imperial kind. He wields power, plenary, whole and entire, and so enjoys above all others authority, prerogative and jurisdiction. 'God has not only made us King,' he proclaims, 'but has given us wisdom of policy, and other graces in plentiful so necessary for a prince to direct his affairs to his own honour and glory.'

I stared at Henry, his great bulk overspilling the chair, the towel wrapped around his head slipping down, his face all twitching, lips still moving. I wondered what he was dreaming about. Was he truly sleeping, or was his brain teeming like a box of squirming worms devising some devious stratagem? If that was the case, someone would die. I gazed around the chamber, so luxuriously opulent. Glowing tapestries, a maze of many colours, covered the walls, silver and gold candlesticks, spigots, precious cups, goblets and dishes caught the eye. So much death had been plotted here. I shivered, rose, crossed to the hearth and placed two finely cut scented logs on the dying fire. A jakes pot in the corner caught my attention; its linen covering had slipped to reveal the squalid filth inside. I went across and pulled the cloth back over, but the smell was so offensive I hastily snatched a pomander and held it against my nose. I walked across to the thick, mullioned-glass window, which shimmered in the light of countless candles. I pressed my face against its cold surface. In the courtyard below, councillors were arriving. I glimpsed the white lion of Norfolk in the fluttering torchlight. Steel gleamed, the sound of voices and the stir of horses carried faintly. Snow was falling, thin, meagre flakes to wet the ledges and cornices.

'Some wine, Will?' Startled, I turned quickly. The King, now very much awake, was staring at me curiously. 'Have you eaten?' He gestured at a tray of sweetmeats next to a flagon of German wine, the jug carved in the shape of a dolphin. I went across, carefully filled a Venetian fluted glass and brought it over to the King. He gulped the sweetmeats and greedily drank the wine. He thrust the glass back into my hand and spluttered, staining my hands with the contents of his mouth, at the same time declaring how both jug and glass had once belonged to Edward Stafford, Duke of Buckingham.

'You wouldn't remember him, Will, a great lord. He hated Wolsey the Red Man, and Wolsey hated him. One day Buckingham had to act as ewerer. He deliberately poured the water over Wolsey's purple silken slippers. I cut his head off, Will, snipped it as you would a flower.' The King brushed his lap, snapping his fingers. 'Bring me the chess board.' I did so. Henry, all energetic, balanced it on his lap, sweeping the pieces into a bowl half full of mouldy fruit. He grabbed four of the crown pieces, placed them on the board and gestured at me to draw closer, as if we were two conspirators in some dingy tavern.

'Here am I.' He took the largest piece and placed it on the board. 'Thirty-seven years a king, now in my fifty-sixth summer. Physician Huicke tells me I might die.' He snorted through his nose. 'One day I will, and so shall he, sooner than he thinks if his care doesn't improve. Next in line,' he picked up another of the chessmen, 'the golden boy, Heaven's own child, my darling son Edward. Nine years old, fair-haired, grey-eyed, with a pointed chin. The say he is the very image of his mother, Queen Jane, a Seymour through and through but still a Tudor. Do you know, Will, there is a vicious story that I was so desperate to have a son that I ordered the physicians and midwives to rip open the Queen's stomach and pluck him out.'

'Did you?' I asked before I could stop myself. The King's fist, fingers now all decorated with heavy rings, smashed into my face, a stinging, cutting blow just beneath the left eye. His lips were curled, his rotting yellow teeth more like fangs, spots of anger high in that flour-like skin. And those eyes: no longer narrow like those of a pig, but fully open in their raging fury. I fell to my knees.

'Your Majesty. I jested.'

Henry rocked backwards and forwards in his chair.

'Are you keeping that journal, Will? The one I asked you to write at the beginning of this week?'

'Of course, Your Majesty.' I felt the King's hand on my head. He grasped my scrawny brown hair, forcing me to look directly at him. The fury had faded. He released me and gently stroked my bruised cheek.

'I need you, Will.' Tears filled his eyes; his jutting lower lip trembled. 'I need you to listen to me and give me good advice. You are my Everyman. Oh, go on. See to your face.' I crossed to the lavarium, dipped a napkin in the cold water and, holding it to my cheek, returned to the stool.

'Edward is nine,' the King continued conversationally. 'Soon I will create him Prince of Wales, yet it will be five or six years before he can beget an heir, whilst his constitution is not strong. He is tutored in the faith I want.' I was tempted to ask what that was; Henry's faith changes every day. Instead I kept my mouth firmly closed and nodded wisely.

'Should Edward die,' Henry moved another piece on to the board, 'there is Princess Mary, but she has Spanish blood and is an avowed papist. Apart from the Norfolks and Stephen Gardiner, Bishop of Winchester, she would regard members of the present Council as her sworn enemies, traitors to herself, to her church and to the memory of her allegedly blessed mother. Then there's Elizabeth, the child of contention, whose legitimacy is suspect, whilst her mother, according to gossip, was nothing better than a goggle-eyed whore.'

I tensed. Henry was no longer meandering or wandering but studying a problem that had hounded him for most of his life. He grasped my arm as if we were the closest of friends. 'Just over sixty years ago, Will, my father crushed the Yorkists at Bosworth and killed the usurper in mortal combat. We Tudors came into our own. But time passes. Master Luther called me Squire Tudor, nothing better than a Welsh farmer. Look at our Council! You see my suspicions? If a Tudor can become king, why not a Dudley, why not a Seymour . . .?'

'And above all, why not a Howard?'

'Aye, Will. Why not? Norfolk's grandfather fought for the Yorkist Richard at Bosworth. God knows what dreams the Howards dream as they creep and crawl towards the throne. They offered two of their women, Anne and Katherine, as my wife and queen. They dream dreams about inviting Cardinal Pole home, of restoring ties with Rome. Perhaps they even plot a marriage between a Howard and one of my daughters? However, let us not forget the others, such as Edmund Dudley, Viscount Lisle, Lord High Admiral, so fervently supported by my brother-in-law Edward Seymour, who wrote to me recently,' the King closed his eyes, '"I can do no less than recommend the Viscount Lisle to Your Highness, as one who has served you heartily, wisely, diligently, painfully and obediently as any man I have ever seen."' The sneer in the King's voice was clear and stark. 'Dudley! I executed his father. I threw his head to the people to please them. Has he forgiven me and forgotten that?' Henry's voice crackled. I sensed the danger he was hinting at. Would Dudley invoke the blood feud? That was the ongoing difficulty: so much bad blood between all of them. 'There is division. The reformists, Dudley, Somerset, Wriothesley and that master of secret practices Sir William Paget; and on the other side the Romanists, the Norfolks and their good friend Gardiner.' The King raised his hands as if weighing something in the scale, his smile rich in malice. 'Which ones first, eh, Will? But enough. Go.' He gestured. 'See to your face. At the appointed time join us in the Council chamber.'

I withdrew from the royal presence. The gallery outside was dark and cold, lit by lantern horns and oil lamps placed in niches. There was a rank smell. A sense of menace cloaks that long, glittering gallery, dappled in shadows, the light juddering and flickering. In dark

46

recesses and shadowy corners stand the Spears, the King's personal halberdiers; their presence proves a grim reminder of swift arrest and even swifter punishment. I walked quickly, my footsteps echoing like a drum beat. A figure darted out of one of the chambers to my right. Sir William Paget grasped my shoulder and pushed me into the Chancery of the Secret Seal, the King's own writing office. Dark and closed, the walls panelled in stained oak, the floor covered with special rope matting over which thick taffeta had been stretched to deaden sound. Across the room, beneath a small oriel window filled with painted glass looted from Peterborough Abbey, where Catherine of Aragon's corpse lies interred, stood the King's great chancery table. A clerk bent over this, busy with a roll of vellum, beside his elbow a carved wooden block. Paget coughed, even as the bell in the King's chamber rang out its demands. The man glanced over his shoulder; I recognised William Clarke of the Chancery. Whatever he was working on swiftly disappeared into a black leather bag bearing the Royal Arms.

'Your royal master calls.' Paget tried but failed to keep the sarcasm out of his voice. The clerk jumped up like the startled rabbit he resembled, with his snub nose, twitching mouth, thinning hair and bulbous eyes, which sometimes have the stare of a mad March hare. He scuttled out of the room; Paget closed the door behind him, his clever, secretive face a mask of concern. The Chief Secretary of the Council was plainly dressed, a buttoned cap over his thick auburn hair. A lockram falling band, coarse but clean, circled his throat. He wore a brown coat tied with a belt of white horse hide whilst his breeches of russet sheep's wool stretched down to stockings of white kersey thrust into battered leather boots. He removed his heavy gauntlets and placed these in a wicker basket close to the hearth, where a merry fire crackled.

'Gardening.' He answered my enquiring look. Paget is a keen horticulturist. A man who plots as he prunes, who conspires as he cuts, who will walk a garden and be busy plotting his own secret way through a maze of intrigue. I stared at the window, against which white snowflakes floated.

'In this weather?' I asked.

'Not planting, Will. Now is not the time for that. As Ecclesiasticus says, there is a time for planting and a time for pulling up.' He let the menace drain from his voice and grinned. 'In truth, I have just taken possession of some apple trees, which those galleys at the King's Steps have brought from France. Nothing like planting.' He winked. 'Or planning.'

'Or plotting?'

'True, Will, the future always beckons.' Paget fumbled at a hanging thread on his coat; he loosened the horse-hide belt. I became distracted by the beautiful ruby, no bigger than a coin, deeply embedded in the oak panelling just above his head. I recognised the Ruby of France taken from Becket's shrine at Canterbury. A precious stone of unique powers. The writing office was dark, the light from the capped candles fitful, yet the scarlet radiance of that precious stone shone like a beacon through the shifting shadows.

'All things change, Will.' Paget followed my gaze.

'For the better, I hope, Sir William. What do you want with me?'

'The King, His Majesty?'

'Ask him yourself.' I stared at this smiler who always carried a dagger beneath his cloak.

'I will do so tomorrow. What agitates His Majesty?'

'People who ask questions, Sir William, so why not do it yourself?'

'Will,' Paget leaned forward, his saturnine face creased in a frown, 'I am not your enemy.'

'Are you my friend?'

'I could be. Sooner or later you may need one.'

'I have friends.'

'Ah yes, the Lady Jane, the innocent, the fool, the jester in Princess Mary's household. She who likes to wear blood-red petticoats.'

I simply stared back.

'And you also consider the Princess Mary to be your friend?' Paget rounded his eyes. 'She too has friends. She also has agents, couriers, men dispatched from her ally, Cardinal Pole in Venice.'

I kept my face impassive, concealing my unease. Paget rose, walked to the desk and returned with a scroll. He undid the red ribbon.

'This is a report from one of my agents in York. You know how the northern march, the border shires still lie bruised from His Majesty's forceful suppression of the Pilgrimage of Grace ten years previous, when Norfolk, with his son Henry of Surrey, caused such dreadful execution upon a goodly number of its inhabitants.' Paget shook his head. 'Norfolk swept through the rebels with sword and fire, hanging them on trees, disembowelling and cutting them, their quarters boiled and tarred, festooned in every town as a fearful warning. Men and women were hanged on poles in their own gardens, from the signs of village taverns, on the branches of churchyard yew trees or along the highways beyond.' He clicked his tongue. 'Most of the victims were poor men, their womenfolk being forced to creep out at night to steal back the corpses. They then kept these cadavers shrouded and hidden in their cottages until the royal levies passed, even though the corrupting flesh spread further pestilence amongst the living.'

Paget paused and crossed himself. I did not reply. He was quietly reminding me that my family, the Somerses, not to mention my former patron Sir Richard Fermor, had been caught up in this bloody tempest, as had the kin of my sweetheart, the Lady Jane Bold. Worse, I knew Balaam had been, and still is, active in those northern parts. Paget was threatening me ever so subtly.

'His Majesty still fears the north and a possible alliance between the border shires and the Scots,' he murmured. 'Resentment at the King and his Council continues to seethe along the marches. A broadsheet was recently pinned to the door of Durham Cathedral, a centre of unrest in the great rebellion.' Paget glanced down at the report. '"Since the realm of England was first a realm", this begins, "there never was in it so great a robber and pillager of the Commonwealth as our present king. We of the spirituality" –' he glanced up, grinning, 'the writer poses as a former priest – "are oppressed and robbed of our livings as if we were his utter enemies as well as those of Christ, guilty of our Saviour's death."' He tutted under his breath before continuing. '"In such an ungodly way this king handles innocents as well as learned and goodly men, not only robbing them of their livings and depriving them of their goods but also thrusting them into perpetual prison. It is too great a misery to bear and more to be lamented than any good Christian here may abide."' Paget paused. 'Can you believe this, Will? Listen, it goes on: "This king has also pillaged his nobility, using their wealth to construct towering palaces in which he enjoys and revels in his filthy pleasures. Our king is mired in vice, more vile and fetid than a sow which wallows and befouls itself in every stinking place. He has given himself up to the filthy pleasure of voluptuousness. He violates every woman at his court, neglecting the sanctity of marriage, and has taken to himself the wives of fornication."' He stared at me.

'Treason,' I conceded. 'What happened?'

'His Majesty's justices and commissioners in those

parts were furious. They tore down the broadsheets and organised the strictest search for its author, who proclaimed himself as Balaam, son of Beor, the oracle of the prophet, the man with the far-seeing eyes, the one who hears the Word of God. He sees what Shaddai makes him see. He receives the divine answer and his eyes are open.' Paget shrugged. 'Balaam's pursuers were not successful, and so Balaam, that man with the far-seeing gaze, struck again. A masque was staged in the great space before Durham Cathedral, the spectators drawn in by proclamations and rumours. The players gathered all visored and cloaked to perform a parable of the times. They even produced forged licences from the Council to warrant this. The stage was set up, great casks rolled out in front of the cathedral door. On one barrel sat God, clothed in white with a glorious sun mask. A pilgrim, garbed in dusty grey, face all painted red, approached God's throne. The pilgrim pointed to the cathedral, recently pillaged by the reformists and stripped of its statues, pictures and reliquaries.

'"How is it, Lord," he asked, "that you are alone? What has become of all your saints?"

'God answered, "They've all left, there are none here. They have departed to Spain, France, Flanders, Italy and Portugal."

'Pilgrim then replied, "Well, since you are alone, I shall not stay here either. I want to go to a place where you are surrounded by a more merry company." He turned to the other barrel, where Lord Satan sat enthroned, cloaked in purple, a gold mask on his face, a silver crown on his head. He too was alone, so the pilgrim asked him:

'"How is it that you are alone? What has become of all your devils?"

'To which Satan replied, "They've all left because they have so much work to do in England!"'

Paget glanced at the light fading against the oriel window. 'Balaam is a troublemaker, an agitator, a man who will end up being burned, boiled or hanged at Smithfield. I was in Smithfield this morning, Will. I watched Dr John Ashdown, a papist who won't take the oath, being burnt alive. They took him to a gibbet between two platforms and tied chains around his waist and hung him up suspended by the middle. He begged to have his hands freed, which they did, before starting a fire beneath him. The air turned smoky black, bitter-sweet with the reek of burning flesh. The skin of the poor man's legs bubbled and broke. I could hear the hiss of his body fat wetting the flames. Only when the fire reached his chest did the victim cease his writhing and hang still.'

'God have mercy on all such sinners,' I prayed. 'You must be greatly discomforted, Sir William. No wonder you plant apple trees, a soothe for your soul?'

'Or my belly. I retired for dinner to a nearby tavern and fed fairly well on a beef pie sopped in ale and capon sauce. Afterwards I returned to Smithfield; the crowd had dispersed and the gibbet was nothing but a smouldering, blackened wreck. Ashdown's remains had been taken and buried in the nearby hospital, though certain ladies, faces masked, were digging with pots and spoons about the execution spot, searching for scraps and globules of the dead man's corpse to preserve as relics.'

Paget watched the effect of his words on me, smiling with his mouth, eyes unblinking.

'I don't like seeing people die, Will. Nevertheless, I was His Majesty's witness, and today he determined that if he showed himself hard on papists and Romanists, he must be equally ruthless with reformers. Lambert came next, late in the afternoon. A leading member of the reformist party, he had openly attacked the sacrament, claiming the presence of Christ was only symbolic. He was questioned cruelly by the bishops but refused to recant. Condemned to burn, he was taken out of prison at four in the afternoon and carried to the house of a certain lord, deep into the inward chamber, where he was admonished for the last time because his end was near. He remained cheerful, however, and comforted. On being brought out of the inward chamber into the hall, he saluted the gentlemen present and sat down to sup with them, showing no manner of sadness or fear. Once the meal ended, he was immediately carried off to the place of execution. I was there, standing on a bench beneath an elm tree with some pie crusts in a napkin. Lambert was lashed to a stake on a high platform and the fire lit, but the flames were not allowed to do their worst swiftly and expediently. After his legs were burnt to the stumps, the fire was doused to no more than a few fiery coals. Guards either side used their halberds to raise Lambert on their pikes. The flames were then strengthened, and Lambert, his finger ends flaming with fire, was lowered to burn until the inferno reached his chest, before being raised yet again. The stench of the billowing black smoke, the screams and the horrid sounds proved too much. I gave my crusts to a beggar man and left.'

Paget picked up his gauntlets, examining them as if for the first time. He shook his head as if genuinely grieving. 'Nobody is safe, Will, be they sane or moonstruck. Take the case of Mr Collins, recorded in the Acts of the Privy Council. He had a wife of excellent beauty and comeliness, but notwithstanding that, she was light in her behaviour, of an unchaste condition. She left her husband for another. Mr Collins took this very grievously, more heavily than reason would allow. At last, being overcome with exceeding sorrow and grief, he became quite mad, and entered a church where a priest celebrating mass was about to raise the host. Collins, being out of his mind, and wishing to imitate the priest, took up a little dog by the legs and held it over his head, shouting out to the people. For that, despite the poor man's senses being turned, the King ordered him to be examined, tried and burnt at Smithfield, the dog alongside him.' Paget fell silent. I knew his reference to those who are moonstruck or witless was a jibe at me. My status as a fool, as the King's jester, would not save me from Henry's wrath. This dark soul and master of politics was making his presence felt. In that chamber I secretly acknowledged that of all the wolves gathered around my failing master, of all the wild hogs snouting at the royal trough, this man, together with Chancellor Wriothesley, was the most dangerous.

'And there are other dangers, aren't there, Will?' Paget persisted. 'The settling of grudges and grievances. You have heard the story about Robert Packington, a man of substance, discreet and honest? No? Well, Packington dwelt in Cheapside, the main thoroughfare of this city, graced with shops, stalls and the stately mansions of the wealthy. Surely a place of safety – yes? Well, every day at five o'clock, winter or summer, weather fine or foul, he would go to pray at a church once called St Thomas Acres, recently renamed the Mercers' Chapel. One grey, misty morning, Packington was crossing the street from his house to the church when he was brutally murdered with a pistol, its discharge being heard by a great number of labourers standing at the end of Soper Lane, though they did not glimpse the assassin. Only later did Dr Incent, Dean of St Paul's, confess on his deathbed that he, growing tired of Packington's railings against Romanist clergy, had hired an assassin for sixty crowns to kill the merchant.'

'Master Paget.' I moved restlessly on my stool. 'You

have now alerted me to all the dangers. Are you finished, or is there more?'

'Will, I am trying to be your friend; I wish you were mine. I am trying to warn you, or shall I say advise you. I know all about Balaam, as he calls himself, son of Beor, the man with the far-seeing eyes, who sees what other people can't see. That's how he describes himself, isn't it? A man who flits like a little fly, a veritable will-o'-the-wisp. Was he Packington's assassin? Whether he was or not, one day Balaam will be caught. He will be racked in the dungeons beneath the White Tower and he will confess.'

'To what?'

'To whatever I tell him to.' Paget waved a hand at me. 'Perhaps he may tell me about how you, he and the Princess Mary's fool and jester, the Lady Jane Bold, meet in a tavern in Whitefriars. What is it called, the Bowels of Hell?' He paused. 'You do most tenderly care for the Lady Jane, don't you? You always have. Both she and you support the Princess Mary, Catherine of Aragon's daughter. You all think you are safe.' He shook his head. 'Very few people have studied our king as I have. They think they can play with the Great Beast. Well, you were absent when this occurred.' Paget was now talking quietly, as if to himself. He glanced under his eyebrows at me. 'Of all men I reckoned to be safe, surely that would be Thomas Cranmer, Archbishop of Canterbury, the priest who brought about Henry's divorce from Catherine of Aragon so he could marry the great lust of his life, Anne Boleyn. Now, as I said, you were absent from court when this happened, the King having dispatched you on some errand or another. Anyway, despite all the archbishop had done for him, the King allowed Gardiner and Norfolk, those two cheeks of the same arse, to launch an attack on Cranmer. Oh yes!' Paget wagged a finger at me. 'They came into the King's presence and accused Cranmer most grievously. They alleged that he and his learned men had so infected the whole realm with their unsavoury doctrines that almost all the land was becoming diseased with detestable heresy to the great danger of the King, as it might produce the same commotion and uproar as it had in Germany. They insisted that the archbishop be committed to the Tower so that he might be more closely examined.' Paget pulled a face. 'His Majesty was most reluctant in granting this demand, but they persisted, claiming that no man dared level an accusation against Cranmer unless he was first committed to prison. Once this was done, they assured the King, men bold enough to tell the truth according to their consciences would come forward. Upon this persuasion, His Majesty reluctantly agreed that they should summon the archbishop next day before them and, if they found just cause, commit him to the Tower.'

Paget refilled his goblet. I had heard rumours of what he was telling me. Once I'd asked the King himself, but he simply lifted his cane and shook it at me. Paget was correct. If Cranmer could be threatened, the Keeper of the King's Soul, why not his fool, his jester? Henry might beat me, but he is also my shield, my bulwark. I am his creature, but there again, so is Cranmer, so was Cromwell, and all that trail of ghosts who now haunt His Malevolent Majesty. Would Henry sacrifice me upon the altar of fickleness? And if he died, would others consider me an embarrassment, to be dealt with in a welter of blood-letting? Terror prowls Henry's court, and in that shadowy chamber, I felt its fingers brush my soul.

'The King, however, had designs of his own.' Paget continued. 'At midnight on the day the archbishop was to appear before the Council, Henry sent one of his confidants to my lord at Lambeth demanding that Cranmer immediately adjourn to the royal presence. The archbishop was in bed, but rose straight away, dressed and repaired to the King, whom he found in the gallery at Whitehall. Once he had arrived, Henry revealed what he had done. How the Council wanted to commit Cranmer to the Tower on certain charges levelled against him. "I have granted their request," the King declared, "but as to whether they have done well or no, what say you, my lord?" The archbishop humbly thanked the King that he had given him warning before-hand. However, Cranmer added, he was very content to be committed to the Tower for questioning on his doctrines so that he might be heard. His Majesty was astonished at this and immediately cried out: "Oh Lord God, what fond simplicity you have, to commit yourself to be imprisoned so every enemy of yours can take advantage against you. Don't you know how, once they have you in prison, three or four false liars will soon be sent forward to witness against you and condemn you? These same accusers, because you are now at liberty, dare not open their lips or appear before you. Oh no," the King continued, "I have better regard for you than to let your enemies overthrow you. So tomorrow, after you come to the Council – and have no doubt they will send for you – when they reveal this matter to you, demand that, being one of them, you have as much favour as they would enjoy themselves. Insist that your accusers be brought before you. However, if they refuse and persist on committing you to the Tower, then appeal from them to me and give them this ring," which he handed over to the archbishop. "By this token," the King added, "they will know what I mean. I use this ring for no other purpose than to revoke matters from the Council to myself." And with this good advice ringing in his ears, Cranmer, after his most humble thanks, departed from His Majesty.'

Paget sat, head cocked to one side, as if listening to sounds from outside. He was telling the truth. I knew about this ring and the King's use of it. I also felt a cold dread. I confess that deep in my soul I always thought I was safe, inured to the King's dreadful games of the soul. Was this what Paget wanted to disturb?

'Listen now.' The King's Chief Secretary leaned closer. 'The next morning, according to the King's warning and his own expectations, the Council summoned Cranmer to be at their chamber by eight o'clock. When he came to the Council door, however, he was not permitted to enter but was told to remain outside for at least three quarters of an hour, many others going in and out. The matter seemed most strange to the archbishop's secretary, so he slipped away to inform the King's physician, Huicke. Huicke, not believing this, hurried to the antechamber and found it to be true that Thomas Cranmer, Lord Archbishop of Canterbury, had been forced to wait outside the door like some menial servant. The physician went directly and informed the King. "What is that?" exclaimed His Majesty. "By the mass, so my lord of Canterbury has become a menial, a serving man, to stand for almost an hour before the Council allow him entrance? How dare they serve my lord so?" Then His Majesty in a fit of rage lifted his hand, pointing his finger at the ceiling. "I shall talk with them by and by."' Paget now had his eyes shut, reciting what he had apparently learnt by heart. I feverishly searched my own memory about his whereabouts. Hadn't he been absent on an embassy to Paris?

He opened his eyes. 'Shall I continue, Will? Eh? A lesson for both of us?'

I nodded.

'The Lord Archbishop was summoned before the Council. They revealed that a most serious complaint had been levelled against him, both to them and the King. How he and others of his household had infected the whole realm with heresy so it was the King's pleasure that they should commit him to the Tower, where he could be carefully examined on what he had written and preached. Cranmer insisted that his accusers appear with him there and then before any further punishment was imposed. Although he argued most eloquently, he could make no headway, and they insisted that he be confined to the Tower. "I am sorry, my lords," Cranmer eventually declared, "but you drive me to this necessity. I appeal from you to His Majesty, who by this token has taken the matter into his own hands." Opening his wallet, he took out the ring and showed it to them. Immediately one of the council, Lord Russell, swore a great oath and said, "Did I not tell you, my lords, that ill would come of this matter? I always knew the King would never permit my lord of Canterbury to have such a blemish and be imprisoned unless it was for high treason."

'The Council, now terrified out of their wits, immediately adjourned to the royal presence, taking with them Cranmer and the ring he had produced. When they came into his privy chamber, the King said, "Ah, my lords, I always thought I had a discreet Council, but now I see I am much deceived. Why have you handled my lord of Canterbury so? What are you making of him? A slave? Shutting him out of the council chamber amongst the serving men? Would you like to be trapped like that?" After such taunting words the King added, "I would have you all consider my lord of

Canterbury as faithful a man towards me as any in this realm and one who in many ways is cherished by the faith I owe to God. Therefore," the King tapped his chest, "whoever loveth me loveth him."

'The Duke of Norfolk immediately went down on his knees and answered for the rest. "Your Grace," he declared, "we meant no harm or hurt to my lord of Canterbury. We only requested that he be confined to the Tower so that he might, after his trial, be set at liberty to even greater glory." His Majesty simply smirked and tapped Norfolk gently on the side of the head. "Very well, very well," he replied, "but I pray do not ever use my friends so. I can clearly see how the world goes amongst you. There is a lot of malice from one to the other. Let this be avoided, I warn you." Then, turning on his heel, he left the royal chamber. The Romanists on the Council had no choice but to shake hands, every one of them, with the archbishop, against whom never again did they raise a word.'

'Were you one of those, my lord?'

Paget scratched his ear, rubbing his lobe thoughtfully. 'I simply describe what happened. I learnt a most valuable lesson that day.' He held up finger and thumb slightly apart. 'So close, Will. Never mind the royal praise; Cranmer was that close to joining all those others our king has used and abused, be it Buckingham, Wolsey or Cromwell. Good Lord, the list gets longer by the year.' He rose and crossed to the dresser. He filled a goblet, thrust it at me. 'My father was a bailiff, Will.

Strictly speaking, a serjeant at mace, employed by the City of London; now I am Chief Secretary to the King's Council. I believe,' he went back and sat on his chair, 'that one should never tell a secret to more than one person, and that includes my beloved wife. The present secret is that our king is weakening; he can't even relieve himself without the use of some assistance.'

'Be careful, Master Paget.' I deliberately used the common term. 'His Majesty might not be as ill as he seems.'

'But one day he will die. What is so pressing is what he will do before he dies. Whom might he remove? And after His Majesty does join his fore-fathers, what might then happen to a jester whom nobody wants? Who consorts with the Princess Mary and her Spanish, Romanist ways. Who is besotted with that same princess's maidservant, the Lady Jane Bold. The jester who knows the true identity and whereabouts of this mysterious Balaam, the man who commits heinous treasons.'

I glanced up at that ruby glowing through the dark. 'What do you want, Master Paget?'

'His Majesty, I understand, talks about the princes, the sons of the Yorkist Edward IV who disappeared into the Tower?'

'Yes?'

'Will, my good man, His Majesty is deeply worried not about long-dead children but about his own: the Spanish Mary, Boleyn's daughter Elizabeth and his son young Edward, not yet ten years old. When Henry dies, will they be swept into the Tower and,' he shrugged, 'die of a fever or some other fatal accident?'

'And who would do that?'

'More importantly, whom does the King think might commit such heinous treason?'

'I cannot say, can you, Master Paget?'

'Why, the family His Majesty always fears: the Yellow Jackets, the People of the White Lion, the Howards of Norfolk. Look,' Paget stilled my protests, 'do you really think any of us are safe from Norfolk, a seasoned commander, and his son Surrey, England's proudest boy? All his life Henry has feared their shadow. He has tried to dominate them. Two of his wives were Howards, and they betrayed him. Worse, he believes they made a public mockery of him. The King has not forgotten that, and why should he? The Howards of Norfolk are even more dangerous now, with the King failing, his heir a minor. Remember the verse: "Woe to the kingdom whose ruler is a child"?'

'And what has this to do with me?'

'Why, everything! You, like everybody at court, must choose your side. One day the reckoning has to be made.' He blinked. 'And where your heart lies, so might your head.'

He paused at the ringing of the bell from the royal chambers, followed by the scurrying of feet along the gallery outside. 'Warn the King about the Howards.' He stretched out a hand. 'You will keep me informed of what you do and where you go? You will tell me on which side of the fence you stand? Time is short, Will.' He pushed his hand closer. 'Yes?'

'Yes.' I clasped his hand even as I breathed a prayer against my own lie.

'Good.' Paget rose, rubbing his hands. I am not the fool he thinks. He was clearly not convinced. He turned, staring at me from heavy-lidded eyes. 'Shall we see you at the Council meeting?'

'I am not a member.'

'No, no, you are not,' he agreed. 'You are certainly not.'

Dismissed, I slipped back into the gallery, now filling with retainers hurrying here and there. I needed to withdraw from the bustle of the court. Soft as a shadow, I scuttled up the various staircases to the chamber the King has allocated to me. A restful place, its walls painted with the story of the Prodigal Son, whilst two new tapestries describing the tale of Noah and his Ark decorate either side of the door. Woven matting covers the floor, stretching to a small four-poster bed draped with deep red silver-fringed curtains. All around the room stand coffers and caskets, chests and trunks, their lids thrown back, spilling out the robes I still like to wear. I have my own close stool specially provided by the King, a New Year's gift made of iron with a removable brass basin beneath its velvet-covered seat, beside this a small lavarium with bowl, jug and linen cloths.

The palace gong farmers had been busy that day and I wanted to ensure that they'd done their task as well as I had done mine. They had. I eased myself, then washed my hands and face, savouring the beautiful smell from the small tablet of Castilian soap Princess Mary had given me on my name day. I slipped into the quilted-back chair that serves my chancery table. I do like my room, I am proud of it, my home, my manor house. I have searched it thoroughly; no eyelets or peepholes have been carved for people to spy or eavesdrop. I enjoy the warmth of the fire and the glow of light from the constantly burning great lantern horn on its table. I closed my eyes, breathed out, then stared around my little kingdom. I dress soberly, though I love to receive doublets of worsted lined with samite, coats, capes and hoods of Lincoln green fringed with red craul, or heavy cloaks of blue wool lined with weasel fur. Another chest holds my painted costumes for court revelries, a crown and mask, together with a gilded mace and chain for my days as Lord of Misrule. Suits of brocaded silk edged with red linen, armour of flimsy board and even a fine hobbyhorse are all mine. Such items litter my chamber, deliberately so. I can tell at a glance if any Judas man, some court spy – and God knows they thrive like fleas on a turd – has been busy sifting through my possessions. Not today.

I picked up a posy from a basket on the desk and sniffed its fragrant aroma. I should be – well I am – a contented man. I have progressed far since I left the service of Richard Fermor of Easton Neston in Northamptonshire. I have undoubtedly prospered. I have gold and silver coins hidden away against any lean times with the goldsmiths along Cheapside and Poultry. Three fine horses and two sturdy sumpter ponies are housed in the royal stables, mine to use whenever I wish, on personal business or when King and court move from one palace to another. Friends are many, or so it would seem. I can pick and choose, for people regard me as the King's fool but also as the King's favourite. Above all I have the Lady Jane Bold, well cared for in the household of Princess Mary, a resident for the last eleven years, having once served Anne Boleyn, that woman of infamous memory. After she went to the headsman's block everything became ruined, dark, deceitful and morose.

I fished beneath my jerkin, took out the locket, snapped it open and stared at Lady Jane's sweet face. Vain as a peacock she is. Like me she spends her money on costly raiment: striped purple satin gowns, their pleats lined with buckram, bodices of fustian or crimson satin; kirtles striped with gold, jerkins of blue damask. Behind all this love of glorious show, Lady Jane is a closed book. She talks little about her past, be it personal or her time at the court of Tarquin and Semiramis, as she refers to the tyrant Henry and the lustful Boleyn. Jane is of medium height, with lustrous brown hair and bright dark eyes. She has perfectly formed features except for her pretty mouth, which she always twists in a slight pout, as if disapproving of the world. She is deft in conversation, skilled at listening and, whatever her mood, looks most interested. Oh she can act the simpleton, yet she is shrewd of wit, sharp of tongue and eagle of eye. She can mimic and imitate, be it a prattling preacher, a counterfeit crank, a drunken doxy or a boisterous bawdy basket. I recall her once turning on a buttery man who tried to steal a kiss from her. She called him a pickled lard and said he should do a tub fast: doused in a hot tub of water for an entire day whilst being starved of food and drink, the cure for anyone suffering from the French disease!

Jane and I are more than close. Once, during a royal progress to Dover, we secretly met before a hedge priest and exchanged our pledges. Now I drew her recent letter from my pocket, scrawled in the deepest black ink. We had not met for days. Jane wondered if I was playing truant with my bed. I recognised the cipher contained within the strange lettering. She wished to meet with me along with Balaam, Princess Mary's agent, that will-o'-the-wisp, mischief incarnate, the Devil in taffeta. I do not know his real name. Balaam has Moorish features, Hispanic, with jet-black hair, glittering eyes and a narrow sallow face. A dagger man born and bred. Jane believes his family once served Catherine of Aragon. Certainly he hates the King with a loathing beyond all comprehension and, as Paget described, never fails to stir up malicious mischief against the Great Despot.

A true scurrier in the cornfield is Balaam, hither and thither on Princess Mary's business, not to mention that of Cardinal Pole, who keeps in constant communication with the Romanists, the papists, the secret Catholics who yearn, as Norfolk does, for the old ways. Paget is correct. If Balaam is ever caught, it will be Tyburn or Smithfield for him. Nevertheless, he is the master of disguise, a true shape-shifter. Last time I met him he was pretending to be a physician, a herbalist, glittering gorgeously like the man on the moon. Bracelets decorated his wrists, his beringed fingers boasted St Vincenza's rocks, a silver case for instruments hung from his girdle with a gilt spatula thrust in the ribbon band around his feathered hat. When we met, he was audacious and bold, strolling into the Bishop's Mitre in Gracechurch Street, a tavern well furnished with all kinds of comfort, a place constantly frequented by sheriff's bailiffs, council men and their horde of hangers-on, spies and informers. On entering, he immediately demanded that the tavern master put an end to the din in the great yard beyond, where mastiffs had been set on a bear and a bull. I must admit, the noise was hideous: the cheering, the growls, the hellish barks and yelps as the mastiffs were tossed, their fall broken by their masters armed with sticks. Balaam's effrontery carried the day. He then proclaimed to all those gathered in the packed tap room that he was not the type of physician who gloried in the juice of a hung tortoise, the scrapings of an alligator or some other ill-shaped fish. He promised he would eschew all such ploys. 'Fingers are the best instruments for a physician,' he declared. 'Why, he should have a lion's heart, a lady's hand and a hawk's eye. I do not believe,' he added, 'that a tumour can be removed by stroking it with a dead man's hand, or that the skin of a salamander protects the flesh from the sun or that a spider swallowed alive in treacle is a sure protection against the ague. Nor do I accept that a steeple struck by lightning is the work of the Devil seen entering through the belfry window . . .'

I smiled at the memory but wondered how Balaam could be so elusive. Paget was undoubtedly hunting him, be it in London or in the north, which brought me back to that secret furtive meeting in the royal chancery office. Paget had been trying to frighten me, as well as discover where my loyalties lay. He was not so much hostile, but reminding me that nobody was safe. He was speaking the truth. Saintly Thomas More once said, long before his fatal clash with the King, that if it could win Henry a town in France, his head would roll. John Fisher of Rochester had been confessor to the King's own grandmother the redoubtable lady Margaret Beaufort, but that had not saved him from the axe. Richard Whiting, the eighty-year-old Abbot of Glastonbury, had been revered by the King as a living saint, but Whiting was dragged on a hurdle to the top of Glastonbury Tor and hanged like a common felon. Hadn't the King of France muttered how he would not let Henry of England marry one of his dogs, let alone a French princess? Paget was a realist; he was trying to elicit my help but he was also warning me not only about the present but also the future.

I also wondered about William Clarke, the chancery clerk with Paget. What had he been working on before he scuttled like a rabbit out of the light? However, a knock on the door disturbed me and a tousle-headed page bawled that the Council was about to gather. I greedily drank a pottle of beer and hastily ate some of the hardened bread left on a platter. Then I hastened out along the torch-lit galleries, the dark oaken rails, balustrades, panelling, newels and banisters gleaming in the light. Shadows moved, prompting memories. I paused briefly at the top of the stairs, recalling a recent visit to Hampton Court. How the servants there complained about the ghost of Katherine Howard, who had lost her head because of Thomas Culpeper. She had been confined there, hysterical with fear. On discovering the King was in the chapel, she had raced along the galleries to beg for his mercy, only to be caught and dragged screaming back. The servants claim her ghost still haunts the path she took, and her screams have woken many at the dead of night. But that is Henry. Where he goes, a whole legion of ghosts dolefully follow. I glanced out of the window. Darkness was falling. Smells floated, the savoury tangs from the kitchens mingling with the perfume and fragrance from herb pots and capped braziers. I continued on and reached the great council chamber. Anthony Wingfield, Captain of the Spears, glimpsed my pass, confirmed by the King's own seal, and I entered that long, cold room.

Torches, candles and tapers had been lit. Catherine wheels, their spokes lined with glowing cubes of beeswax, had been lowered. A fire roared in the carved double hearth. Candelabra placed along the centre of the great oval-shaped table glowed magnificently, yet for all this, still a cold, sombre room. Brilliant tapestries glow in a myriad of rich colours, but I am always fearful of that chamber. Whatever the hour, whatever the season, a sense of impending danger dulls the spirit, a malevolent malice, constantly lurking in the perpetual shadows. I hastened to the King's end of the table and climbed the stairs to the music loft, murky and ill-lit, though a place that provides an excellent view of the entire chamber. Henry often places me there, asking me to watch, to note the expressions and attitudes of his councillors, the glances between them and who whispers to whom. I once protested that I wasn't his spy. The King promptly beat me and banished me to my chamber, saying I would be whatever he wanted me to be. I was not his spy, he later breathed at me. (I remember the gin fumes; God knows he loves that drink.) He praised my memory and said my quick eye and sharp wits would catch what he might miss. I replied that in which case I should be the King and he the fool, upon which Henry promptly cuffed my head and tweaked my ear until I screamed in pain.

The tide of such protests has passed. I am the King's

creature. The Princess Mary has begged me never to forget that. So I stood cloaked and hooded in the shadow of that music loft. I sensed something would happen as the wolf pack gathered. Oh, they all swaggered in, jewelled bonnets and caps on their heads, heavy cloaks not quite covering their decorated, embroidered stomachers and waistcoats of silver cloth or quilted with gold. The light picked up the jewels on their doublets as well as the water on their cloaks. Gauntleted and booted, they stamped their feet and clapped their hands against the cold. A cheerful, merry group, like powerful merchants gathering for a banquet in the Guildhall, but this was different. The Dark Lords, the Masters of the Twilight, the Shadow-bringers were clustering in all their pomp and might. Thomas Cranmer, Archbishop of Canterbury, was the only visible exception, dressed in a white surplice under a heavy black mantle, a square cap of the same colour and material on his ageing head. A grey man Cranmer, with his seemingly colourless eyes, his dull shaven face always twisted into a mournful pull, lips pushed forward as if his tongue is too big for his mouth. He wore the archbishop's ring and rested on a silver-topped ebony cane. One crow amongst the peacocks, all a-glitter with their precious rings and collars.

Bonnets, hats, gloves and cloaks were doffed and thrown at waiting servants. Mulled wine richly garnished with cinnamon, mace and cloves was served in elegant pewter goblets wrapped in snow-white napkins. Trays of soft bread, buttered and covered in diced meat, were also offered. The lords of the Council, busy in their preparations, ordered their chancery clerks to place their writing cases on the table. Each seemed to know his own place. Greetings and salutations were exchanged, hands clasped, lips curled in smiles, heads shaken in knowing nods, confidential morsels softly whispered. All this was shadow and no substance, a mere ritual. The pack was simply milling about. The smiling faces hid devious, sharp minds. Wits were being honed. Opponents secretly but carefully scrutinised for any weakness. Everyone kept an eye on the door through which the King would enter. Physician Huicke appeared dressed in his costly black furred robes and physician's cap. Diamonds winked on his fingers, broad gold bracelets shimmered on his wrists and the silver medallion on his filigreed necklace glittered with the jewelled snake of Aesculapius. This too was only a pretence. Huicke's narrow, ill-tempered, whiskered face shimmered with fear. Truly the hunt at court was on, but who was hunting whom?

I moved to get a clearer view of the rest. The Seymour brothers, Edward and Thomas, the former newly created Earl of Hertford, bristling men of war who would take to fighting on land or sea as a bird does to flying. Hertford is fresh out of Scotland, where he has been busy burning, slaying and ravaging to his heart's content. Thomas has been roaming the seas chasing pirates, though court gossips claim he is no better than the men he hangs. Edward and Thomas are so alike, with their broad brows, staring protuberant eyes, thick sensuous lips and luxurious hair and moustaches. Both men stood gossiping with that other leader of the pack, John Dudley, the Viscount Lisle, his harsh, lean, bony face all shaven, his hair cropped close like the soldier he boasts to be, claiming that he is more at home on the battlefield than he is at court. Dressed completely in black, Dudley has the look of a Tower raven, constantly moving, head turning to watch the rest of the Council. The King enjoys the company of these three because he also likes to act the bluff, sharp-tongued, cynical soldier himself. He loves to challenge them to dice, hazard or cards whilst gossiping about the conduct of war. However, if present chatter is correct, His Majesty is not too favoured with the younger Seymour, a rash, impetuous man, a roué and rake who'd be more at home in the French court, where the dissolute gallants leave the corpses of hanged men in the beds of their mistresses as a clever conceit. English courtiers are more brash and aggressive; their tempers flare more easily. They breathe harsh words and commit violent acts. Dudley once exchanged fiery words with the Bishop of Winchester and struck him full in the face, for which he was expelled from court for an entire month. My lord of Hertford, the elder Seymour, also exchanged violent, injurious words with Wriothesley, the Lord Chancellor, though he did not suffer any such exile.

In truth, my king loves to watch his dogs curl and

fight. Chief Secretary Paget has the measure of our royal master. He realises that Edward Seymour, Earl of Hertford, uncle to the king-to-be, will take the ascendancy and, according to gossip, has persuaded Hertford to follow his advice in all proceedings. Paget uses Hertford as his dog to menace the Romanists and their mastiff Henry Howard, Earl of Surrey, son of the old Duke of Norfolk. Surrey is a poet who believes he is free as the air he breathes. He has already spent a month in the Fleet for challenging Sir John Leigh, the King's Justice, to a duel. He has also clashed with Hertford, striking him violently within the precincts of the court, for which he nearly lost his hand. Despite these strictures, he cannot restrain his heady will. Years ago, he went on a night attack against the wealthy of London, breaking their windows and hurling obscenities at them. When confronted with his crimes, Surrey retorted that he'd acted so that his victims might learn from the stones passing noiselessly through the air and breaking in suddenly upon them about the punishment that, as Scripture tells us, divine justice will inflict on impenitent sinners. Surrey is a wayward, haughty soul who led his troops to defeat before the walls of Boulogne. So frenetic did he become at his misfortune that he demanded his officers stick their swords through his guts and make him forget that day. Many now wished they had. His soldiers blame their defeat chiefly on him, their leader, whose head and heart are swollen with pride, arrogance and impetuous confidence in his own unreasoning bravery. Little wonder Paget has abandoned Surrey the hot-head and turned to my lord Hertford, who can act so moderately in all things (apart from dealing with my lord Surrey) that all believe him to be their own.

In fact the two Howards, Norfolk and Surrey, and their ally, Stephen Gardiner of Winchester, were the last to arrive in the council chamber. The three stayed away from the rest as if eager to inspect the cupboards of plate studded with precious stones and pearls that stand further down the hall. I've closely studied Master Holbein's painting of Norfolk. The duke is shown in all his glory grasping the golden baton of the Earl Marshal in one hand, the Lord Treasurer's white staff in the other. A sallow, clean-shaven face, the dark hair unfashionably long, a hawkish visage with hooded eyes, finely shaped brows and pointed chin, lips tight as a miser's purse. Thomas Howard is one who hides his seething ambition. A petty man in so many ways, he is deceptive and deceiving, well steeped in the dirty devices of the court and most skilled in weaving sinister designs. He complains constantly of a queasy stomach and loose bowels, yet lives to prove the English proverb that 'a creaking gate hangs longest'. He is like a tree that bends to every storm, a gambler who took up primero, a game introduced by Henry's Spanish queen, and became so skilled as to empty His Majesty's purse many a time. Norfolk is a reed shaking in the wind but one that has dug its roots deep, long and tangled. His own wife

Elizabeth, daughter of Edward Stafford, Duke of Buckingham, said of him: 'He can speak fair as well to his enemies as to his friends. He neither regards God nor his honour.' He can change like a loosened weather-cock on a village steeple. A man of contrasts, he'll feed the hungry yet wears his dressing gowns until the fur is rubbed clean. He once proclaimed, 'I've never yet read scripture, nor ever will read it. It was merry in England before the new learning came. Yes, I wish all things were as in times past.'

In so many ways Norfolk is a memory of things long gone. He wears relics around his neck and revels in his ownership of fifty rosaries. Nevertheless, whatever his coarse boasting, he patronises scholars such as Skelton the poet, Leland the historian and the great classics scholar John Clarke of Magdalene, who introduced Norfolk's son, Henry of Surrey, to the beauties of Petrarch and other poets of that ilk, as well as grounding him firmly in Latin, French, Italian and Spanish. It was Clarke who set Surrey along the road to be the great glory of His Majesty's court, as well as the most arrogant man in England. Surrey is tall like his father and so is easily recognisable. He has a long, serious face, thick auburn hair, tightly compressed lips and a slightly flared nose. What is immediately striking about him is the cast in his right eye, a defect he feels most sensitive about. I have read some of his poetry where he makes reference to it. In his paintings they try to disguise such a defect, because an eye turning outwards, according to popular lore, indicates cunning, deceit and treachery. He will need all such vices in this present time.

I noticed that Paget, now dressed in his satin and silks, a jewelled bonnet on his head, did not greet the Norfolks, seemingly busy moving from one councillor to another. Wriothesley, the Chancellor, that viper incarnate, did sketch a bow towards them, and to his former patron Gardiner. Thomas Wriothesley! Now there's a man I truly fear. Yes, I, William Somers, formerly of Northamptonshire, the fool, the jester, the innocent. I am a soul who at times loses all wit and sense, the sort of fool who will add water to the sea or bring a firebrand to a burning house. True, I make mistakes and take false shams for true substances. Yet I can also be discerning, and that is a thing to be at Henry's court! I live in times when one Christian tears at another in those darkened chambers beneath the Tower. Yes, those dungeons, with their so-called licking walls, because the damp on them is the only refreshment available to the dry lips and cracked throats of the prisoners. Often the only reason they are there is because they no longer believe that God kissed Mary in Galilee, or they deny that royal Henry has the same power as the Bishop of Rome. Such prisoners are at the mercy of wall-eyed, fiendishly faced torturers, who hack and tear in the name of the gentle Christ who himself was hacked and torn. I truly admit, as I would on a book of the Gospels, I do not understand the heart of it. Such days of terror in a world of uncertainty.

I love my Jane. I would become truly hand-fast and warm with her in bed, but we are fools, innocents, and what might she conceive? That troubles me. When I am away from her I have to listen to the poisonous pourings of a half-mad king who seems to delight in dispatching all those his love touches to a violent death. Nonetheless, that same king, at certain times, will sit upon the floor of his bedchamber and sob like a child for what he has done and must do again. Little wonder I become anxious and afraid. Fear turns both belly and bowel to water. Demons in human flesh prowl my waking hours, and none is worse than Thomas Wriothesley, he of the dark russet hair pressed down under its flat-rimmed bejewelled cap, that curly beard and moustache cultivated in an attempt to hide his aggressive jutting jaw, and his eyes, milky blue, like those of a baleful cat.

Now and again in my teasing mood I have asked the great lords of the Council what they desire. Good governance? Honour? Titles? Lands? Wealth? Power? All are there. I asked Wriothesley the same question, only once, in the gardens of Hampton Palace. Swift as a snake, he grasped a bee in his thick gloved hand, squeezed it until it cracked and dropped the corpse at my feet. 'To crush my opponents, Will,' he murmured. Wriothesley is absorbed with death. Like all such men, strangely enough, he couples this with a detestation of women. He loves to interrogate, to question: a man who fences with his own shadow, a hell-hound who lives to hunt others to a gruesome death. A smiling villain, a dove-feathered raven, a wolfish ravenous lamb. He is false of heart and bloody of mind, a pig in sloth, a snake in stealth, a wolf in greediness, a dog in madness and a lion in hunting. I secretly call him Legion because his soul must house a veritable mob of demons. Nowhere is this more apparent than when some poor woman falls into his power.

Anne Askew was one of these; Balaam told me the story. Askew was young, beautiful and learned, of honourable birth and ancient lineage and a convert to the reformist faith. She was, for that reason, ejected from her Lincolnshire home by her husband. She then resumed her maiden name, journeyed to London and devoted herself to the propagation of that faith, for which she was patronised by the Queen's sister Lady Herbert, the Duchess of Suffolk and other great ladies of the court. Indeed, report has it that the Queen herself received books from Askew in the presence of Lady Herbert, which would have brought both under the penalties of the statute against reading heretical works.

Now the opinions of Mistress Askew are neither here nor there, but when Gardiner and Wriothesley learnt of her relationship with the Queen, they promptly ordered her arrest. She was cruelly confined in prison, where the ladies of the court, perhaps even the Queen herself, made the mistake of sending her monies, goods and other items for her sustenance. Immediately Wriothesley closed in. Askew was put to the rack to reveal the names of those who had sent her money. She refused to answer, only saying that it had been delivered by 'a man in a blue coat', whilst another 'dressed in a violet coat' had brought a purse, but she could not say who had sent these. Wriothesley racked her cruelly because she refused to confess or name supporters at court. The racking continued until the strings of her eyes and limbs were strained and she swooned into a dead faint. The then Lieutenant of the Tower, Sir Anthony Knyvett, ordered her release.

Once they had roused her with water, they made her sit for two long hours on the floor with Wriothesley, who whispered false promises and threatened bloody menaces if she did not tell him exactly what he wanted. He enjoyed it, rocking backwards and forwards, sometimes solicitous, at other times threatening. Askew was racked again, pinched and hurt until her joints popped out. Eventually Sir Anthony Knyvett intervened and instructed her to be taken down. Wriothesley, not at all happy that Askew might be released without confession, commanded Knyvett to strain her on the rack again, but the lieutenant refused, saying the weakness of the woman would not bear it. Wriothesley turned on him cursing, adding that he'd report his disobedience directly to the King. Knyvett still objected, so Wriothesley, throwing off his gown, actually manned the rack himself, questioning Askew closely but unable to break her and only ceasing when her bones and joints were almost plucked apart.

Finally Wriothesley gave up his attempt and returned to court. Sir Anthony Knyvett, upset and frightened by his threats, took a swifter barge to speak to the King before Wriothesley did. Ushered into the royal presence, Knyvett went down on his knees and sought His Majesty's pardon, then showed how the whole matter stood. How he had stopped the racking of Mistress Askew and had been threatened by the Lord Chancellor with His Majesty's displeasure. The King, patting Knyvett on the shoulder, said he'd done right, granted the lieutenant pardon and ordered him to return immediately to supervise his charge.

His Majesty, of course, was once again playing the two-faced Janus. He expressed his greatest displeasure that a female, a lady, should be exposed to such barbarity, yet he did not condemn or punish the perpetrators, nor did he intervene to preserve Anne Askew from further tribulation. In truth, according to Balaam, the King himself had ordered Anne Askew to be stretched on the rack, being furious against her for having brought heretical books into the palace and imbued his queen and others with her false doctrine.

Wriothesley and Gardiner then spread their net wider. Certain gentlemen of the court – William Morris, the King's usher, and Sir George Blagge from the privy chamber – along with Lascelles, a gentleman from Nottinghamshire, were arrested, confined to Newgate and warned by Wriothesley's men how they were all marked for death and so should pay heed to their lives.

So confident were Gardiner and Wriothesley that they could purge the court of all reformists that they struck hard and high. George Blagge was a great favourite with the King, who would honour him in moments of familiarity with the endearing appellation of 'his little pig'. Apparently His Majesty did not appear to be aware of Blagge's arrest until it came to signing the warrants for execution. He immediately sent for Wriothesley and berated him for arresting a man like Blagge and daring to interfere with retainers of the royal privy chamber. He instructed the Chancellor to draw up a pardon. Blagge was promptly released and swiftly trotted off to thank his royal master, who on seeing him cried out:

'Ah, my little pig, you're safe again.'

'Yes, sire,' replied Blagge, 'but if Your Majesty had not been better than your bishops, your little pig would have been roasted long ago.'

Mistress Askew was not so fortunate. Tortured and broken, she had to be carried to Smithfield on the day of execution in a chair because she was unable to stand on her feet. Two others died with her. Anne Askew was lashed to the central stake, bound around her middle with a chain to keep her upright. A priest came forward to deliver his sermon. Mistress Askew shook her head, saying, 'There really is no use.' The priest persisted, despite the cries and protests of the crowd, which proved so strong the execution ground had to be specially railed off. I, the King's witness, was close by on a bench near St Bartholomew's, where Wriothesley, Norfolk and the others had gathered. There was some alarm because the rumour spread that the victims had gunpowder about them. The lords were frightened that any explosion might send the faggots flying about their ears; Norfolk however pointed out that the gunpowder was not laid under the wood but about the victims' bodies, so there was no danger from the fire at all.

Once again Anne Askew and her companions were invited to recant. All refused. The Lord Mayor stood up and shouted: *'Fiat iustitia!'* – 'Let there be justice'. Then the fires were lit. Askew and her two companions were soon consumed by the flames. Wriothesley stayed till Askew was no more than smouldering ash. He savoured that.

Wriothesley was also the King's choice to send to Hampton Court when Queen Katherine Howard fell from grace. That silly popinjay, with a host of women from both her chamber and household, was swept into prison. Wriothesley interrogated them all about the Queen's passionate trysts with Dereham and Culpeper. Oh how he enjoyed himself! He took the greatest pleasure in almost frightening to death the aged Duchess of Norfolk, Lady Rochford and the rest. He would enter their chambers with the torturers jangling their chains behind him. He would listen to their screams, occasionally jumping up and down, dancing with pleasure, before leaving to regale the court with what he'd done. Once, overcome with revulsion, I conquered my fear and asked him why he took such delight. He just stared at me, that great chin trembling, those milky blue eyes full of dreadful joy.

'Master Somers,' he replied, 'I am the King's rat-catcher. I trap rats for him, and who cares about them?'

Well I did, and I told him so. Wriothesley pushed me along the gallery where we'd met, grabbed my shoulder and pulled me into a window recess.

'Will,' he whispered, eyes rounded in mock innocence, 'your Lady Jane was in Boleyn's household. You know, the great goggle-eyed whore. What did Jane know about those nightly trysts with Master Smeaton, Sir Henry Norris and even Boleyn's own brother George? I mean, while we are investigating queens, shouldn't your friend be seized and taken in a sealed barge to the Tower? Oh, the ladies hate that! Katherine Howard, all fearful, kicked her lovely legs till the tops of her stockings showed, her thick lacy petticoats going back. Oh Will,' Wriothesley closed his eyes as if savouring a delicious meal, 'how that firm, queenly little body struggled against mine.' He opened his eyes, chin thrust forward, 'So what did the Lady Jane know about all that, and what did she tell you?'

I broke free of his grip. I confess, perhaps I don't know how to love; that feeling is difficult to describe and even harder to explain. But hate? Oh, thanks to Wriothesley, I know how to hate. If he ever falls, I want to be there when he's dragged kicking and screaming from the barge as it docks before the great gates near St Thomas's Tower.

Nevertheless, standing there in the music loft above the council chamber, I also took great comfort in how I had thwarted him over the present queen, Katherine Parr. Gardiner and Wriothesley certainly failed to trap Cranmer, but they were not finished, and engaged in further wicked intrigue towards their real quarry, the Queen. The Queen's sister Lady Herbert had already been secretly denounced to Henry as an active instrument in subverting his edict on heretical works. Wriothesley subtly pointed out that Anne Askew, the recently burnt heretic, had also been patronised by Lady Herbert and others of the Queen's chamber. The King was not pleased. The attack had gathered strength, a subtle malignant plot. Wriothesley fed His Majesty information that his consort received and read books forbidden by royal decree. Time and again Gardiner and Wriothesley continued to argue that everything the Queen expressed or insinuated must be seen in the light not only of heresy but of treason.

Now I know our king; I have studied him most closely and I have very good reason to do so. Henry's anger is always the most deadly when he broods over an offence, and as I assure myself, this king does brood. It nearly cost Katherine Parr her life. The Queen had become accustomed during those hours of domestic privacy with her husband to converse with him on theological subjects, in which they both took great delight. Naturally they disagreed, but the ready wit and honeyed eloquence of the Queen only gave spice to these discussions. I have it from the gossips amongst the ladies of the chamber, as well as a gentleman in the King's household, that His Majesty was at first amused and intrigued by such debates. Katherine gradually became aware not only of her husband's physical sickness but of his deep guilt over a horde of unrepented crimes, in particular about Catherine of Aragon of blessed and beloved memory. Her Grace proved keen to provoke her husband to a sense of sorrow, a realisation that one day he would have to account for what he had done. Moreover, the Queen was swift to realise that the King was neither Romanist nor reformist but wished to mould religion in the light of his own conscience and will, which she herself could not accept.

Now, as God, his angels and my good self realise, anyone who tries to advise His Majesty with spiritual advice, be it Romanist or reformist, treads a very dangerous path. John Fisher, Bishop of Rochester, tried and paid the price. Thomas More, once Lord Chancellor, attempted the same and lost his head. Cromwell, Anne Boleyn and others had all stumbled along that murderous runnel leading to execution in or around the Tower. Her Grace the Queen thought she could avoid such danger and quietly challenged the King's infallibility, pointing out that he was assuming for himself what he condemned in the Bishop of Rome.

One day, in the malignant presence of Wriothesley, the Queen tried to discuss with her husband a proclamation the King had recently issued, forbidding the use of the translation of scripture, which he had previously licensed. The King was tired and depleted, the ulcers in his legs inflamed and painful. The Queen, unknowing of this, persisted in the matter too closely, even though the King showed tokens of anger and abruptly cut the matter short. Her Grace then made a few other pleasant observations and withdrew. Once she was gone, the King's fury erupted.

'A good hearing it is,' he shouted, 'when women become such clerks. Much to my discomfort in my old age, I am to be taught by my wife!'

I do not know whether the King was trying to trap the Queen or not, but Wriothesley, along with Gardiner, could not resist the opportunity and began to breathe a malice which, only a few days earlier, they'd kept so well hidden. They flattered His Majesty, I witnessed this, on his theological knowledge and judgement, declaring that the King 'excels the princes of his age and every other age as well as all the best doctors of divinity'. Consequently it was most unseemly for any of his subjects to argue with him so impudently as the Queen had just done. Indeed, it was most grievous for any of his councillors to hear it, since those who heard such bold words spoken in defiance would themselves not scruple to act so disobediently. Gardiner, hard eyes watching the King, added softly that he could make great discoveries about the truth if he was not deterred by the Queen's powerful faction. And chattering the like, Wriothesley and Gardiner so filled His Majesty's suspicious mind with fears that he gave them permission, under warrant, to consult with others about drawing up articles against the Queen to charge her with heresy and treason.

Wriothesley of course thought it was best to begin with the women of her chamber, particularly Lady Herbert. He proposed to accuse them of breaking the Act of Six Articles, which defines this kingdom's faith, and so organised a search of their closets and coffers. He hoped to find incriminating evidence against the Queen; once he had, she could be taken by night in a sealed barge to the Tower. The King agreed, and the matter was secretly carried forward, though the Queen had no knowledge of the dangers gathering about her. Despite my pleas, His Majesty continued to behave politely whilst Gardiner and Wriothesley drew up an act to attain his wife, a bill for her impeachment in Parliament. I decided to act, and anonymously sent her clear warning of the horrid danger.

The Queen, once informed, fell into a hysterical agony. She was accustomed to occupying an apartment close to the King and lapsed into one fit after another, her shrieks and cries reaching his ears. The King, incapacitated with pain, sent me to visit her. I comforted her and returned to inform His Satanic Majesty that his wife was dangerously ill, her sickness being caused by a malady of the mind. I urged him to see her. The King immediately insisted that, because his legs could not sustain him, he be carried into the Queen's chamber, where he found her heavy with melancholy almost to the point of death. The Queen however had the wit and shrewdness to show a proper degree of gratitude for the honour of the royal visit, which, she assured His Infernal Highness, greatly revived her spirits. She then confessed how distressed she was at having seen so little of His Majesty lately and that her apprehension had deepened as she may have unintentionally given him offence. The King, fat face beaming goodwill, replied graciously and encouragingly with many tender touches. The Queen, as if tutored, behaved in a humble and ingratiating manner, supplicating the humour of her husband.

Once he had left, the King turned to me and Huicke, quickly informing us in great detail about what was being plotted against the Queen. I have no proof of this, but I suspect that Huicke immediately went to Katherine and advised her about the great danger still threatening and how she might escape it. Our queen is no fool and recognised the source. Her own ladies have no love for Wriothesley; one of these owns a pet dog called Riotously, which she teases and taunts outrageously in public.

The Queen certainly felt under threat. Once the meeting with the King was over, she ordered new locks for her coffers and boxes, whilst the religious books that had been brought in by her ladies, those donated by Anne Askew, were either hidden in the garderobe or smuggled out to a safer place. There were other dangers. Katherine Parr, Lady Latimer as she once was before her marriage to His Majesty, was a widow. She is a pretty piece, small, pert-faced and dresses so elegantly. Now a comely widow with a rich inheritance is as attractive as a honeycomb, and no lesser person than Sir Thomas Seymour, brother to the Earl of Hertford, paid court to her. In my view, and those I trust, Katherine Parr was much taken with Sir Thomas. Under different circumstances she would have married him, but of course, the King's eye and favour fell on her and she had no choice but to bow to his imperial will. Sir Thomas, under the prompt direction of his elder brother and Master Paget, decided to quit the field and leave His Majesty to his pleasures. Now Katherine Howard, late queen of this present king, was executed for not revealing previous amours and relationships with young men of the court. Gardiner and Wriothesley hoped they could discover the same about Lady Parr, but could not.

I do sense a shifting danger in all this. One day our King of Hades must join his forefathers, but who will manage the kingdom for his heir? The Council? Yet there again the Queen-widow has rights; could she not be appointed regent? And if she is made regent, does Sir Thomas hope that he can control her and so master the young king? The younger Seymour is a bloodsucker, a bottled spider, twice as fit for Hell as any of them; his tongue could out-venom a viper and he is a danger to the Queen. Only the good Lord knows whether

Wriothesley, that royal rat-catcher, mentioned Seymour or the Queen's childlessness to further disturb the King's humours.

I did my best to mollify such rumours. The King had visited his queen and shown he was benevolent towards her. The following evening the Queen found herself well enough to reciprocate and so visited the King in his own privy chamber. She came attended by her sister Lady Herbert, the King's young niece Jane Grey carrying the candles before them. His Infernal Majesty welcomed his wife most courteously but slyly turned the conversation to the controversy regarding religion, hoping perhaps to draw her into further heated debate. The Queen – and her flattery would have choked me – cleverly avoided the snare, declaring that she was but a woman, imbued with all the imperfections natural to the weakness of her sex. Consequently, in all matters of doubt and difficulty she must refer herself to His Majesty's better judgement, because God, she continued her face all prim and proper – and the Lord only knows how she kept it so – 'has appointed you to be the Supreme Head of us all, and from you, next to God, will I learn'.

'Not so!' our royal hypocrite retorted. 'Aren't you becoming a theologian, Kate, to instruct us and not to be instructed by us, as sometimes recently we have seen?'

'No, Your Majesty,' the Queen replied. 'If Your Majesty has so construed my meaning, how much mistaken! For I have always maintained that it is preposterous for a woman to instruct her lord. Moreover, if I have ever presumed to differ with Your Highness on religion, it was partly to obtain information for my own comfort regarding certain finer points on which I stood in doubt. At other times because I understood that, in conversing with you, you were able to pass away the pain and weariness of your present infirmity. All this encouraged me to boldness in the hope of profiting from Your Majesty's learned discourse as well as soothing you.' Oh, clever, subtle woman! I learnt that evening how cunning Katherine truly is.

'Then if this is so, sweetheart,' our King of Pharisees replied, 'we are the most perfect of friends.' The Devil's own liar then kissed her with much tenderness and gave both her and her ladies permission to depart.

Wriothesley and Gardiner had no knowledge of this meeting and continued their plot, singling out a time for her arrest. On that day the King, recovering from his ailments, sent for the Queen to take the air with him in the gardens. She came attended by her ladies. The royal couple walked and talked, but then Wriothesley, with forty of the guard, entered the garden with the hope of carrying the Queen off to the Tower, the Chancellor having not the slightest information about how the King had changed. Our ever-fickle Majesty received Wriothesley in a burst of indignation and saluted him with the unexpected address of 'Beast!', 'Fool!' and 'Knave!' then sternly ordered him to withdraw. The Queen, when she saw the King angry with his Chancellor, had the sense to intercede for him, saying that she'd become a humble suitor for Wriothesley as she deemed his fault was occasioned by a mistake.

'Poor soul, Kate,' retorted our mendacious monarch, acting his much-loved Solomon role, 'you little know how much evil this man deserves at your hand. On my word, sweetheart, he has been a very knave.'

Afterwards I remonstrated with the King that Wriothesley should be severely punished, even removed from the Council. Henry, for his own strange reasons, disagreed.

'Gardiner, Bishop Gardiner of Winchester, is the prime mover,' he declared. 'He is the one to be punished.'

Wriothesley suspected, God knows how, that I had been instrumental in saving the Queen. I waited for another opening to strike at him, but none occurred. The weasel-souled rat-catcher decided to make his own submission. Grinning at me with his eyes, he knelt solemn-faced before the King, stretched out his hands and pleaded, 'I shall have good cause to be sorry to my innermost heart for all my life if the favour of you, our most gracious master, fails me. I pray, I beg, I plead your clemency will temper that.'

Only the Lord and his angels know who put Wriothesley up to that. He knew he had done a wicked thing and he was no more sorry than the cat who'd swallowed the cream. Henry of course loves to appear merciful and compassionate, especially when he is accosted personally. I remember one dire story of a man whose son was hanged. The King passed him at court and stopped. 'If you had pleaded with me,' he remarked, 'I would have pardoned your son.' And then he passed on. The King loves such occasions just as he never forgets an enemy. He had certainly not forgotten Gardiner, nor the fact that Thomas Seymour had secret designs on Katherine Parr.

My sleepy meditations and reflections in the music loft were brought abruptly to an end by the ostentatious entrance of the wand-bearing royal chamberlains, resplendent in their livery. These loudly announced the imminent arrival of the King, who shuffled into the chamber, a great, hulking shadow, breathing noisily, face all creased, leaning on a staff that rang like the beat of a funeral drum as he edged into the light. Henry was garbed in a beautiful long robe powdered with gold and silver crowns and lined with snow-white fur, velvet buskins on his feet, the bejewelled flat cap on his head sporting a blood-red plume. He stomped across the floor to his waiting chair. Assisted by his chamberlains, not speaking a word to anyone, he lowered himself down on to the thick cushioned seat. I was standing behind him. I could not see if he winced at the shooting, burning pains of his haemorrhoids or the suppurating ulcers on his legs. The Council were also denied such pleasure. Once the King entered, they doffed their hats and sank to one knee. Henry kept them waiting. He snapped his fingers and snatched at the goblet of white wine a chamberlain hurriedly brought; he slurped this noisily, belched loudly then slammed the goblet down on the table before him.

'My lord Cranmer, my good friend,' the King emphasised the last three words, a warning to the Romanists, 'intone the prayer.'

Cranmer, in a shaky, reedy voice, began the 'Veni Creator Spiritus', which the rest of the Council soon joined in. Once finished, however, Henry kept them kneeling, even as the Spears, the royal halberdiers, the King's own bodyguard, filed ominously into the council chamber, the naked steel of their pole-axes glinting in the light. That constant sense of dread deepened. These royal axemen had accompanied so many who had enjoyed Henry's favour to a waiting black-draped, sealed barge on the Thames. The councillors continued kneeling, bonnets off, heads bowed like those who had to kneel on the scaffold on Tower Hill. Henry breathed out, a noisy gasp, before greedily sipping from his goblet. I stared down at that great frame, a doom-bearing mound of festering flesh, cunning brain squirming like an eel in the muddy, sluggish waters of court politics. The silence grew baleful. Some of the councillors such as Norfolk, the knobbly joints of their old legs straining against the pain and discomfort, found it hard to maintain their genuflection. Somewhere in the palace a bell boomed, followed by a loud cry, which abruptly died.

'My lord Thomas Seymour,' the King rasped, 'you are no longer sworn to this Council. You have no need to stay. Begone.'

The younger Seymour raised his head. Paget, kneeling beside him, gently touched that blustering, lecherous soldier on the arm. Seymour's brother Edward coughed, a warning to his impetuous sibling to rein in both his tongue and his temper. Everyone knew the reason for Thomas's abrupt dismissal. Queen Katherine Parr resided at Greenwich, exiled from the royal presence. Seymour still carried a torch for her in his heart. He had stupidly interceded for her to join the court to keep a merry hall at Westminster over Yuletide. This was the King's response. Seymour rose, bowed from the waist and walked to the door, the high heels of his riding boots rapping the floor.

'My lord Seymour.' The errant nobleman paused. 'If I were you, and I am certainly not,' Henry did not even turn in his chair, 'I would tread much lighter.' Seymour almost tiptoed from the chamber, the King's guarded warning ringing like a death knell over the heads of his councillors.

'My Lord Chancellor?' Wriothesley raised his head, face all fearful. 'Did I not,' Henry was now pointing at Gardiner, who, to ease himself, was leaning back on his heels, 'did I not command you, my Lord Chancellor,' Henry kept jabbing his finger at the hapless bishop, 'how that person can no longer be amongst us?'

'Your Majesty,' Gardiner gabbled, 'I simply came to

offer money, benevolences from the clergy.' He gestured with his hands as if supplicating the very air.

'Then I accept it,' Henry replied.

'Your Majesty,' Gardiner babbled on, 'my apologies, my humble entreaties . . .'

'Had your previous doings been as agreeable as your present fair words,' Henry bellowed, 'you would have no cause to speak.' The King raised a hand. 'As it is, we see no reason why you should bother us any further.'

Now Gardiner is a fearsome man, with frowning brows, deep-set eyes, a nose like a buzzard and great paws like the Devil. They say that when he passed through Winchester recently, he grew deeply offended when the people didn't pull off their caps for him and make courtesy at the cross carried before him. He turned to his servants, saying, 'Mark that house! Take this knave's name and have him imprisoned!' No doubt Bishop Gardiner harks back to other days, as he himself said, 'when the realm lived in faith, charity and devotion. When God's word dwelt in men's hearts and never came abroad to walk on men's tongues. Now jesters, railers, rhymers, players, jugglers and simpering prattlers take upon themselves the duty of both administrators and officers to set forth God's word.'

Gardiner did not act so confident now. He staggered to his feet with no one to assist him and bowed towards the King, who, having downed more wine, belched in the bishop's direction. Gardiner scurried from the chamber.

'He has gone,' Henry bellowed, 'because my lord bishop cannot be managed. He is like a horse or a mule without bridle. Moreover, I know things about my lord Gardiner.' He nodded, finger wagging. 'Discord!' he thundered. 'Discord here, discord in Parliament. Tell my beloved commons I thank them for their recent subsidy in defence of Boulogne. Yet,' the King continued, 'the perfect love that should bind ruler and subject is being bitterly marred by disputes amongst themselves. Charity and concord are not even found amongst you,' the King bellowed, 'but discord and dissension weigh heavy in every place, even here. One calls the other heretic, an Anabaptist, whilst the other replies with "Romanist hypocrite". Are these tokens of charity amongst you? Are these signs of fraternal love? So all men are in discord and few, or none, preach truly and sincerely the word of God.'

Some of the councillors, I am sure, must have been sorely tempted to retort that the King himself was a constant source of such discord, but silence is best. His Majesty then went on to reprove his kneeling councillors for their lack of order, for allowing others to slander priests and bishops, for failing to seize those who rebuked and taunted preachers in the pulpits with their fantastical opinions and vain expositions. The King reminded them how, although he'd permitted his subjects to read Holy Scripture, this was only to inform their own consciences as well as to instruct their families and children; it was certainly not to make scripture a railing and taunting stock against priests and preachers. The Bible was meant to enlighten; 'Instead,' His Diabolic Majesty thundered, 'that most precious jewel, the word of God, is being disputed to rhyme, song and jangle in every ale house and tavern.'

Henry let his words roll like a volley of cannon. He then lapsed into silence. He had seized an issue as he would his cane and lashed his fighting dogs.

'Now, my lords, I have spoken my mind. Pray take your seats.' He snapped his fingers. 'Some wine? Sugared wafers for my Council. Sir Anthony,' he turned to his captain of halberdiers, 'I no longer have need of you.' He paused. 'As yet.'

The Council, hiding their groans and moans, took their seats. Paget's creature, William Clarke, hastened in. More lanterns and candles were lit. Chancery satchels were opened. The King now acted all courteous and kindly, addressing several members, though I noticed that he did not even glance at the Howards. The formal meeting began. Paget soon proved his reputation as the master of dark politics! I scrutinised him carefully. Although he proved to be the busiest, he acted pliant but not petty, cautious but not cowardly, popular but not people-pleasing, correct but not condemning. In truth, Paget is a realist. Our king will die, that is a fact. Young Edward will succeed, that is a fact. The elder Seymour is the young heir's uncle, with an entree to the royal privy chamber denied to others. Dudley is a soldier who can whistle up and deploy the thousands of mercenaries garrisoning the royal castles and ports. Paget, I suspect, will not try to control the Council or the heir apparent, but he will control those who do. In the meantime he will flatter the King.

Paget began with news from France. How the King's great rival Francis was sickening, his body swollen with the pox, the effect of consorting with so many women, for King Francis, Paget murmured, did surely sup at many fountains. He reported how the French king was now racked by dreams and fantasies of his silvery youth and persisted in visiting certain rooms, forests and glades where he had carried out his greatest conquests. How he became angry when he heard that his sons were already toasting his death and plotting what to do next. He lost his temper and went to their chambers to find his sons had fled, leaving nothing but soiled table linen, napery, unwashed cups and platters, which Francis hurled from the window.

Henry pronounced himself delighted, as he always is when he hears about the ailments and discomfitures of his rivals, especially the King of France. 'I should send him good Dr Huicke.' He coughed in his laughter as he gestured at Huicke sitting so forlornly at the end of the council table. 'Now . . .' The King turned to the business in hand.

I watched and waited for at least an hour. The price to the King for this display of royal power was costly. Once the Council meeting was over, Henry returned to his own secret chamber, the room all neat and sweet-smelling. He dismissed his household men, even Huicke, who only stayed to prepare a certain potion, then stripped for bed, pulling over his bloated, blood-blotched torso a thick linen nightshirt with a matching purple woollen mantle; around his balding head he wrapped a towel, clasping the folds with a brooch, then, cursing and retching, he lowered himself on to the close stool. He sat straining, head forward, those narrow little eyes unblinking. Once finished, leaning heavily on me and grasping the polished walnut post, he climbed into the great four-poster bed. For a while he just lay back against the bolsters, savouring the goblet of white wine I served. I thought he was drifting off to sleep, but he stirred and abruptly asked what I had thought of the council meeting.

'You frightened them,' I replied. 'Which was your intent.'

'Terror more likely, Will. Horror piled upon horror.' He gave a twisted smile. 'I must leave this kingdom safe, yet look at me now.' He leaned forward and ruffled my hair. 'Only you do I trust.'

He paused as the door of the chamber opened and John Roberts, Yeoman Extraordinary of the Secret Chamber, a sly-eyed rascal whom I do not trust, allowed in the King's spaniels. Yapping furiously, these circled the bed, unable to jump such a height, for which the King was grateful, as these excited little dogs often tread on his legs. At last I quietened them to lie on their cushions in the corner. Behind me, Henry was bemoaning the loss of Catullus, his favourite spaniel, who'd died suddenly two weeks earlier, found in a pool of vomit on these same cushions.

'Will?' he called out. I crossed to his bedside. Henry had slipped on to his red, swollen nose a pair of those German spectacles he orders by the dozen, as he often loses them. 'Will?' He passed me a docket ordering thirteen items in gold and silver gilt, mazers, goblets and jugs, from Morgan Wolf the royal goldsmith, and asked me to decipher a number on the docket, as his sight was failing. Ever since I entered his service, over twenty years ago, the King has been impatient with clerical work, hence his utter reliance on Wolsey, Cromwell and the rest.

I clarified the entry for him and noticed how the docket had been signed with the King's dry stamp. This was a small, carved wooden block impressed on parchment by a special hand-press, which would leave an imprinted imitation of Henry's signature to be later ink-filled by William Clarke, that ubiquitous clerk of the Privy Seal, and witnessed by Sir John Gates, or Sir Anthony Denny, another of Paget's creatures. Now to uphold probity, all such transactions are recorded in a special ledger inspected by the King. Both stamp and ledger are kept in a black, leather-bound casket held by Henry himself. Previously I had witnessed nothing untoward; now my thoughts milled like a shower of falling arrows. I recalled Clarke busy with Paget in the royal chancery, his sly furtiveness. The King was growing weaker, his eyesight was failing. He was impatient, as he always has been, with the outpourings of his writing office. Did he – could he, I wondered – control the dry stamp? Were there two stamps, one the King used and another fashioned by Paget and his agents for their own devious, secret reasons? To forge the King's seal and signature was high treason. I had no proof for my anxieties, just a hidden fear. After all, if my suspicions proved correct, the Council could use such a dry stamp to snuff out a person's life like the wick of a candle.

'Will? Will?' I broke from my reverie and stared at the King's swollen, vein-streaked face. 'Go back into the City tomorrow,' Henry pleaded piteously. 'Discover what you can. Snatch up the gossip about me.' He lay back against the blood-flecked bolsters. 'Afterwards cross the river with Huicke to Greenwich. Visit my queen. I do miss her lithe white body, fresh and warm, ever so obedient. She reminds me of Boleyn, my little night crow. She is not stale or frozen, yet I do not trust her. During these days, I will not have her close, but watch her!' Henry's lower lip thrust out, trembling; his narrow, bloodshot eyes brimmed with tears. 'Will, I trust no one except you.'

'Your Majesty, the dry stamp?'

'Oh fool, what about it?'

'How do you know that you see every document sealed with that?'

Henry waved a hand. 'Not for now, fool. More pressing business. My queen, does she expect to be regent? Is that snake Seymour hoping to slide between her thighs? Oh why am I without friends?' He squeezed his lower lip between finger and thumb, peering plaintively at me.

'Why did they get rid of poor Cromwell? Ah well,' he sighed, 'go out, sniff about and come back, little dog. Discover the mood of the City. I draw my strength from it. Remember!' He gripped my wrist. 'Once you leave the Queen, do not let Huicke out of your sight.' Henry stretched back against the bolsters. 'I must sleep now.'

And so he did. I lay down on the cushions amongst the spaniels. I was woken in the early hours. Henry was shouting and crying, bellowing at the cowled, empty-hooded shapes he claimed were crowding around him.

'I was in Mount Grace,' the King gasped, his sweat-soaked face glittering in the nightlight. 'You know, Will? The Carthusian house up on the Yorkshire moors? I was standing in the nave. Along its transepts either side ranged a row of hanged men, bodies twirling, the nooses attached to brackets in the wall. A cold breeze swept the ruins and ruffled their robes. Then they began to chant, I think it was them, a hymn from Maundy Thursday, "Tenebrae Facta Sunt" – "And Darkness Fell". That was it, Will, "a great darkness over the whole earth". My horse stood alongside me. I went to climb into the saddle when more ghostly shapes emerged like columns of black smoke pouring out of the ground.' Henry gasped and sighed.

I did my best to comfort him, dabbing his face with a napkin soaked in rose water. I made him drink a little opiate mixed with wine. Eventually he slept, and so did I.

Yeoman Roberts roused us early the next morning. The King roared at him to take the spaniels, now all frisking and yapping, and stay outside until he'd finished his matins.

'Will, Will!' Henry whispered like some little boy conspiring against his tutors. 'Come here, come here!' I went and sat on the edge of the bed.

'Your Majesty is comfortable?'

'His Majesty's arse is paining him with all the fires of Hell. I woke again to lay siege to the close stool.' He grabbed my shoulder and squeezed it until I yelped. 'You were sleeping like a babe. I stood over you, Will.' His eyes glittered with a malicious glee. 'No, no, I didn't piss on you as I've done before. I was tempted to, but why spoil a good jerkin, eh? Instead I looked down at poor Will Somers, hair sweat-soaked against his scrawny face, that small hump on your back that makes you look like a snail all curled up.'

I did not reply; Henry was in an ugly mood.

'Now,' he thrust a small purse into my hand, 'I shall tell Huicke to meet you in what tavern, at what time?'

I glanced across at the hour candle Roberts had trimmed the night before. I wanted to be free of Westminster for a while.

'The Lamb of God in Cheapside, opposite the Guildhall, when the market horn sounds for the last quarter of the day.'

'Good. Accompany Huicke to Greenwich, where he will meet my sweet queen, then escort him back here. Do not let him out of your sight once you have seen the Queen.' The King wiped his fingers, their cracked skin seeping blood on to my jerkin. 'Go, Will.' He smiled. 'Who knows, you might meet the Lady Jane . . .'

'Tonight, after dark. I will meet her . . .'

'Just be careful. Now go.'

4 December 1546

I left the royal quarters, pushing my way through the throng of retainers, servants and others gathering in the galleries and antechambers beyond. Within the hour I had washed, changed and left the palace. I showed my letter of pass to the halberdiers who patrolled everywhere. I was intrigued by Henry's forced jollity; it meant he was plotting. I also wondered what he meant by the warning to be careful. Did he know about Balaam, Princess Mary's man, slipping like a weasel in and out of the city to cause mischief and to bring his mistress letters of support and encouragement from the Emperor Charles V or Cardinal Pole and other exiles abroad? Was he concerned that I might betray secrets to Balaam? But what secrets did I really know, except that Henry was plotting? As usual, everything he did was dappled in light and shadow. Was he plotting mischief against his queen? At the previous night's council meeting he had struck at the Romanists, removing Gardiner, the bishop who dared to conspire against Katherine, from his royal presence. Yet the younger Seymour had also been exiled, and why had Paget been so keen to probe and question me?

Such questions could only be posed, not answered. 'Sufficient for the day is the evil thereof' and '*Carpe diem*', 'Seize the day', are my mottos. The King wanted to know the mood of the City, and so did I. His Majesty uses me. If I have one gift, apart from my jests and sallies, I am a good listener who prompts confidences. In many people's eyes I am like the old and infirm; I don't really exist. Small in stature and slightly hunched, I pose no threat, real or imagined, against anyone. I recall Thomas More's famous dictum: 'I think no man evil, I say no man evil, I do no man evil.' A good rule to both live and die by.

Today, with Advent drawing on and the Christmas festivities fast approaching, I immersed myself in the City. First I talked to the watermen along the Thames, especially those commanding the royal barges (one of which is still reserved for my use), beautiful craft: the glass windows in their resplendent cabins exquisitely ornamented with painting and gilding, made even more gorgeous by garlands of artificial flowers of green sarcanet, their branches of eglantine powdered with blossoms of gold. These watermen informed me how the King is failing; that is why his craft lie berthed and idle at Whitechapel Steps. They loudly bemoaned the lack of business along the waterways. The gilded barges of the London Mysteries, which always accompany the royal entourage in a joyful and ear-splitting cacophony of trumpets, drums and flutes, with guns and squibs hurling to and fro against the blackness of the night, also lie silent. The steeples of the score of churches lining the Thames remain eerily peaceful: the wardens have no reason to call out their ringers to salute the King and afterwards pay them threepence to quench their thirst.

The river certainly seems to reflect the sombre mood of this city. Winter's high tides have brought flooding and muddied the water, so thick you can pluck haddock with your hand from beneath London Bridge; the fish float upon the water, their eyes blinded by the heavy river sludge. Some of the watermen hoped the Thames would freeze as it did ten years ago, so hard that His Majesty and his wife-queen Jane Seymour, now cold in her coffin beneath the paving of St George's Chapel at Windsor, crossed in sumptuous pageantry from Westminster to Greenwich. Yet this December of God's year of 1546 is bereft of such frozen beauty. The swollen Thames is used only by those who have to man the tilt barges that nose their way forward, their deep hulls crammed with livestock for the markets: boars (live 8p, dead 4p), calves (5p live, 2p dead) and poultry (5p for 20 or 3p for the same number dead). Such bills demonstrate how high prices have risen, another complaint of the riverside people as they sit in the warm fug of the Fisher of Men tavern just south of Westminster.

The watermen have certainly noticed the changes, especially the ominous silence now shrouding the steps to Whitehall and Westminster Palaces. Not even the great barges of the ambassadors of France and the Empire have been glimpsed. Whilst the guards, as one bargeman dramatically proclaimed, have been doubled, and throng so thickly that the dim light of winter glints off their pikes, morions and breastplates.

I was intrigued by this character. Narrow-faced and hot-eyed, a man educated in his horn book. One of those emerging preachers who has studied the scriptures, newly translated, and believes that God has inspired them to proclaim true religion, which, if the facts be known, has more to do with Master Calvin and the Genevans than Archbishop Cranmer and Lambeth Palace. This waterman had assumed the name of Ezekiel, which, I am sure, was not his true title conferred at his baptism. He was certainly full of ale and ready to pontificate on all things, human and supernal. He trusted me, and as I've written, who sees any danger in a grotesque? Moreover, council spies and Judas men would soon be recognised in such a tavern and immediately tossed into the freezing river.

'And the King?' I asked. 'His Majesty's silence?'

'I can only report what other tongues wag,' Ezekiel replied lugubriously. 'The rumours have begun: "The King is dying! The King is dead!" The brothels, whore-houses and strumpet shops recently closed by royal decree, those abodes of filth and debauchery,' his lips became slobbery and wet, 'now thrive joyously. They know the King is failing and his council too divided to act. Once again red candles glow behind latticed windows, inviting customers to share the joys of the sisterhood in all their satin and taffeta, that glorious throng of city prostitutes with their bare breasts and painted nipples.' This self-proclaimed prophet was now thoroughly enjoying himself. 'My dear mother of blessed memory would mourn such decadence, but she lies dead for many a day, buried beneath the harsh coldness of St Michael's, Cornhill. She always warned me against these bath-houses and molly shops.' Ezekiel wagged a bony finger in my face. 'Such places boil, stew, then spread all forms of gossip about our king and this seeps out to the surrounding alehouses and taverns. The talk is always hushed, since the Law of Treasons, recently amended, has made it a heinous crime to even imagine the King's death.'

I sat round-eyed, mouth gaping, as if awestruck by his knowledge and skill. Others now joined in. The cause of His Majesty's weakness was hotly discussed; the conclusions reached would certainly not have pleased my hellish master. The King, so one waterman whispered, was a wasteful dissolute in all his ways, a deflowerer of virgins. He, the great lecher, who banned all lewdness in the stews, kept his own privy cupboard of prostitutes and procurers in a solar above a gatehouse. Yet the fellow could not even inform us where that gatehouse stood!

Such chatter, I reflected on leaving the Fisher of Men, spreads like a deadly pestilence, heavy in the air. Nothing can stop it, not even the fog-bound river, for rumours creep across London Bridge, the only span over the Thames, eight hundred feet long, connecting the City with Southwark at Fish Street. I constantly marvel at its grandeur. The bridge certainly proclaims London's darkening mood. The magnificent gatehouse on its southern approach is a forest of spikes thickly festooned with the heads of executed traitors; these range black and gaunt against the sky like onions on toothpicks. On 15 November 1546, no fewer than thirty-five heads, eyes and lips pecked sharp by the kites, decorated the gatehouse rim to peer sightlessly in all directions. Those who live in the handsome, well-built mansions along the bridge whisper that there is certainly room for more, a tale taken up by the pin-makers who have their stalls there. I pretended to purchase and eavesdropped on their words. They claim the King is dying and the Great Lords are gathering, whilst the City mob, that beast with many heads, is ever ready for mischief. These same pin-peddlers talk most comfortably, their treason cloaked by the sound of the Thames. The river thunders through the twenty stone arches, lacing the protective starlings with all the dirt it carries. The thudding of the water competes with the soaring water-mills, their great fans clacking noisily as they fight to harness the tide. Words are easy to hide beneath such clamour, whilst the bridge is always a place of darkness. The houses and shops built on either side lean across like conspirators to block the light, the only break being a few ancient cornerstones, each called Jesus, where the drawbridge waits to be raised for some high-masted ship. The common chatter here is whose head will next decorate the spikes. Whoever it is, the skull will rot away to softness. Eventually some enterprising trader will take it down and hollow it into a drinking cup, to be sold as a sure remedy against noxious fumes to metal workers at the Tower mint.

What else did I learn? I listened and observed sharply. I have found that rumour moves like an army pillaging a city. It breaks into strands, snaking up the narrow rutted lanes past the posts and chains at Holborn Bar, across muddy ditches and foulsome streams full of the greasy bones of measled hogs as well as the heads, entrails and hides of pig and calf. More importantly, the clacking gossip creeps along Fleet Street, that land of ink, to form an invisible bridge between the broadsheet sellers who work with dirty fingers at their printing presses and those more skilled who sell such news at St Paul's and Westminster. Naturally, few dare put their names to what they think. Government men swarm like fleas over a diseased carcass, whilst those who know add that the King has been ill before and still recovered. Nevertheless, rumour piles upon rumour. Tower troops apparently guard the roads leading in and out to the City, while a strict watch is being kept at Queenhithe and along the other City wharves. Couriers, armed and swift, have been sent to the ports, where the council surveyors are out in force. Speculation about the King boils feverishly in the one-storey cottages as well as the three-level mansions of loam and lath along the twisting trackways of Pudding Lane, Bread Street and Milk Street. People claim to know someone who knows someone else, whose nephew is a friend of an ostler in the royal stables. He was the one who definitely told them about the King's health in the Mermaid in Pater Noster Row, or was it the Pegasus along Cheapside or the Bull's Head in East Cheap? It's always the same: 'The King is dying.' The gossipers stay wary and weasel-eyed. They do not want to be arrested by the bailiffs with their iron-tipped staves and hauled off in Newgate fashion to rot in that ancient gaol close to London Wall. Once there, they are doomed. They will only leave to make the final journey to the derelict leper house at St Giles Field, where they'll sup their last refreshment from a deep-bowled cup before being hanged to strangling on the Tyburn gibbet. They will choke and dance whilst the executioner, with all the skill of a flesher, plucks out their steaming bowels to the horrified delight of the crowd.

No matter how humble your station, I discovered, a gossiping tongue can bring pain and humiliation. I walked down Cheapside, marvelling at the wealth of this city and what can be found there: sweet wines of Crete, oil from Calabria, Moorish carpets, buttons and bells, hats and spices, hawks' bells, birch rods and candles, condiments and sweetmeats. London truly is an array of contrasts. The ground about these richly stacked stalls is infected with the entrails washed from the nearby scalding houses, whilst I glimpsed a beastly body shamelessly defecating in the open street. Further down Cheapside, at the Standard, two women, one heavy with child, were being nailed by the ears to the stocks for calling certain parsons 'puffed up porklings of the Pope'. London is like a vast sea, full of gusts, dangerous shelves and fearful rocks, ready at every storm to sink or cast away the weak and inexperienced.

Perhaps I should not be so prejudiced. I recently received news from Paris, where, even in the royal lodgings, chamber pots are rare and, for want of any alternative, men have to urinate on the fire. They do this everywhere by night and day. Indeed, the greater the nobleman or lord, the more readily and openly will he do it. Nor must I forget the noble French king's celebration of the winter solstice on the day following Christmas last. The city authorities erected in the Place de Grève a towering pyre around a sixty-foot-high tree stacked with kindling and straw. On top were placed a barrel, wheels, flowery garlands and baskets containing two dozen cats and a fox to be burned alive for the king's pleasure. Trumpets blared as His French Majesty sparked the conflagration with a wax torch wrapped in red velvet. Afterwards he sat down to enjoy the spectacle whilst dining on a confectionery of dried fruits, scented sweet tarts and other sugared delicacies. Cities change, human nature does not.

Life in this city continues as normal, or apparently so. The water flows through the lead pipes and conduits in Hog Lane, Cheapside and elsewhere. Traders barter, metals are tapped, tubs hooped, pots cleaned, coaches and carts rumble along the narrow streets, the houses on either side, sagging with age, supported by posts and poles. Taverns are busy, be it the Sun in Splendour or the Face in Heaven. The streets, at least until the curfew sounds and the beacons flare in the church steeples, ring with cries of 'Hot peas!', 'Small cords!', 'Milk fresh as the dawn!', 'Clear water!', 'New brooms!', 'Sweetmeats!' Beggars swarm like shoals of fish. The bold-eyed cross-biters and pimps search for conies: customers desperate for a feverish tumble in some dark corner before moving back to the taverns where the horse boys hold the mounts of those too precious, too tender or too idle to work. Such young gallants always bring gossip.

Others, wanting to be more knowledgeable, slink into that den of thieves, the cathedral of St Paul's, the haunt of nips and foists, the trading ground of butchers, ale-conners and fishmongers, as well as costly courtesans in the company of their apple squires. Here the curious can bathe in a river of chatter whilst keeping a wary eye on the delators, the professional informers clustering thick as lice on a foul hog's hide. The old St Paul's is gone, the glory dismantled. Of all its former chapels, shrines, paintings, carved marbles, work of silver and gold, gilt-edged relics, nothing is left. Only bare white-washed walls and a few crumbling stone tombs. A bleak place where people speak of the winter being so harsh it affects men's moods, including the King's. The air is so cold, deer have been found frozen in Epping Forest, to the north of the city. There is talk of the last summer, so very hot, with the sweating sickness, and of fresh diseases rife in the capital, be it a postume on the brain, swelling of the head, terrible dreams, the falling evil, the palsies, the cramps, limpness of limbs, bloodshot eyes, scabbiness and itch, diseases in the ears, sneezing out of measure, breathing with a wheeze, colic and rumbling in the guts, worms swelling the navel, the pain of a stone, pissing in bed, consumption, leanness or bleary eyes. The air is thick with pestilence. Indeed, the Angel of Death hovers so close, priests have grown busier than doctors.

I was so taken up with my observations I startled in alarm as a figure brushed by me and a piece of parchment was pushed into my hand. The shadow was gone before I could even exclaim. I unfurled the scrap. Balaam had struck, providing the time and place of our meeting later that day. I am sure he disappeared, though I felt I was being watched, even followed; just a suspicion, a prickling along the nape of my neck. However, even when I stopped and turned quickly, I could see no one. Slipping and slithering on the frozen mud, I walked on, deeper into the noisy, smelly throng of Cheapside. Smoke fumes, odours and fragrances swirled in the freezing air, so cold even the beggars strove to cover every piece of flesh against the nipping frost. The feast of Christmas is approaching, yet in that busy thoroughfare I detected a real change, a sense of mourning and consternation that the old ways had gone. Many churches have lost their statues and relics. They do not know what to do. Priests, parsons and vicars are confused; the Church is now the Tower of Babel rather than the sheepfold of unity. They cannot decide if mumming, carolling and all the rest of the festivities are permitted. If the music of sackbut, viol, schawm and other instruments is allowed. They wonder if it is acceptable to stage a tableau depicting Gabriel meeting Mary, or to dress in tawny coats, red hoods and silver masks to play out the visit of the Magi. Is the Blessed Sacrament reserved? Should there be a sanctuary lamp and bells be rung, and if so, when? Can the altar be incensed? What vestments may be worn? During mass, when the bread and wine are consecrated, are they truly the body and blood of the risen Christ, or only tokens of Our Lord's Last Supper? Can there still be wrestling in the churchyard during which church ales are served, and is it right to bestow a bleating ram on the champion wrestler? What vestments, if any, should be worn in God's Acre? May the faithful bring flowers and candles to pray for their dead? Is it permitted to re-create the stable of Bethlehem in figures or in masques? Is this still valid or popish idolatry? After all, it was encouraged by the Franciscans, who, because of their deep hostility to Henry, have been dissolved and banished.

I felt this deep confusion as I moved among the crowds coming out of churchyards and cemeteries, listening to their chatter and whispering. Now and again some fiery speaker like Ezekiel would deliver a short homily on what he thought should be happening. Of course such sermons were always brief, over and done with before the sheriff's men arrived. Some churches still ring out the Angelus bell, reminding the faithful of devotion to the Virgin; many now reject this as superstition. Even the dead are caught up in the confusion. Some coffins are borne to their last resting place with taper, candle, incense and psalms, beadsmen finger their rosaries and whisper an Ave. Others are hurried along the frozen lanes without pomp or prayer as if the mourners are ashamed of their dead. In the cage on top of the Cheapside Tun, an imprisoned nightwalker had collapsed. Someone had placed a bowl of water on his chest as well as a feather beneath his nose to discern whether he was still alive and breathing. An argument had also broken out about whether a priest should be called. One bailiff shouted that the fallen man should be shrived, whilst another ridiculed such papist nonsense.

I passed on and reached the Lamb of God, where Huicke, all resplendent in his dark robes, was waiting patiently for me. The physician is a strange character, a fellow of Merton, principal of St Alban's Hall. According to Balaam, he alarmed the university authorities by dismissing the old schoolmen as destroyers of good wit, though he was later appointed to the Royal College of Physicians, their censor no less. Like the master, so the servant; Huicke had attempted to divorce his wife Elizabeth. Dr John Croke trialled the case and found in favour of the wife. Huicke then appealed to the Privy Council, and the case was heard by my lords at Greenwich. After listening to them both face to face, the Council exonerated Elizabeth of any blame and vigorously condemned her husband's cruelty and deceit. The King, a patient of the good doctor, could not resist mischief. He used the occasion to become his own physician's comforter, confessor and councillor. Huicke trusts the King, truly the mark of a fool! No better proof of the proverb that 'nothing masks deceit better than soft and tender flattery'!

We decided to leave immediately for Greenwich. A hideous journey across the freezing, fog-bound river with craft warning each other off with bells, horns and flaring lanterns. The Thames was ugly, grey and swollen. I was pleased that Huicke had arranged our passage in one of the royal barges with cushioned seats, albeit soaking wet, beneath a protective stern canopy. The swell of the river, the barge sinking and rising before juddering sideways, rendered me sick. Huicke made matters worse by chattering about how dry seaweed was a sure preventative against the mal-de-mer. When he started to describe how to chew it, I held up a hand and, turning away, vomited generously over the side, much to the amusement of the oarsmen. Never was I so pleased to glimpse the red-roofed turrets of Greenwich Palace and pass through its majestic yawning water gate. I leapt like a deer on to the narrow quayside, where servants carrying torches escorted us up the slippery steps into the palace. For a while we waited in an antechamber, where we were served mulled wine and portions of apple tart. I balanced these sitting on a stool next to Huicke, fending off the Queen's greyhounds, their wet muzzles buttering my fingers. Huicke chatted about how we would not be long; later that evening he must attend a meeting of the Privy Council to be held by Seymour in his mansion on the Strand.

'A meeting of the Privy Council,' I exclaimed, 'in Seymour's house! All council meetings must be held in the palace.'

'That is what His Majesty ordained.' Huicke's voice turned officious. 'So that's the way it should be.' I nodded wisely, as I am expected to, and so often do. Naturally I wondered why the King had given his consent. My heart skipped a beat. I know Henry as well as any man does, I recognise the signs: the tears, the swift changes of mood, his devil-may-care attitude to matters of state, only to turn abruptly, spinning like a coin. Henry was plotting something, and this visit to Greenwich was part of it, as were my instructions not to let Huicke out of my sight. However, the greyhounds were pressing even closer, so I gobbled my apple tart and drained my posset. A chamberlain came for us and we were ushered into the Queen's privy chamber.

Queen Katherine Parr is rather small, with delicately marked features. She has hazel eyes and auburn hair and was wearing a round crimson velvet hat (she had been recently walking in the park) edged with pearls under a gold band studded with jewels, which kept her hair in place under a white veil. A double row of pearls shimmered around her slim throat. She was garbed in a richly brocaded dress of silver and green with a girdle of gold hung with jewelled pendants around a still slim waist. She was reading a book of her own thoughts, 'The Lamentations of a Sinner', which she presented as a gift to Dr Huicke. The Queen smiled obligingly at me. The lady does not really know what debt she owes me from when Gardiner and Wriothesley were hunting her. I never told her, whilst the King's memory is always shaped to suit his whim. How can he confess that his own fool was sharper than he – or had more compassion towards her?

For a short while we discussed certain herbs and poultices on which she is an apparent authority. The Queen however seemed ill at ease, eager to be alone with Huicke. Now and again she'd break off as if distracted by the bedchamber itself, with its richly carved black oaken panelling and tapestries of brilliant beauty. She seemed particularly taken with a gorgeous central hanging. I, being sharp of eye and keen of wit, studied this intently. At the centre of the tapestry was a medallion surrounded with flowers wrought in twisted silk and bullion. Above this a spread-eagle floated, around its throat an imperial crown, whilst in each corner of the hanging reared heraldic dragons in red, purple, crimson and gold. This long, heavy tapestry hung down the wall where there was no wainscoting. I noticed it move as if shifted by some secret draught and wondered if the hanging concealed a hidden door.

I was then dismissed, told to sit in the small antechamber with only one of the Queen's henchmen present. I remembered the King's instructions not to leave Huicke's side, but what choice had I? The room had been cleared; it was truly deserted even of the Queen's beloved greyhounds (nourished on milk) and her parrots (fed on hempseed), whilst nowhere to be seen were the many minions she had constantly around her. Once I was ushered out, the door to the Queen's bedchamber both closed and locked behind me, I grew even more intrigued. The chamber-man offered me some mead in a gilt cup. I, in return, proffered a coin and said I would sip provided the fellow joined me. Of course he did. I performed the office, filling both cups and sprinkling a little potion into that of the chamber-man, a mild sleeping powder which, because of my constant attendance upon the King and his sudden moods, I always carry with me. A short while later the servant was dozing in his chair. I swiftly locked the door to the antechamber and pressed my ear against that of the bedchamber. I heard chairs being moved, the clink of jug against cup, murmured greetings followed by laughter as more logs were placed upon the fire. Others had secretly entered the bedchamber through that hidden door. I heard many voices and, beneath the hum of conversation, recognised one: the younger Seymour.

I strained to hear. The conversations were whispered, though I heard Surrey's name. Balaam had reminded me previously how Surrey and Seymour had clashed when they had fought together before Boulogne. Balaam believes, and I agree, that the recent attack on the Queen had its origins in the Howard faction; were the Seymours now plotting their revenge? I heard footsteps, the click and crick of a door being opened, more voices, but these remained muted. I listened keenly and heard two men speak, then the Queen answer. I am sure I caught the drift of words about 'the death of the screech owl'. I wondered if I had misheard, but the phrase was repeated before the voices faded to a whisper. I then stepped back, though in such a way that I could see into the chamber when the door was opened. Eventually it was, and Dr Huicke, all flushed and hot, strode out. I am certain that in the chamber beyond I glimpsed the shadow of a man standing very close to the Queen. Huicke, however, was all bristle and bustle, snapping his fingers at me to follow him out of the palace.

We had to wait a while for a royal wherry. Huicke was full of talk about the King, chattering like a bird of the dawn about the royal symptoms as if eager to divert me from his recent meeting with the Queen. He confided that some people thought the King suffered from the French disease, the Great Pox; he waved an admonitory finger beneath my nose.

'They say His Majesty suffers from that.' He tapped my right nostril. 'How there's a bruise or mark on the King's face here, a sign of the disease, but that is nonsense! His constant fevers are due to the ulcers on his legs caused by a fall from a horse some twenty years back. Look at his children,' Huicke continued, 'no trace there of the pox. A fable.' He snapped his fingers and shouted at the wherryman to hurry. 'A sheer fable based on a story about how the late Cardinal Wolsey, the Red Man, tried to infect the King with such a contagion. Yes, yes,' he continued, 'that's how the indictment put it: "that the same Lord Cardinal, knowing the foul and infectious disease of the Great Pox had broken out upon him in diverse places on his body, came daily to His Grace whispering in his ear and blowing upon his most Noble Grace with his most perilous and pestilential breath to the great danger of his Highness. But God, in his infinite goodness, provided a better cure and protection."' Huicke seemed very satisfied with that. He glanced away, rocking backwards and forwards on his feet, whispering to himself. I truly wondered why he should raise the matter of the Great Pox. Had such a scourge been discussed during this secret meeting in Greenwich? Was the Queen herself concerned that in her ministrations to the King she might have become infected? I decided however not to press the matter further. We climbed into the wherry and took our seats under the hooded canvas covering near the stern.

Physician Huicke remained all a-tremble and once again explained how the ulcers on the King's legs were the source of his ill-humours. Recalling what I had glimpsed in the Queen's bedchamber just before we had left, I diverted the conversation back to Her Grace. Did she not have a love of herbs and skill in physic, having had to nurture two old men, previous husbands, in their dotage? Huicke rejected that, pointing out how Lord Brough had been the same age as Lady Parr when they'd married some seventeen years ago but he had proved sickly and died. And Lord Latimer? Huicke smiled grimly. The royal physician seemed eager to extol the virtues of the Queen. He described how ten years earlier, during the Pilgrimage of Grace, the great rising in the north against Cromwell and all his doings, Latimer had been taken hostage by the rebel leader Robert Aske and forced to be his mouthpiece during Aske's most treasonable negotiations with the King. (Balaam of course has told me all about that, as he became a gentleman in Aske's company, though one swift enough to avoid the royal pursuivants when Aske was taken, hanged, quartered and disembowelled.) Latimer, Huicke explained, was compelled to go south and treat for the rebels with the King. His Majesty furiously demanded that this hapless envoy reject Aske and submit to royal clemency. Latimer did so, but once the rebellion was over, he was a broken man, remaining in London to be nursed by his wife.

Huicke was now gossiping so much, I suspected he had swiftly drunk a deep bowl of claret, but why? What was the physician frightened of? He kept chattering how the Lady Parr, as she was then, first won the King's attention by pleading for a kinsman, Sir George Throckmorton, a victim of Cromwell's rapacity. Indeed, she'd been visited by the King and given presents by him months before her husband's lingering death. And my lord Thomas Seymour? (I decided to test the waters.) Hadn't he also been hot in the pursuit of the soon-to-be-widowed Lady Latimer? Huicke just smiled knowingly and, tapping his nose, turned the conversation back to the King and the treatment of his ulcers. He dipped into his wallet and drew out a script of parchment detailing a poultice the Queen herself had drawn up. I would have liked to study this, but Huicke thought better of it, putting it away, whispering how the Queen was concerned that His Majesty might return to the hunting park at Oatlands to try and hunt the stag during the grease season, which would do his health no good.

Still gossiping, we disembarked at the King's Steps and were at once approached by the Norfolks, father and son. Of course both ignored me but chattered for a while with Huicke, explaining how they were leaving London before the Christmas festivities 'on king's business'. Surrey, arrogant and impetuous, the cast in his eye most marked, discussed the condition of his wife, Lady Frances, who was expecting their child. Norfolk, his long, cunning face twitching, kept dabbing at his dribbling mouth, bemoaning how cold Westminster felt and how he looked forward to keeping merry hall at his own palace of Kenninghall. I was tempted to ask if it was more the warmth of Bess Holland he was pining for, that brazen-mouthed, big-bosomed strumpet he'd installed in his bed to the exclusion of his wife Elizabeth, daughter of the great Buckingham. Eventually they moved away. Huicke, whispering to himself, preceded me into the warren of galleries leading back to the royal chambers. Servants were busy pushing paste balls soaked in herbs into the mouse holes at the base of the wall panelling. The corridor reeked of a tang that reminded me of the salt pans along the coast.

When we reached the King's privy chamber, Henry was sitting in his scarlet and gilt throne chair looted from Fountains Abbey. The abbot's thick winter robe, lined with ermine, was wrapt closely about his shoulders, his head protected against the cold by a flat jewelled bonnet which Catherine of Aragon had taken from the corpse of James IV of Scotland at Flodden Field. The King glanced up from the makeshift bed table across his lap. Paget and his creature Denny were with him. Denny is all sweet-faced and earnest, a handsome man with copper-gold hair, moustache and beard; his merry eyes crinkled in welcome, though Paget glowered like the basilisk. I smiled and bowed at Denny. I rather like him, especially as he does me no hurt. A

Norfolk man, a scholar, he once confided in me: 'If two deities did not command me, the King and my wife, I would surely return to my studies at St John's College, Cambridge.' He certainly served his wife, the Lady Joan; they have ten children. To house them all Denny was, as Keeper of the Palace, given custody of three mansions close to Westminster named, rather appropriately, Paradise, Purgatory and Hell. I always tease him about which of the three shelters the Lady Joan. A born courtier, Denny had comforted the King over his mockery of a marriage to the German Anne of Cleves, declaring: 'The condition of princes on matters of their marriage is infinitely worse than that of poor men, for princes have to accept what is brought to them whilst poor men are most commonly left to their own choices and devices.' Henry was profoundly impressed. Denny could do no wrong because he had portrayed Henry as the victim. Poor Cromwell, who'd arranged the marriage, climbed the scaffold at Tower Hill while Denny was given a strong hand up the ladder of royal preferment.

I heard a cough and glanced across the chamber. A man, dappled by shadows, lounged in the window seat. He was dressed like a soldier in leather jerkin and thick serge hose, one booted leg swinging, spurs clinking faintly. I peered closer and recognised the bald head and unshaven face of Sir John Gates, the King's roaring boy. If politics should ever come to swordplay in a darkened runnel, or a dagger beneath the arras,

Gates is your man. He can whistle up his ruffians to form a posse: mercenaries from Spain, Portugal, Italy, the Rhineland duchies and even a sprinkling from North Africa. At Henry's court, danger swirls like a perfume; you can grow so skilled at its detection that you can pluck it from the very air. I sensed it then. The whisperings at Greenwich about the screech owl, Norfolk and Surrey leaving the court just before Seymour held a meeting of the Privy Council in his own house. And now these three cunning courtiers closeted with their king.

'I really must do something about his corpse.' Henry broke the silence. He had taken the bonnet off his head and was inspecting its rim.

'Who, Your Majesty?'

'Why, Paget, James IV of Scotland. After Flodden Field, old Norfolk brought his corpse to London, beautifully embalmed, and it was never sent back. It still lies here, in one of the cellars.' Henry peered at me. 'You've seen it, haven't you, Will?'

I recalled that cadaver embalmed like a doll lying in its casket in a wine cellar to the north of the palace, a sombre, dreadful sight: the corpse of a once magnificent king left lying like a piece of old furniture.

'You should send it back, Your Majesty,' I agreed. I watched those shifty eyes blink. 'The servants say that James's ghost haunts them, crying for burial.' Henry grinned. He has no intention of ever sending that corpse back to Scotland. James IV once held a resplendent court. A warrior much loved by the ladies, he had dared to challenge Henry by invading England, only to meet the bloodiest defeat. Of course what rankles with Henry is that the great English victory was not won by himself – he was busy chasing French horsemen around Normandy – but by old Norfolk, the present duke's father, and Henry's queen, Catherine of Aragon.

'Ah well.' Henry closed the jewelled calfskin-bound ledger he had open before him, placing it in the black coffer. 'The dry stamp is being handled validly.' The King winked at me. 'Gentlemen, I must ask you to withdraw. Good physician Huicke, please leave what you have brought from Her Grace the Queen. Somers, stay for a while and amuse your king.'

The rest withdrew, Huicke backing out bowing. Denny smiled at me; Paget gave me that hard, calculating gaze of his whilst Gates rose and swaggered across reeking of leather and sweat. He still wore his sword belt with his hanger, a long stabbing dagger in its brocaded sheath, a rare concession, a mark of trust since very few are allowed to carry weapons into the King's presence. Gates gave me an arrogant look; he reminded me of a falcon on its perch, those cruel eyes, that hooked nose and narrow slit of a mouth. Outside in the antechambers and galleries voices rose and fell as Paget issued orders. Henry sat up in his chair, head back, face all shadowy.

'Your Majesty.' I broke the deepening silence. 'What is happening?'

'We have seen the days, Will, haven't we? Do you remember old Wolsey and the tricks you used to play on him? How he once asked you to better yourself and you promised you would. He asked how. You replied that you'd live in Ipswich and be a butcher's boy like he was.' Henry sniggered.

'And do you remember,' I retorted harshly, 'how John Dudley was only six years old when you executed his father, *your* father's loan collector. You killed him and his comrade in sin, Empson; you did it to please the people.'

'One of these days, Will, your head will fly.'

'Your Majesty my feet will be swifter. I am not the threat. I fear some trickery with the dry stamp. The Privy Council meet in Seymour's house tonight. Your own physician Huicke will be present.'

'Let them be. Cromwell became Earl of Essex, vice regent of the Church of England, and where is he? Wolsey was a cardinal, he even sought the triple crown of St Peter, and where is he? Buckingham was the greatest duke in England with his host of spears, and where is he now? As for Huicke, he is my spy, not the Council's, so I will know what happens. Now, you were with him at Greenwich?'

'Not all the time.' The white wand came hissing out of the darkness, striking my shoulder, a searing blow scraping my cheek. I screamed, jumped to my feet and backed away.

'I commanded you.' Henry leaned forward, his

swollen face contorted, the folds of fat so creased his eyes became small black pebbles in a pasty waste of puffy skin.

'Your Majesty, I had no choice. Your wife the Queen was insistent. She wanted to consult with your physician, Huicke, on a personal matter. I—'

'True, true.' Henry threw himself back in the chair, the cane slipping from his hand. 'I am still master of the game, Will. I know what I am doing. Huicke will tell me. Now,' the King indicated the piece of parchment listing the ingredients for the poultice, 'you can swear that from the moment you departed the Queen's chamber that scrap of parchment never left his hands? Whom did you meet?'

'The Norfolks, for a brief while on King's Steps.' Henry simply groaned, waving a hand. I picked up the Queen's prescription: linseed, vinegar, rosewater, long garden worms, scrapings of ivory, pearls powdered until they are fine, red lead, red coral, honeysuckle water, suet of hens and fat from the side-bones of calves.

'Your Majesty?' I glanced up. 'Is there anything wrong?'

'Tell me, Will, what happened at Greenwich?' The King listened carefully, nodding his head quickly, as was customary whenever he concentrated. 'The screech owl,' he whispered. 'Who is that? Is it Surrey, Norfolk's brat?' Just the way he spat these words out created a stab of fear. I recalled him ignoring the Howards at the recent council meeting, their exclusion from the proceedings at Seymour's house, their haste to leave Westminster.

'Surrey's arms boast an eagle,' I offered. 'The reference to a screech owl could be an insulting reference to that.'

'Tell me, Will; you know the lore, the folk tales. What is the screech owl?'

'According to tradition, the bird acquired its name from its cry because its mouth speaks what overflows from its heart; what it thinks inwardly it utters with its tongue. It is regarded as loathsome because its roost is filthy from its droppings, just as a sinner brings all who dwell with him into disrepute through the example of his own wicked behaviour. The screech owl is heavy with feathers to symbolise an excess of flesh, and like an evil spirit is always bound with a heavy laziness, the same laziness that renders sinners idle and unwilling when it comes to doing good. The bird lives day and night in cemeteries, just like sinners who revel in their sin and the stench of human corruption. It also hides in caves like a sinner reluctant to cast off the darkness, hating the light. If other birds see the screech owl they make a great cry and attack him vigorously, just as a sinner recognised in the light becomes an object of mockery for the righteous as he struggles in the toils of his own sin. Other birds tear out his feathers and wound him with their beaks, as the righteous who hate the fleshly deeds of a sinner curse and attack his excesses. The screech owl is unhappy because its heart is heavy with the habits and vices it nurtures.' I enjoyed reciting that. I know all about the bestiary, be it the basilisk or the unicorn. I also entertained my own suspicions as to whom it really referred. The King sat silent.

'Is it,' he asked, as if he could truly read my thoughts, 'a reference to me? Is that how my goodly wife, that bastion of prim virtue, truly regards me? You suspect Thomas Seymour was with her today, don't you?'

'Possibly, Your Majesty. If he was, that makes Huicke a traitor.'

'Or a very frightened man,' Henry replied. 'And Huicke can easily be frightened. They are all terrified of the Seymours. Though one thing at a time. Unlike you, Will, I am no fool. The court expects my death. The Council discuss it daily.'

'Even though it is treason? Sir Walter Hungerford was condemned to death for speculating about your death.'

'Don't quote him,' Henry snapped. 'So many do! Hungerford was exceptional. He bribed two priests to raise demons to inform him of my death. He was a born fool. He was executed the same day as Cromwell.' The King yawned, revealing yellowing black stumps in blood-tinged gums. I glanced away.

'Hungerford was executed not just for treason.' Henry yawned again. 'He also buggered a servant and raped his own daughter.'

'Huicke could be replaced,' I declared, eager to divert the King.

'And who would fill his place? Physician Wendy, who in turn will be threatened and bribed? No, no,' Henry sighed, 'I realise how these things go with them – I mean my courtiers. I am just suspicious.' He paused. 'The Act of Poisons was enacted some fifteen years ago, wasn't it? After Richard Roos, for his own wicked, damnable reasons, tried to poison the entire household of the Bishop of Rochester.'

'Oh yes, I remember him. Roos was boiled alive in Smithfield. You forced me to go and witness it.'

'Did you?'

'No. I sheltered in a nearby tavern; that was bad enough. Roos's screams were horrific. Smithfield, I understand, stank of boiled fat for days afterwards. Why?' I was becoming increasingly alarmed at this macabre conversation. 'Do you believe you are being poisoned?'

'Catullus,' the King replied, 'my dear dead spaniel. He gnawed on a poultice after it had been smeared with one of the Queen's recipes. I left it on a stool; the dog chewed it and died.'

'But sire, there are many medicines that can be applied to a wound but are not to be swallowed.'

'So you are a physician now, Will?'

'No, I am trying, as I often do and fail, to be your conscience. Are you really saying your queen is trying to poison you?'

'Or her would-be lover, Thomas Seymour?'

'You have proof?'

The King's lower lip began to quiver, fat jowls shaking, tears starting.

'Will,' he began to sob, 'how do you think I feel? I have proof that my beloved wife is pining for another man, waiting for me to die, hoping she will be left as queen regent. If that is the case, why should she, or Seymour, baulk at shortening my life?'

I was tempted to reply that this was also a queen who had cared tenderly for him and had been walking in the garden when Wriothesley and the Spears arrived to haul her off to the Tower. How Wriothesley would have loved to bully such a fine lady into a hysterical fit. I kept my lips sealed. I recognised the danger.

'Over seventy years ago, Will, we Tudors won the crown by the edge of the sword! Why shouldn't someone else do the same, sweep away little Edward and my daughters?' Henry's whole bulk heaved. He reminded me of an old mastiff preparing to attack. 'But who?' he demanded. 'The Howards? The Dudleys? The Seymours? I have cared for them all, favoured the Seymours because of Jane, their poor sister. I have overlooked Dudley's lowly, tainted origins. As for the Howards, they fought against my father, yet I made Surrey the constant companion of my bastard son, Henry Fitzroy, Duke of Richmond. I even married Fitzroy to Norfolk's daughter, and now they betray me.'

'Who does, sire?'

'They all pull lady faces and wag lady tongues but they have dragons' hearts; they are wolves garbed as lambs, hawks who act the dove. Never mind, never mind.' Henry's voice became brisk. 'I have much to attend to; my Council will be returning here.'

Dismissed, I returned to my own chamber and drew out Balaam's message, thrust into my hand earlier in the day. Balaam and Lady Jane would come suitably cowled and visored to the Bowels of Hell, an ancient three-storey tavern close to the old friary of the Carmelites, Whitefriars, not far from Puddle Wharf and the Temple Gardens. Balaam promised to be there after the witching hour, waiting for me in the Vespers Chamber overlooking the garden at the back of the tavern, a suitable place for escape should flight become necessary.

I left after lamp-lighting. I hired two armed luciferi to carry lanterns before me as I hurried through the crooked, narrow lanes. Darkness had fallen, an icy blackness that drove all good citizens from the streets and melancholy wastes. A bristling breeze sent the tavern and shop signs creaking eerily. The only light was the occasional flaring pitch torch pushed into some crevice or holder. Here and there bonfires raged as the rubbish heaps were soaked in oil and fired into a furious conflagration which drew in the legion of beggars from the mean streets and lanes. On doorposts tallow dips in their lantern boxes glowed a dull yellow, their cheap odour mingling with the insidious stench of refuse, dung and above all that stink of rancid oil that seems to drift everywhere. We passed open doors revealing narrow nooks of rooms, their walls blackened by time: pillars and rafters worn, floors tainted and sticky with rotting straw, windows mere slits stuffed with old rags and pieces of rubbish. I was nervous because such a night-time foray is a rare event. Nevertheless, the creatures of the dark, the night-stalkers and sewer squires, glimpsed the steel of my escort and slunk away.

Eventually we reached the Bowels of Hell, a stark, forbidding tavern standing on the corner of a trackway leading down into the heart of Whitefriars. Of course the curfew means nothing here. I knocked on the side door and it quickly swung open. A shadowy figure led me across a gloomy taproom. The place reeked of rancid cheese; the rushes underfoot were a squelching slush through which vermin scampered and squeaked. A rickety staircase led up to the main gallery. My shadowy guide knocked on the door to the Vespers Chamber. Balaam, he of the long dark face, cynical eyes and mocking mouth, was waiting. He was sitting at the head of a well-scrubbed table where platters of dried meat, fresh bread and pots of hot herbs and vegetables mixed together had been laid out with goblets of water and a stoppered jug of white wine. He rose to greet me. He was dressed in a dark brown robe like that of a Benedictine monk, whilst the chamber he had hired seemed like his cell. Its walls and floor were clean and free of any covering; a Spanish crucifix hung over the hearth where a fierce fire roared. Pots of incense curled scented smoke, which provoked memories of masses offered.

Balaam whispered his greeting and we exchanged the kiss of peace. He then went to the door and his escort brought up the lovely Jane Bold, my sweetheart, my true reason for living. Oh Lady Jane! Small and petite, her face even prettier framed by its furred hood. I gave her the warmest hug and a saucy kiss on those lovely lips. She gazed bright-eyed at me and we kissed again until Balaam coughed. I took the Lady Jane's hands, brushed them with my lips and escorted her to a chair. All three of us gathered around the table.

For a while we satisfied our hunger, Jane, in her soft country voice, telling me how she felt and what she had done, how she had brought her mistress's greetings. I listened intently and grasped what she wasn't saying. All power now lay at Westminster. The households of Princess Mary, the Princess Elizabeth and the Lord Edward were isolated, allowed to sink into a boring, humdrum existence. Winter had sealed the roads, whilst the Council determined what messages travelled along them. In return I told the usual tales. How Henry's mood was improving. How he missed his elder daughter. How he hoped to travel to meet her and looked forward to sharing the festive season with her. Jane nodded as she listened; she knew it was fiction, as would her mistress. Everybody was waiting to dance to Henry's tune, as they had for the last thirty years, only now Henry had hidden himself deep in shadows. This time

Balaam would demand the stark truth on other matters. I fed the Lady Jane sops of food until Balaam tapped the table with his goblet.

'The Lord be with you,' he breathed.

'And with you too, brother,' I retorted.

'Master Will, the King, how is he? Please be blunt.' He grinned. 'Even treasonous! The Princess Mary is being starved of all real news.'

'I shall speak directly. The King's torso is obese, gross. The fat around his neck threatens to choke his breath and he has a great hump here,' I half turned, indicating my own back, 'between the shoulder blades. His skin is yellowing, thin and as easy to crack as a communion wafer. Wounds and cuts heal very slowly if at all. His face is now moon-like, dragged down by folds of fat beneath his eyes; the same swell around his hips. He complains of constant soreness to his ribs and back; his bowels and anus ache so much, the pain of easing himself licks like tongues of flame.'

'And his mind?'

'Sharp as ever. Just as changeable. Just as dangerous. He trusts no one, but sometimes gives the impression that he trusts everyone. They are all fearful. Henry has a nightmare that when he dies, all will be swept away.'

'And the Council?'

I told Balaam everything I had seen and heard in the King's secret chamber. This was not betrayal; I could tell from Jane's face that if the King was fearful, so was the Princess Mary. I relayed my conversation with Paget, particularly his description of Cranmer's brush with death.

'I have heard of that,' Balaam murmured. 'Rumours, snatches of conversation. Now that would disturb the humours of a man like Paget. Dudley and the Seymours are soldiers, but Paget is a true student of Machiavelli. He has studied Henry closely. In many ways Paget reminds me of Thomas More without his saintliness.'

'But why discuss the King with me?'

Balaam toasted me with his goblet. 'Will, you are the King's close companion. Paget wishes to see which way you will jump. If he has approached you, he probably has had similar conversations with other members of the Council. I would wager a purse of silver that Paget is prepared, should the King die, to concede supreme power to Seymour and Dudley on the one condition that they are guided and advised by him.'

'Paget is also hunting you,' I warned.

That master of shadows simply smirked. 'Cromwell tried the same, and where is Cromwell?'

'Where is this leading?' Jane demanded. 'Surely it is the King's mood that is all important?'

'Shall I tell you?' Balaam shuffled his feet. 'If Master Paget studies our king, then so do I, and that includes the paintings. I have glimpsed one; you may have seen it, Will: Henry seated in all his glory under a cloth of state. On his right stands the Prince Edward, Henry firmly grasping his hand. On his left, Queen Jane Seymour, as if she has been lifted from the funeral hearse and made to stand beside her king and her seven-year-old son whom she hardly glimpsed before she died. Further away, to the right and left of the King, stand his two daughters, Mary and Elizabeth, almost indistinguishable.'

'I have seen this painting,' I broke in. 'I cannot recall who executed it; a strange painting, timeless. Young Edward is depicted much older than he was at the time. Queen Jane died in childbirth, yet she is there, as if summoned back from the dead. Even more curiously, at either side of the painting there is an arch leading into the great gardens of Hampton Palace. Under one arch stands you, Jane, in your red petticoats, in the other myself garbed in a green jerkin and rough hose.'

Jane too was nodding excitedly. 'I too have seen this,' she murmured. 'It hangs in the presence chamber at Whitehall.'

'And there is the other painting,' Balaam declared. 'On one occasion, Will, you described it to me, from the King's book of hours, very peculiar.'

'What is this?' Jane turned to me.

'A curious painting,' I replied, 'where the King is depicted as old, ill and overweight. Shown in the guise of King David, he squats close to a Welsh harp, one of the instruments His Majesty is most skilled at. In the foreground stands myself, the King's fool, with my back to him in an attitude of rejection. I am dressed in a coat of green cloth, its hood lined with fur; on my belt hangs Cromwell's purse. My hair is cropped, my face unshaven. On my left shoulder perches a monkey, which is searching my scalp.'

'Master Balaam, why do you mention paintings?' Jane asked.

'They show the King's mind,' he retorted. He paused, listening to the wind whipping the shutters and carrying the dull cries of the night.

'How?' I started at the hideous screech of a rat caught in the jaws of a cat along the gallery outside.

'Remember, Will, remember, Jane.' Balaam was not being pompous, but voicing something he'd milled and sifted in his own devious brain. 'Remember,' he repeated, 'all paintings have to be approved by our king. The first painting is significant. Henry in his splendour with his long-dead wife next to him and his son brought to boyhood. Queen Jane just stands there like a statue, whilst Henry grasps Edward's hand to demonstrate complete ownership. On either side, much further away, his two daughters, whom Henry really didn't want but who he will tolerate and use to his best advantage. Nobody else is depicted except, my respects to both of you, the two court fools. Do you represent, at least in Henry's eyes, the rest of the world? Look at that painting again, Will. Jane is correct: it hangs in the presence chamber at Whitehall. There is no cross, no crucifix, no altar, no bishop, no priest, no clerk, no courtier; nothing but Henry, his queen, his three children and his fools. Nothing else exists for him; that's his world and how he regards it.'

'And the second painting?' Jane asked. 'The one in the book of hours?'

'Henry is neither Romanist nor reformer but simply the King,' Balaam declared. 'The verse in this painting is from Psalm 52: "In his excess the fool said there is no God." The painting underscores this. Will is the fool who represents those who hold that no God exists and so turn their back on the true God, so evident to see: Henry and the royal house of Tudor. Henry,' Balaam concluded, 'has the arrogance to assume the role of King David, God's anointed, a man, as scripture says, after God's own heart. David's bloodline is sacred because from it came Christ the Lord. Henry sees the same replicated in his own lineage.'

'A prince who had many women,' Jane murmured, 'who slew his enemies but remained God's beloved.'

'That's why Henry allowed himself to be depicted as old and overweight – it's the truth, but so are the King's claims to be what he most desires.'

I touched Balaam's hand. 'Which is precisely what?'

'His Majesty,' Balaam replied, 'believes in neither the God of Rome nor that of Luther, Calvin and Zwingli, but only in himself. He is obsessed with his own lineage and house; he will destroy anyone who threatens them.' He went on to say that if the King survived his present illness and returned to government, he would carry out reforms and purges the like of which had never seen before. He would destroy everyone: the Howards, the

Seymours, Dudley, even Cranmer. No one would stand in his path.

Balaam maintains that His Majesty the King is approaching the same form of princely madness as the emperors of Ancient Rome. Henry believes he is God, or at the very least, God's will on earth, and therefore cannot be checked or opposed; hence his depiction as David of scripture. Outside of Henry the king, there is no God, so he will dictate the true tenets of established religion.

'Remember,' Balaam sipped at his goblet, 'this is nothing new. The seeds were planted many years ago. In 1530, so the Princess Mary tells me, the King held a meeting of the English church in St Edward's Chapel, Westminster. They discussed the translation of the Bible. Henry asserted that the welfare of his subjects' souls was his, not the bishops' responsibility. He would decide on what translations, if any, were to be made and how they would be distributed. No other monarch has ever claimed such a right.' Balaam gave that lopsided grin. 'A few more steps,' he murmured, 'from being the keeper of God's word to being that word himself.'

He went on to say that the screech owl was not Surrey but the King himself, a dark, lonely, dangerous soul. His councillors had now recognised the lurking danger and were plotting furiously to counter it.

'Once,' Balaam declared, 'I stayed in Rome. I visited a haunted house where, allegedly, two statues of cardinals of the Santa Croce family descend from their pedestals at night to walk dolefully in a rattle of chains. I investigated that house. I discovered an oubliette lined with sharp pointed stakes, all around a mass of skeletons, one of them in armour with a dagger driven through the helmet. I also found an embalmed corpse walled up in a niche.' He paused, clicking his tongue. 'It's the same here,' he murmured. 'England is a haunted house full of devious devices, traps and secret cells with corpses hidden away and ghosts that walk the dead of night.'

'A ghost story!' Lady Jane exclaimed.

'England is a ghost story,' I retorted. 'The court is its haunted place. Ghosts lean against the wall, stand by the threshold and peer through the window.'

'Old resentments,' Balaam declared, 'buried griev-ances, dashed hopes, murderous resentments, Henry knows all this. He will not exorcise the ghosts but will try and kill them. I truly believe that. He will turn on one party then the other. The one he believes to be the most vulnerable will be smitten first.'

'And who is that?' I asked.

'Why, the Howards of Norfolk!'

'And what charge could the King or the Council level against them?'

'Not from without, Will, but from within. Holy Scripture says a house divided against itself cannot stand, and the Howards are riven with dissension.'

'True, Norfolk is alienated from his wife. Surrey has clashed with both his father's mistress Bess Holland

and his sister, the widow of the King's bastard son, Henry Fitzroy, but how can this be treason?'

Balaam was about to reply when a clatter of steel echoed from outside in the freezing night air. The chamber fell deadly silent. Balaam hurried across to a window. He pulled back the shutters, slashed a cut in the stretched pig's bladder covering the narrow gap and peered out.

'Men, hooded and visored,' he whispered. 'They carry staves and pennants. Council men! Somehow our meeting has been betrayed.'

I felt a chill. I was responsible. Paget knew of my visit here. We had done no wrong, but if we were taken, questions would be asked. I rose, and was gesturing at Jane to follow when the chamber door was flung open. A group of men, heads and faces covered in white sacks with rents for eyes, nose and mouth, slipped like ghastly nightmares into the chamber. Lady Jane gave a scream, cut off as Balaam pressed a gloved hand against her mouth.

'No fear,' he whispered, 'no fear. These are my men. What news?'

'Council men,' one of the masked men replied. 'About twelve in number. Mine host is keeping them dancing on the threshold. They carry no warrant but demand entrance to search. We had best leave, but not through the garden.'

He led us out of the chamber, along the ill-lit gallery then down stairs and shaky steps until we reached the dingy, smelly cellars beneath. The floor was slippery and stained by the beer and wine that had leaked from the barrels, tuns and vats, the cold night air broken by the constant squeak of mice and rats. Torchlight flared. We waited anxiously whilst a great cask was pushed aside to reveal a door built into the wall; that was quickly thrown open. Balaam, sword in one hand, a flaring torch in the other, led us into a warren of evil-smelling passageways and ancient sewers cut beneath London's streets. We fled like bats down those dark tunnels. Now and again, I am certain, we passed skeletons, a heap of snow-white bones glittering in the passing light before the darkness swallowed us again. On one occasion Balaam made us stop, the blackness all around us, to ensure we were not being pursed and there was no danger ahead. I stood clutching Lady Jane's hand, eyes tightly closed. Balaam's ghost story and the sights we'd glimpsed had upset my humours. I was not sure whether I was dreaming or not. Faces came out of the dark. Edward Seymour with his craggy features and popping eyes; Thomas his brother, with his bristling moustache and beard; Dudley, fox-like and predatory; Paget, slapping those garden gloves against his thigh whilst studying me intently. Balaam murmured, tugging at my cloak, and we moved on.

Ghosts haunted that place of shadows. I abruptly recalled a story of how the King had apparently entered a chamber at Hampton Palace and come face to face with all his victims: Anne Boleyn, sharp-featured and laughing shrilly; Katherine Howard clasping her neck to show how small it was; Cromwell clutching his beads and pleading piteously for mercy; Wolsey in his purple cardinal's robes weeping that he had served his king better than his God; More and Fisher all reproachful; the Carthusians of Charterhouse in their bloody robes. Henry had fled screaming like a demented child. Such a memory rendered me highly anxious. I was so relieved to be free of that gloomy vault, out through the taproom of a riverside tavern and on to the snow-swept quayside. We made our hasty farewells. I embraced Jane, whispering my love into her ear, kissing her on the lips, cheek and brow before Balaam plucked her away, ordering some of his escort to see me safely back to Westminster.

I slept fitfully and woke famished, so I rose and, pushing aside all cares, broke my fast on a chine of beef, a joint of mutton, buttermilk, six eggs of chicken and a pottle of beer followed by a little salted fish with melted butter poured over it. I tried to see the King but I was turned away from the privy chambers by that arrogant oaf Roberts on the orders of Sir William Paget. The yeoman curtly informed me that I was not needed and should look to my own affairs. I replied that I had gossip from the city for His Majesty. Roberts just shrugged. He said he had his orders and I had mine. I had no choice but to return to the kitchens and my good friend Master Bricket, the master cook. Bricket knows my weakness.

I love the life of the kitchens. There is nothing more soothing than to be swept up in the lavish preparations for the King's table. I helped to prepare the royal meal: soup, roast capon, boiled beef, chicken pasties, roast pork, fish, almond tarts and baked apple. In the evening we prepared stewed fruits, and oysters from Colchester augmented with eggs, cream, butter, onion and herbs. Bricket surpassed himself making subtleties of almond paste and sugar in the shape of the Virgin and the Angel Gabriel. A minstrel, hired by the Lord Chamberlain, joined us. I listened to his stories about a bleak castle set in the middle of a wild forest where outlaws prowled clothed in Lincoln green, but soon grew tired of this and asked for something romantic, a lilting country tune so I could evoke the past. Afterwards I went to the palace bath house, its roof and walls hung with sheets, the bath itself warm with rosewater, herbs and a sponge for me to sit on. I cleansed myself and returned refreshed to my own chamber.

I was content to relax and reflect on what Balaam had said. If Henry was about to move, and he certainly was, on what grounds could he strike at the Howards? They were powerful. They had done nothing to incur the King's anger except by being who they were. How could Henry find evidence against them? They had their estates, their palaces, their retinues. I glanced at a painting on the wall and felt a chill of apprehension. The picture showed a married couple, long-dead courtiers, husband and wife sitting so amicably close together.

I recalled Balaam's words about how a house divided against itself could not stand. To outsiders, the Howard family are like a fortress, but within, have not Norfolk and his wife gone to war? I have glimpsed Norfolk's wife Elizabeth, daughter of Stafford, Duke of Buckingham, at the Howard house in Lambeth. A fine-boned, full-faced lady with reddish hair and eyes as sharp as a jackdaw, a pleasant visage though with a slightly receding chin. She has long, slender fingers; I remember them grasping a scarlet missal with a gold cross in the centre. She wore a hood in the English style edged with a band of jewels, peaking high in light red velvet from which fell a full train of dark material. I recall it well because an acquaintance, someone who'd served Chapuys, the former Imperial ambassador, remarked how the duchess's appearance evoked memories of Catherine of Aragon, the very source of all that redoubt-able woman's troubles. Such a chance memory empha-sised Balaam's prediction. When the King moved against an opponent, he always destroyed them from within, be it Anne Boleyn's musicians or Katherine Howard's ladies. Norfolk's household would be a fertile furrow to plough, the source of dissension being the old duke's rejection of his wife.

At first, according to court gossip, Elizabeth's marriage to Thomas Howard seemed happy enough. She bore him three children, Henry, Mary and the younger Thomas, but the bane of her life was Cardinal Wolsey, whom her father Buckingham hated with a passion beyond all others. Buckingham publicly called Wolsey a butcher's churl and, as royal cup bearer, refused on one occasion to pour water for him, instead spilling it all and spoiling the cardinal's purple silk shoes. Hatred for Wolsey was common amongst the lords. Howard himself drew a dagger on the good cardinal and, on another occasion, declared he would tear Wolsey apart with his teeth. Howard could dissimulate; Buckingham, however, could not; little wonder Emperor Charles called him 'the proudest Buck in England'.

Eminent for his high birth and large revenues, Buckingham built a fantastical pile at Thornbury on the Welsh march, a monument to his own greatness. He rode high in the councils of the King, but was ruined by his ever-clacking tongue. Believe me, at the English court Fate never undoes a man without his own misdirection, and when it does, its first stroke is always at the head. Buckingham preened himself so magnificently that people considered that if the King should die without a male heir, the duke might easily obtain the crown. A dangerous saying. His Majesty took note. Buckingham was arrested and arraigned before Norfolk's father, the victor of Flodden, for plotting the destruction and death of the King. The Norfolks wept at the thought of Buckingham being condemned but still pronounced the verdict of death. Buckingham had to surrender to the sheriffs and a guard of five hundred men. On Tower Hill he recited the penitential psalms, took off his gown and, blindfolded, laid his head on the block, where he died miserably but with great courage. The Norfolks, both father and son, wept and wailed, then comforted themselves with large portions of Buckingham's chattels and estates. This was slightly before my time, but the story was common knowledge. Henry often comforted himself by personally itemising the fallen duke's personal possessions, which he kept close about him.

Elizabeth, the duchess, so common report has it, never recovered her wits after her father's brutal and sudden fall. Perhaps she glimpsed for the first time the deep hypocrisy of Norfolk, her husband, who emerged as one who had conspired with both king and cardinal to bring him down. Buckingham did not go like a lamb to the slaughter but, from the bar of his court, rounded on those who had plotted his destruction, declaring that of all men living he hated Howard the most, regarding him as a man who had done his utmost to disgrace him in the eyes of His Majesty. Elizabeth never forgave nor forgot; some thirteen years later, as the King began to press for a divorce from his Spanish queen, she proved resolute in her defence of Catherine. Norfolk once warned Thomas More that the wrath of the King meant death, to which More replied that if that was the case, the only difference between them was that he would die today and Norfolk tomorrow. Such was the Duchess Elizabeth's attitude. She did not fear the King's wrath. She had no time for political subtleties or pastime with good company, the joys of the tennis courts, tilting yards, bowling alleys and dicing tables, of bawdy doggerel and games of courtly love. The constant masques, dances and banquets in the royal palaces, with their unalloyed service to Venus and Bacchus, repelled her. The duchess loudly proclaimed that she had no patience for those who showed her fair face to conceal false heart, who cried 'All hail!' when they intended all harm. Men and women of the court who'd doff their bonnets to her in greeting, but who would quietly pray to see her head leave her shoulders. Courtiers who would make a leg to her and bow with all reverence yet would have those same legs broken to see her dead and hurried to the grave.

She herself was guilty of no such deceit. Angry at both king and husband, she openly espoused Queen Catherine's cause, and that of the Princess Mary, so I hold the duchess's name in the highest regard. Lady Jane once informed me how Norfolk's wife filched letters from her husband's own chancery which provided information about the King's secret designs to have his marriage to his first wife annulled. The duchess carefully copied these and sent them to the Queen cleverly concealed in an orange. She publicly informed the Queen how Boleyn's court strove to entice the duchess over to theirs and declared that even if the world tried, she would remain faithful to her. She encouraged Catherine to stand firm, telling her to have good courage for her opponents were at their wits' end, being further off from their design than the day they first began. The Duchess of Norfolk openly realised she could be the ruin of her family, and her fidelity to the Queen certainly cost Norfolk dearly. She was eventually exiled from the court, judged as speaking too freely and declaring herself for Catherine more than was liked.

Lady Jane was party to all the gossip and rumour learnt by her mistress the Princess Mary. She narrates with great gusto how there was even a secret plan for Anne Boleyn, when the King's cause seemed weak, to marry young Surrey. A marriage of convenience to satisfy Boleyn's ambitions whilst allowing the King free rein with her. Norfolk always tried to weave his family close to the Crown, and his wife's persistent refusal to even consider such a squalid arrangement enraged him further; to be sure, my lord of Norfolk's fiery temper is more hasty than is needed. Duchess Elizabeth remained obstinate in her stubbornness. She refused to bear Boleyn's train when she was elevated to the title of Marchioness of Pembroke, and ignored the summons to join that same lady's retinue during her crossing to France. She did not attend Boleyn's coronation or the christening of her child, the Princess Elizabeth. Norfolk, distracted out of his wits and fearful of the King, begged Henry Stafford, his wife's brother, to take her back. Stafford refused, saying his sister's wild language was constant and he had no power to prevent it, whilst her presence in his house might cause great danger for him and all his kin. He did not deserve that and he could only pray that God would send his sister a better mind.

Matters were certainly not helped by my lord of

Norfolk, who was greatly seduced by the charm and beauty of Bess, the daughter of Lord John Holland, his chief steward. Bess eventually became the lady of the house at the duke's principal manor of Kenninghall. This proved too much for Duchess Elizabeth, who turned on her rival, calling her 'a churl's daughter, a washer of nursery pots, a drab, a quean, a harlot'. Twelve years ago, during Passion week, all thought of Christ's suffering and death was ignored in the duke's residence. The King, smirking behind his hand, told me the story. The duchess refused to suffer the Holland bawd and her harlots, so the duke locked her in a chamber, taking away all her apparel and jewellery. On hearing this, the reformist Bishop Latimer openly preached at court how it was part of the penance of being a woman to suffer in bearing children, as it was to be subject and subservient to their husbands, because women were underlings and, as such, must be obedient. The duchess certainly refused to accept such advice and her husband became lost in a marvellous sorrow and indignation at her obduracy.

The duke was already mired in controversy. Unable to help either the King or Boleyn, he had become Anne's enemy. She openly resented him, especially his remarks about how the conflict over the King's divorce from his Spanish queen was caused by Satan and nobody else. How Satan had been the inventor and source of all that dispute. Norfolk, fearful lest Anne Boleyn and her faction would turn the King's heart from him, banished his wife to Redbourne, one of his Hertfordshire manors. Even there, the duchess sustained her litany of sorrows and objections, dispatching letter after letter to the King, Master Cromwell and her husband. She insisted that Kenninghall belonged to her and not to Holland; that she, the duchess, was a noblewoman by birth and raised to live daintily. She described physical attacks on her when Norfolk sent Holland and other harlots to bind her until blood seeped out of her finger ends. How they tortured her and sat on her breast until she spat blood. So ill was this treatment that it had weakened her health; she became sick in autumn at the fall of a leaf as well as the spring of the year. She protested how she'd only married Norfolk out of duty to her father, as her real love was Neville of Westmoreland, and how her husband, even when she was pregnant, had assaulted her. She received no comfort from her children and publicly proclaimed that no mother bore so ungracious an elder son and so unnatural a daughter. The duchess fled to the King when he was hunting outside Dunstable, but what could His Majesty say about the holiness of marriage vows? In truth, and I was the King's audience, Henry secretly but gleefully recounted Norfolk's woes. He and his drinking companion, the one-eyed Sir Francis Bryant, laughed at the duke's misery until their cheeks were wet and their sides ached. Elizabeth, despairing of the King, importuned Cromwell for protection, claiming that even if she was allowed to go home, she might be poisoned because of Norfolk's love for his harlot Bess Holland.

The duchess had chosen well. Norfolk hated Cromwell, the upstart blacksmith's boy from Putney who in turn twisted and turned to trap Norfolk as Wolsey had Buckingham. Cromwell was ever greedy for any morsel of possible treason by Norfolk. The duke had to swallow, even choke on his pride and account to Master Cromwell for what he regarded as the truth of the matter. Surely this must have been the bitterest egg to bite! The duchess arrived in London and stayed at Austin Friars. Cromwell wrote to Norfolk that perhaps he should also come so Cromwell could mediate between the two. How Henry laughed at that! Norfolk, furious, dismissed his wife as wilful, saying that he would never come into her company because she had wrongly slandered him, claiming that when she was in childbed with their daughter for two days and nights, he had dragged her out of that bed by the hair of her head, thrown her about the house and, with his dagger, scored a wound to her head. Norfolk protested his innocence. He claimed to have witnesses that the scar on his wife's head was from fifteen months before she was delivered of the said daughter; it was in fact a cut by a surgeon in London for a swelling when drawing two teeth.

Henry was beside himself with merriment at such details. He cuffed my ear and said he would replace me with Norfolk and his wife, for such a masque was better than anything I had ever presented. On one occasion, at Greenwich, deep in his cups, he insisted on playing such a drama out. Closeted in his chamber, he made Bryant, who could mimic all he met, take the role of Norfolk, with me as Bess Holland and himself as the duchess. I grew tired of such revelry so Henry struck me, loosening a tooth. Bryant drily remarked that now I and the duchess had something in common. Henry roared with laughter, gave me a purse of silver and, drunk as a sot, declared we should all make peace before collapsing on the bed with his spaniels.

In the end, Master Cromwell realised that Norfolk would never take his wife back and, at the King's secret order, conceded he could do no more in the matter. The duchess, in full despair, wrote to Cromwell shortly afterwards saying that, from now until ever, she would never petition the King or any other to ask for her husband to receive her. The King thanked God for that! The duchess proclaimed that she had made her plea and received nothing in return. She insisted that she had done no wrong except reveal her husband's shameful handling of her and concluded that she would never go home, for if she did, her life would be short. Henry, now bored with the proceedings, ignored her protests. However, he would never forget. Norfolk's most dangerous enemies were in his own household. Henry, like the predator he was, would study this. The great Buckingham was destroyed by his own son-in-law. Could circumstances repeat themselves?

23 December 1546

When Henry strikes, it's always swift, like a peregrine swooping from the clouds. The victim does not even realise the danger until the talons close about it. Anne Boleyn was busy with her May Day celebrations. Cromwell joined his fellow councillors after dinner. Queen Katherine Parr was tending to her sick pained husband. And so it is in these last of days. I kept no journal for a while as there was nothing to describe, nothing to note until late this December the Year of Our Lord 1546. I had been excused, increasingly so as the King became closeted with Dudley and Seymour. Life became still, if not serene. The King locked in his chambers would host neither wife nor children, so why should he see me? I thought he was resting, plotting or both, only to discover that the carnival of blood was picking up pace. The Howards of Norfolk have fallen! Swift and brutal, both father and son were taken up and committed to the Tower. Henry Howard, Earl of Surrey, had come up from his country residence to Whitehall. The King, much recovered, ordered his arrest, telling the captain of his guard to take the earl most secretly and swiftly. On Thursday afternoon, 9th December, entering the palace after dinner, Surrey glimpsed Sir Anthony Wingfield, Captain of the Spears, walking towards him down the stairs of the palace.

'Welcome, my lord, to Whitehall,' Wingfield declared. Nearby a dozen Spears waited in an adjoining corridor. The captain was eager to take the earl towards that trap, well away from his own household men. 'I want you to intercede for me with the duke your father,' Wingfield continued, plucking at the earl's sleeve, 'on a matter in which I need his favour. If you would be so kind as to listen to me . . .?'

Surrey graciously conceded. They had hardly disappeared from the hall when the guards ran out, seized the earl and hurried him without attracting notice on to the quayside and the waiting barge. He was taken to Blackfriars and then up to Ely Place in Holborn to the residence of Lord Chancellor Wriothesley, the man with the milky blue eyes of a cat. Here he was detained for ten days, interrogated and questioned most closely. Thomas, Duke of Norfolk, on hearing this, hastened to London from his palace at Kenninghall to enquire after his son, only to be seized himself. Some allege that father and son had some ambiguous discourse about the King whilst the latter was ill some weeks ago; the object of their discussion seems to have been the government of the young prince. Any hope of their liberation is very small. The duke was deprived of both staff of office and his Garter before being taken to the Tower by water. According to Balaam, who learnt this from a gentleman in Wriothesley's retinue, the Imperial ambassador van der Delft declared it pitiable that persons of high rank and noble lineage should have undertaken so shameful a business as to plan the seizure of the government of the King by such treacherous means. Others gossip about a Howard plot to murder either the King and his heir or the entire Council; the evidence for this is a letter written by Surrey to a certain gentleman full of threats and menaces. The case against Surrey certainly presses hard. Even though he has always been so generous with his countrymen, there is no one well disposed enough to regard him as innocent.

The fall of the Howards is proof enough that the reformist coven have obtained such influence over the King as to lead him according to their fancy. Indeed, in the days since I last wrote, courtiers who used to refer foreign envoys directly to the King are now of a different aspect and inclined to please the Earl of Hertford and Lord High Admiral Dudley more than anyone else. Indeed, these two have entirely obtained the favour, grace and authority of His Majesty. Nothing is done at court without their intervention. Council meetings are regularly held in Lord Hertford's mansion on the Strand. Balaam, that greedy gull for information and rumour, claims the custody of the young prince and the government of the realm are being daily entrusted to Hertford and Dudley, whilst the misfortunes that have befallen the Howards spring directly from them. Rumours fly as thick as the snowflakes that now carpet the palace gardens. How Surrey has been taken on two principal charges: first that he had the means of seizing the castle of Hardelot when he commanded His Majesty's forces at Boulogne, and neglected to take it; the other that he said there were some in England who made no great account of him but that one day he trusted to make them very small. Whether he intended, plotted or wished the death of His Majesty or his son is not certain. I regard such accusations as false and spurious; the Princess Mary, Balaam and Lady Jane would swear the same.

The reformists are certainly gleeful. They view Norfolk and Surrey as the bitterest enemies of their word and claim that both are guilty of secret attempts to restore the Pope and the monks. This latter allegation masks a greater danger. I, Balaam and the Lady Jane secretly met a gentleman of the Princess Mary's chamber, a former priest, Lydgate, who, so it is said, is the princess's envoy to Cardinal Reginald Pole. According to Lydgate, many Romanists believe that in the eyes of God, the young prince has no right to succeed. Henry was solemnly excommunicated by the Pope, and his marriage to Lady Jane Seymour was clearly against the law of the Church; thus any child from such a marriage could never be a true Christian monarch. It is hinted that Surrey, England's proudest and most foolish boy, has been confined because he might stir up such a commotion against the young prince after his father's death. Indeed, it is claimed that he was already hot on this business, hence his unexpected return to London with certain henchmen of his household, all armed and ready for war. I do not believe this. Surrey always had such young bloods in his company.

Now, excluded from the royal presence, I haunt the royal kitchens, warm and friendly and a deep well of juicy gossip. Scullions and spit boys, servitors and pastry cooks do not, as with myself, exist in the eyes of the great lords of the soil. Naturally, such lowly people snout out rich truffles of gossip. Stories about Surrey's henchmen echo chillingly true. How two of them were found garrotted behind the stews along Southwark side. How another was knifed over a game of hazard in a tavern nearby whilst five more took a barge close to the Priory of St Mary Overy but never reached Queenshithe. River accidents, especially when the sea mists roll in thick and heavy, are common enough. The corpses of all five young men, frozen blue and bloated with filthy water, were plucked by the scavengers from the reeds further north and given hasty burial in some common place for strangers. The warning was clear. No Howard, retainer or henchman, was welcome in London.

Surrey himself and his father are certainly not ill-used.

The earl is confined to comfortable house arrest at Ely Place. As for Norfolk, I visited the Bosom of Abraham, a spacious tavern that serves the garrison at the Tower. Mingling there with warders and other minions, I learnt that Norfolk is not imprisoned in some fetid hole but in Beauchamp Tower, chambers usually reserved for the King and the royal family. Certainly he is not hidden away. He is even provided with pens and manuscripts. Sir Walter Stonor, the new Lieutenant of the Tower, has allowed him to keep two servants close to him, whilst buckets of sea coal are provided for the fire in his chamber, together with at least six dozen candles, yards of black satin, furred buskins and tapestries to warm the walls. Norfolk has a feather bed with a bolster, two pillows, thick blankets, quilts and sheets, as well as special utensils including a flagon, salt shaker, cups and goblets from the King's own jewel house, and is served hot meals from the Tower kitchens.

Nonetheless, the axe has truly fallen. The Howards are taken. They have fallen so low that Wriothesley and his allies on the Council could dispatch a party of horsemen, led by Sir John Gates, that royal bully-boy, Sir Richard Southwell and Wymand Carew, to Kenninghall to plunder the Howard palace. Of course they realised there would be women and children present, so Dr Huicke was included in the comitatus issued by the Council on Sunday 12 December between three and four o'clock in the afternoon. They reached Thetford on Monday night and were at Kenninghall by daybreak on the 14th. They galloped up to the gatehouse with the startling news that the duke and his son were taken. The steward was absent organising some form of muster, so they called the almoner and ordered that the gates at both front and back be locked. They then demanded to speak with the widowed Duchess of Richmond and Bess Holland. These had only just risen but nevertheless hurried down to meet their unexpected visitors in the dining chamber. Huicke, on his return, informed me how the young duchess was so perplexed and trembling that she was on the point of collapse. On recovering, she reverently knelt and humbled herself to the King, saying that although by nature she must love her father, whom she always regarded as a true subject, and her brother, whom she believed to be a rash man, she would conceal nothing but declare in writing everything she could remember.

It was not a pretty sight. Huicke offered his ministrations, but Sir John Gates – and no man's pie is free from *his* greedy fingers – was merciless. He and the others, all booted and spurred, cloaked and cowled, stood in the dining chamber with these women on their knees and advised them to use truth and frankness but not despair. My foreboding was correct. Henry had marked down the Howards for destruction, but the means were not a legion of Judas men and council spies; rather Howard's own family. He had studied them all and knew what keys to turn in which locks. If admissions of treason were elicited from the likes of the King's own former daughter-in-law, how would the Norfolks fare?

Gates and his coven were greedy for confessions but also for plunder. They became frustrated when they ransacked the Duchess of Richmond's coffers and closets to find nothing worth taking. The duchess explained how she had sold her jewels and all her precious objects to pay her debts. However, when they turned to Bess Holland, Norfolk's mistress, they found a wealth of girdles, beads, buttons of gold, pearls and rings set with diamond stones, which they swiftly listed. At the same time they sent servants to the duke's other houses in Norfolk and Suffolk warning the retainers there that a careful audit would be made. They also dispatched couriers to Bess Holland's well-furnished house in Suffolk. Afterwards they visited Surrey's residence on a hill outside Norwich called Mount Surrey, where he had built a great palace to his own honour and prestige.

Once these plunderers and ravishers had returned to London, the attack on Surrey began in earnest. At Princess Mary's secret request, I tried, I truly did, to plead with the King, but he was obdurate. My exile from his chamber had been imposed by Paget, that master amongst the shadows, who was weaving his own dark web whilst the King was busy with his. Henry lapsed into a sullen mood of deep sulks and terrible threats. He chose to completely overlook how Norfolk's own daughter, the Duchess Mary of Richmond, was the widow of his beloved bastard, Henry Fitzroy, who in turn had also been Surrey's close companion, whilst the earl's reputation as a warrior and leading poet of his day was never even considered. So why should I expect compassion from this King without mercy? This is the same Henry who openly rejoiced when Catherine of Aragon died in that haunted, benighted manor of Kimbolton. The same Henry who proclaimed his daughters as bastards and banished them from his sight even when he resided at the same palaces as they did. The chatter-mongers claim that our sinister king nourishes a hideous anger. Oh no, it's something much grimmer. There are occasions when Henry's soul simply dies; no hate, just nothing, a yawning cold emptiness. In his eyes, at such a moment in time, no one exists except Henry and God, perhaps not even the latter.

Yet while the King ignored my pleas, he ordered me to attend the hearing at Wriothesley's house in Ely Place where the wolf pack had gathered. Sir Thomas Wriothesley, his twisted face wreathed in smiles, posed as the lead questioner whilst the Seymours, Dudley and the others looked on. At first Surrey protested, but Wriothesley badgered him with questions, first asking about the earl's residences, particularly his palace at Mount Surrey and what he meant by such glories. He listed for Surrey what Surrey already knew. How his wardrobe boasted a gown of black velvet embroidered with a border of Venice gold; another lined with black velvet and satin from Bruges; a riding coat of green satin with a fringe of silver; hose of black velvet embroidered with Venice gold and a whole fur of sables. How Surrey also owned hats, jewels and brooches as well as decorative swords, daggers and knives, collars with knots of crown gold and a George medallion set with diamonds. Surrey, sitting in that long panelled room lit only by faint candlelight, seemed puzzled as Wriothesley plucked up one piece of parchment after another, detailing items such as an image of St George standing upon a dragon with his sword, spear and shield weighing forty ounces, and a vast array of golden chandeliers, basins, ewers, pots, flagons, dishes, spoons and bowls, as well as certain tapestries boasting the stories of Moses, St Louis and the Jesse tree.

Wriothesley then went on to describe Mount Surrey, with its remarkable view of Norwich, and its three pavilions designed to resemble fortresses, all decorated with military insignia and ornamental cannon. How the Howard lion was depicted everywhere, be it on walls, windows or plate; even on the banners flying from the crenellated towers of his residence. Again Surrey just shrugged, perplexed, as Wriothesley went on to describe curtains and quilts panned with red and yellow silk and a chair of state upholstered in purple velvet and satin, as was the canopy of his bed, which was embroidered with silver lions. Why, Surrey had even bought Turkish carpets, Spanish blankets and bedsteads from Flanders, whilst the walls of his house boasted tapestries that would cost more than a fully rigged and armed warship, all of the finest quality, displaying garlands of flowers, pomegranates, cucumbers, grapes and birds.

Surrey sat at the end of the long refectory table tapping his fingers impatiently. I, standing with the rest in the shadows, watched Wriothesley pause, long neck down, jutting chin pressed against his chest, then heard him whisper the words 'The residence and possessions of a prince, perhaps even a king?'

Surrey snorted with laughter, head going back. He was all tight with pride and honour, his right eye even more notably askew. He glared around and the real taunting began. Wriothesley touched on the question of Lady Jane Seymour, the King's third wife and mother of Prince Edward. How she had declared that she had no greater treasure in the world than her honour and would rather die a thousand times than tarnish it. Had not Surrey heard those words and mocked them? Had he not spread the story that the King had forced Master Cromwell, now adjudged a traitor and executed, to vacate his lodgings so Lady Jane could occupy them and use the private passage to the royal apartments? Had not Surrey implied, by such malicious words, that Henry's beloved late queen, mother of his darling heir, was no better than a Cheapside strumpet? Surrey hotly denied this.

Wriothesley then turned to the Pilgrimage of Grace, the great rebellion in the north against the King some ten years earlier. Had not John Fowberry, a servant of Surrey, taken part in this insurrection? To this Surrey just laughed out loud, saying that Fowberry, a rebel at first, had later redeemed himself by informing the Howards of the rebels' plans to take Hull. Wriothesley moved smoothly on, proclaiming how Surrey had twice listened to a song in support of both the Pilgrimage and the rebels, yet refrained from punishing the singer. Again Surrey just scoffed, indicating that he had heard many such songs; if every singer were hanged, there would be no men left alive. Wriothesley made a wry mouth and turned to Surrey's poems, most of which he had read. Had not Surrey composed a poem about an ancient king of Syria, a ruler steeped in blood who had fed and gorged himself on the plunder of his victims? Was he referring to any prince alive? The earl just glanced away. Oh, I could see the dark path opening up, leading to the pits, traps and morasses. Wriothesley was acting on behalf of the Seymours and Dudley, and behind them, the dark, menacing shadow of the King. The stage was set for the drama to be presented: Surrey was to be depicted as a truly dangerous traitor who saw himself perhaps not only as the protector-in-waiting but even as England's new prince. For this he was being hunted to death.

Wriothesley sighed and pronounced himself satisfied for a while, summoning servants to pour wine and serve sweetmeats. He and the others sat talking quietly amongst themselves, leaving Surrey at the end of the table to tap his fingers and stare wildly around. I and the other retainers murmured amongst ourselves. I heard the swell of damning whispers. How Edward Seymour, Earl of Hertford, had always been Surrey's bitter enemy. He too had served in the retinue of Henry Fitzroy, in the lesser office of master of horse. After the Pilgrimage of Grace, Hertford, amongst others, had expressed doubts about Surrey's loyalties. Surrey, learning about this, had hurried to Hampton Court, where he'd found Hertford walking in the park and had struck him, challenging him to a duel. Of course to strike a man at court, in His Majesty's presence, warranted the bloody penalty of losing one's right hand. Surrey was not punished in such a way but closely confined for a time at Windsor Castle. I studied Surrey. Did he, like Cromwell, Wolsey and the rest, not understand the real danger? He had not even been tried but was already condemned.

Once the wine and sweetmeats were served, Wriothesley rang his small handbell. The door in the far corner of the room opened and in came Sir George Blagge, the King's 'little pig', the same who so narrowly escaped being roasted as a reformist at Smithfield. Surrey pushed back his chair and would have risen, but Wriothesley's guards stepped from the shadows so he sat down again.

'Do you not remember George?' Wriothesley taunted. 'And your argument with him at Whitehall recently? You were full of venom against my lord Hertford. Master Blagge reminded you that those whom the King appoints shall be the most suitable to groom the prince in the grievous event of the King's death. To which you, my lord Surrey, replied: "My father is most suitable for such a task both because of the services he has done and because of his high estate." Do you remember that?'

Surrey, glaring at Blagge, refused to answer, so the King's little pig spoke up. 'You may remember well, my lord, because I answered that if that was so, the young king would be evil taught. Indeed, I declared that if the prince should be under the government of your father, or even yourself, I would thrust my dagger into you.'

'I do remember,' Surrey replied quietly. 'And then you fled.'

'Yes, my lord,' Blagge retorted, 'and because I opposed you, you took sword and dagger and hurried to my lodgings. Fortunately my house has a stout door, which withstood your efforts to break it down, but you stood outside, shouting that I had been very hasty with you and you meant to teach me better ways.'

Before Surrey could protest further, Blagge was dismissed. Wriothesley, enjoying himself immensely, preened and shook himself like a cat ready to pounce. Oh how I hate that man; my heart seethes with fury at him. A good friend of Cromwell, at least until he fell from grace, Master Wriothesley is a disrupter and an iconoclast. At Winchester he revelled in shattering the cathedral's precious statues and ancient painted glass. Later, out of fear of the local inhabitants, he stole back into that same cathedral during the dead of night and demolished a tomb much loved and visited by pilgrims, that of St Swithun, whose feast day, so it is said, determines the weather of our clammy island. Worse, once finished there, Wriothesley took horse to nearby Hyde Abbey and, with the utmost sacrilege, destroyed and desecrated the tomb of England's first and some say greatest king, Alfred the Saxon. There's something horrid in Wriothesley's soul, if he has one: a destroyer who, I suspect, would dance with joy if the world caught fire.

At Ely Place Wriothesley posed like the master of the masque from the School of Night, a strutting player determined to delight his audience with fresh horrors. No sooner had Blagge left the chamber than Wriothesley rang his infernal little bell again. The door opened and another figure slipped in. Those gathered there, myself included, gasped at the arrival of Sir Richard Southwell, a supposedly close friend and neighbour of Surrey. He took his seat in the pool of candlelight and, at Wriothesley's prompting, declared that he knew certain things about Surrey touching his loyalty to the King.

'What things?' purred Wriothesley the cat.

'I saw it myself,' retorted Southwell, blood-red face all sweaty. 'On the seventh of October last at Kenninghall and again at Mount Surrey, a coat of arms treasonable to the King.'

'How so?' Wriothesley sighed as if cut to the heart.

'Because Surrey's arms were quartered with those of our saintly King Edward the Confessor.'

'But they have silver labels,' exclaimed Surrey,

recovering from his shock at seeing this Judas so eager to lead him up the garden path of treason. 'I have, my family has, always carried such arms; the labels show their difference from the royal insignia.'

'Silver labels or not,' replied Wriothesley, an expert in heraldry, 'such arms are still identical to those of the Prince of Wales.' He stilled the hum of conversation with a dramatic gesture. 'Are you, my lord, proclaiming yourself to be an heir to the throne, to have a claim on royal power?'

Surrey's passionate temper gave way to violence. He sprang to his feet and strode forward, affirming that he was a true man, demanding to be trialled by combat, offering to fight Southwell in a duel, armourless in no more than his shirt. Only then, I do suspect, did he begin to perceive the cloying web closing about him. Wriothesley, on behalf of his masters, had worked hard and well.

With the light fading, Wriothesley wanted to finish that day's business with more spectacles. No sooner had Southwell, Howard's Judas, disappeared than Judas' sister, Norfolk's mistress Bess Holland, swept into the chamber in a gown of tawny sarcanet that matched her auburn hair. A bold-faced, hot-eyed woman worried sick that the treasures seized from where she'd concealed them at Kenninghall might never be returned. A true treasure hoard: diamonds, rubies, white sapphires, gold, silver and pewter brooches depicting images of Our Lady of Pity, the Trinity and Venus Arising. Necklaces and bracelets, jewel-encrusted crucifixes and a valentine of gold with five diamonds, three rubies and eight pearls. Other chattels included ivory sandalwood tables, silver spoons and other such utensils, as well as a row of girdles all strung with precious stones. Bess the Harlot wanted them back and would sing any song for their return. In that shadow-filled room, before her lover's son, who had little time for her, she confessed all the gossip and chatter of the Howard family. Care and tribulation must have pierced Surrey's entrails, a growing fear seized his mind, a cold dread drenched his soul. What hope for him from such a false heart and lying tongue? He held up a hand, interrupting Bess's opening words.

'And the Lady Frances?' he demanded. 'How is she?' Surrey's wife, Frances de Vere, daughter of the Earl of Oxford, was enceinte, only six weeks off delivery.

Wriothesley replied, words dripping soft as melted butter, something about the Lady Frances being well comforted. In truth we had all heard about Gates's ruffians. Surrey's children had been placed with others, whilst Lady Frances had been unceremoniously hustled into a chariot. When she complained about the cold, a nightgown of black satin, much worn and edged with squirrel fur, snatched from the old duke's wardrobe, was thrown about her.

Surrey heard Wriothesley out, then whispered loudly how this 'brace of lying knaves' would have their day against him. He joined his hands, head bowed, as Bess

Holland, who had held her peace during the interruption, proclaimed her grievances in a voice like brass. How the old duke had told her that none of the King's council loved him because there was no noble born amongst them and because he truly believed in the sacrament of the altar, which they did not. How the duke considered that the King did not love him either because Norfolk was popular in the country, which was why he was not a member of the inner Privy Council. How His Majesty was so sick he could no longer endure and the realm was divided by differing opinions. 'The King is much grown in body,' Norfolk had confided, 'and cannot go up and down stairs but has to depend on devices.'

Surrey lifted his head at this; so far Bess had said nothing about him but only about his father imprisoned in the Tower. However, Wriothesley had summoned her for a purpose. She was closely questioned about Norfolk himself bearing an illegal coat of arms. She claimed she knew nothing about that; only that the old duke had found fault with his son's heraldic devices. There, I saw the deadly snare. Bess Holland would portray even Norfolk himself as deeply affronted by his own son's conduct.

'The old duke liked them not,' Bess confessed, 'and did not know from where they'd come.' She went on to explain how Norfolk had claimed that Surrey himself had the family arms wrong and ordered Bess to refuse to weave such a motif into her needlework. Because of that, Bess Holland declared, glaring down the table, the Earl of Surrey did not love her much.

Once Bess Holland was gone, Surrey shouting that she would stifle in her own midden heap of lies and calumny, certain councillors pressed forward, bending over Wriothesley, whispering to him and pointing at the window. Wriothesley shook his head and gestured towards the door through which Bess Holland had left, talking swiftly and excitedly, as if there were certain businesses that had to be finished on that particular day. He waited. The silence in the chamber deepened. All eyes were on that long table, the sheen of the candles glowing along its polished surface. Wriothesley, arrogance seeping through every part of him, slouched in his high-backed chair at one end, the Earl of Surrey at the other, like jousters in a tilt yard waiting for the next run. Further down the room, deep in the shadows, stood the rest of the Council, listening intently. Surrey asked for something to drink. Wriothesley lifted a hand, snapping his fingers. A servant placed a goblet brimming with wine in front of the earl, who gently sipped it, then glanced around and leaned back in his chair.

The door opened again and a woman entered the chamber. Only when she stepped into the pool of candlelight did Surrey suddenly rouse himself as if from sleep. He started forward, staring in disbelief as his own sister Mary, the widowed Duchess of Richmond, took her seat on Wriothesley's left, turning slightly to face her brother. A pretty, comely woman, the duchess was dressed in a dark blue cloak with a mantle of the same colour around her shoulders; a hood, slightly pointed, covered her hair. She pushed this back. Her gloved hands were first kept hidden, but she betrayed her nervousness by rubbing the top of the table, peering anxiously at Wriothesley though never once glancing fully at her brother. Surrey put his face in his hands, shoulders shaking, his sobs clearly heard. Wriothesley sat and watched. Surrey took his hands away, wiped his cheeks with his fingers and crossed himself.

Wriothesley, that purple-hued malt worm, was cunning. He did not question the duchess but simply gestured with his hand, saying that Her Grace had information that was of great value to the Council and of deep interest to His Majesty. The duchess began to talk like someone who'd learnt a speech by rote. She spoke loudly, her voice betraying little warmth, as she described how her father had wanted her to marry Sir Thomas Seymour, Hertford's brother. Surrey had also desired that, but not for her happiness or that of Sir Thomas; instead he had insisted she should endear herself to the King and so win his affection and rule there as others had. She had protested bitterly and refused such a task.

The duchess paused, playing with the fringes of her gloves as what she had said was savoured and digested by those listening. In truth I found such an allegation difficult to believe. That the Duke of Norfolk and his son wanted their own daughter and sister to prostitute herself to the King through marriage to another man! Wriothesley of course had schooled her in her statement, as he knew such an arrow would not miss its mark. Since the death of his bastard son, the King had always had an appreciation for the pretty young duchess and perhaps at a better time in a better place might not have refused her favours.

Surrey sat shocked, his back against the chair, head lightly twisted, mouth opening and closing as if he wanted to shout his denial but could not. The duchess then continued explaining how her father would also have liked her brother to marry the Earl of Hertford's daughter, but he had refused, saying that he would have nothing to do with such an upstart family. That these new men hated the nobility, and that once God called His Majesty away, Surrey would make them smart for their arrogance. Indeed, the duchess continued, her brother hated them all since he had been imprisoned at Windsor Castle. She then paused as if forgetful. Wriothesley leaned forward and whispered something. The duchess lifted her head and talked about heraldry. How Surrey had assumed the arms of his grandfather the Duke of Buckingham, an adjudged traitor. However, instead of the duke's coronet, he had put into his livery a cap of royal purple with powdered fur, whilst the crown, in her view, looked much like a royal crown, and underneath it a cipher that she took to be the King's 'HR'.

She gabbled on, saying that Surrey had confessed

how the King did not like him because of his failure at Boulogne; that he had dissuaded her from reading the scriptures and added that God must give his father long life, for once the old duke died, the Council would have Surrey's head as he had so bitterly cursed some of its present members. Eventually Wriothesley tapped the table, a sign that she had said enough. Even those hostile to Surrey realised the duchess was only rehearsing and repeating what she had been instructed to say. Once she had finished, she fled from the room, leaving her brother, a faint smile on his face, staring down at Wriothesley.

Surrey murmured something. Wriothesley leaned forward, cupping his ear.

'My lord, what did you say?' he demanded. 'Eh? Eh?'

'Just a line from a poem,' Surrey replied, 'about the froth of folly, the scum of pride, the shipwreck of honour and the poisoning of the nobility.' He lapsed into silence.

'What mean you?' Wriothesley shouted. 'What mean you by that? Do you have a mortal malice against these in this chamber?'

Surrey refused to reply.

'Is it true, my lord,' Wriothesley pushed back his chair, 'that you have a painting of yourself depicted full length, standing under an archway against a rural landscape?'

'I hired William Scrots, a Dutchman, the court painter,' Surrey replied, as if thinking about something else.

'And in that painting,' Wriothesley continued, 'are you not leaning on a broken column, your left hand resting on your hip, your right hand clasping a white glove?'

'I remember that.'

'And did you not ask the artist to paint a miniature of His Majesty's dead son, the Duke of Richmond, on the column plinth?'

'I did.'

'Why?'

Once more Surrey refused to answer.

'Why, my lord? Why should you put on a pillar, in a painting of yourself, an image of His Majesty's dead son? Are you alleging that you and he were the same? Are you implying that your relationship with the dead prince gives you a power and status that you would exploit if His Majesty, God forbid, should die?'

'It was a painting,' Surrey retorted. 'I have never abrogated to myself kingly or princely powers.'

'Do you not, sir,' Wriothesley plucked up a piece of parchment from the table, 'do you not remember how three years ago you lodged at Mistress Millicent Arundel's house in Laurence Lane? Is that true?'

'You know it is.'

'And do you remember that night of Sunday the twenty-first of January, the Year of Our Lord 1543? How, when the beacon lights had been lit, the curfew signalled and the bell of St Mary-la-Bow rung, you and your companions ran amok through the streets of Cheapside?

Armed with stone bows, you shattered the windows at the home of Sir Richard Gresham, former mayor of this city, and then abused others along Cheapside, Poultry and the Stocks Market. Afterwards you commandeered boats and barges rowing along the river, shouting obscenities and shooting missiles at the prostitutes who ply their trade along Southwark bank.'

'My lord,' Surrey leaned forward, 'that was hot-headed foolishness for which I answered before the Privy Council.'

'For some of it you did,' Wriothesley declared, 'but the maids of Mistress Arundel, Alice Flanner and Joan Wetnall, made depositions against you. They reported how the armorial bearings above your bed in the chamber you hired from Mistress Arundel were very similar to those of the King. Is that not so?'

'I cannot remember.'

'And when Mistress Arundel bought a knuckle of tainted veal from the butcher's, you sent it back with a sharp rebuke, saying that no one should mock a prince such as you. Are you a prince, my lord?'

'I cannot answer for what tavern wenches blather.'

'No, you cannot,' Wriothesley continued, 'but where did they get these imaginings from? How could a tavern wench blather that if anything happened to the King and his beloved heir, then you, my lord Surrey, would be king after your father?'

Surrey protested most vehemently once more. But for Wriothesley the day's proceedings were finished. The

Council had done its task most efficiently – or at least I thought they had. The Howards were divided and chance remarks were being turned into weighty matters of law. What concerned me, and this must have occurred to Paget, was whether the King would be satisfied with their destruction. Would he turn on someone else? If so, who? I hurried back to Westminster, but the King refused to see me.

In the days following, the interrogations continued, but now they were following a well-beaten track. Wriothesley received fresh depositions, the most damaging that of Sir Gawain Carew, who claimed that the Duchess of Richmond had informed him that Surrey had actively encouraged her marriage to Sir Thomas Seymour. How she should dissemble the matter and use it as a means for His Majesty to speak to her. How she should not refuse such invitation but leave the issue to rest so His Majesty would take occasion to speak to her again and again. Consequently, by passage of time, the King would take a great fancy to her. The duchess would become his mistress and rule both King and court like Madame Destampes did in France. Surrey had argued how this would help not only herself but all her friends and family. The duchess, however, had defied her brother. She said her family could all perish, that she would rather cut her own throat than consent to such villainy. Similar statements were made by others. Edward Rogers, an acquaintance of Surrey, repeated the established story.

How Surrey hated the new men on the Council and believed that when the King died, the protection of the young prince should lie with the Howards.

Such charges and depositions were repeated time and time again until Sunday 12 December, the vigil of St Lucy, a day popular in this city, with lights and candles and much gathering around the stalls and shops. The Council chose that day for Surrey to be taken to the Tower through Holborn, not riding with banners flying but walking surrounded by guards like a common criminal. Wriothesley's arrow sped true. He wished to divest the earl of any trappings of power, publicly proclaiming him a criminal, dispatched to the Tower to await judgement.

Only then did Balaam and I meet secretly in a tavern chamber. He sat warming his fingers above a chafing dish, his face much drawn and tired. He acknowledged that Surrey's cause was finished. Balaam was hot against the King, exclaiming that if all the pictures and patterns of merciless rulers were lost to the world, they might again be painted true to life in the story of His Despotic Majesty. He was certain that Surrey, now he was in the Tower, would never be freed or receive royal mercy.

'You see,' Balaam lifted his hands like a storyteller, 'imagine the mix they've prepared for him. Listen, Will. Surrey is accused of mysterious paintings, of changing his armorial bearings, of hinting that he is a royal prince. Above all, he stands arraigned of whispering that if something happened to His Majesty and his son Edward, then perhaps the Norfolks are the true heirs. Even so, if His Majesty dies, then it should be Surrey and his father who govern the young prince. Wriothesley, that father of villainy, has mixed this meal and served it to His Majesty, that swollen parcel of arrogance lurking in Westminster.' Balaam crossed himself. 'Remember what you told me of the King's mumblings about the blood of innocents? He is haunted by the princes in the Tower. He is fearful that his own son may become a similar victim, a young prince once seen and quickly forgotten. Can you imagine what His Satanic Majesty must feel after all these years of intrigue, of lechery, of divorce, of seeking an heir? Within days of his own death such plans might simply be smoke wafted away by the cruel winds of politics.'

'But the evidence against Surrey?' I asked. 'Surely it is meagre? That alone may weaken all charges.'

'Perhaps. There is another story,' Balaam declared, 'which is coming to light. How Surrey had a picture painted where the arms of his father were joined to those of the King surrounded by the Garter of St George. Where the motto of the Garter should have been, "*Honi soit qui mal y pense*", Surrey has inserted the phrase "Till then thus". Till then thus?' Balaam repeated. 'That could be viewed as a threat! That Surrey was biding his time until the right moment for his planned treason, the King's death. Surrey is supposed to have ordered the artist to put another canvas over it so it looks as if there is no other painting there. He shared all this with his sister, the Duchess of Richmond. She told the duke her father, who called his son aside and fiercely berated him, to which Surrey replied, "Father, our ancestors once bore those arms, and I am much better than any of them, so do not grieve about it." Norfolk retorted, "My son, if this comes to the ears of the King, he'll accuse both of us of treason, so keep it secret." "No one knows it, Father," Surrey replied, "but you and my sister. The painter is a foreigner who has now returned to his own country." The duke replied, "God grant my son that no ill may come of it. Do not tell your younger brother Thomas, he is too young to be trusted and might tell someone else who might accuse us. Bring the painting to me and let me see it." To which the earl replied, "Sir, that is impossible, another painting is over it."'

I was surprised: in all the gossip I had sifted, such a tale had not been told. I shook my head in disbelief, but Balaam assured me the story might well be true. More importantly, Surrey's sister, full of anger at her brother's marriage plans for her, did go to the King and informed His Majesty that her brother had such a painting. The King immediately summoned Paget and Hertford and told them what intelligence had come to his ears, and so the order was issued for the earl's arrest.

'Surrey,' Balaam concluded, 'may well have had a painting executed in which he allowed his fantasies full play; that is enough to send him to the headsman's block.'

I could only wonder at Henry's cruelty and cunning. He had used a Norfolk to trap a Norfolk. The Duchess of Richmond would be terrified witless. Whether she liked it or not, she had been cast as a woman urged to seduce the King into adultery. After all, was he not married? And was not such a proposal part of a Norfolk plot to seize government? This was treason on so many counts. What pity could the Duchess of Richmond expect from a monarch who'd considered poisoning his first wife, executed two others, cruelly rejected a fourth and diligently plotted the arrest of a fifth for treason? Margaret Pole, the Countess of Salisbury, and Lady Rochford had been shown none of the tenderness owed their sex. Others might blame Paget, Seymour or Dudley, but I recognised Henry's hand as the guilty one. He was using the same device against the Howards as he had against the Poles over a decade earlier: terrifying one member of a family in order to accuse the rest of treason.

'And now?' I asked wearily.

Balaam lifted his head. 'According to the Princess Mary, Surrey must escape and I must help him.'

'Why?' I asked. 'Why must Surrey escape? True, I feel sorry for him, and God knows he is guilty of foolishness and a devilish pride, but if that is treason, then we'd all dance at Tyburn. He is innocent . . .'

'Surrey is condemned already.' Balaam's face was all mournful. 'His trial will be a sham of shadows. Henry wants him dead and probably his old father too. The

Council also want the Howards and their Yellow Jackets destroyed before the King dies.'

I held a hand up. 'Master Balaam, I am a fool by profession, that is my trade. I am not foolish in wit. Why not state it clearly? The Howards of Norfolk still pine for the old days and the Church of Rome. They will be the best defence for the claim of the Princess Mary should young Edward die without heir. You know that, the world knows that. I am not a physician,' I continued remorsefully, 'but for God's sake, look at Edward, frail of body and not yet ten years old. London is swept by plagues and ailments. The Council are not only frightened of the Howards when the King dies, but terrified lest his heir follow him swiftly into the grave. Mary's claim is next. I know your mistress, Balaam. Cardinal Pole will return as papal legate. There will be peace with Rome, but above all, the Princess Mary will deal out judgement to the gods of Egypt. She will demand a bloody reckoning with these men of the reformed faith. Dudley, Seymour and their ilk would not survive a season.'

Balaam gave a lopsided grin and nodded. 'The Princess Mary,' he whispered, 'has given me my orders. I must attempt Surrey's escape.' He stretched out a hand. 'You are with us on this?'

I stared back. Balaam lives on intrigue; I'm simply its spectator. I watch His Malignant Majesty as I would that fierce lion in the Tower menagerie, fascinated yet frightened, but my heart's blood loyalty? This is to Lady Jane Bold and so the Princess Mary.

I clasped Balaam's hand. 'To the death.'

There, I was committed. I had crossed Paget's line. God help me. God help us all.

17 January 1547

Christmas, Yuletide, the New Year, Epiphany and the Feast of the Kings have all come and gone. Presents have been exchanged. Greenery placed on rafters and along sills and ledges. Hobby horses and fantastical creatures have danced and carolled with the Master of Revels and the Lord of Misrule. Yuletide logs have been cleared of snow and pulled into feverishly hot kitchens to be dried and prepared for the fire. Sweaty, red-faced cooks have wielded their axes and fleshing knives on legs of mutton, capon, venison and beef. Pheasant royale and princely goose have been prepared, along with a boar's head gilded gold, its mouth stuffed with boiled apples, all carried on precious plate escorted by cooks and their underlings from steam-hung kitchens to this great table or that. Now the mummery has gone like silver tinsel which shrivels and blackens. Christ has been born anew but is still ignored. The court observed both ritual and the rite, yet the message was lost. Masses were sung, but all were uncertain about what these actually meant and what was their use. Change and more change is imminent; what is doctrine and liturgy this year might be heresy and treason the next.

I met the Lady Jane secretly and gave her my presents: spice boxes, jewellery and a heart-shaped pendant. We kissed and cuddled, then kissed and cuddled again stretched out on some tavern bed. She brought me news about how the Princess Mary kept a merry hall over Christmas. I could give her little in return except that our plotting prince was busy, busy. It was as if the King had abruptly recalled who he really was, of the blood imperial and God's viceroy on earth, so why should he converse with a poor, lonely, witless hunched-back creature such as Will Somers? If Henry did not say that, I am sure Paget and Wriothesley did. Both had seen me at Surrey's questioning. They know full well where my sympathies lie. On the morrow of Epiphany, Wriothesley passed me in the gallery outside the palace chapel. He drew his dagger and pushed me into the deserted, incense-filled nave. He slammed the door shut, then shoved me so close to a window the Christmas holly along its ledge scratched my face.

'Mannekin.' He grinned down at me, pale lips curling back like those of a dog to display yellow teeth. I flinched at his stale breath. 'Mannekin, be careful. Do not put your trust in foreign princesses . . .' A reference to the Princess Mary. 'Restrain your prying and your peering. Do not upset your betters. Remember you are no safer than the Howards, or anyone else you might choose to name.'

I had little choice. What concerned me particularly over the Holy Season was the way Henry's mind seemed to have turned against his family. Neither the Queen nor his children were invited to spend the Christmas festivities with him. All doubts about Huicke appeared to have been put aside. He and others of his ilk, such as Physician Wendy and Thomas Alsop the apothecary, together with their legion of assistants, were busy in their attendance of the King, who proclaimed himself to be fine and in full fettle. I was left to my own devices. The weather had turned bitterly cold, with thick snow carpeting Westminster and both banks of the Thames. I had little opportunity to travel after the Christmas season so I joined Master Bricket, the King's chief cook, in his own steam-filled empire. I nicknamed Bricket 'Herod the Great' because, I jested, 'He rules the roast and is a pitiless murderer of innocents as he mangles poor fowls with unheard tortures, sparing neither hen nor chick and being particularly merciless to the newborn capon.' Never a true Christian until a hissing pot of strong ale has slaked him like water thrown on a glowing grid iron, Master Bricket is a redoubtable man, a true terror who scowls till his tarts quake, his custards quiver and his jellies shake. His kitchen is a merry place and a very useful refuge, as well as a fount of gossip. I learnt how His Majesty, on the day after

Christmas, had asked his council to produce the royal will, drawn up some three years earlier. When it did so, the King was swift to pounce, roaring that the version produced was not what he wanted and there was certainly one of a much later date. What this will decreed, however, I could not elicit, being dependent on gossip three times removed.

The other reason I frequented the kitchens was to meet Balaam, that cunning man of subtle wit. If you wish to hide and go in disguise, then do so in a crowd. The royal kitchens, butteries, pastry chambers, scolding rooms and store chambers are ideal. Such places are thronged with the many officers of the household, be it 'the serjeant of the King's side of fresh fat deer roasted' or 'the keeper of the white puddings of hog's liver': officious little men who thrive on flattery and obsequious-ness. Balaam was in his element amongst them. He arrived suitably dressed in honest but coarse garments, a black woollen hat and broad-toed leather shoes. He would chatter to me and yet who could study him in a haze of smoke or eavesdrop in a place where stillness was as rare as a thin priest? Of course the brimming news was Surrey and the plans to aid his escape. Balaam informed me all about this . . .

There is a chamber in the Tower of London built on the first floor in the western half of St Thomas's Tower overlooking the moat near the water postern that people call Traitor's Gate. Within that western wall is a large shaft that runs its entire length down into the moat.

This comfortable room was refurbished some fifteen years ago to accommodate Anne Boleyn as she prepared to journey to Westminster to be crowned; little did she know that she would be returned to that very same chamber to await execution. Surrey was also imprisoned there. He was well treated and, unlike poor Thomas More, was given pens, ink and parchment. The hapless poet boy returned to composing sonnets based on the psalms, writing about his desire for wings to escape the stormy blast that threatened to engulf him. Escape in fact was the only choice he had. The Londoners were cowed. Surrey's henchmen had either cooperated fully or were hiding in their lonely Norfolk manor houses. The memory of the malignancy that had befallen those henchmen who'd accompanied Surrey into London remained very fresh in the minds of many.

At Westminster the King, narrow black eyes sunk even deeper into the folds of his fatty face, ignored me and urged his Council on to another act of bloody, judicial murder. Surrey became completely isolated. Nobody wished to serve him. I have noticed this before. Whenever some unfortunate falls from grace, brothers, sisters, indeed all the victim's relatives, flee as if from the plague. Queen Katherine Howard had a gentleman of her privy chamber brought to her bed every night. There was so much puffing and blowing her maids could scarcely sleep. On one occasion the intruder was almost surprised by the nightwatchman, and when he grew more cautious, Katherine taunted him that she had a stream of lovers waiting outside other doors. At the time Katherine and her lover were feted and praised. Nevertheless, when they were swept up by the storm which overwhelmed them, the brothers of both these victims of Henry's anger, garbed in their finest clothes, paraded around London on horses openly rejoicing, a public show to demonstrate how pleased they were that royal justice was to be done. A means of proclaiming that they did not share in the crimes of their relatives and, more importantly, that they remained faithful and loyal to their sovereign.

And so it was with Surrey, England's proudest poet, the King's own champion outside Boulogne. Once he fell, no one came to stand beside him. Accordingly, Princess Mary, through her agents such as Balaam, found it very easy to use her good offices to introduce an adventurer, a Spanish mercenary called Martin, into Surrey's prison chamber to act as his servant. Neither the lords of the Council nor the King would like it if Surrey – and he certainly would – were to proclaim at his coming trial that he had been ill-treated. This Martin was under secret orders to assist him with any plan. He was a Spaniard, or of Spanish extraction, so it was easy to depict him as free of any Howard influence or allegiance.

Of course I wandered out to listen to the chatter, and the best place for that is the taverns and ale houses that throng Petty Wales and the area around the Tower. Here the keepers, turnkeys, grooms, ostlers and maidservants rub shoulders, eat, drink and revel. Naturally gossip about prisoners is rife, especially about the likes of Surrey. Apparently he soon grew to trust his new manservant and the plot to escape developed very swiftly, all being planned in a day and a night. Martin brought the earl a dagger, and Surrey decided to escape through the shaft in the western wall serving the garderobe; this ran down to the moat, which in turn was cleansed by the river. At times the tide came up, at others it receded, leaving the ground beneath almost dry. Surrey noticed how the lowest point of the tide was around midnight for that time of year. The only difficulty was that his two guards slept in the retiring room which housed this garderobe. Nevertheless, Surrey considered this shaft to be his only hope. Once he had the dagger, he revealed the particulars of his escape. He asked Martin to go to St Katherine's Wharf and wait for him there shortly after midnight. He was to hire a boat and stay until Surrey appeared. In the meantime, he was to approach Surrey's younger brother Thomas and ask for a certain amount of money to assist him.

On the chosen night, Surrey hid the dagger in his bedstead and waited his chance. He pretended he was ill and declared he would retire early to bed. The guards wished him well, adding that they would do their tour of duty before their return. Once they had left, Surrey prepared himself. Shortly before midnight, when the tide was at its lowest, he pulled back the closet lid and lowered himself down. At that very moment the guards returned. Surrey was unable to defend himself with the dagger he had secreted and was easy prey for the guards, who then called to others for help. The earl was ignominiously dragged out of the closet and placed in shackles. Martin the servant disappeared and was never heard of again. I learnt all this with sinking heart when I met Balaam in the Palm of Jerusalem, not far from the King's Steps. He assured me that he had made careful search for Martin, as had soldiers from the Tower, who had swept the quayside looking for any barge or wherry equipped to take Surrey away.

'I found nothing. They discovered nothing,' Balaam hissed. 'I don't know what happened to Martin. Was he seized and secretly murdered? I don't know. But both he and any money he may have collected from Surrey's younger brother have disappeared.'

'But if he was captured?' I urged. 'Could he not betray you and others of Princess Mary's household?'

Balaam shook his head. 'No, no,' he replied. 'Martin was met and paid deep in the shadows. He would not be able to recognise me or anyone else. We regarded him as a desperate man, hungry for money.'

'Then he was well fed!' I snapped.

I felt deeply uneasy about the so-called escape and the way it was so swiftly foiled, but I left it at that. Of course I tried to intercede with the King once again, but Henry was preoccupied. Now this tyrant King loves nothing better than preparing an indictment against those he has marked down for death. Henry appeared stronger, his wits keen, his mind sharp. No longer bed-ridden, he dressed in a simple blue, red and gold robe, stomping about his chamber. He had chosen his quarry and, like any predator, was simply measuring the distance between himself and his victim. In the King's eyes, Surrey had usurped royal authority, proved by the Howard use of the royal arms and insignia. The King became feverishly busy on establishing this, assisted by the court cat, Wriothesley, who considered himself an expert on heraldry. Books and manuscripts were produced. The King, fingers all bloodied, spectacles perched on his nose, drafted questions and objections to what Surrey had done. He only half listened to my pleadings, until on one occasion he abruptly paused and stared at me over the spectacles as if noticing me for the first time. God be my witness, I have never seen him look at me like that before, as if he was measuring my worth and found me totally wanting. His cold, soulless eyes peered at me, lips slightly twisted, and I knew someone had done me terrible damage. If I did not suspect already, I soon discovered who.

The King promptly dismissed me. I walked down the gallery, then jumped at the hand on my shoulder. I turned. Wriothesley beamed down at me.

'My lord?' I asked.

'Martinmas, Will? Isn't that the season when the lambs are slaughtered?' Wriothesley gave a crooked smile, eyes half closed in amusement, and walked off.

Martin! Wriothesley was hinting at so many things,

perhaps claiming that Surrey's servant Martin was his man, while the reference to the slaughter of the lambs was Surrey's planned execution. Surrey was truly beyond all mercy and compassion. He had been imprisoned, provoked to escape and captured.

Urgent dispatches were sent to the lords at Westminster. Surrey was more closely confined, put in irons, yet he still protested his innocence. Wriothesley, Dudley and the rest of their coven visited him in the Tower, urging him to confess, but without any profit. The Council had waited long enough. They were determined to convict Surrey yet equally scrupulous to achieve this by publicly honouring the process of law. Of course it was a travesty. Surrey had allegedly committed his crimes in Norfolk, so the bloody charade began there, in the great snow-bound hall of Norwich Castle with its lowering black beams draped in the banners and pennants of the Crown. An indictment of treason for appropriating the royal arms was presented to a grand jury assembled on the benches before the gold-festooned dais. The jurymen had been carefully selected; not a true friend of Surrey amongst them, a veritable gaggle of Judases. They had little difficulty in reaching their conclusion. The foreman, in ringing voice, declared the indictment to be *billa vera*, a true bill. A special commission of oyer and terminer, 'to hear and to decide', was established to sit at the Guildhall in London. Royal couriers, horses splashed with muddy slush, thundered to Westminster with the news. The rats poured in together. Surrey, shackled in the Tower, remained defiant, but his father, Norfolk, Thomas Howard, now in his seventy-fourth year, was different.

I tried once more to plead with the King. By now Henry was wary and suspicious of me. Wriothesley had done his job well. The King's mind had been turned. I recalled the fate of old Skelton, a former jester. How Henry had favoured him until Skelton went too far and Henry beat him to within an inch of his life. When I did meet the King, he was much improved and looking forward to the usual pre-Lent festivities. I enquired as to what revelries would be staged, what masques would be presented. The King just smiled to himself, tapping his fleshy nose and saying he would think about that. I asked him about the Queen and his children. Would they be joining him and wouldn't it be good if they lodged at court? Again the King tapped his nose. I suspect he would have liked Edward to visit him, but he could not invite his son without issuing an invitation to his daughters and the Queen.

Because I do not like Paget, or trust him, and I had dismissed what he'd told me at the royal chancery about the King's secret scheming. On reflection, I now beat my breast. Henry is certainly involved in some subtle strategy, but, as ever, I cannot decide what direction it will take. No doubt the Queen is out of favour. Henry does not wish to either see or meet her. He no longer requires her as his nurse. So what does he intend? I tried one final time to plead for Surrey and his father.

I will be honest: I did so at the Princess Mary's behest. In truth, the Howards of Norfolk may not be my friends, but they have never proven to be my enemy. Indeed, old Norfolk, when he used to gamble with the King, always gave me something from his winnings. On another occasion, before he and the King left for Boulogne, I made young Surrey laugh, a rare event, with a story about a Norfolk squire who made himself a fool over a milkmaid, a story I borrowed and refashioned from Chaucer. Surrey instantly recognised that. He rubbed my head, gave me two silver pieces and said it was a subtle conceit. I have pleaded for prisoners before and won the King's mercy; Henry likes that. Nothing soothes his pride more than to have someone on their knees begging for their life or someone else's. Isn't that how Katherine Parr saved herself? When Katherine Howard fell from grace, Norfolk sent a letter to the King distancing himself from his errant kins-woman and throwing himself on the King's mercy. I did the same, kneeling before the great throne-like chair, hands clasped. And my reply? The King pressed his foot against my shoulder and gently kicked me away. He did not even raise his eyes. He said he had no further need of me, and if he did, I would be summoned.

Others of course had also reflected. If the lords of the Council could not break Surrey, then they would try with his father, the great survivor. Norfolk has a gift of saving his own skin. He has lived through turbu-lent times. He was born in the year after the furious fight at Tewkesbury when the Yorkists annihilated their Lancastrian foes, wiping them out as you would a dusty slate. Thomas of Norfolk has seen it all. A page at the glorious court of Edward of York, he witnessed the treachery of Clarence, the mysterious death of King Edward, who died at such an early age whilst boating on the Thames, and the violent usurpation of Richard. His grandfather fought for that same Richard at Bosworth and was killed, whilst his father was carried off the battlefield a grievously wounded prisoner. But, as I have observed, the Norfolks survive, and Thomas Howard is the finest example of this. All his enemies – Buckingham, Wolsey and Cromwell – have been dispatched to ignominious death. Indeed, if Norfolk had had his way and the King not listened to me, poor Thomas Cromwell would have been burnt alive at Smithfield. I don't think that even Cromwell, for all his cunning, realised Norfolk's deep treachery; he can smile when he wants and be ever so humble. On one occasion he wrote to Cromwell, 'Since I saw you last you have most lovingly handled me. You will always find me a faithful friend.' A short while later he invited Cromwell to Kenninghall, and even promised he would find a 'buxom wench with pretty, proper tits' for his entertainment. Yet when Cromwell was arrested, Norfolk was the one who beat him down and humiliated him. When I frustrated Norfolk's attempt to turn Cromwell into a living torch, the duke secretly arranged for the most inexperienced executioner to be assigned to sever the head of the disgraced minister. In this he was successful. The creature Gurrea, along with his assistant, chopped at Cromwell's neck and head for nearly half an hour.

Now imprisoned in the Tower himself, Norfolk is no doubt wondering how he will survive the present crisis. As soon as he was arrested, he sent the most supplicant letters to Westminster. Such pleading letters to both King and Council continued, signed 'His Highness's most poor prisoner. T. Norfolk.' I read copies of these missives. Henry, however, would not be moved. Wriothesley constantly dripped poison into the King's ear. No, that's wrong. The greater truth is that this King believes what he wants to believe. He has determined on the destruction of the Howards.

I soon learnt to keep a still tongue, reverting to what Henry wants me to be, his congregation, his audience. I act like a dumb, submissive wife in a malicious, squalid marriage. He is the master and I am the slave. I become the part, nodding my head, gazing in admiration at his profound wisdom and insight. Henry has grown stronger, I recognise that. He stands as he used to, feet apart like some colossus, belly thrust out, great body encased in his robe. Such occasions sharpen my memory. Henry neither forgets nor forgives anything. Oh, I listened to the habitual tirade about the Norfolks at Bosworth. How they gained the great victory at Flodden. This was followed by the usual ranting and raving about the Norfolk women, Anne Boleyn and Katherine Howard, how both had made a fool of him. The honest answer would be that never was a man so eager to be gulled and wear the cuckold's horns. Henry gave such vent to his spleen about the Howard women, I did wonder if the rumours were true. We all know that Mary Boleyn, Anne's sister, was the King's mistress for a while. Rumours abound that she had a son by him, born short of wit and weak of mind. However, Henry then began to talk salaciously about Anne's mother, Elizabeth Howard. He even recalled a joke he'd made with his drinking companion, Francis Bryant, who had teased him about having both the hen and its chick. Other ugly jealousies and resentments emerged. Surrey's ability to compose beautiful poetry, his bravery in battle and love of show. God forgive me, I have served this King for more than twenty years. I have made one hideous mistake. I have underestimated that cancer of the heart, his aptitude for hatred.

Henry allowed the Council their way and they left Norfolk to wallow like a becalmed ship in some dreadful limbo. They'd already made their decision, or Henry had made it for them, that they would use the father to destroy the son. Wriothesley led the pack. This time he included the two Chief Justices, Sir Richard Lister and Sir Edward Montague. They decided to visit Norfolk in the Tower. The King, cuffing me sharply about the ear, told me to join him. I asked him why. I even gently teased him that he had lost confidence in me. Henry grinned maliciously. I was being sent for a host of reasons. I was the King's audience; he knew I would report back. He also wanted me to see his cunning at work, and above all, he was being cruel. He wanted to demonstrate that all my pleading had come to nothing. He recalled the old legal dictum that he used to pun about, 'The will of the King has force of the law.' Or, to paraphrase it, 'Will, I am the force of the law.' Henry is like that. Poor Margaret Roper, Thomas More's daughter, wanted to give her father honourable burial. After all, More was dead, head severed from his body. She still had to negotiate with the executioner and snatch her father's remains from London Bridge. Oh yes, Henry likes such grisly conclusions. He always insists that the relatives of his victims are not spared the consequences of royal decisions, so I was off to the Tower to witness this for myself.

A bitterly cold day. Snowflakes coated our faces and stung our eyes as we clattered through Lion Gate and into the inner bailey, dominated by the soaring White Tower. They were all there: Wriothesley, Dudley, Paget and the Seymours. They had summoned their ally, Sir John Gates, and set up house in the great refectory in the Tower's royal lodgings. They grouped around the banqueting table on the dais, close to a fire which roared up the stack and exuded a blast of heat supplemented by spluttering braziers and chafing dishes of sparkling charcoal. We broke our fast on capon, sliced and drenched in herb sauce, white currant bread, dishes of stewed vegetables and goblets of mulled wine heavily laced with nutmeg and cinnamon. Of course they ignored me. I was of no more interest to them than the two greyhounds nosing the rushes. Strange, I remember their names: Sallyforth and Parryswiftly; their keeper, a young boy, kept begging me for morsels of food to feed them. On one occasion I caught Paget studying me rather sadly. I glanced away as if interested in the greyhounds.

Only when the hawks were ready for their quarry did they summon Norfolk. He was brought from his chambers in a furred robe all stained and moth-eaten, shabby slippers on his feet. A veritable scarecrow of a man, no more haughtiness, his dirty grey hair and beard all a-straggle, blinking eyes deep-set in that long, furtive face. Ave beads and miniature reliquaries hung around his neck and hands. He shuffled into the refectory, hands outstretched in supplication.

Wriothesley stepped off the dais and exchanged the kiss of peace with this noble he truly despised. Indeed, if he'd had his way, Norfolk and his son would be kneeling with their necks exposed on the blood-soaked scaffold on nearby Tower Hill. Then he offered Norfolk a cup of posset, pouring it himself before taking the duke over to a deep window embrasure so the old man could be questioned by Huicke, who had also accompanied us. In truth, the lords of the Council hoped that Norfolk was failing and that the damp, dire miasma of the Tower would be more deadly than the headsman's axe. This was a strong possibility. The old duke complained loudly of constant catarrh, rheums in his joints, a bubbling belly and bowels as loose as water, an ailment, he added plaintively, contracted in the service of the King along the northern march. Once the physician was finished, Wriothesley invited Norfolk up on to the dais. An air of jollity and calmness reigned. The Council's bully boys and henchmen clustered near the door and around the hearth. More posset was poured, then Wriothesley led the assault on the old duke. He recalled Norfolk's years of court service, emphasising the King's generosity and magnanimity, particularly over Anne Boleyn and Katherine Howard, the duke's two errant nieces.

'I was swift to condemn them,' Norfolk protested.

'As you were to recommend them,' Wriothesley interrupted. 'But come, my lord, you know the treasons of your own son?'

'No I do not. I . . .' Norfolk fell silent as Wriothesley rapped the table. I watched that sly man with his reddish hair, moustache and beard, pale face and sloe eyes. He stabbed at the heart of the matter.

'My lord of Norfolk, even if you and your son are innocent, that is not important. What is pertinent is that the King believes you are guilty. You have served him long and well. You know what I say.'

Wriothesley let his words hang like the clanging of a mourning bell. Norfolk sat as if struck by a bolt, hands out on the table, fingers splayed, shoulders shaking as he tried to suppress a sob.

'Buckingham thought he was innocent,' Wriothesley

continued remorselessly, 'Wolsey considered he had done no wrong. What about More and Fisher? Thomas Cromwell, whom you hounded to the death, always believed he was the King's good servant.' He paused. He was closing off all the other paths, leaving only one gate free to open.

'Others, my lord, have openly and unreservedly acknowledged their guilt or thrown themselves on the King's mercy. Remember Cranmer, whom you hoped to take? He went to the King at the dead of night. Or Queen Katherine Parr? Didn't she save her neck by pleading on her knees, openly acknowledging her failings? Or your good friend Bishop Gardiner, before he was exiled from the King's presence for good? You must recall how the late lamented Charles Brandon, Lord of Suffolk, had the King's permission to take Gardiner off to the Tower. Indeed the order was issued, the death barge prepared, the halberdiers summoned. Gardiner's friends, however – you must have been one of these, my lord – informed our good bishop about the real and pressing danger. You must recall what happened? No? Well, our cunning prelate hastened to the King and humbly confessed to all the accusations levelled against him. He earnestly pleaded for His Majesty's pardon, which the King graciously granted. The following morning my lord of Suffolk protested to the King, who replied: 'You should have kept him from me. You know what my custom and nature is and always has been on such matters. I am consistent in pardoning those who neither dissemble or deceive but truthfully admit their transgressions.'

Wriothesley slowly sipped from his goblet. The trap was opening. Every other gate was locked fast against Norfolk; the only escape was what Wriothesley offered. God forgive me, God have mercy on us all. Norfolk walked straight into the snare and the trap slammed shut behind him.

'This,' Wriothesley pushed a parchment before him, 'contains all the allegations levelled at you, my lord. God be my witness, the case presses heavily against you. You, your son and your family have only one resort – His Majesty's clemency and pardon.'

'And I will be able to see the King?' Norfolk pleaded. He was now a broken man. From the moment of his arrest he had defended himself, but the ominous silence from Westminster had broken him. Now these lords of the Council were his only salvation.

In a matter of an hour it was finished. Norfolk had studied and signed his confession. By the following morning copies would be posted at the Cross at St Paul's and the Standard in Cheapside. The confession is not so much proof of treason but testament to the utter collapse of the house of Norfolk. And so it was done, signed by Thomas Norfolk and witnessed by the hounds who'd brought the old tusked boar to bay. Once the proceedings were over, Wriothesley picked up a mazer of sweetmeats. He thrust this into Norfolk's shaking hands and, one arm round the old duke's shoulders, escorted him from the refectory and pushed him into the hands of Sir John Gates's bully boys. The ruffians led Norfolk, the premier duke of this kingdom, off like a schoolboy who has not excelled but been awarded some piffling prize as a petty consolation. Good Lord, it would have brought tears to any eye. The door had hardly shut behind them and Wriothesley was organising his couriers and clerks. What can I say? I have read the documents. Norfolk had confessed to the same so-called treason levelled against his son, the misappropriation of the Royal Arms. In truth it is nothing but arrant nonsense.

The pack, however, were not finished. For a while all was business in the refectory, men entering and leaving. A bell chimed through the freezing air. I felt restless. I always do when I visit the Tower; that grim, narrow place provokes sharp memories. I left the refectory and wandered about. Frosty and freezing, the ice sparkling along the sills and coating the woodwork and cords of the great war machines, the catapults, mangonels and trebuchets so beloved of Henry. I went across to study the massive cannon and mortar but became distracted by the ravens, those sleek black birds, their cruel yellow beaks constantly spearing the ground. I heard shouts and cries coming from the refectory; soldiers and archers were assembling, gathering together with the Council's henchmen. I hurried back inside, taking my seat just before a figure cloaked and cowled like a monk was led in. The door slammed shut behind him. The mysterious figure, escorted by Gates's retainers, pulled back his cowl to reveal Henry Howard, Earl of Surrey. He stood defiantly, feet apart, hands hanging by his sides, his long, bony white face sharply offset by his russet hair and beard. He was the very opposite to his father, face full of pride, glaring fiercely at his gaggle of accusers, the cast in his eye even more pronounced.

'Your father the Duke of Norfolk has confessed,' Wriothesley yelled, 'to a whole litany of treasons.'

'No he has not.' The earl's voice was calm but carrying. 'He has been tricked, as have I.' He turned his back on them and walked to the door.

'We have much to talk about.' Wriothesley sounded shrill, white foam staining the corners of his mouth.

'I have nothing to say to you,' Surrey shouted back over his shoulder. 'Not here, not ever.'

God bless him, but the lords still had their way. The following morning, Thursday 15 January, the Year of Our Lord 1547, Surrey was committed for trial. An ice-bound morning which marked the end of the Howard family, their opponents eager to render it as degrading as possible. Surrey was not deemed a parliamentary lord; his earldom was a courtesy, so he was not to be tried in the solemn grandeur of Westminster Hall, where King's Bench and the other great courts sat next to both abbey and palace. Instead he was to be dispatched at the Guildhall like any other common felon, be it a housebreaker or violator of the King's peace. I had not been summoned back to the King, so I crossed to Greenwich and then returned to take lodgings in the Puddlicot, a tavern adjoining the ancient gateway of Westminster Abbey.

Surrey was roused early that Thursday morning and his chains removed. He had been stripped of his possessions, so the Lieutenant of the Tower brought him a black satin cloak lined with coney fur. Once all was ready, he was marched out through the Tower's Lion Gate, the noise of the royal beasts echoing like some discordant chant. At the gate he was handed over to the sheriffs' men; these formed a cordon around him, and they processed along the frost-hardened lanes. Crowds had gathered, not only at the mouths of alleyways and the windows of taverns and houses but on corners, church steps, even climbing on to the market crosses, braving the buffeting wind and the icy, slippery stonework. Immediately before Surrey walked the headsman, holding his execution axe with the blade to the front. If and when Surrey was convicted, the blade would be turned back towards him.

Snow was falling as the three hundred halberdiers, weapons at the ready, marched through the heart of London. If Surrey's enemies hoped to stir resentment against their foe, they were bitterly disappointed. Surrey was popular in the City even though he had been a scapegrace, a roaring boy who had feasted, revelled and rioted long after the chimes of midnight. The crowds, braving the bitter cold and sharp snow flurries, remained ominously silent. The procession reached the great cobbled yard of the Guildhall, dominated by the life-size statues in their frescoed porches: Christ in majesty, two bearded men representing Law and Learning and four female figures depicting Justice, Discipline, Strength and Moderation. Inside, the dimly lit court hall was ready, the galleries around it packed with people, including myself and Balaam, all anticipating the unfolding drama. The judges sat on their great throne chairs along the dais: Wriothesley, Paget, Dudley and Seymour. Immediately to their right were the jurymen who had been empanelled at Norwich Castle. To be sure, these included former friends of Surrey, but others, like Sir John Gresham, had clashed with the earl. The Greshams had never forgotten Surrey's frenetic revelry in London four years earlier, when the drunken earl and other rioters smashed the windows in Gresham's Cheapside mansion.

Surrey was escorted to the great bar before the judges. A bell tolled mournfully, marking the ninth hour, and the trial began. The clerk rose and, in a ringing voice, asked Surrey to raise his right hand. Once he did, the indictment was read: how Henry Howard, Lord of Surrey, had 'falsely, maliciously and treasonously' assumed the royal arms of King Edward the Confessor. Neither in law nor fact was there any justification for this because such arms, by right and law, pertained only to His Majesty the King. By his actions, therefore, Henry Howard had encompassed the 'peril, scandal and disinheritance of the said Lord King and the overthrow of this his realm of England' and was therefore a public enemy; the devil had seduced him from his allegiance and he deserved death. Surrey heard this out. He had been the first to offer to fight without armour to prove his innocence, so sure was he that God would protect him; now he was prepared to fight with words. When the clerk asked, 'Henry Howard, how do you plead?' The 'Not guilty!' reply echoed like a trumpet call of defiance through that cavernous, oak-beamed court.

'And how will you be tried?' asked the clerk.

'By God and the country.' Surrey delivered this in a tone that eloquently conveyed how the true verdict on him would be decided in years to come and not on this bleak January day surrounded by his enemies.

Only then were the jurors sworn in. Surrey could not challenge these, as the recent Treasons Act had abolished the defendant's right to question a juror. He could only defend himself, and he did this brilliantly for almost eight hours, until five o'clock in the evening. When Sir Richard Rich opened the case for the prosecution, Surrey rounded on him. 'You are false,' he shouted, 'and to earn a piece of gold you would condemn your own father!' He continued in the same vein: that he had never intended to usurp the King's arms, whilst everyone knew the Howards had a right to certain insignia. 'Go to churches in Norfolk,' he boasted, 'and you will see such arms; they have been ours for hundreds of years.'

'Hold your peace, my lord,' Paget interrupted. 'Your

intent was to commit treason, and as our king is old, you thought to become king yourself.'

'And you, Catchpole . . .' Surrey paused, allowing those in the gallery to laugh quietly at the earl's allusion to Paget's father, a mere city bailiff. 'What do you have to do with this?' He continued. 'You should hold your tongue. This realm has never been the same since the King put mean creatures such as you into its government.' Paget fell silent, and even from where I stood, I could see his deep discomfiture.

Dudley came next, accusing the earl of trying to escape from the Tower, an act which proved his guilt.

'I tried to escape,' Surrey swiftly retorted, 'to prevent myself coming to this situation in which I now find myself. You, my lord . . .' He was now quietly reminding Dudley about his own father. 'You, my lord,' he repeated, 'should know full well that however right a man may be, they always find a fallen man guilty.'

Surrey was like a hawk swooping on all the judges, pecking at their weaknesses, in each case the same: the father of the man accusing him. For the rest, he trusted in the classic defence: not to dispute the facts but to establish what were his motives. He was impressive. The mood of the court subtly changed. He established himself as a man of deep understanding, sharp wit and the most remarkable courage. He changed tactics, sometimes denying the accusations as downright lies and so impugning the credibility of his accusers, at other times demonstrating how his words could be interpreted to pose no threat and so casting the prosecution as feverishly lying.

He dealt with witnesses in a similar fashion. One of these described an argument with Surrey, who had used hot words against him. Surrey simply pointed out that the man's conduct was so disgraceful he richly deserved what he received. When the allegation that he tried to persuade his sister to become the King's mistress was levelled, he did not bother to deny it but posed an angry question: 'Must I be condemned on the word of such a wretched woman?' He struck at the very heart of a key witness: not what she said but what she had become, a woman prepared to send her own brother to the headsman's block.

Surrey outfoxed his opponents so cleverly that a member of the commons, a gentleman of Essex, voiced the attitude of the spectators that Surrey had depicted himself as a man of great parts and high courage with many other noble qualities. Most of the jury tended to agree. If Wriothesley and the rest thought the play was finished and all the rehearsed lines delivered on cue, they were bitterly disappointed. On their retirement the jury could not, did not reach a verdict. The judges became so nervous that Wriothesley was dispatched to Westminster to confer with the King. An interesting development as His Majesty must have been alert and very expectant about the outcome of the trial. He had apparently demanded to be closely apprised of any development, and a recalcitrant jury was one of these.

For judges to interfere with a jury's verdict they would need the royal assurance of protection, which they very swiftly received.

Wriothesley hurried back to Westminster and visited the jurors in their chamber. Of course it was a foregone conclusion, and what I write here I learnt from Sir John Clere, a juror, a former friend of Surrey, a firm adherent of the Princess Mary, a man who is highly regarded in many parts of Norfolk. Once Surrey's trial was over, Clere went straight to Greenwich and sought an audience with the princess, where Lady Jane was present. He related the sorry tale. Apparently the jury had found for, not against Surrey. At the time I accepted that was obvious, but to my astonishment, Clere revealed to Princess Mary that the judges also agreed with this. However, they insisted that Surrey had to be condemned, not because of the King, but 'that it was sufficient cause to make them say guilty because Surrey was not a man to live in a commonwealth'. I have reflected carefully on this; I catch its drift. Henry had struck at the Howards but the lords of the Council did not perceive it in that fashion. They were already reflecting on what would happen when the King died. Were they plotting a change of governance? Would this governance be Crown or commonwealth? Did the lords see themselves like the council of Venice or those other republics in Germany and northern Italy?

At the time, I understood what they preached: whatever his defence, Surrey was to be condemned. The jurors returned to the courtroom; even then they were not allowed to speak. When summoned by name, each replied that Seymour would speak for them, a subtle subterfuge; like Pontius Pilate, they washed their hands of any guilt. Seymour relished the part. After each juror stood, he shouted in Surrey's face, 'Guilty and he should die!' The verdict was greeted by shouts and cries of protest. Once order was imposed, Surrey broke the silence.

'Of what have you found me guilty?' he demanded. 'Surely you will find no law that justifies you. However, I realise the King wants to be rid of all the noble blood around him and to employ none but the lowest people.' He kept up this tirade until a guard silenced him. Then Chancellor Wriothesley, head, neck and shoulders veiled in black, rose and pronounced sentence.

'Henry Howard, you are to be taken to the place from whence you came; from there to be dragged through the City of London to the place of execution called Tyburn. There to be hanged, cut down while still alive, your privy parts to be cut off and your bowels to be taken out of your body and burnt before you. Your head is to be cut off and your body divided into four parts, the head and quarters to be set at such places as the King shall assign.'

The headman's axe was turned towards Surrey as he left the bar, the halberdiers closed around him and he was led back through the City to the Tower.

*　　*　　*

I finished this last entry to my journal late the following day, after Surrey had been condemned. I visited the Lady Jane at Greenwich and she informed me of what they knew about the machinations of the jury. I felt sick at heart and indeed sick in body, tired and depleted. I returned to Westminster. The situation has not changed. The King has no need of me. I spent two days in bed wrapped in blankets against the iron cold outside. To be honest, I am also frightened. Whatever the King is planning gathers pace. He will see nobody except the Council, and they are hot on finishing what they have begun. The Howards have been destroyed; the Romanists severely checked. Gardiner languishes in exile, locked firmly under house arrest. A Bill of Attainder has been introduced in the Lords proclaiming Norfolk and Surrey 'High Traitors' and ordering the complete forfeiture of all titles, houses, chattels, offices and lands. Norfolk has not saved himself; his confession was simply a trick to entrap. No mercy has been shown. No compassion or pardon exercised. From what I understand, the old duke's death warrant awaits signature.

19 January 1547

God forgive me, but today, 19 January in the Year of Our Lord 1547, saw the destruction of Surrey. Yesterday evening John Roberts, escorted by one of Gates's ruffians, banged on the door of my room. My heart leapt. Perhaps the King was summoning me. That was not the case. Henry was turning the knife. The writ Roberts thrust into my hand made it very clear. I was to be one of the King's witnesses at Surrey's execution the following morning. I could not object. Roberts waved a hand around my chamber.

'It will be very early.' He spoke matter-of-factly, as if he and I were planning to rise and journey to some fair. 'Master Somers, you'd best go to the Tower now. You must not be late. My good friend here,' he patted the ruffian dressed in half-armour, a man whose horrid soul was clear in his cruel eyes, 'will make sure you arrive safely.'

I was tempted to plead sickness, but that would be

ignored; this would prove to be a winter's evening in more ways than one. I packed a few belongings in a set of panniers and my escort took me down to King's Steps and the waiting barge. The river journey along the Thames is always to be feared, but never more so than in the depth of winter, the breeze sharp as a knife, the river swollen black and ugly. Thank God we kept close to the shore. I drew comfort from the beacons glowing in their steeples and the roaring bonfires of rubbish along the quaysides. We passed under London Bridge without harm and docked at Tower Wharf. Soldiers, men-at-arms and archers, all wrapped in thick cloaks, their weapons at the ready, guarded every approach, gateway and postern door. Torches flared merrily along the battlements. Despite both the hour and the season, I glimpsed the sheen of armour. The Tower had been put on a war footing, as if expecting an enemy fleet to come sailing up the river or an invading army ready to circle it about. I walked doggedly. I was aware of the various courtyards and narrow gulleys we passed through. Fires glowed. Braziers crackled. People hurried here and there, slipping on the ice. Shouts and cries. The neigh of horses in the stables and the barking of the guard mastiffs were all drowned by the roars and snarls from the royal bestiary.

I was given a chamber in the Salt Tower, with two guards outside. A spit boy brought me a surprisingly hot and delicious meal from the Tower kitchens: venison freshly slaughtered and well cooked, soaked in a spicy sauce with a mess of chopped vegetables, good white bread and a jug of the heaviest claret. I ate well and drank deeper. I did not change, but stretched out on the bed, falling into a deep dark sleep until I was aroused the following morning. Surrey was woken in his cell at the same time, the first faint light against the sky, and briskly informed that he was about to die. Poor boy; he protested, but the decision was made and sentence passed.

I waited outside with the other witnesses, stamping our feet, clapping our hands, drinking the posset that had been served on trays and pecking at the bread and salted bacon offered us on platters. Now and again one of the witnesses would walk away to ease themselves at the latrines. Guards and servants came hurrying up full of gossip about what was happening at St Thomas's Tower, where Surrey was being hurried towards his death. The fallen earl was not even given time to itemise and bequeath the paltry possessions he'd been allowed to keep in his grey-walled cell: a feather mattress, bolster, blankets and quilts, a silver flagon, and a gilt-edged salt shaker. Dressed in the same black satin robe lined with coney fur as he had worn at his trial, boots on his feet and a soft cap on his head, Surrey retained his dignity as the Lieutenant of the Tower, Sir Walter Stonor, bluntly informed him how the King, out of the depths of his mercy, had commuted the dire punishment for treason to simple beheading. After this he was brought down to us in the bailey.

Torches flared. Cresset torches spurted, their flames leaping eerily in the icy half-light. Surrey kept his face like flint. I glimpsed his pale skin and those strange eyes, a man almost hiding himself in the clothes he wore. He did not even glance at us but turned his back, staring up as if studying the parapet walk along the Tower. Orders were issued. We proceeded to the gatehouse. A freezing dawn, the snow and ice underfoot hardening while the river mist hung as thick as wool, turning the torchlight into a hazy yellowy glow. At the drawbridge Surrey was handed over to the two waiting London sheriffs, Richard Cernas and Thomas Gurlin, as the City of London owns the execution ground of Tower Hill adjoining the fortress. Retainers and henchmen of the lords of the Council were there, a few foreign ambassadors and some local tradesmen. I listened intently to the sheriff's men. The execution party was under strict instruction to proceed as swiftly as possible. Surrounded by City serjeants carrying torches, and preceded by the headsman, the blade of his axe held high towards Surrey, we walked along the line of the Tower to the black-draped scaffold, four feet high and reached by nine steep steps.

Surrey walked purposefully and climbed the steps, the executioner and sheriffs assembling behind him. The halberdiers promptly ringed the scaffold. A drum roll sounded, threatening and ominous. Surrey strode to the edge of the platform and began to address the small crowd. He was not going to submit or admit to being justly condemned. He never asked forgiveness from either God or the King, and all the conventional rituals were ignored. As during his trial, he loudly protested his innocence. He wasn't allowed to speak for long. The wind whipped away his words. Torches moved on the scaffold. A voice shouted and any further speech was drowned by another roll of drums. The drama of death swept on. Surrey held his hands up as if in prayer and loosened the clasp of his cloak. The executioner, as expected, knelt to beg his forgiveness. Surrey gave that; then he too knelt, to be shriven by a priest. Once finished, he was offered a blindfold. He refused. He lay down, stomach pressed against the black, water-soaked drapery covering the boards. He loosened his shirt further and stretched out his hands. Even as he positioned his head more carefully on the block, the executioner's axe swung up, a sliver of glistening steel, and the thud of its fall echoed down the hill.

Surrey was gone. England's premier poet and greatest earl, one of the kingdom's bravest men. The waiting death wagon, black and stark against the lightening sky, draped in funeral cloths and carrying the arrow-chest coffin, drew closer. Torchlight moved. Both corpse and severed head were lifted, the executioner wrapping the latter most tenderly as if he was swaddling it. I turned and walked away as the cart pulled off to the simple burial ceremony in All Hallows by the Tower.

*   *   *

I made my way back to Westminster. The sheer, bleak fog of death weighed heavily on me. Surrey's death was murder by another name. An earl, a leading poet, an audacious warrior had been executed for the sheer silliness of a foolish boy. Henry's court truly was a masque, a carnival, a sham, a pretence, and I had been part of the illusion. Henry the Magnificent, the Champion of the English Church, the Defender of the Realm against the power of Rome. Bluff Hal! Yet when I now look back down the passage of the years, I see it crammed by steaming corpses. What did it all amount to? A string of severed heads on the poles above London Bridge? The Mouldwarp manifesting his misery to the multitude around him?

The city I passed through was dark and filthy. No beauty caught my eye, but rather the frozen middens populated with vermin, scavenging dogs and snouting swine. Blood-soaked fish and meat stalls watched carefully by the nest of beggars in alleyways and runnels, their children waiting to snatch a gobbet of raw flesh, ready to risk their lives by scampering beneath the iron-shod hooves of the stable-fed stallions ridden by the great merchants and lords. On that day London seemed to be a city of the damned, bathed in the half-light of a winter night that would never fully pass. The freezing cold, the sour smells and hideous sights frayed my soul further. I avoided the pillories and the stocks, the whipping post and the bailiff's cart. I stopped at a tavern to down a goblet of wine. At the same time I tried to remember my love for the Lady Jane, lying with her under the sun in some green, supple-grassed meadow. My thoughts, however, kept going back to Surrey and the pack of wolves that had brought him down. When I was young I could never understand the hermits, the anchorites, the recluses who hid themselves away from humankind. *Oh Jesu miserere*, now I do! If you live alone, there's no other, no pain, no struggle for power, no victory, no submission, no hurt, no harm.

I was terrified, finished with a king and court where no one was safe. I drained my goblet of wine and downed another, then quickly made my way back to Westminster, determined to flee. Sir Anthony Wingfield, Captain of the Spears, prevented that. He was waiting in the gallery below my room, two of his men lurking in the stairwell. He must have guessed I would return, and God knows, that man can wait like a cat ready to pounce.

'His Majesty,' Wingfield leaned down, watery blue eyes glaring at me, 'His Majesty, God knows why, wants to see your ugly face. No,' he grasped my arm as I turned to go down to the royal privy chambers, 'not there. Follow me.'

I had little choice in the matter. The Spears, the royal halberdiers, swarmed everywhere and Wingfield is a man you do not cross. Red-faced, bristling and bustling, he is a man for orders; if instructed to fight the sun, he would do his best to comply. He led me through the warren of courtyards that make up the old palace. A place where time seems to have paused some hundred years ago. A dark, ill-lit maze of ancient chambers, rooms and halls. Paintings, their gilt frames decaying, the canvas faded, hang slightly askew. Here and there ancient weapons are nailed against the wall, such as the war axe of the Black Prince or the sword of his grandfather, dulled and chipped, put up as trophies and left to fade as dim memories. Cobwebbed statues stand in niches, now ignored under the new religion, the flower pots beside them full of dirty water, the flowers long corrupted to a black smelly mush. Lamps and candles glowed fitfully, making it a place of dancing shadows even though it was not yet noon. We crossed overgrown frozen gardens past sheds with turf for roof and ox-hide curtains for doors and shutters, the squalid hovels of those hired to rake and weed the ice-hard soil. The air was thick with the acrid smoke of their fires and sour with the stench of human refuse from the makeshift latrines. Thin-ribbed dogs barked and yawned at us. Mangy cats slithered out, then fled. The hide curtains were pulled back by grimy fingers holding cracked food bowls; pallid faces, framed by hoods and cowls, peered out at us.

We left one such garden, entering a gallery where the oak gleamed as it caught the shifting light, the air rich and sweet from the aromatics crushed and sprinkled on the many braziers. We were now on the opposite side of the palace, where the great storerooms of the Exchequer, Chancery and Court of Augmentations are supervised by an ink-stained tribe of clerks who scrambled aside at Wingfield's approach. Eventually he paused and opened a door; the steps inside leading down to the cellar were railed and covered with thick rope matting. The cavernous chamber below was well lit by a host of flambeaux and warmed by a row of glowing braziers. At the bottom of the steps halberdiers stood on guard; beyond, slumped on a great cushioned seat surrounded by huge chests, iron-bound coffers and metal-studded caskets, sat the King. On the floor next to him lay his two great walking sticks. He was dressed in a heavy blue and scarlet robe powdered with gold and silver, woollen purple buskins on his feet, a bonnet sporting diamond, rubies and pearls pulled down firmly over his head. He glanced towards me, peering through the murk, beckoning at me. Even from where I stood, I could see the blood glinting on those fat, splintered fingers.

'Come, Will,' he said throatily. 'Come join your king and sit amongst the dead.'

I did not understand what he meant. Wingfield pushed me forward and continued to do so until I reached my grim master. I immediately genuflected and felt a stinging blow to my right cheek. I glanced up at Henry; smirking from ear to ear, he slapped me again.

'Your Majesty?'

'Not for being what you are, Will, but for what you do.'

'Your Majesty?'

'Oh, I cannot be bothered,' Henry sighed, dropping a purse of coins before me, tapping me on the face, incensing me with his blood as he gestured that I should pick it up. I did so wearily and the King punched me on the shoulder.

'You saw him die?'

'You know I did.'

'Bravely?'

'You know he did.' Henry lunged at me, but I scrambled swiftly backwards.

'Sit down, sit down.' The King was breathing heavily. I looked around, and as Henry probably intended, my gaze was caught by the corpse, embalmed and gowned in a dark woollen robe of murrey, lying within a lead coffin. Startled, I rose and went to stand over the unburied remains of James IV of Scotland, killed that cruel day, 9 September in the year 1513, at Flodden Field, above ground now for almost thirty-four years. I stared at the reddish hair, clipped moustache and beard, the snow-white skin and faint pinkish lips. The dead king's hands were long, the fingers tapered, his cheeks slightly sunken. The smell from the remains was fragrant, like the aroma of a herb garden. In the dancing dim light it looked as if he was asleep.

'Your Majesty should bury him.'

'They started it,' the King murmured.

'Who did?'

'The Howards,' Henry replied. 'Thomas Howard now awaiting death in the Tower, the father of the traitor we killed today. Years ago, Will, he was Lord High Admiral and took two Scottish ships off the Downs. I refused to punish their captains or return the goods. James of Scotland saw this as cause for war. Come here, Will.' I did so tentatively. The King grabbed my arms, fingers digging into my flesh; I yelped at the pain. From the other end of the crypt I heard the sound of weapons being drawn and glimpsed the glitter of steel.

'No, no.' Henry pulled himself up close to me, grinning down like some moonstruck lover. 'No, no!' he repeated; his voice was strong, echoing off the grimy stonework. 'Will is no danger, just a prop.' And with one hand on my shoulder, the other gripping a silver-topped walking cane, Henry pushed me aside so he stood close to the lead coffin. He stared down at the preserved corpse.

'I come down here to talk to him. Do you know, Will, they dragged his half-naked corpse from the battlefield after someone recognised it? Others disputed that. You see, James . . .' Henry broke off as if addressing the corpse directly, 'was not wearing that iron chain around his middle. The chain of penance for rebelling against his own father.'

'Your Majesty?'

'A man for the ladies, weren't you, James?' Henry wagged a finger. 'You young fool. He crossed the northern march because the Queen of France, stupid woman, sent him her ring on the tip of a spear. She begged him to be her champion and invade the northern shires.' Henry stood rocking on his feet, hand firmly clasping my shoulder. 'Some people claim that James escaped from the battle, but he did not. I have him here. So strange!' His voice sank to a whisper. 'The Norfolks brought him to battle, trapped him at Flodden. He fought like a man possessed and got within a spear's length of Norfolk before he was cut down. A mass of wounds; his right hand hung only by a strip of skin. They disembowelled and embalmed him at Berwick. Look at him, Will, and weep! A prince whose throat once burst with rich words and vivid images. A poet, a troubadour, a warrior, but where is that now? Where is the chivalry, the minstrel song, the full-boobed wenches with their scarlet baskets of cherries? The Howards finished that, father and son,' he hissed. 'And they would have done the same to me. The fate of princes, Will. James was killed in battle, his father James III was murdered. He tried to put down a rebellion and failed. He fled and hid in a mill. He begged a peasant woman to fetch a priest to shrive him. God knows who the priest was, but he heard the old king's confession, then cut his throat.'

Henry gripped my shoulder and turned me towards another chest. 'Look too at the grandeur that was!' I stared in amazement. The deep, iron-studded coffer was filled with some of the sacred relics looted from various shrines. For a while he regaled me with scandalous stories about abbeys, monasteries and convents. How at Swaffham the Benedictine nuns were ruled by Prioress Joan Spilman, who had set up house with a runaway friar and sold all the convent's goods. After Henry dissolved the house, Joan had turned witless and lived out her life in an underground cellar in the local vicar's garden. Henry, hobbling from casket to coffer, then described some of the relics. There was the phial of the Holy Blood from Hailes Abbey: 'Nothing but honey mixed with saffron,' he muttered. He gestured at the Black Virgin of Willesden, an ebonised statue revered by former kings and queens. The golden jewels from the tomb of St Edmund. Mary Magdalene's girdle from Farleigh. The Rood of Grace from Boxley and the miraculous blossoms from Maiden Bradley.

Muttering to himself, the King moved slowly around the various chests. I watched him intently. I recalled the rumours of how he was accustomed to come here and talk to the embalmed corpse of King James. The cadaver should have been sent back to Scotland; it had first been entrusted to Henry's great friend Charles Brandon, the Duke of Suffolk, who sent it to the Carthusians at Sheen before it was moved here. I recognised that Henry was fascinated by James, a true ladies' man, married to Henry's ugly frump of a sister Margaret, a king so fertile in the sons he had produced, both legitimate and bastard. Henry's fascination with relics was also understandable; these were the bridge back to the old religion of his father and mother.

'Your Majesty,' I tried to keep my voice humble and suppliant, 'why have you brought me here?' I suspected he wished to justify himself. Henry hobbled back to his cushioned chair, gesturing at the stool close by.

'James of Scotland was once a great prince, feted by France, the papacy and the Empire, yet he died on a wind-blasted hill, his corpse now lies in a London cellar and his orphan child rules Scotland, or at least tries to. And the relics? Once they held sway over kings and queens and tens of thousands of souls. Now look at them. I read Augustine's "Confessions" recently. He argued how we are a veritable bag crammed with all sorts of fears, influences, memories and dreams. I was five, Will, five years old when Cornish rebels in their thousands occupied Blackheath. My father fought one pretender after another. Ten years ago the north rose in rebellion against me. Danger on every side.' Henry gestured at the lead coffin. 'What happened to James could happen to me and mine.' He leaned closer. 'Do you really think that the Howards would suffer the Council? There would be civil war, and if the Yellow Jackets were victorious, how long do you think my little Edward would last, or pretty-faced Elizabeth or your own brooding mistress, Princess Mary?'

'And how long do you think they will last with the lords of the Council?' I retorted, pushing back the stool, fearful of the King lashing out. He just smiled, the grin of a greedy, spoilt boy who was already plotting fresh mischief.

'I tell you, Will,' he leaned closer again, whispering hoarsely, 'there will be one king, one realm, one religion. So don't weep for Surrey or his father. Staring at that corpse, going through these so-called relics is a reminder of what can happen if we don't succeed and matters fail.' Then he added, almost to himself, 'I have not yet finished.' He held out a hand for me to kiss. I did so, and he drove his knuckles hard against my teeth.

'Go, Will. Wingfield will take you back.' He gently touched my face and stared sadly at me. I rose, bowed and turned away.

'Will?' I glanced back. Henry was grinning at me. 'Remember, I have not yet finished.'

Sir Anthony Wingfield escorted me back to my chamber. That was three hours ago. I have sat here and had food brought up by my friends in the kitchen. I have reflected on what the King said. He has often talked about fickle fortune, of his determination to rule and be ruled by no one else. At first I thought he might be expressing guilt, yet Henry never feels guilt. He often asserts how he lives in peace with his conscience, which is on excellent terms with God. No, I concluded, he was drawing strength for something else, but what? More remarkable was Sir Anthony Wingfield's conduct as he led me back. Wingfield is Henry's man body and soul, in peace and war. He has no dealings with anyone, yet something amiss occurred as we passed the royal chancery chamber. Wingfield was accosted by Paget's creature William Clarke; a hushed conversation followed. I am certain Clarke passed over a heavy pouch, a purse of coins, which Wingfield swiftly took. So why would that be?

4 February 1547

enry is dead! The King is dead! The Great Monster, the Prince of the Sun, that vast-framed man is no more! The Mouldwarp of ancient legend has gone into the dark. No longer will we hear his booming voice. Never again will he stride into a chamber and make all who wait there shake with fright. A prince who cuddled and cosseted me, who laughed uproariously at my jests and sallies, who showered me with gifts yet at the same time would beat, pummel, pinch and humiliate me. A lord whom I loved and served and at other times loathed with all my heart.

He died, according to reports, at two o'clock in the morning of Friday 28 January. On this matter alone I have to grieve, at least for a while. Death soothes many a pain, yet it is a heavy price to pay for peace. Whatever the King's sins, my heart still harbours memories, and these come sweeping back. Images and thoughts. Henry in his prime. Henry the King in his robes of silk slashed with different colours, a jewelled bonnet on his head, his great body encased in gorgeous robes sparkling with precious stones. Henry swaggering along a gallery, filling it with his presence, or standing on top of some steps, feet apart, hands on hips, carefully scrutinising all before him. Seasons and feasts: Christmas, Easter, Midsummer and Michaelmas. Banquets opened with the blare of trumpets as a gilded, painted boar's head was presented to the King. Masques and revelries where mummers leapt and danced, their faces visored, their painted bodies covered in coney skins and furry tails. Henry galloping on his beautiful stable-fed warhorse. Henry in the tilt yard. Henry in the forest. Gorgeous mock battles with Morris men armed with pikes and cross-bows. The sudden explosion of miniature sacks of gunpowder through which devils fled pursued by angels intent on strangling them. Henry roaring with laughter and throwing food, coins and precious goblets as a reward. Crowded halls at the dead of night, the torch-light battling against the inky darkness as he refused to leave the board for bed. Or like some mysterious paladin from Arthur's court, Henry entering the lists on the tournament grounds to joust and break a spear. He would abruptly appear in black armour, purple plumes nodding in the breeze, no escutcheon or insignia on either his breastplate or the huge kite-shaped shield which I sometimes carried as his squire. Henry emerged as a fearsome figure, some hell-born vision sitting firm as a rock in his high-horned leather saddle,

241

his satin-coated warhorse black as night, its sharpened hooves pawing the ground. The spear would be slowly lowered, knight and warhorse moving in an ominous rattle, the lance, feathered with pennants, now fully couched, aimed directly at his opponent's heart. Oh the awesome beauty!

And these last of days. That powerful voice, those piggy eyes blazing with fury, snarling lips spitting a white frothy rage, the heavy footfall, the nipping, the beating, the pulling and pushing, and then the abrupt change of mood, the sly glance, the giggling behind the hand. *Kyrie eleison, Christe eleison, Kyrie eleison.* Lord have mercy, Christ have mercy, Lord have mercy! Whatever the nightmare he became, he was still my king. At times a good and generous lord, a man of vaulting ambition with the talent to match. I mourn his death. I grieve for what he might have been and, in the end, for what he truly was. Some might say I could have done more to soothe his fiery rages, temper his malice, check his pride. I ask you in all truth, what could I have done? I, scruffy Will Somers the fool? I did what I could in the circumstances, as I do now. I have recited the Dirige psalm, David's song of mourning. I have arranged for requiem masses to be offered privately by a chantry chaplain garbed in blue and gold, purple-tinted candles spluttering against the darkness, in the side chapel of St Michael's church. My present lodgings are draped in funeral cloths. I will perform the three-day fast. I will light tapers before a statue of the Virgin, if and when I find one.

So how did this all happen? How was I taken unawares? *Mea culpa! Mea culpa!* My most grievous fault. My own arrogance. My confidence that I was safe. Ah well, Satan fell like lightning from Heaven and so did I! On the morning of Saturday 22 January I left the palace to stroll in Westminster's crooked, narrow lanes. The guards had been strengthened. More cannon hauled from the Tower. Horsemen milled in the courtyards. I returned a short while later. I wanted to see the King, but Roberts, together with two of Gates's ruffians, turned me away. I went to my own chamber. I had hardly taken off my cloak and boots when the door was flung open and Paget and Wriothesley sauntered in, Gates dressed in half-armour behind them to guard the door. All three were casually and coolly arrogant. Wriothesley sat on my bed. Paget on my high leather-backed chair. Gates's burly figure filled the doorway. Menace and threats seeped from all three. Paget peeled off his elegant doeskin gloves, beating them against his thigh as he stared around.

'His Majesty is not well,' Wriothesley declared. 'He does not seek your company. We do not want your company, fool.' He wetted his lips, chin jutting out like a weapon towards me. 'Scuttling little Somers, hither and thither like a will-o'–the-wisp over the marshes. Well, my mannekin, now you are caught and held fast.' He grinned falsely at me. 'No more scurrying or scampering. You are detained.'

'On what charge?'

'Possible treason.' Wriothesley smiled, wiping his eyes. 'Treason.' He shrugged. 'Perhaps misprision of treason.'

'Nonsense!'

'Speculating on the King's death. You, little fly, are not fit company for His Majesty.'

'I want to see him.'

'He does not wish to see you,' Wriothesley murmured with mock sweetness. 'You are a fool, Somers.'

'And you are not a wise man,' I retorted, 'and what folly I commit I dedicate to you.' I pointed at his face. 'You wear your wit on your chin and your guts in your head.'

'I would cut out your tongue.' Wriothesley got to his feet.

'And sir, I'd still talk more sense than you.'

Wriothesley's face paled, those soulless eyes unblinking. Gates took a step away from the door. Paget, watching me closely, stopped playing with his gloves.

'All of you . . .' I could not control my temper, 'glass-faced flatterers. You are so full of oil even Satan doesn't want you. You'd set Hell on fire. Your very tears are Judas's children. You do not care for His Majesty. You are busy preparing a mess of malicious mischief. The Norfolks were your enemies, not the King's. Now you are rid of them, your malice plots more mischief against whomsoever,' I stopped for breath. These clever, subtle men had conspired well. At the time I did not know what they were plotting, but they had already sprung the trap.

'You will stay here,' Paget declared. 'Food and drink will be served. There's a garderobe in the gallery. Sleep, eat, drink and be merry, but stay here, Master Somers. Try and escape,' he pulled a face, 'and you will be one corpse amongst many fished from the Thames.'

Wriothesley sauntered towards me scratching his ear, then he lunged like a dog, driving his fist into my face. 'For your impertinence,' he snorted.

Then they left. Outside in the gallery I heard Gates's henchmen assemble to stand on guard. I nursed my face and accepted there was nothing to be done.

From then on, for the next nine days, I was a prisoner. The gallery outside was constantly thronged with Gates's city rifflers and a few Spanish cut-throats. One of these worthies of Spain brought me my meals, his scar-crossed face a mask of contempt about why he should serve someone so small and ugly. I was allowed to use the garderobe at the end of the gallery. I was permitted no visitors. I could not detect or discover any news except that from the mist-bound courtyard below, night and day, echoed the clatter of horsemen leaving and arriving.

The first I knew that something was seriously amiss was the cannon fire from the Tower booming through the frosty air, the first public signal that Henry had died. This was late in the afternoon of Monday 31 January, just as Seymour, Dudley and Sir Anthony Browne, Master of the King's Horse, galloped into the city. In their loving care, or so I was told later, was the King's only son and heir, Prince Edward, surrounded and protected by three hundred horsemen and a host of banner bearers. They rode directly to the Tower to be greeted by fresh salutes from the fortress's walls as well as from the warships moored strategically along the Thames. In the greying, misty fastness of the Tower, Prince Edward was proclaimed king.

At the same time Thomas Wriothesley, Lord Chancellor, that mummer from Hell, gave his finest performance before Parliament. He appeared all grieving and in deep mourning, tears soaked his face, emotion tightened his throat. He solemnly announced the King's death and declared Parliament to be dissolved, but not before Paget, equally stricken to the heart, read out the principle clauses of the King's will, declaring the succession to be his son Edward and, should he die without heir, then Mary by default, then Princess Elizabeth. In the meantime there would be no queen regnant; Katherine Parr was completely ignored. A regency council would wield power; the names of this council were obvious to everyone.

I learnt all this on the morning of 1 February. Wriothesley, this time more distracted, entered my chamber. Halberdiers crowded the gallery outside. The Lord Chancellor, pale-faced and red-eyed, was vicious as ever, but wary. I wondered if all was well with the wolf pack. In the end, after staring malevolently at me, he gave me an hour to leave Westminster Palace.

'Where should I go?'

'Your mistress, the Spanish Mary, resides at Greenwich with the widow queen.' Wriothesley stared at me, those milky blue eyes full of malice. 'Do you know, mannekin, I am not yet finished with you or with . . .' He caught himself. 'One hour,' he repeated. 'Master Bricket in the kitchen will provide both cart and carter. Do not come back.'

'Wriothesley?' At least he turned. 'The King? His Majesty?'

'One hour,' he repeated, then he was gone.

Thanks be to God, Bricket proved to be a good friend. He whistled up his legion of scullions from his steam-strewn kitchens. They helped me pack and carry coffers, chests, panniers and caskets, rolls of cloth and my chancery bags down to the cart in the main kitchen yard. Bricket warned me with his eyes and signs not to speak or question him. He whispered how he'd sent a courier across the river to advise the chamberlains at Greenwich that I was about to arrive, adding that he had already arranged for me to be conveyed there in his own small barge. A strange experience being released from that chamber. Once a part of my life; now I'd been thrust out like some dishonest servant.

The Council were certainly making their presence

felt. Captain Wingfield and the Spears thronged everywhere. I also noticed how important doorways and
galleries were guarded by Dudley's henchmen, wearing
his livery of the bear and ragged staff. He must have
whistled up every single able-bodied retainer. The more
I watched, the more I realised that Dudley and Seymour
had assumed precedence over the rest. Perhaps that was
why Wriothesley seemed apprehensive. The royal
quarters remained closed and sealed. I gazed despair-
ingly at a doorway that I used to casually walk through.
Bricket, however, gripped my shoulder and guided me
out of the palace, down to the freezing quayside, where
the cart containing my possessions was already waiting.
Only then, with the mist swirling about and the cries
of the riverside strangely dulled, did he whisper about
what he knew, and that was very little.

'On the Sunday, the day after you were imprisoned
in your chamber, everything continued as normal. Food
was cooked, served and taken to the royal dining room.
Some of it was even carried up into the King's privy
chamber.'

'By whom?'

'Roberts, Huicke, Alsop the apothecary. On a number
of occasions even Dudley and Paget themselves. But no
one except those sworn of the Council were allowed
anywhere near the King. The Seymours particularly
were very busy, especially Thomas.'

'But . . .' I gazed back through the drifting snow at
the lords' retainers crowding near the main gate. 'Is

Thomas Seymour now sworn of the Council? You know, I know, everyone in the palace knows how the King deeply resented him.'

'I pretend to know nothing,' Bricket whispered, catching at the cuff of my jerkin, 'but on the twenty-fourth of January I learnt that Thomas Seymour was indeed sworn to the Council. Now come, Judas men swarm everywhere, it's time you were gone.'

I cannot really recall that journey across the tumul-tuous Thames, I was so deeply locked in my own thoughts. Servants awaited me at Greenwich. I was led like a dream-walker down galleries and passageways. I was shown a chamber in the royal quarters and told this comfortable, warm room was mine. Porters followed carrying all my luggage. Jane appeared. Once the room was empty, we just lay wrapped in each other's arms on the four-poster bed, its heavy, gold-fringed drapes and gleaming walnut posts capturing the light of the candles on their prickets. We lay together until a servant knocked shouting how Her Grace was waiting. We prepared hurriedly and left.

The servant ushered us into the privy chamber, where the Princess Mary greeted us. She was dressed in black taffeta lined with white lace at neck and cuff; a veil of similar colour and fabric covered her reddish hair. Small and quick in movement, Princess Mary finds it difficult to sit still; her unpainted face showed she'd been crying, those gentle grey eyes all red-rimmed. The King's elder daughter has her own unique beauty, though her harsh, deep, almost male voice does jar on the ear, and when she is angry, her furious shouting reminds me so much of her own dread father. Restless and irate, she explained how she had only been informed about her father's death late last night. Queen Katherine Parr had also been overlooked, having been given the news about the same time. Distraught and unsettled, the Queen had retired to her own chamber to quietly grieve. Mary however was furious at Wriothesley and others.

'I cannot tell you much, Will.' She forced a smile and ran a finger down my face. 'His Majesty, my father, is dead. I mourn, I grieve. My chantry priests will sing the requiems.'

'How?' I replied. 'Your Grace, how did your father die? When? Who tended him?'

'I do not know, Will.' Mary's voice fell to a whisper. 'The very tapestries of this palace have eyes and ears.' She sat down in a chair, shifting her Ave beads from one hand to the other. 'We must wait until Balaam arrives. He is busy as a ferret in a warren.'

Balaam did not keep us long. Later that very day he came swift and sudden like a storm sweeping up the Thames. Mary summoned myself and the Lady Jane back to her privy chamber, where the fire had been built up, chairs and small tables placed close to the roaring flames. Balaam was frozen through, quietly cursing the snow, vowing he would seek warmer climes. Nevertheless, once he had doffed cloak and boots and loosened his sword belt, he described what he had discovered since the day of my arrest. Apparently, on that same day almost to the hour, the King's chamber at Westminster became closely guarded, even more so than usual. Balaam, one hand extended towards the flames, the other holding a deep-bowled goblet of posset, described how he learnt this by mingling with the henchmen and retainers of the great lords in and around Westminster. He described how during these secretive days matters had been helped by the thickest mist of the winter curling along the river and shrouding everything in a dense veil of freezing greyness. Horses, hooves muffled, slid out of this gate or that. Couriers and grooms appeared no more than shadowy wraiths visored and cowled. Outside the palace, the few torches did little to disperse the gloom. Orders were also issued forbidding bonfires or the movement of carts without Wriothesley's permission. Inside the palace itself, passageways, galleries and stairs were also bereft of light, places of deep gloom, full of an inky blackness where candles and torches had either been doused or allowed to splutter out.

'Why?' Lady Jane asked.

'Simple enough,' I replied. 'Only those who know the palace well could move around stealthily and easily. Some furtive stranger, a spy or someone curious to discover what was happening, would stumble and slip and certainly arouse the attention of the guards. Like an army camp when the enemy is close, if the light is poor it means no one can thread the picket lines and move about at will.'

'That is true,' Balaam agreed. 'The palace was like an army preparing for battle, silent and secretive, guards and halberdiers patrolling everywhere. There was a sense of perpetual night; that and the icy weather reduced everyone to the same cowled figures. The guards were most vigilant. Everyone, even councillors, was stopped and ordered to show their passes.'

Sitting almost knee to knee in Princess Mary's chamber, thinking we were safe, again an arrogant mistake on my part, we listened to Balaam describe the dense fog of secrecy that spread and curled through Westminster. How entry even into the courtyards was subject to a special pass. I asked about Bricket and the cooks.

'Oh,' Balaam replied, 'they are all now terrified. Very few people are allowed to enter. No one is permitted to leave unless they carry a special warrant.'

'From whom?' I asked. Balaam just shrugged.

'Will, when was the last time you saw the King?'

'The day Surrey was executed, sometime in the afternoon of the nineteenth of January.'

Balaam nodded. 'Did he discuss what was happening?'

I recalled that macabre meeting in the Westminster cellar. 'Just his imaginings,' I murmured.

'According to what I have learnt,' Balaam drank some posset, 'the King was troubled about his will. He intended to include some who were not named before and put out the likes of Gardiner, whom Henry continued to curse as a wilful man not fit to trouble the King, his son or the Privy Council any more. Van der Delft, the Imperial ambassador, was trying to meet the King, as were others. Rumours were rife that His Majesty was ill. Others claimed his legs had been cauterised and the ulcers closed. Would that be true, Will?'

I replied how I had met the King in the royal cellars at the other end of the palace, which at least proved he was able to walk. Balaam nodded, saying that all this agreed with what he had learnt. How the King had appeared very alert, deeply concerned about the English garrison at Boulogne and their lack of supplies. He was also interested in his gardens, especially some apple trees recently imported from France.

'Did he,' Princess Mary asked, putting her hand to her face, 'ever ask to see his children?'

'No.' Balaam smiled sadly at her. 'Your Grace, as far as gossip has it, the King your father did not ask to see the Queen or any of his family, certainly not before that last week when Westminster fell under the iron grip of the Council. To be honest, Your Grace, God only knows what the King said or did during those last days of his life.'

The Princess Mary held a hand up for silence, staring into the fire. God forgive my arrogance, yet I could sense what she was thinking. The bittersweet, and not so sweet, memories must float like dark smoke through her soul. Once Henry had hailed her as the greatest treasure of his kingdom. Yet when locked in his lust for Anne Boleyn, he would not even speak to her. He declared her illegitimate, exiled her, humiliated her and, on occasion, left her vulnerable and exposed to the malice of others, who, if given leave, would certainly have executed her.

'Perhaps he was not in his right mind?' Mary shifted in her chair.

'The King,' Balaam soothed, 'must have been in great pain.' He sat chewing his lip

'What!' Princess Mary demanded. 'What did you hear, Balaam?'

'Oh, Your Grace, there are stories, vague imaginings, tittle-tattle, scraps of gossip. How the King's secret chambers and apartments were sealed for days.' He took a deep breath. 'Of course you heard the cannon fire from the Tower?' He didn't wait for us to agree. 'Well that was the first public announcement. Here,' Balaam stretched in his chair, 'is where we walk on firmer ground, but,' he paused, 'remember this is what is being proclaimed to all and sundry.' He rubbed the side of his face. 'You know how it goes. If enough people repeat a story time and again, then lo and behold, it is the plain and unvarnished truth.' He paused to collect his thoughts. 'It's common knowledge that the King met the French and Imperial ambassadors on the seventeenth of January. They were told not to tarry long as the King was greatly weakened. We know Surrey was executed on the nineteenth. The King was active enough. Silence descended till Thursday the twenty-seventh, when Parliament passed the Act of Attainder against the Howards, both father and son. The King approved of that; he also took the Eucharist from his confessor, John Boole. Now all this,' Balaam waved a hand, 'is the official story. On that same day the King weakened considerably. Rumours abound that his ulcerated legs had become a squelching mess, that he'd lost control of bowel and bladder, that the light hurt his eyes, his skin crackling yellow like cheap parchment all dried out.'

'So,' the Princess Mary intervened, 'once the attainder against the Howards was approved, my father's state worsened. He slipped swiftly towards death.' She shook her head. 'If Norfolk was condemned, why hasn't the sentence been carried out?'

'Perhaps the Council do not want the young king's reign to begin with the execution of an old man, England's premier duke. Or,' Balaam pulled a face, 'Norfolk is over seventy. We have had enough drama with the Howards. Perhaps Wriothesley and the Council just hope he will rot away in the Tower and die like some neglected old man in his hovel. They have what they want. Surrey is dead. The rest of his family terrified, their property, estates and movables all seized.'

'And my father,' Mary insisted, 'if he died early in the hours of the twenty-eighth of January, surely somebody warned him of his impending death?'

'No one dared. According to rumour, Wriothesley

and the others hung like ghosts on the threshold of the privy chamber. Late in the evening of the twenty-seventh, Sir Anthony Denny, First Gentleman of the Privy Chamber, entered and knelt beside the King's bed. Henry asked what the matter was. Denny informed the King that all human help was in vain and it was now time for His Majesty to review his past life and seek for God's mercy through Christ.' Balaam paused as if listening to the sounds of the night. 'I must be gone soon,' he suddenly whispered. 'The city is under close watch.' He rubbed his hands. 'Soldiers have raised chains on the streets. Barricades have been set up. Horsemen patrol Cheapside. War barges float along the Thames. Your Grace, it's best if I not be seen.' He grasped Mary's hand, raised it and kissed it like the good troubadour he was.

'Finish your tale,' Mary insisted. 'Although whether it's the truth is another matter. It seems to be . . .' she searched for words, 'so much hearsay.'

'After Denny had warned him,' Balaam decided to continue, 'Henry struggled to reply, asking him what judge had sent him to pass this sentence. "Your physicians," Denny answered. Henry promptly summoned these. They arrived with their trays of medicine but Henry, gasping and fighting for breath, demanded they leave. "After all," he rasped, "once judges have passed sentence on a criminal they have no need to trouble him any further, so begone." Denny then invited the King to confer with some of his prelates. "I will speak to no one except Cranmer," the King replied, "but not yet. Let me rest for a while and then I shall decide." He slept fitfully for about an hour, and when he awoke was feeling very weak. He ordered that Cranmer, who had withdrawn to his palace at Croydon, be sent for with all haste.' Balaam drained his goblet. 'Cranmer is no swift courier. It was now the dead of night, the weather was freezing, with savage flurries of snow. By the time Cranmer entered the King's chamber, Henry was speechless. Cranmer stretched out on the royal bed and grasped the King's hand. He begged Henry to testify by some sign that he still hoped in the saving mercies of Christ. The King stared at him, pressed Cranmer's hand and, a short while later, passed from this life to the next.'

Balaam paused at a bell booming through the mist-hung evening. I heard doors opening and shutting. I glanced at Princess Mary. She just sat staring into the fire, eyes brimming with tears. As for myself, I was more intrigued by Balaam's story. The princess was correct, it was like a scene from some miracle play: the Norfolks had been silenced and then the King's condition suddenly worsens. However, no one really talks to him, no one summons his wife and children, whilst hours are spent fetching Cranmer from Croydon.

'My father died early on Friday morning. They kept his death quiet for almost four days. Why?'

'Your Grace, they will argue that certain preparations had to be made. Your illustrious brother was brought into London, ports were sealed, the roads closely watched. The Council had to deal with its own schedule of business.' Even as I spoke I realised my own words sounded hollow. Such matters might take one or two days. Nevertheless, the King died in the early hours of Friday and his death was not made public until Monday. What did happen in those secret chambers at Westminster? More importantly, had the King, my royal master, really died in this rather peaceful way? I turned to the princess.

'Cranmer,' Balaam murmured, 'says he will not shave his face as a sign of mourning.'

'Will?' the princess asked. 'What were you going to say?'

'What must have occurred to your Grace, to Balaam, to Lady Jane and indeed everyone.' I emphasised the points with my fingers. 'First, the King said nothing before he died except that he felt unwell and would like to see Cranmer. Second, there are no witnesses to his death. Cranmer is summoned when it is already too late. The Queen and the King's children are not alerted. No one is allowed to view the corpse. Is that not so?'

'I have dispatched messengers to the palace. I am informed I cannot view my father's corpse; it is now being embalmed and prepared for burial. I believe the same reply has been sent to the Queen.' Mary sighed noisily, 'For the moment, there is little more to be done.'

We had just risen, preparing a collation of cold meats and bowls of hot stewed vegetables to be served on a table near a window, when the sound of pounding feet in the gallery outside startled us. The door was flung open and one of Mary's Spanish servants, the steward I think, burst in and fell to his knees in front of his mistress. Even as he spoke I heard the clash and clatter of steel, the sound of wood breaking, the shrieks of serving wenches. The steward was chattering in Spanish. Mary quickly silenced him with a gesture of her hand and turned to us.

'Wriothesley!' she declared. 'Wriothesley is here with Wingfield and a company of the Spears.'

Balaam at once drew sword and dagger, checking for escape routes. There was no other door. The chamber windows, shuttered against the cold, were too narrow for any escape. Already the halberdiers were in the gallery, the door crashed open and Wriothesley sped like some hunting dog into the chamber, Wingfield and his escort pouring in afterwards. Instantly I knew why he was here, or at least I thought I did. Princess Mary shouted her protests, spots of anger high on her cheeks. I caught the same passionate, flaring fury of her father. She demanded to know by what right they invaded the palace and forced her chambers. Of course this was Wriothesley. Our chancellor does not care for courtesy, honour or title. Swathed in a heavy coat with a ridiculous-looking bonnet on his head, he leered at me and the Lady Jane, who now huddled close beside me. He produced a warrant even as Wingfield drew his own sword and, accompanied by a group of Spears, halberds lowered, advanced threateningly on Balaam. I heard a clatter as Balaam's sword and dagger fell to the floor. Mary snatched Wriothesley's warrant.

'It bears the Council's seal,' Wriothesley bellowed. 'It gives me the power to search any house, palace or not, and to seize any persons suspected of being involved in treason.'

'Not here!' Mary snapped. 'My lord,' her voice became more placatory, 'my father the King is dead. I have just received such doleful news. I do not think this is either the time or the place.'

'Your Grace,' Wriothesley bowed, 'I mean no ill, but this present time is truly perilous, especially in a place like this, a royal palace. Your brother has yet to be crowned, this city seethes with unrest.' He pointed at me and Lady Jane. 'They have not been accused. No indictment has been laid against them, but I'm afraid I must take them into custody.'

'Custody!' the princess cried. 'What custody?'

'Your Grace, I am sure a few questions will clarify matters.'

'Then do it here.'

'No, Your Grace, that is not appropriate. Sir Anthony?'

Despite the princess's strident protests, the Spears closed in around us. Jane was clinging to me for life. Wriothesley was truly enjoying himself; that demon soul revels in such mischief. Deep in my heart I knew he might harm me but not the Lady Jane. Her terror was that she did not recognise that.

'And who is this drawer of weapons?' Wriothesley stepped round me. To my astonishment, Balaam lapsed into a tirade completely in Spanish, acting the part, flinging his hands in the air and shouting at the Princess Mary, who just as swiftly replied in her mother's tongue.

'What is this, what is this?' Wriothesley demanded.

'Master Hugo,' the princess replied, 'is an accredited envoy in the retinue of the Imperial ambassador. His Grace will not be pleased that one of his household is accosted and threatened.'

'Your warrant?' Wriothesley demanded.

Balaam correctly played the surprising role he'd assumed. Voluble in Spanish, he ignored Wriothesley and, hands extended, conversed with the princess as if he did not know what was happening, though clearly resenting Wriothesley. I was astonished. True, I was terrified by Wriothesley's arrival but I was equally startled at this abrupt turn of events. Surrounded by halberdiers, with the Lady Jane clinging close, I found it difficult to turn and watch what was happening. Nevertheless, the Chancellor's demand to produce the warrant was swiftly answered. Acting the interpreter, the princess explained what Wriothesley wanted. Balaam pulled a face, shrugged, scratched his head and muttered something beneath his breath. Neither I nor Wriothesley understood Spanish, but it was obvious that Balaam was cursing our intruder with a spate of filthy words. He looked as if he was going to refuse. Ignoring the Spears, he slowly picked up both sword and dagger and resheathed them, then opened the wallet on his war belt, took out a square of parchment and tossed this at Wriothesley's feet. The Chancellor picked it up and walked over to a lantern box. He read the document before carefully scrutinising the seal.

'The dry stamp,' he called over his shoulder. Balaam had the sense not to reply. Wriothesley was certainly suspicious. He scrutinised both seal and royal signature again, pronounced himself satisfied and handed the document back.

'Take these.' Wriothesley gestured to Lady Jane and myself. Princess Mary shouted protests. Balaam also contributed to the clamour, which echoed in our ears as we were pushed along the gallery and down the stairs. A thoughtful servant hurried up with our cloaks, then we were out in the icy cold half-light. We were hurried along the quayside down to the waiting barge and a nightmare journey across the Thames. Lady Jane, wrapped in both her cloak and mine, trembled like a babe. I shivered until Wingfield, a look of compassion on his harsh face, snatched up a rug the barge master had provided to cover his legs and threw it at me. I squatted, watching the lantern horns either side on the prow rise and fall. A trumpeter kept blowing his horn, a mournful, echoing sound, warning other craft to stay away.

At last we reached Queenhithe, where we disembarked and trudged through the streets to the hulking, ugly, evil-smelling mass of Newgate tower. 'The Stone

Jug' and 'the College of the Damned' are just two of the names given to that sprawling fortress of heinous horrors. I have reflected on what happened that evening. One day, God willing, I will reread it. Perhaps I will teach Lady Jane or some other close friend my cipher and allow them the same. Somebody should know what happened and learn a little more. Certainly I speak the truth. If there is a hell on earth, this can be found in Newgate. If there are degrees of torment in hell, Newgate will certainly display them. The prison is a living death, a grave, a tomb where you are buried before you are dead. A place of sweating filthy walls, its paved cracked floor crackling with the lice which multiply like the plagues of Egypt upon the putrid clothes and filthy bodies of the hordes of unwashed prisoners crammed into its squalid chambers, cells and holes. The reek and stench are suffocating. The clamour, the constant shouting and screams of those incarcerated there din the ear and chill the heart.

We were at once taken to the master's side, where Wingfield's halberdiers were replaced by burly, leather-aproned turnkeys. Wriothesley shook his head when the chain clerk produced the Black Book to record our admission. Now, though that demon did not recognise it, I took great comfort from that. Many years ago, I was hauled off to Newgate for some petty crime. The keeper and his gaolers are like carrion crows; they batten full and wax fat on their victims. They like to number every one and assess his worth so they can exact the fullest tribute. Wriothesley's refusal demonstrated that we might not be there for long, and I began to suspect that he did not enjoy the full authority of the Council for what he had undertaken. He did not want a written record explaining the reason for our arrest and committal to prison. Indeed, the more I studied him, the more I could detect behind his bluster and malice a strident nervousness, as if he too was frightened, but of what?

Wriothesley talked quickly and quietly with the keeper and we were taken to a narrow, cobwebbed room, its floor covered by a dirty, slushy straw which formed a mess around our feet. I sat on a bench opposite the door, pulling Lady Jane down beside me. I murmured comforts as Wriothesley slammed the door shut, grabbed a stool and sat before us. He continued to play his game of Hodman's bluff. He seemed hasty, impatient, and of course he would be. Princess Mary had her father's temper; she would not stand idle but be voluble in her protests. Already couriers would be hastening across to Westminster. I also wondered about Balaam. How could he have a diplomatic warrant? Who arranged that for him: the Princess Mary, the Imperial ambassador or someone else? At the time, that was not my prime concern. I just prayed the winds of this storm would shift swiftly and we would soon be released. I fought to steady my breathing, to calm my nerves. Princess Mary might protest, but this was still dangerous. If Wriothesley could trap us into treason, he would justify his actions. Of that I was truly afraid. Nevertheless, I underestimated the Chancellor's malice. He could not resist spending valuable time on indulging his own cruelty and resentment.

Wriothesley was distracted by Lady Jane, slim and pretty, a maiden in distress, a comely damsel terrified out of her wits, his natural prey. For a while he berated us, our status, our patronage, 'two deformations' who had no right to be at court. A spate of furious, filthy insults spurted from his mouth until he paused, dabbing his fingers at the creamy froth on his lips. He lifted a hand as a chilling scream from elsewhere in the prison pierced the air. Lady Jane, now beside herself with terror, began to chatter nonsense. I was deeply concerned. My beloved is small and well formed, she can be merry and sharp of wit, but those wits can be easily shattered. She can become highly anxious, fretful, sometimes collapse at the confusion that rages within her. I was frightened this living nightmare might truly turn her humours.

'Hush now, hush now,' Wriothesley mocked. 'That's only a prisoner in the press yard suffering peine forte et dure. Some wretch who's refused to plead. He lies in the yard under great paving stones, starved of every-thing except foul water.' The Chancellor grinned. 'It might be him screaming, or there again,' he shook his head, eyes blinking as if genuinely perplexed, 'it might be his accomplice, some stupid wench, a doxy having her ears nailed to the pillory board.' He paused, sniffing noisily as if waiting to sneeze. 'The prisoner will eventually plead, then he will be taken to Tyburn Elms, where he will be half hanged, disembowelled and his entrails burnt in front of him. Afterwards he will be beheaded and his body quartered; that's what traitors suffer. You may wonder, as many do, how a man can survive being ripped open. Well, the executioner ties certain strands within the body so his victim will survive long enough to watch—'

'Wriothesley!' I screeched. 'What is it you want? Why are we here? You know we are no traitors.'

Wriothesley, jaw jutting, wagged a finger. 'Just one question, Will, only one.' His change of tone and mood surprised me, even more so as I caught a flicker of fear; there truly was more to this. Wriothesley delighted in frightening and terrorising us, but this masked something else. He swiftly glanced over his shoulder at the door, then back at us. 'The monster,' he hissed, 'is dead! Screaming and begging he was, Will!' He raised an eyebrow as if expecting applause.

'What!' I demanded. 'That's not what we heard. Are you out of your wits? Are you babbling about the King?'

Wriothesley leaned across, slapped my face then poked Lady Jane on the shoulder like some spoilt, malignant child. I resolved then as I do now: if I can, if I am able, I will kill this man. For a while he just sat staring at us, clucking his tongue. I held his gaze, wondering if this man was truly out of his wits. Ill, evil or both? I also felt strangely reassured. Wriothesley had brought us here to play some hideous game. In his narrow, soiled soul, if he has one, he truly hates myself and Jane not for what we do or say, but for what we are. He considers us freaks, less than human. Years of watching us being fussed and patronised had festered and now spilt over. Yet there was something else. Wriothesley could have seized me at Westminster, pummelled and harassed me there, so why not? Because he needed Lady Jane, to use her to frighten me, whilst he was also concerned about being overheard. He didn't want us in Newgate just to vomit his filthy spleen, but for something else. And what did he mean about the King screaming and pleading? Oh how the world changes so swiftly! A few days earlier he would never have dared say that. Wriothesley continued to stare at me, rocking himself gently backwards and forwards as if the Lady Jane's gentle sobbing was a sweet cantata to his ears.

'You should hasten,' I taunted, 'you really should. Princess Mary will be sending urgent messages to the Council. Our release is only a matter of time. What do you really want to know, Wriothesley?'

'What our late king said to you about me.'

'You should have asked him yourself.'

'Did he ever intend to move against me, I mean with Dudley and Seymour, or discuss any secret plans involving me?'

God be my witness. That poisonous snake of a man! I truly wondered what he was talking about. Of course, like any snake on the move, he twisted and turned.

That's Wriothesley. He had been with Cardinal Wolsey and deserted him. He should have gone to the Tower with Cromwell but saved his neck by testifying against his former master, who had taken him into his own household. Gardiner had been his ally, but Wriothesley deserted him in his hour of need. Perhaps that was it: had the King been plotting his downfall? I tried to cover my confusion, deciding that honesty was the best path.

'I know nothing,' I blurted out. 'I know nothing at all.'

'You could be questioned.'

'By what right? Where is your warrant?'

'I could frighten you,' he pointed at Lady Jane, 'or her, your little friend. Or,' he spread his hands, 'you could tell the truth.'

'I know nothing. Question me, torture me, I will still know nothing. You could bribe me with a house, lands and a pot of gold, my answer will be the same. But Master Wriothesley,' I deliberately used the same common term which the King would have done when he censured this man, 'you have miscalculated, haven't you? You are nervous and you should be. You were once Gardiner's friend and ally; do you think Dudley or Seymour will forget that? What guarantee do they have that you will not whisper council secrets to the Bishop of Winchester?'

Wriothesley abruptly stood up; I secretly rejoiced. Apparently all was not well with the late king's fighting dogs: they would turn on each other, and this sinister soul might be their first victim. He walked to the door and peered through the grille. He was agitated, plucking at the costly belt around his waist, muttering to himself, fingers fluttering the air. I do wonder if Wriothesley suffers fits of lunacy.

'What do you know?' He turned on me.

'Nothing you don't know yourself,' I taunted, 'and if I told you that, you wouldn't be any wiser for it.'

'Riddles.' He smiled. 'Riddles . . .'

A pounding on the door startled him. The hammering was repeated. Wingfield shouted for the door to be open. Someone echoed that. The door was flung back and Wingfield, accompanied by William Clarke, Paget's creature, strode into that miserable cell. Clarke at once produced a document, which he pushed into Wriothesley's hands.

'A writ of liberate!' he shouted. 'Signed by the Chief Secretary, Lord Paget himself. These two are to be released unharmed and delivered into the care of Princess Mary's household.'

'Sir Anthony?' Clarke turned to Wingfield, who'd retreated back to the doorway, the keeper of the prison behind him. 'Sir Anthony, if necessary, enforce the writ.'

Wriothesley examined the document, kicked the stool over and stormed out, muttering under his breath. Clarke stood like a sparrow, head cocked slightly to one side, a smile on his lips as he listened to the clash and clatter in the passageway outside. Once this had faded, he snapped his fingers and led us out of that hellhole along a warren of putrid passageways, across filthy courtyards, through the iron-bound gates on to the great concourse before Newgate prison. We had to wait momentarily, as the death carts had just arrived back from Smithfield and Tyburn Elms crammed with the cadavers of the hanged. A truly gruesome sight with their ghastly faces, twisted necks, limbs sprawled all frozen in a cruel death. Relatives and friends were pushing forward to claim their kin, only to be beaten off by the hangmen and their assistants, whose faces remained hidden behind macabre red masks.

Jane huddled close. I shielded her eyes from such ghoulish sights. Once the carts were gone, we followed Clarke into the fleshers' markets. The day's trading was done, the market horn had sounded. The butchers had taken down the gutted flesh of pig, chicken, duck, pheasant and calves. The offal tubs were being rinsed and the misty air reeked of salt, blood and rotting meat. Bonfires, lit to consume the rubbish, had drawn in the beggars with their scraps of mucky meat that they had managed to scoop up from the cobbles. Now fastened to makeshift cooking rods, these morsels were thrust into the flames, turning the air rancid with the reek of bubbling fat. Clarke led us past, striding down Cheapside, now and again looking over his shoulder to make sure we were not being pursued, and straight into the Lamb of God, where Balaam was sitting in the inglenook, toasting himself before a roaring fire. Clarke waved us towards him as he handed over a pouch.

'Two warrants from the Council,' he grinned, 'properly sealed. These will allow you to journey without impediment or obstruction,' he paused, 'as retainers in the Princess Mary's household, both you and your woman. But,' he held up a bony finger, 'not in any other.' Then he was gone.

Balaam acted all solicitous. He could see I was wary of him; indeed I marvelled at the change. The excitable Spaniard had disappeared; now Balaam was very much the master of the scene. He called for the wash-boy to fetch bowls and napkins so we could cleanse the filth from Newgate from our faces and hands. Lady Jane was beginning to recover from the horrors Wriothesley had inflicted. Still pale and shaking, she greedily drank a deep-bowled goblet of the richest burgundy, ate some diced chicken and manchet bread and promptly fell asleep. Helped by Balaam, I carried her to the cushioned settle to the right of the hearth, then we returned to the table.

'Spanish?' I abruptly asked. 'Are you Spanish, Balaam? Are you a friend of the Council? All of them, or just one or two? Does the Princess Mary know? No,' I brushed aside his interruption, 'as I have said before to many a person, I may be a jester, but I am not stupid. To be recognised as a member of the Imperial ambassador's household you need a warrant signed by the King – if it is the dry stamp – and ratified by the Council.' I extended a hand. 'Show me that warrant.'

'Will, Will,' Balaam smiled sadly at me, 'I cannot, not now. Perhaps one day, I assure you. I have already revealed too much.'

'Why not now?' I demanded of this shifter amongst the shadows.

'Wriothesley has just apprehended you. He had the arrogant insolence to invade Greenwich Palace, force the Princess's chambers, arrest you and throw you into Newgate. I suspect he threatened and menaced you; he certainly terrified her.' Balaam gestured at the settle. 'The Lady Jane is still suffering from shock. I know people locked in Newgate for a day and a night who came out baying at the moon. What if Wriothesley or even someone else tries again, subjects you to harsh torture, peine forte et dure? You would, as I would, as any of God's creatures would, break and tell them everything they wanted. These are murky times. We are like swordsmen in the darkest room, stumbling about, lashing out. We cannot distinguish between friend and foe.'

I drank my wine. Despite the turbulence in my heart, I recognised that this enigmatic man spoke the truth; Wriothesley had proved that.

'You could be as white and as pure as rain-washed bone,' Balaam leaned closer, 'and still be guilty. Days of thunder, Will, where you could be met by a sudden shoal of ferocious furies, a swarm of menace and malice. We all walk on the edge of death's dark park. Sin and charity stand thick together in the same field; the only time we can tell the difference is when they blossom, and that time may well be close. So tell me what Wriothesley wanted.'

Satisfied that Balaam was speaking the truth, I described everything that had happened, from our leaving Greenwich to the welcoming arrival of Clarke.

'I sped hastily,' Balaam murmured. He stared pitifully at the Lady Jane. 'I was anxious lest she break.'

'Wriothesley frightened her into abject silence.'

Balaam thrust his hand out for me to clasp,; I did so and he held mine fast. 'I swear, Will, by all that is holy, if Wriothesley ever falls, I will be there.'

'God hasten that hour.'

'Amen.' Balaam withdrew his hand. 'The Council seem united except for Wriothesley.'

'He cannot plot against them,' I replied. 'He doesn't have the skill, a bully who terrorises women . . .'

'No, no.' Balaam shook his head. 'Not him, Will. This has its roots, I am sure, in that mysterious silence that clouds His Satanic Majesty's death. I just wonder what . . .' He paused. 'You know the hymn well enough.' He waved a hand. 'Henry used Wolsey to destroy Buckingham, Cromwell to destroy Wolsey, Richard Rich to destroy More. Norfolk brought Cromwell down and Henry used Howard's own family to destroy Norfolk. Subtle and sly was our late but not lamented king. Norfolk himself is not executed.'

'He was saved by Henry's death.'

'Was he?' Balaam smiled. 'I wonder. Then there is

Gardiner, abruptly exiled by the King but never really punished, and finally our good friend Wriothesley.'

'What do you wonder?' I asked.

'Was Henry cut off in the middle of yet another of his murderous plots? Is that why he ranted and raved?' Balaam drained his cup. 'Here,' he got up, 'let me help you and Lady Jane reach Greenwich safely. The night is dark and cold. A few of my roaring boys will escort us.'

15 February 1547

In the succeeding days we were all swept up in the funeral preparations. I remained anxious about the Lady Jane, who still had waking nightmares of Wriothesley and that dank, dismal cell at Newgate. No invitation to visit the royal coffin to pay their last respects was issued to the widow queen, Henry's heir or his two daughters. Mary remained silent on that, white-faced and thin-lipped. Apparently no one was allowed near that cold, rotting royal corpse. Balaam reported how the chief apothecary, Thomas Alsop, and his minions had been given a veritable treasure to buy oil and herbs for when the body was embalmed: cloves, oil and balm, musk, myrrh, cinnamon, crushed rose powder and various other spices. A lead coffin within a huge solid elm casket was also constructed. Balaam tried to question those involved in the grisly task of embalming. My master was over six foot three, whilst the weight of his body must have been well above twenty stone at his death. He had rottenness in his legs, catarrh and rheums in his nose and corruption in his belly. Surely the cleansing of all this would cause some chatter and gossip? Yet, as Balaam admitted, he might as well have asked a stone statue to sing the 'Salve Regina'.

'They are fearful,' he reported to Princess Mary. 'They will neither say nay or yea, except for what a servant girl reported. One of the halberdiers was sweet on her. He told a story of how hundreds of pounds was also spent on oil of roses and other perfumes to sweeten the air around the royal privy chambers; how a hideous stench, an offensive reek polluted the air. More than that I cannot say.'

Balaam went back to his searches but could discover nothing else. The Council was tightening its grip on both city and kingdom. Ports and harbours were under surveillance, all roads into London closely guarded, whilst the Council's Judas men were as busy as rats in a hayrick. He did discover that old Norfolk, that duke of infinite cunning, had cheated the headsman's axe by a mere breath. His death warrant had been signed by the dry stamp on Thursday 27 January; the death of the King, or so it was said, had prevented it from being served.

'I heard another story as well,' Balaam declared. 'How Norfolk had bequeathed his lands in their entirety to Prince Edward, and how the King was delighted with this. In the end, they have left him to rot.' He rubbed his hands and stretched them out to the fire burning in the great hearth of Princess Mary's chamber. 'They'll let the cold, damp rigour of the Tower drain both life and health from him.'

'I wonder,' the Princess Mary declared. 'So smooth, so serene.' She answered my quizzical look. 'I mean for Wriothesley and his coven.' She pointed at me. 'Do you really believe it, Will, the story about my father's last illness and death?'

I thought of Westminster sealed and closed like any trap, horsemen galloping here and there. Dudley hastening to Hertford. Young Edward's swift arrival into London. Beneath it all a prickling unease, that matters had been, and still were, cunningly contrived.

'No, no.' I shook my head.

'*Flectamur nec flectimur,*' Mary murmured. 'Let it go. Let us bend and bend very low lest we break, then we shall see.'

I was reluctant to talk with Balaam present. I was still deeply concerned about his loyalty. I could understand the logic of what he'd claimed in the Lamb of God, yet here was a man who had posed in the northern shires as a rebel, an outlaw, a traitor put to the horn, hunted by the likes of Paget, but who still carried that warrant signed by the King and sealed by the Council. Little wonder, I reflected, that he had never been caught. Memories came and went of how he could slip so easily in and around the city and never be taken. I recalled King Henry once discussing certain spies in France; he had bitterly joked how he was not too sure where their loyalty lay, only to answer his own question by suggesting that it probably was for the prince who paid them the most. Was Balaam one of these turncoats? On one occasion I tried to speak to the Princess Mary about it, but she simply gave that cold smile, her usual sign for a polite refusal.

Something nagged at my soul like an importunate beggar. It was like trying to recall a nightmare; it plagues your sleep but you cannot recall the details. Lady Jane eventually jogged my memory. She soon recovered from her ordeal, returning to her usual pursuits. Now the Lady Jane likes nothing better than to learn and recite poems and sonnets which catch her heart. Copies of the late Earl of Surrey's commentaries on the psalms, written during his last weeks in the Tower, were now being sold by the various print shops in the City. One morning I found her reading Surrey's commentary on Psalm 73. She was sitting in the princess's pew in the small chantry chapel made available to her mistress at Greenwich. I sat beside her as she recited the verses in that pretty clear voice of hers. The words invoked Surrey in all his passionate energy. I recalled the way he had so bravely defended himself, then I abruptly started, so much so that I sprang to my feet, staring at the Spanish crucifix, all heavily wrought and intricately carved, placed on the black-and-gold-draped altar.

'Will?'

'Spanish!' I exclaimed. 'Martin, the man who was

supposed to assist . . .' I broke off and stared down at my beloved, then kissed her absent-mindedly on the brow and left the chapel. I found a lonely window seat overlooking the gardens, still held fast in a heavy winter frost. What if, I wondered, Balaam had been Spanish Martin? He had proved he could certainly act the part, a true shape-shifter, a master of disguise. If he had, and I was becoming more certain that he did, a patron or ally on the Council, he would have found it very easy to secure the post as Surrey's servant. After all, during those last days, the earl had been deserted by friends and family. Balaam could have disguised himself as Martin and been placed at the young earl's service, but what then? Had he urged Surrey to escape and then betrayed him? But why would he show such callous ruthlessness? In truth I could find no solution to the mystery; all I could do was promise myself to be more circumspect and wary with the man with the far-seeing gaze.

I have decided to continue this journal. I want to record what truly happened from the very start of all the mystery shrouding the last days of Henry. I agree with the Princess Mary. The official story of the late king's death is both *faux et semblant*, false and dissimulating. I pick at the story as you would loose threads on a piece of cloth. I have nothing else to do, and the mystery weighs more heavily on me than the King's actual death. For all the horrors he could heap upon his own subjects,

Henry had a deeply morbid fear of death. Did he truly slip away like some shadow under the sun? I cannot understand the business of Cranmer. According to the Council, Henry had been weakening, yet they delayed sending for Cranmer, allegedly at the King's request, until it was almost too late. They claimed Cranmer was in his house at Croydon, but what was he doing there in the depths of winter? Thomas Cranmer was the King's special confessor and confidant, Archbishop of Canterbury, the man who presided over his church. He had been in Westminster on 27 January when Parliament had passed the Bill of Attainder against the Howards. Surely, I argued to myself, Cranmer would have made constant enquiries about his patron and friend the King? Why didn't he stay in Westminster to be close to his ailing master? He could have lodged at the palace, at Whitehall or any of the royal residences. Moreover, if Cranmer did not make enquiries, which I would find very strange, surely the Council, of which he was a member, would have at least informed him about the approaching crisis. Instead, like some sorry actor in a play, he was kept hidden away deep in the shadows until summoned to play his part.

And what a dramatic role was assigned to him! Hastening into London in the dead of night, reaching the King at that very moment when Henry had lost the power of speech and was slipping into death. Yet who would challenge the word of the King's friend and confidant, the Archbishop of Canterbury? Few would know that only recently Henry had toyed with the idea of sending the archbishop to the Tower, a churchman whose leanings towards the reformists in Europe were making him less and less palatable to his king. Perhaps Cranmer was not the King's favourite after all? True, he and Cromwell had helped Henry break with Rome, divorce Catherine of Aragon and marry Anne Boleyn. He had ghosted the King's conscience during the crisis. However, he had also, for a short while, tried to defend Anne Boleyn, until the King snarled at him, and had been one of those who brought Henry dire news about the loose morals and lewd living of Katherine Howard. Henry would not forget that.

The King would also have been alarmed at stories about Cranmer's private life. How his supposedly chaste archbishop, when he was a scholar, had fallen in love with a maid at the Dolphin in Cambridge. Cranmer had married her secretly and, some claimed, carried around his 'holy wench', as she was described, in a stout chest pierced with holes. Perhaps the relationship between king and archbishop had grown colder. For his part, Cranmer, for all his humility, would not have forgotten how close he had come to following the likes of Bishop Fisher of Rochester and Houghton of the Charterhouse to the Tower. Consequently, if the story of Cranmer's arrival at the royal bedside well after the eleventh hour was a fable, Cranmer himself must have been party to such a fiction. Despite all the claims of close friendship, had the archbishop grown fearful of his king? And what would that fear induce him to do? Be party to a conspiracy involving others on the Council about the last days of their dread royal master? Was this what Wriothesley meant by his enigmatic reference to 'the monster' screaming and ranting during his final hours? Or was this just the vain imaginings of a sick, sad soul?

Moreover, why were Henry's wife and three children never brought to see him, either alive or dead? Were the Council trying to hide something? Even criminals condemned to death are allowed the courtesy of a visit from family and kin. To be sure, Henry's relationship with his wife might not have been harmonious, but his beloved son and heir? Mary and Elizabeth, whose rights he had so jealously safeguarded in his will? I recall Balaam's words about those paintings of Henry that emphasise the importance of his family. I could also plead my own case; I was close to the King but still cruelly excluded from his last hours.

I continued to listen carefully to chatter about the funeral preparations. Henry had published detailed plans for his burial in St George's Chapel, Windsor, the resting place of his grandfather, the Yorkist Edward IV, as well as of his beloved Jane Seymour. Wolsey, God rest him, had chosen the same place and commissioned the construction of a massive black marble sarcophagus. Henry had promptly seized this for his own use, yet all this was to be ignored. Henry would be laid to rest next to his beloved Jane, her brothers would see to that, but the coffin would be that speedily constructed lead shell in its elm wood case. There would be no lying in state, no viewing of the corpse. Haste was the order of the day. According to the published account, the apothecaries, surgeons and wax chandlers went swiftly about their business, sponging, cleansing, waxing, embalming and furnishing the royal corpse. By 1 February, the dead king's bowels and entrails had been removed, hastily encased in a chest and swiftly buried beneath the flagstones of Westminster Palace chapel. I could only imagine the embalmers busy digging and cutting the mouldering, messy flesh. Nonetheless, I was deeply surprised at their speed. The embalmed corpse, wrapped in thick velvet and samite sheets and bound with silk cord, was sheeted in its lead shell and placed in its wooden casket.

On the eve of Candlemas, 2 February, the entire coffin under its rich gold pall was brought to the prepared and lavishly decorated royal hearse standing in the royal chapel, the entire church hung in black cloth of the most precious fabric decorated with the King's arms and royal insignia. The hearse was ringed by eighty candles, each two foot high; all about it hung more banners, pennants and other heraldic cloths depicting the royal descent. The floor of the chapel was covered in black cloth, whilst at each corner of the hearse, more gorgeous tapestries celebrated the lives of St George, Edward the Confessor and others. An altar bearing a weight of silver and gold holy vessels stood at the foot of the hearse so that requiem masses could be celebrated continuously. The massive rail around the hearse also included twelve pews or stalls, three on each side, for the twelve principle mourners, led by that nonentity Henry Gray, Marquis of Dorset, garbed like the other eleven in special mourning habit, hood, mantle and gown.

Such preparations pricked my suspicions. The royal corpse left the King's secret chambers late on the afternoon of 2 February. Henry had died early on Friday morning of the previous week, but this had not been made public until the Monday, 31 January. Now of course preparations for the funeral may have been initiated secretly; even so the haste must have exhausted the apothecaries, carpenters and other workmen. Or had Henry really died much earlier? I was also surprised that Bishop Gardiner was designated as the chief celebrant bishop, ostensibly because he was the leading prelate in the Order of the Garter. More pertinently, he was a Romanist in persuasion and would not refuse to celebrate the sacrifice of the mass. Cranmer, Latimer and the other reformist bishops certainly would have refused. On reflection, the Council was playing a subtle game. They had tightly controlled the King, both alive and dead, during that last week of January. Now that he was gone, the breath out of his body, his corpse so swiftly hidden away, Dudley, Wriothesley and the rest seemed eager to draw in others. They deliberately did not appropriate rank and status for themselves in the funeral obsequies, but ceded these to other nobles such as Dorset, Oxford and Shrewsbury.

In the end, the King's coffin lay in state at Westminster Palace chapel for days, draped in gorgeous cloths brilliantly lit by thousands of pounds of sweet-smelling beeswax. Again the Council seemed eager to distract attention from those secret, furtive days at the end of January. No expense was spared. Ceremonies were ornate and rich. The mourners regularly gathered, suitably garbed in the pallet chamber, the bishops in all their pontificals in the sacristy. Requiem prayers were recited. The Dirige and Placebo psalms were sung. Both coffin and hearse were incensed till they were hidden beneath the sacred smoke. The Norroy King of Arms would repeatedly declare, voice ringing through that chapel: 'Of your charity pray for the soul of the High and Most Mighty Prince, our late Sovereign, Lord and King, Henry VIII.' I certainly did. Clustered with the Princess Mary and her small retinue I stood in that magnificent chapel bathed in half-light, clouds of incense drifting, bells clanging ominously, the sparking of flames shimmering in the oak and elm of the hearse and glittering in the costly silver and gold thread of the splendid funeral drapes and tapestries. The solemn requiem masses were sung, followed by votive masses to Our Lady, the celebrants vested in white, then those of the Trinity in the liturgical blue, followed once again by black-garbed priests chanting the continuous requiems.

Outside, in the City, thousands of poor Londoners gathered in Cornhill and Leadenhall to receive the royal alms of a groat each in memory of the King, a prompt to pray for the repose of his soul. This almsgiving lasted for most of the day, whilst the churches in every ward of London observed the funeral rite; this was followed by a similar liturgy in churches throughout the kingdom as couriers galloped along the roads spreading the news. The same messengers also carried orders to clear the highways between Westminster and Windsor of over-hanging boughs, overgrown hedges and anything else that might impede the planned progress of the royal coffin. Bridges were to be checked and repaired. Huge panels, decorated splendidly with the royal arms, were dispatched to scores of parishes along the route, along with sacks of grain to dole out to the parish poor so they would pray for the dead king's soul. God knows, he would need every prayer.

On 14 February, the funeral cortege left Westminster. The coffin was carried on a great gilded chariot, on its top a life-size effigy of the King. At Charing Cross an escort garbed entirely in rich black livery gathered to conduct the coffin out of the City, a majestic column of over a thousand mounted men and a similar number on foot all carrying torches. I, following the Princess Mary, was able to get close to the hearse to pay my respects, the closest I'd been since my imposed exile. Once again I was struck by the lavish preparations. If I had had my doubts about the Council's treatment of the King, I was now cynically convinced that they were determined to honour him in death, or at least publicly so. The effigy was dreamlike. A direct imitation of a king, on its head a black satin night cap over which had been placed the Crown Imperial, with collars of the Order of the Garter around its throat and thighs; gold bracelets, studded with pearls and jewels, circled each wrist. On one side of the King lay his sword, whilst in either hand rested the orb and sceptre of state.

We left Charing Cross, porters armed with heavy staves going before the funeral procession to clear the way. Hundreds of beadsmen garbed in funeral weeds chanted the psalms for the dead. Behind these came the banner men, their gorgeous standards displaying the red dragon of Tudor, the greyhound of Lancaster and the King's own household banner. A mass of people followed these: standard-bearing heralds with grooms leading the King's destrier, caparisoned in flowing cloth of gold, all ringed by the Spears dressed completely in black, halberds resting on their shoulders. Nonetheless, a cold, bitter, nerve-jarring journey. I kept myself cowled and cloaked as we processed across a countryside frozen in the icy grip of a frost so harsh it seemed it would never break.

17 February 1547

I have just reread what I have written. It was a pageant well devised by those cunning cozeners of the Council, I am sure it was. They were eager to divert attention from the secrecy surrounding the King's death with this public display over his burial. It was also a prologue to what was about to be played out at Syon on Thames, where the King's corpse rested on its final journey. We reached the former Bridgettine convent early in the afternoon, passing through lines of London aldermen to the great west door of the church, under its double arch and into the nave. Here the coffin was placed on the prepared gilded hearse. Standards were raised, candles lit, psalms sung and masses celebrated. Darkness fell and the horrors erupted.

The King's coffin was left on its hearse in that convent chapel. I considered the place to be an ironic choice: the King had roughly dispossessed its nuns, whilst his disgraced queen, Katherine Howard, had been imprisoned there after the scandal of her amours became public. Indeed, the King's coffin arrived at Syon on the fifth anniversary of that hapless queen's execution. Such a bloody memory quickened my own sense of deep dread at entering that ghostly place. I was lodged for the night with Princess Mary's household. I could not sleep, but tossed and turned. Eventually I made my way to the church, where the corpse door hung open. Inside, the nave was clothed in the deepest darkness except for a circle of light around the elaborate hearse and the coffin it supported. Countless candles fed this floating pool of glowing light. Other mourners had entered the church to conduct their own private death vigil. None of the lords of the soil; perhaps just the curious who wanted to tell their grandchildren how they had prayed at the midnight hour for the great Henry.

I crouched by a pillar and stared down at the funeral hearse. Once again I was close to my master. I dozed. I pondered memories. I said my prayers. I suppose I was half asleep, so I cannot truly describe what actually happened. I recall pulling my cloak closer around me and wishing I'd brought a blanket. The church was freezing cold despite the braziers crammed with blazing coal that stood around the nave. I moved to be more comfortable on the cushion, my only protection against an icy dampness which seeped through the ancient cracked paving stones. I tugged at the heavy cloak and pulled at my cowl, watching a freezing mist creep under the doors, its tendrils moving like ghostly fingers.

Suddenly I heard a crack, a wrenching from the direction of the glowing candles, followed by a heavy thudding, as if something had slipped and fallen. I half rose. Others, sleeping in their vigil, also stirred. The strange creaking from the candle-ringed hearse continued, then silence. The barriers protecting the coffin were high, providing a broad enclosure around it. As I crept carefully towards them, a most horrid stench caught my nostrils, an odour so foul it made my gorge rise till I began to gag and retch. From the coughing and spluttering echoing around me, others had also noticed this rank, fetid smell. God forgive me. The creeping horror of that nave killed all grief: that monstrous hearse rising up above the glow of candles, the sharp echoing of those strange noises, the foulsome stench of corruption heavy on the draughts that seeped through that ancient place. I stared at the huge dark mass of wood, gold, silver and steel which made up the late King's funeral ornaments. I guessed what had happened. The rotting, bloated corpse had swollen and burst so fiercely it must have wrenched open the lead coffin and the elm wood casket that contained it. I crept closer to the barrier and looked over. The offensive odour was almost impossible to bear. I heard the drip, drip of putrid matter seeping out and glimpsed the filthy puddles which caught the light. I could take no more. I turned, as the others did, and fled.

The following morning, after a fitful sleep in my narrow chamber in the old Bridgettine guest house, I stepped over the sleeping bodies of the two chancery clerks I shared the chamber with. Cloaked and booted, I made my way down across the mist-hung cobbles towards the convent church. A grey, cold morning. The only sound was the raucous cawing of the rooks and ravens that thronged the winter trees, their stark branches stretching like black fingers against the sky. At first I thought everything lay under a pall of silence, only to find the lychgate closely guarded by halberdiers. Through the shifting mist I could see others clustered around every door to the church. The halberdiers were grim and abrupt. No one could enter. I returned to my chamber, unlocked the small coffer I had hidden away and took out some silver. I returned and took up position where I could observe both corpse door and lychgate. The guards were now turning mourners away, telling them that there would be some delay before the funeral procession recommenced, as one of the poles on the hearse had snapped and had to be rectified. Everyone accepted this. I did not.

The morning drew on. The mist lifted. Eventually the corpse door opened and two royal serjeants of the carpentry hurried out. A short while later a local workman, by his smock and leggings, a felt cap pulled over his eyes, also departed. He carried a leather sack in one hand and a basket of tools in the other. I followed him as he left the convent and crossed the trackway. Ahead of him I could glimpse through the bare branches of the trees a tavern sign, the Keys of the Kingdom. By the time I entered the tangy, warm taproom, my quarry was seated on a bench before a roaring fire. It was still rather early; the taproom was fairly empty. I ordered a bowl of hot steaming oatmeal laced with honey and went to sit next to him. He introduced himself as William Consett, plumber. I gave him a false name, gossiped for a while, then put my bowl down. I took out some of my silver coins and placed them on the small trancher across my lap. Consett, red face all blistered by the cold, dark eyes watery, sniffed and gave a wry smile.

'I wondered what you wanted, and it isn't your pots and pans repaired.'

'The coffin in the church,' I replied.

'I was sworn to secrecy.'

I leaned closer and smelt the costly perfume generously daubed on his face, neck and clothes.

'They made you wash your hands and face thoroughly,' I whispered. 'Your gloves and apron were seized and burnt. They sprinkled you with perfume and, of course, you were generously recompensed.' Consett stared unblinkingly at me. 'I was there when it happened during the night,' I continued. 'The wooden casket and lead coffin within burst asunder, didn't they? The stench must have been hideous. You must have masked your nose and mouth with cloths soaked in spices.' I gestured at his blackjack of ale. 'Turned your stomach, didn't it? That's why you are not breaking your fast. The silver is yours. You will not be violating your oath but simply confirming what I suspect. You, my friend, can take the coins and I swear by all that is holy that you will not hear or see me ever again.'

Consett licked his lips, one hand going for the silver; I knocked it away. 'Yes or no?'

'Yes,' he breathed. 'I cannot say whether it was the jogging and shaking of the chariot or,' he glanced over his shoulder, 'the effect of some other cause. Anyway, both lead coffin and casket were ripped open, cut apart, corrupt body fat and putrefied blood seeped out on to the floor beneath. Fortunately the thick black cloths beneath the hearse soaked up this squalid mess. These were pulled away, heaped in barrows and taken out to be buried on the other side of the church. Fresh cloths soaked in all sorts of heavy perfume were brought in.'

'But the corrupt matter must have continued to trickle out?'

'A large tub, the type a washerwoman uses, was placed just beneath where the coffin was cracked. The rupture ran across the top and down one side.' He took a sip of ale. 'It was like working in a cesspit, a slimy mound of human mess. I used heavy cloths and some wood to plug the gap and repair what I could.' He waved his hands. 'Cloths, wood, sacks of sawdust and glue. Once I'd finished, others took over. The crack is now hidden by the heavy funeral drapes. They doused everything in all forms of fragrances, the fabric soaked in crushed herbs; huge pots of smoking incense were also brought in. They will hurry him to his grave now.'

'Who was in charge of this?'

'One lord looks very much like another,' he jibed, 'especially in a darkened church.'

I dug into my purse and brought out two more silver coins and placed these alongside the rest.

'Three in particular,' the fellow gabbled swiftly. 'My lords Wriothesley, Dudley and Paget. There may have been two more.' He shrugged. 'They said very little, at least in my hearing and that of the carpenters. When I had finished, Wriothesley took me up into the sanctuary, forced my hand against the Book of the Gospel and swore me to silence. I am of the old faith, master, and its ancient ways. I am learned in the horn book. Any oath taken under duress has no force either in the sight of God or man.' He moved closer, fingers not far from the pile of silver. 'There is something else,' he whispered. 'I was brought into the church during the early hours. By then, the mourners had been dismissed. They opened all the doors because of the great stink. Now the convent used to house a pack of lurchers; they still haunt their former kennels, more wild than tame. Anyway,' he picked up one of the coins, 'three of these lurchers crept into the church and managed to skulk beneath the hearse. They were lapping up the putrid mess. It took some time to drive them away.' My stomach protested at the gruesome story; no wonder Consett was not eating. I rose swiftly, trying to curb the urge to vomit. I gestured at the silver and hurried to the door leading to the privy.

When I returned, both Consett and the silver were gone.

God be my witness, I was shocked at what he had told me, as well as haunted by a sinister memory. Over a decade earlier, King Henry and his new wife Anne Boleyn had been staying at Greenwich, where the Franciscans had a house. One of these, Father Peto – now Cardinal Peto after he fled the kingdom to escape Henry's wrath – in a sermon before His Majesty compared him to Ahab the wicked king of Israel. Peto had warned Henry to his face how if he did not take greater care, he, like Ahab, would meet a macabre end and the dogs would come to lap his blood. A true prophecy? Had the King's coffin been deliberately damaged to give Peto's prediction a helping hand? Yet I'd been there in that gloomy nave when the corpse had burst asunder. Nobody had approached it. What was the true cause? Particularly if Henry's corpse had been so properly embalmed, crammed with the costliest spices by the most skilled in the kingdom?

I returned to the Bridgettine convent, seeking to speak privately to Princess Mary. We met in what used to be the prioress's cell, a cavernous, shadow-filled chamber with a writhing white Christ nailed to a cross against the wall. The princess, dressed completely in black except for frothy lace at her neck and cuffs, seemed distant. Her long, narrow face was unpainted, her red hair clasped tight to her head under a black veil; Ave beads, her mother's, curled around her fingers. She sat on a box chair with me on a stool before her like priest and penitent at the mercy pew. I told her what I'd seen, heard, witnessed and felt. She dragged thin fingers down her face and muttered in Spanish, blinking swiftly to hide her tears.

'I remember Peto's curse,' she confessed. 'Many would say it has come to pass. But what caused it, Will? What did happen in my father's secret chambers?' She beat her fists against her knees.

'They cannot have properly embalmed him,' I replied. 'Your father, according to the official record, died fifteen days ago. Thousands of pounds were spent purchasing a mass of spices, embalming fluids, herbs and other materials. The most skilled practitioners worked on his corpse. His Majesty was a man of massive proportions. If his corpse had not been prepared properly, then it would bloat, swell and burst, surely, the strength of the rupture so great it would shatter both wood and lead. And yet, as I have said, the body was supposedly embalmed.'

'Or so we think.'

'I agree. Did they really honour his corpse, or was your father's cadaver thrust into its lead shell and wooden casing unprepared and swollen? Your Grace, you did not view the corpse. I cannot discover anyone who actually did. In short, I do not think the circumstances of your father's death are as the official proclamation described them.' I then confessed my doubts about Thomas Seymour being sworn to the Council, whilst the story about Cranmer's intervention well past the eleventh hour also seemed highly suspect.

'This present pandering,' I concluded, 'this charade is to satisfy the public whim. The churching, the prattling of requiem psalms, the masses are a liturgical sham. Where is the black marble sarcophagus your father wished to be interred in? Oh, banners fly, heralds chant, priests pray, but Your Grace, the King's death is proclaimed on a Monday, then, unseen by anyone, his corpse is coffined away by Wednesday. Now of course the Council can take its time. What the eye doesn't see, the heart can't wonder about. What happened last night must have agitated those who know the truth.'

'I agree,' Mary replied. 'Gardiner has told me how the Council have enriched themselves; my father's will virtually bribes everyone. There are gifts and grants to me and the Princess Elizabeth. Queen Katherine Parr may not be regent but she is well endowed and, if rumour be correct, already playing cat's cradle with Thomas Seymour. Oh yes,' she smiled at my surprise, 'have you noticed how the Queen both at Greenwich and on this funeral march has kept very close, deep in the shadows? That is the best way to meet her lover. There's more. According to Paget, the King promised generous grants to others on the Council, lordships of certain manors, estates, rents and revenues. Not only that, all the doctors and apothecaries, commoners like the doorkeeper Roberts, are also to be well rewarded.'

'Except me!' I declared.

'Yes, but they know that you live by the truth, whilst they are practising a great lie.'

'How are they justifying this?' I asked.

'Gardiner tells me all. Old Norfolk is not to be executed; they will leave him to the mercies of the Tower. However, to answer your question, Paget maintains that all these generous grants were recorded in a small black book which the King kept in the pocket of his gown. Of course this book can't be found, but Paget can recall every detail. Seymour is to be made Duke of Somerset, Dudley Earl of Warwick, Wriothesley Earl of Southampton. The Council was to be the protectorate, but according to Gardiner, some of them are already calling Seymour the Lord Great Master; he is set to become regent or protector. The rest of the Council and others will be bribed, more grants lavishly issued under the dry stamp.' Mary rubbed her face. 'The elder Seymour will be king in all but name. Of course that will not go unchecked. The other wolves, Wriothesley in particular, are already beginning to howl in protest.'

'Your Grace, they may have used the dry stamp without your father's knowledge, or even had a second one fashioned unbeknown to him.'

'It does not matter now, Will. Gardiner is correct. Power, money, honours, titles, Crown lands, offices and benefices pour like a waterfall over the Council.' She waved a hand. 'You are right: this farce of a funeral is very clever. The great lords hide in the background. The disgraced Gardiner leads the services, which are Catholic in both form and substance. Cranmer cannot be seen. The likes of Dorset lead the mourners. I want to know what is behind this charade. My father, his death? The dead are dead,' she added wearily. She bent closer; the redness in her cheeks had gone. I could see the dark shadows beneath her eyes; even the gorgeous hair beneath its beautiful bejewelled cap seemed to have faded. 'What they did to my father haunts my every waking moment and troubles my sleep. Did they abuse him? Yet behind that lurks another horror. If they could do that to the great Henry, what about me? Catherine of Aragon's Spanish brat, cast off by her father, once declared illegitimate? Am I to be forced into a loveless marriage to some German princeling in the frozen wastes of Prussia? Will I disappear into the Tower, suffer a fatal accident or rise from a banquet vomiting black bile?'

'Your Grace, Your Grace.' I tried to calm her, but Mary was locked into her mood of desperate imaginings.

'Do you think Dudley, Seymour or Cranmer will let me succeed? Cranmer, who dissolved my mother's marriage and pronounced me illegitimate? Dudley and Seymour, who favour the teachings of Geneva and Zurich? Edward my brother is frail; he may well die without an heir. I don't think they will turn to Catholic Spanish Mary or even my half-sister Elizabeth; Seymour would never accept her, nor she him. His sister caused the downfall of Elizabeth's mother.' Mary wrapped the Ave beads more tightly around her fingers and stroked her nose, a common mannerism whenever she becomes highly agitated. 'We have to be careful, Will, prudent. Tell no one else about what you know.' She rose to her feet. 'Let us finish this charade, this hypocrisy, and await our time.'

I took an oath that day to be careful and prudent. I will be most strict in its observance. The sham funeral with all its mock mourning continued. On Monday 15 February, the cortege left for Windsor to be greeted by a dozen white-coated knights as well as scholars from Our Lady's College at Eton. The coffin moved through the town in a sanctified atmosphere, prayers, psalms, chants, hymns and gusts of incense. In the Chapel of St George, the coffin was placed on its three-storey hearse all draped in black and gold. Masses continued to be offered in the nearby chantry chapels, culminating in a solemn requiem presided over by Bishop Gardiner. The climax of this was when the King's Serjeant of Arms, Chiddick Paul, rode in full armour, except for his helmet, into the choir and placed the King's pole-axe, point down, on the altar, where it lay on richly embroidered cloths. The mass continued. After the Gospel, Gardiner delivered a homily on the frailty of man and how the King's death was a most dolorous and heart-wounding loss. I was standing amongst the Princess Mary's ladies in the choir loft and could hardly keep a straight face at the sheer hypocrisy of being told I should thank the Almighty for having bestowed upon us 'such a Virtuous Prince'.

This Virtuous Prince, this much-trumpeted Mirror of Justice was finally laid to rest. The elaborate effigy was moved to the sacristy. Gardiner and his bishops chanted the verse 'The snares of death have surrounded me' as they left the altar. The chapel vault was opened to reveal Queen Jane Seymour's coffin. Fifteen strong Yeomen of the Guard in parties of three used coiled linen ropes to lower Henry's massive coffin down into the darkness. The bishops scattered the dust of Ash Wednesday as they loudly recited the ominous verse 'Remember man that thou art dust, and unto dust thou shalt return'. God be my witness, if there was one verse Henry didn't remember, let alone reflect on, that was it. Members of the King's privy chamber, led by Paget, then broke their white staves of office above their heads and hurled the shards into the vault. I watched Paget and Gates. Oh, they played the part, their faces heavy with sorrow, loud sighs, mumbled words of grief as the tears rolled down their cheeks. To be honest, I suspect these were more due to genuine relief than any mourning. The vault was then covered with planks. The business was finished. There would be no black marble sarcophagus, no elaborate monument or finely carved statue fashioned by the finest craftsmen out of Italy; nothing at all!

The Garter King of Arms, surrounded by all the other heralds, proclaimed the accession of Prince Edward, but already the grooms of the King's chamber were grabbing at the costly funeral cloths of precious material woven with silver and gold and studded with miniature diamonds. They would later share these out. Even as the trumpets blared gloriously for Prince Edward, Dudley was crossing the chapel to claim the great ceremonial chair draped in purple velvet and silk with its three blue cushions of precious taffeta. Others, hungry for food and drink, were bustling towards the door and the gallery leading down to the castle refectory. Here the lords of the Council gorged themselves on the finest wines and delicious food. I watched them stuff their maws, then, bellies full and warm, they collected their cloaks, went down to the bailey, swung themselves up into the saddles of the finest horses from Henry's stables and thundered swiftly back along the road to London.

Later that day, with the falling snow freezing hard and a grey dusk moving swiftly in over Windsor, I left my narrow chamber in one of the garden towers and made my way back to St George's Chapel. All was in disarray. Chairs and stools lay overturned, scraps of parchment littered the floor. The King's once magnificent effigy rested face down in the sacristy. I turned it over. This effigy was a goodly image, similar to the late king in all aspects, but now it looked battered. The black silk cap, gold crown and precious garters around throat and thigh had been torn away along with anything else of value. Someone, as a grim joke, had gouged out the eyes in the waxen mask and inserted two small roundels of charcoal, pulling down the lips on either side so it looked more like the face of a hell hound than anything else.

The candles were guttering out, though there were so many, the light was still strong. I crossed to the burial vault, moved the planks, took the workmen's ladder from the sacristy and thrust it down into that burial pit. Then I grabbed a sconce torch and carefully descended into the icy blackness. The vault is about eight feet wide and the same deep. I reached the bottom and stood holding up the torch, its glow glittering on the purple pall of the coffin. I rolled this back. Even as I did, I caught traces of that same filthy stench I had smelt at Syon. I lifted the torch. The top of the casket had been roughly and swiftly repaired. I touched the extra pieces of wood inserted in the crack and felt the bulge along the top of the coffin, proof enough that both the corpse and its lead sheath within had swollen, then erupted. I took my hand away and carefully sniffed at where the repairs had been effected. The stench was strong but so was that of the aromatics hastily packed into every crevice. I pulled back the pall, positioning it correctly, then closed my eyes and crossed myself. I had come to pay my last respects. I opened my eyes and stared at the coffin. Here lay a king, a monster I had known and served for over twenty years. All his passions, his lusts, his loves, his hates, his dreams of empire had ended here in this lonely, dark, freezing vault.

'Sic transit gloria mundi' – 'Thus passes all the glory of the world' – and 'Remember man that thou art dust, and unto dust thou shalt return'. Henry, the fearsome, ferocious, fickle lion, lies dead and buried, his plotting brought to a sudden end, his death sprung like a trap. I suppose I was obsessed with him as you would be with a half-remembered fear-drenched nightmare. He, in turn, was obsessed with himself and his kingdom to the point that Henry became England and England Henry. Now he is gone, what shall I do? Hide, probably; hide well away from the wolf pack. My days of courtly dalliance are over. Henry is gone and he will never return.

'I am sorry.' I spoke out loud. 'Your Majesty, I am so sorry that I could not make a proper farewell.' I thought of his councillors, bellies full, bodies warmed, galloping back to London to celebrate their new-found wealth, power, status and titles. 'God rest you. God bless you,' I whispered. 'God assoil you, Henry of England.' Then I crossed myself and climbed the ladder, pulling it up after me.

I returned to this chamber, warming my fingers over a chafing dish, reflecting on what had happened and wondering what the future held. Henry is dead. I promised to keep a journal. Now that he is gone, there is no need to continue, not unless I learn the truth. I shall end it here, 17 February, the Year of Our Lord 1547, at Windsor Castle.

29 September 1553

Queen Mary is crowned! England's rightful monarch is triumphant! The plotting of vipers and the cunning of other serpents has been brought to nothing. On 27 September, the day before her coronation, my beloved Queen Mary rode through the City of London to Westminster, sitting in a chariot of cloth-of-gold tissue, drawn by six horses caparisoned with the same. She was attired in a gown of purple velvet, furred with powdered ermine. On her head a caul of cloth tinsel set with pearls and stones, above this a round circlet of gold, so richly studded with precious stones that its value is inestimable. So ponderous were both caul and circlet that the Queen was obliged to bear up her head with her hand. Over the chariot was a canopy of state borne by yeomen dressed in red and gold . . .

Today, Michaelmas, the day following Queen Mary's coronation, I, Will Somers, dressed in my favourite brown and green cloak fringed with squirrel fur, my hair shorn, my face shaved and oiled, a new pair of Cordovan boots on my feet, a gift from the Queen, sauntered into the Pegasus of France, a spacious red-walled, black-tiled tavern close to the ruins of St Mary Grace's Abbey, a mere arrow shot from the harsh fastness of the Tower. Her Majesty had sent me there with all the warrants I would need to meet that shadow from her household, Master Balaam, fresh out of Flanders, Venice, Madrid, or wherever that flitting shade has travelled on Her Majesty's business. Fortune's wheel has surely turned, spinning violently to set the world upside down. The Seymours, Sir John Gates, Dudley, Denny and others are gone, as is their master, poor Edward the boy king. Bishop Hooper once remarked how the young monarch might become the terror and the wonder of the world, if he lived. He did not. Earlier this year, around midsummer, Edward, already wasting away, his ulcerated body mere skin and bone, lapsed into paralysis and unconsciousness. When he awoke, he coughed black sputum, which exuded the most offensive and putrid smell, and both his hair and nails dropped out. So desperate became the physicians that they foolishly allowed a so-called wise woman to give Edward potions, but these only made his shrunken body puff out and so choked off his vital parts. The poor young man, God rest him, died in agony on 6 July last. John Dudley, Viscount Lisle, who styled himself Earl of Warwick before elevating himself to be Duke of

Northumberland, realised that Edward's death would mean his ruin. Dudley tried to change Henry's will by publishing a so-called 'Device for the Succession', inserting that Edward's legitimate successor should be Henry's niece and Dudley's own daughter-in-law the Lady Jane Grey, and her heirs. A period of turbulence and thunder followed. Soldiers marching the roads, warships gathering off the Thames, castles fortified, the drums of war loudly beating.

In the end no one accepted either Dudley, or the Lady Jane Grey as Queen. I was with the Princess Mary when her brother died. She retreated to Framlingham in Norfolk, where she raised her standard, declaring herself to be true queen, the daughter of King Henry and, by his will and the law of Parliament, the legitimate successor to her brother's crown. The kingdom responded. Ships at Yarmouth declared for Mary. Troops raised in the shires hailed her name. The Council locked in the Tower broke out of Dudley's prison and proclaimed the same. London rose in rebellion, tearing down the usurpers' standards and great cloths of state. Dudley himself advanced to Cambridge, where he acknowledged his failure. Already his allies on the Council had deserted him, riding into Mary's camp to submit on their knees, their own daggers turned towards them. I truly enjoyed that. Paget was one of them!

Now the victorious queen had sent me secretly to this tavern where I was to await Balaam. In truth, I was highly nervous. Since the death of Henry, my beloved Jane and I had sheltered, or more correctly hidden, in the Princess Mary's household, well away from the swirling fog of London and the deadly miasma of the court, moving to Beaulieu and other lonely manors close to the Essex coast. The black water of Maldon, the stony beaches of Walton and the windswept Orwell estuary became as familiar to me as the frenetic busyness of Cheapside and Poultry. Of course we had news and heard the gossip and chatter, yet they were hard, difficult years as Princess Mary fought a lonely battle to maintain her faith, her independence and her rights. Balaam had virtually disappeared. In London he could move easily amongst a shoal of people; he could act the part and stride the boards. But in those lonely Essex manors, every going and coming was brought under the most careful scrutiny of the Council's Judas men.

Balaam, I understood from Princess Mary, became very busy in foreign parts. He played a leading role in the preparations to spirit the princess abroad after she had defied the Council on matters of religion. Dudley and the rest regarded her 'as a runnel whereby the rats of Rome could re-enter the kingdom'. They mocked the bowing and genuflecting of her priests as the gesturing of apes and ridiculed the Sacrament as 'Round Robin' or 'Jack-in-the-box', whilst her chaplains were insultingly dismissed as 'the whores of ancient Babylon'. Mary's agents, couriers and spies like Balaam fared no better, being described as 'the Misty Angels of Satan'.

Rewards were posted on their heads, especially after Corneille Scheperus and eight imperial warships hovered close off the Essex coast ready to take Mary off should she decide to flee. Instead she stood her ground, despite the bullying of the Council, who had the impudence to claim that she was subject to their will and should not attend mass. The princess roundly replied that she was subject to their will only in the matter of her marriage, and if they were right in their remembrance of her father's will as she was, they should have two masses celebrated every day for the repose of the late king's soul. Princess Mary has spent these last six years hurling stones against the wind, yet she has remained constant. Now, miraculously, in three months, her fortunes, all our fortunes have changed. I suspect the man with the far-seeing gaze has played his part in this.

I entered the red-walled garden of the tavern, a sheer square of sweet-smelling beauty. Late September is best enjoyed amongst the flowers as they come to full blossom. I love this season of the year, when you can catch the shift, the bridge between summer and the delicate onset of autumn. I certainly did in that garden, with its aromatic herb plots, brilliant flower beds and small orchard of perfumed apple trees, the fragrance of their full fruit ripening the air with its sweetness. I would have liked my beloved Jane by my side, but ever since that hideous business with Wriothesley in Newgate, the Lady Jane had begged me not to include her in what she calls my 'secret affairs'. She was now happily closeted with the mistress she adores and loves, revelling in her new-found status. The six years and more since Henry's death have been oppressive, so walking into that garden, sure and certain of the full support of the Crown, was like being liberated from a noisy, foulsome prison. I also nourished a ravenous curiosity. I suspected I was there to bring certain matters to a close, particularly the mystery surrounding Henry's death.

Balaam had not arrived, so I hired a small enclave in the garden, secret and private, a three-sided arbour, its trellis fencing covered by the most fragrant-smelling roses. A very comfortable place with stout wooden chairs, their arms, backs and seats cushioned by thick flock pushed into dark blue felt, the table heavy and well polished. Mine host the tavern master brought snow-white napery, gleaming tranchers and pewter goblets for 'the purest water' from the nearby abbey well, together with a jug of the finest Rhenish. I sat cradling my cup, lost in my own thoughts, until a shadow blocked out the sun. Balaam stood in the entrance, dressed like a fighting man in a cream-coloured shirt, a leather sleeveless jerkin and light green hose pushed into the most elegant riding boots. He unstrapped his heavy war belt with its basket-hilt sword and iron-coiled dagger, winked at me and placed these carefully on the ground. He beckoned me to stand. We embraced and exchanged the kiss of peace, then he pushed me gently away, studying me from head to toe.

'You look a little older, Will, though the years have not broken you.'

I stared back. Balaam was darker-skinned, his hair neatly cut like that of a soldier, his cunning, sallow face clean-shaven, oiled and perfumed. He still had that lazy, cynical glance, as if he knew the world for what it was and did not trust it. Oh I have glimpsed him over the years, but until that moment in the garden he was just a shadow scurrying amongst other shadows as the Princess Mary eked out her dangerous existence. But as I have written, the object of this journal is to bring matters to a close; that is why I have returned to it. The full reckoning had yet to be known about my master's death. Deep in my heart I suspected that was why we were there.

For a while Balaam and I just sat and shared the wine, reminiscing and recalling. Balaam had been everywhere, even hinting that he had visited the New World. He was certainly full of stories, so extraordinary I wondered if he was telling tales like any moon man; all the time he studied me sharply, leaning over to grasp my hand or staring at me over the rim of his cup. At last he fell silent, tapping his thigh with his fingers as if listening to music I could not hear. He shifted in his seat, then turned back.

'Will, towards the end you did not trust me.' He jabbed a finger. 'You still don't.'

'For whom did you really work?'

'You will see soon enough.' The thin smile disappeared.

'First, though, I kept my promise. The dog is long dead, his soul thrust down to Hell.'

'Which dog?' I mocked.

'Wriothesley.'

'He died peacefully at his house at Ely Place, Holborn.'

'Oh yes, Baron Wriothesley, freshly created Earl of Southampton after his master's death, mad as a March hare and malicious as a demon.'

'He was disgraced,' I replied.

'True, on some trumped-up charge that could be levelled at any Lord Chancellor: misuse of the office of the Great Seal. He was placed under house arrest.' Balaam put his cup down and leaned closer. 'I visited him late one summer afternoon. I slipped like the vengeance I was into that deserted house, the scene of his former glory. The very hall where he and the other self-devouring monsters trapped and baited the hapless Surrey.' He ran a finger along the rim of his goblet. 'Wriothesley was disgraced, finished. No one truly trusted him.' He waved his hand. 'He hopped like a flea on a hot skillet, this way, that way. He was also prone to lunacy, though when clear-witted was dangerous enough. I am sure you will hear more of that soon.'

'What do you mean?'

'In a while, my friend, but back to Wriothesley. I had not forgotten how he terrified you and the Lady Jane, one of the main reasons for my visit. I pretended to be from the Council. Wriothesley, unshaven, half drunk, blubbering like a babe, welcomed me himself; his servants had long fled, taking whatever they could. Eventually he brought me into that hall; indeed I asked him to. Chattering like a friendly sparrow, I sat where Surrey had sat. I poured the wine. I toasted him to the rafters. I extolled his great work, his endless labours for the Crown. How he had not been truly appreciated, but future glory certainly beckoned. Oh, how he revelled in that! A dismal place, Will. Unpolished and ill-swept, the dust mites dancing like a host of demons in the streaks of sunlight. A summer's day, but that hall was gloomy. I wondered if the ghosts of Wriothesley's victims were beginning to gather. Of course, he just wallowed like a pig in its sty. Sottish with drink, he confessed how his sleep and waking hours were plagued by sweat-drenched nightmares. I cheered him up and told him not be frightened of shadows.'

Balaam fell silent. I closed my eyes. I recalled that long, sombre hall at Ely Place. Yes, it would be thronged by ghosts, especially Surrey's.

'Will!' I opened my eyes. 'I was there for vengeance, for you, for the Lady Jane and for Surrey, but I also came on behalf of the Princess Mary. Now that did startle him. He became sharper-witted; the old cunning returned. He challenged me about being an emissary of the Council. How could I come from both them and the Princess Mary? I told him I wanted to know the truth about the last of days. What really did happen in the old king's death chamber? He refused to reply and became very agitated. He mumbled something

PAUL DOHERTY

about how dangerous it was. He turned in his chair, staring at me out of the corner of his eye. He asked if I had not heard about Sir Anthony Denny, Chief Gentleman of the Privy Chamber; you remember Denny?'

'Of course.'

'Denny was well rewarded after Henry's death, then disappeared from public office and died suddenly at his house. Anyway, Wriothesley was now suspicious. I pressed him hard about King Henry's death, what really happened? Wriothesley began to rant. He sprang to his feet, walking up and down that hall dressed in his long dirty robe. You know the way he was, fingers jabbing, chin jutting, those milky blue eyes frenetic with an unreasoned excitement. He turned on me. He called me a spy, an intruder, how he would go to the Council. I realised I would get no further sense from him so I refilled his goblet and left.'

'And?'

Balaam half smiled and leaned closer. 'You remember my days as a physician fresh out of Salamanca?' He laughed softly. 'Or wherever else it was. Well, I slipped a potion into that last goblet. A few days later Wriothesley was dead, his soul gone to God. No one will miss him.' Balaam paused. 'Wriothesley was quite frenetic. I have studied his history. This behaviour, moon-struck, lunatic, apparently began after the King's death. Oh,' he waved a hand, 'Wriothesley was always vicious, nasty as a viper, but something truly turned his wits.'

'And you killed him?'

'Executed him, Will. I executed a murderer, a torturer, an evil soul. Do you remember Anne Askew?'

I nodded.

'Beautiful woman, fair and graceful. I met her. I was much smitten with Anne. Wriothesley dispatched her to torture and condemned her to a more horrific death than his own, burnt to a blackened stump at Smithfield. If given a chance, if the opportunity ever arose, he would have done the same to you and the Lady Jane. Ah well.' Balaam turned, gazing up to catch the warmth and light of the sun. 'They have all gone into the dark, despite their bustling and busyness. Queen Katherine Parr? Henry died in January; the two turtle doves, Katherine and Thomas Seymour, were already clinging together. Henry suspected that. If he had lived any longer, Katherine would have followed her namesake to the scaffold and Seymour would have joined her. Henry was scarcely in his grave and Seymour was tripping along the midnight paths to Chelsea Place to pay court to the royal widow.'

'Mad as a pot of frogs,' I murmured.

'And just as bad,' Balaam added. 'What did one of his companions say about Seymour? "Fierce in courage, courtly in fashion, in personage stately, in arms magnificent but somehow empty in soul." He and Queen Katherine played a very dangerous game. They were meeting before Henry's death. They certainly did afterwards; betrothed by May, married in June. Then the

Lady Katherine was pregnant within a year of Henry's death. Great passion,' he breathed.

'The other councillors, Seymour's elder brother and Dudley, must have known.'

'Oh yes, they frowned on the marriage. The Council refused to hand back the jewels and property Katherine acquired as queen. The younger Seymour was like an untrained stallion; his new wife was given custody of the Princess Elizabeth but she had to send that young woman away when Seymour began to interfere with the young princess's clothing as well as appearing in her bedchamber at the most unseemly hour. Seymour secretly entertained hopes of marrying either Elizabeth or Mary.'

'I heard rumours about his plots, all brought to nothing.'

'In September five years ago, twenty months after the death of her royal husband, Katherine Parr gave birth to a baby girl and died shortly afterwards. Thomas Seymour became unhinged. Sent to fight pirates in the Bristol Channel, he entered into secret negotiations with them. He then tried to defraud the mint at Bristol and crowned all his foolishness by invading the young king's bedchamber during the dead of night and shooting one of the royal spaniels.' Balaam sipped at his goblet, 'Even his own brother could not save him from the headsman's axe. Bishop Latimer, whom Thomas Seymour asked to deliver his funeral sermon, openly declared that it was clearly evident that God had forsaken

Seymour; indeed, whether he be saved or not was a matter only God could decide. Seymour was certainly a wicked man and the kingdom was well rid of him. According to Latimer, Seymour died irksomely, dangerously and horribly.' Balaam wafted away a fly. 'As for the rest, you must have learnt what happened. The elder Seymour, who made himself Duke of Somerset and Lord Protector, failed in Scotland and stirred up rebellion in England. He was removed from power but was then executed for plotting to poison the entire Council in a banquet to be held at his London house.'

'And now Dudley has gone? What a death! He and his henchman Gates arguing in the death cart on the way to the scaffold!'

'Oh yes. When Dudley reached Cambridge and realised all was lost, Gates tried to change sides and arrest his master when he had his boots half on. In the end, both went to the axe—'

'I was there,' I interrupted. 'The Queen asked me to be her witness. Dudley was executed by a lame swordsman dressed in a white butcher's apron. He died renouncing all the reformist doctrine. He reverted to the old faith. When asked why, he replied that he'd thought best of the old religion but, seeing a new one begin, run dog, run devil, he would pursue it.' I paused. 'How fortune changes. Old Norfolk, freed from the Tower by Queen Mary, presided at Dudley's trial and execution. He enjoyed it. He wanted Dudley's beating heart plucked from his body and flung against his face.

But in the end, Balaam, why all this now? The wolf pack, that horde of mad, wild predators, turned on each other and tore themselves to pieces.'

'True, true,' Balaam soothed. 'And I ask myself would such men deliberately kill a king?' He studied my surprise. 'Oh yes, Will!' His words seemed to hang in that warm, scented air. 'That is why you and I are here. What did happen in that frost-besieged, cold, shadowy palace vibrant with all forms of devilish passions? We are queen's men, Will. We now hold the power, and God be my witness, Queen Mary wants to know the true fate of her father.'

'And how will we discover that in a rose-covered tavern arbour? Do you already know, Balaam? Did your patron on the Council tell you?'

Balaam got to his feet. 'One thing I did not learn was that, which is why we are here. We are going to the Tower, where someone will meet us.' He leaned down. 'Remember this, Will: do not act surprised if I ask you one question.'

'Which is?'

'You will tell a lie. Maintain you heard Dudley's confession after he had been shriven by the Bishop of Worcester on the scaffold. After all, you were there as a Crown witness. Yes?'

I shrugged. 'It doesn't make sense.'

'Don't worry, it shall. I cannot answer every one of your questions, but in justice, you deserve to know what I do.'

'Including Martin, the Spanish servant of the late Earl of Surrey?'

Balaam pulled a face. 'Including him. Come.'

We left that scented garden and went down an alleyway into Petty Wales, that close, narrow place around the Tower. The needle-thin alleyways were thronged with all the low life who prowl there: beggars, coney-catchers, apple squires, sewer squires, penny traders and touting tinkers, a shifting sea of red, brown, green and black. A surging shoal of common folk who pushed and shoved their way past sumpter ponies and purveyance carts, fighting their way under the shabby gable-ended houses that leaned over to black out the brilliant sun in a deep blue sky. Signs creaked dangerously and noisily just above our heads. We breathed a heavy fog of different scents, odours and smells, which ebbed and flowed, be it the steaming, fly-infested midden heaps or the acrid smoke billowing out like the thickest mist from the many cook shops which pander to the poor, selling cat meat as venison and the offal from Newgate shambles as the sweetest stews. Mountebanks jostled with moon people in all their garish finery and cheap glittering rings and collars. An ape, trained to juggle, performed on top of a barrel, watched by no one except a tamer and his pet bear, a black, scruffy-furred animal with sad eyes and tightly tied muzzle. I also sensed the frenetic excitement, a legacy of the stirring times following Queen Mary's entrance into the City, the execution of her opponents and all the glory of her crowning at Westminster. A feeling of relief that the crisis had passed. People no longer felt that they had to draw their horns in. They could now give vent to their feelings, throwing their caps higher than the stars and rejoicing that the kingdom was at peace under its legitimate ruler.

I walked silently beside Balaam, feeding off the City's sights and sounds. Such a stark contrast to where I had lurked for the last five years, those lonely, gloomy manor houses of Essex. We approached the Tower. Our warrants gave us safe and smooth passage through the Lion Gate and all the other sally ports and entrances. The fortress was well garrisoned: troops from Norfolk, squadrons of Spanish musketeers and a host of royal archers. No one bothered us as we slipped along those narrow gulleys under grey, forbidding walls. The soft breeze carried a pervasive stench from the menagerie pens where the tawny-coated lions and the other great cats prowled, growled and snarled, a heart-chilling din on such a beautiful day. We reached the great water gate leading to the river, the docking place for the sealed death barges that brought the victims of Henry's rage to be imprisoned in the Tower. Few of those ever escaped, led up the great steps to where we now stood. I glanced at the narrow barred windows then down into the moat; the river was ebbing and the black, oozing mud reeked of the dead fish lying in its stinking mess.

'Surrey's prison,' I murmured. 'St Thomas's Tower.' I

pointed down at the mud. 'That's where he hoped to make his escape.'

Balaam did not reply. He had a quiet word with the guards, then led me up the steps into Surrey's chamber, a cavernous, bleak room, its plaster-white walls turning a dullish grey, the fire in the narrow hearth long extinguished and crammed with crumbling ash. Windows on either wall provided a view over the river or the Tower. A crucifix was nailed to the wall, although the figure of Christ had been ripped off. There were sticks of battered furniture: chairs, stools, tables and a narrow rope-bound cot bed. The chamber smelt musty and stale, though I noticed the gleaming flagon and goblets on the small table beneath the crucifix covered with snow-white napkins. I walked over to the retiring room which housed the garderobe, opened the creaking door and stepped inside. The room was black and shabby, the latrine primitive, a stony chute that cut down through the wall. The seat over the hole had been removed, the gap left broad enough for a man to climb in, dropping down into the muddy moat once the river had ebbed. I turned and stared back at the door to the chamber. On the night Surrey tried to escape, the guards must have returned, unlocked that door, noticed their prisoner was missing and immediately hurried across to this garderobe.

'Martin the Spaniard?' I demanded. 'That was you, Balaam?'

'Yes, I was Martin. I drifted into the Tower, posing

as one of the many Spanish mercenaries serving in London. Gates gave the impression that he didn't care one way or the other, nor did Stonor, the lieutenant. Nobody, as we know, wanted to be associated with Surrey, who had fallen never to rise again. I liked him, Will, I really did. And he favoured me. Of course he thought about escape.' Balaam pointed to the garderobe. 'That was the only way. He asked me to carry messages to his younger brother Thomas, to assemble men and supplies for him. I persuaded him not to.'

'What!'

'Think, Will. How far would Surrey have run? Who would have helped him? Oh no.' Balaam sat down on a stool. 'I had been indentured so easily into his service. I grew deeply suspicious. Gates had only acted as if he didn't care; I noticed that. When I left the Tower, I was followed. One night I hired a barge and we passed as close as we could to Traitors' Gate, as they now call it. I observed armed men in boats nearby, groups of the same on the quayside down to St Katherine's Dock. Remember, Will, Surrey was first imprisoned in Wriothesley's house in Ely Place, Holborn. Wriothesley brought him here to this prison chamber. He wanted Surrey to escape, he was hungry for it.'

'Why?'

'To draw in any other Howards, as nearly happened with young Thomas—'

'And more than that,' I interrupted, 'Henry Howard, Earl of Surrey, would have been killed trying to escape.

The mad, hot-tempered warrior nobleman. Everybody knew what he was like: his rash temper, his impetuous conduct while besieging Boulogne.'

'True. The accusations against him were feather-light.' Balaam tapped his booted foot against the ground. 'If Surrey was killed whilst escaping, there would be no need for a trial. He was intent on escape. I gave him a knife as a token of my support. However, I warned him that it was precisely what his enemies, especially Wriothesley, wanted. He would be killed, and if any of his family were implicated, they too would suffer.' He paused. 'Surrey, locked in composing his sonnets, finally agreed. He thought it would be better to establish his innocence at a trial and protect what was left of his family. He also conceded that his enemies would depict any attempt at escape as proof of his guilt. On the night in question, when in truth there was no one ready to assist him, he hid in the garderobe, the knife I had given him thrust into his belt.' Balaam spread his hands. 'He just waited until the guards returned. They found him hiding there, and that became the alleged escape – which is why so little was made of it at his trial.'

'But someone else must have informed you about what Wriothesley plotted, someone on the Council?'

Balaam held up a hand; he was staring over my shoulder.

'Of course, Will. It was me.'

I whirled around. A figure had followed us up the steps and stood in the doorway. He came into the chamber slightly lame, resting on a gold-topped cane which tapped the floor. The stranger pulled back the hood of his silver-edged deep blue cloak. I stared into the face of that arch-schemer Sir William Paget, once Chief Secretary of the Council. He had certainly aged, the silver quite plentiful in his once reddish hair, moustache and beard; his smooth pale face was creased, those clever eyes looked tired.

'Put not your trust in princes,' I whispered. 'And I said in my excess all men are liars . . .'

'We are all liars, Will. God knows we have to be.' Paget laughed abruptly. 'Those who live by the truth rarely survive long. Yet we pay the price for our lies. The years have not treated me gently.' He hobbled over, patted me on the arm, then crossed to sit on the chamber's one and only high-backed chair. I glanced accusingly at Balaam.

'Were you a Judas man?' I asked.

'Tell him!' Balaam snapped.

Paget rested both hands on his walking cane and beckoned me to a stool. I sat down.

'Will, I do not dream dreams of power like Dudley or the Seymours. I do not imagine, deep in my cups, that I might wear the Crown Imperial. No, I am the Crown's good servant.' He grimaced. 'Or at least I thought I was. You know the story of Henry's council. We turned on each other as soon as the one great fear that bound us all together disappeared for ever: King Henry of not so blessed memory. Whilst he lived, we were united not so much in purpose as in terror, like sheep who cluster together when the wolf approaches.'

'Some sheep!' I taunted. 'More wolves in sheep's clothing yourselves.'

'I agree. But we were nothing compared to Henry.' Paget pointed at me. 'I served him, Will, because I serve the Crown. Balaam is proof of that. I was determined to maintain close ties with the Princess Mary. Balaam was my man as well as hers. Mary is the Crown, the rightful heir after Edward; Romanist or not, she is our legitimate ruler. Balaam was our link. I could not tell him everything. I had to be careful. If Mary really knew all that was plotted, she might betray herself and eventually us. The likes of Wriothesley and Gates would have strangled me. Fluent in Spanish, Balaam was given false credentials. I issued him with a warrant declaring that he was a member of the Imperial ambassador's household. He could now move as he wished.'

'But you were hunting him. You said that yourself. You threatened me . . .'

'All shadow play. I had to pretend. I also had to discover where your true loyalties lay. I soon found out. Your heart was with the Princess Mary and the Lady Jane. It would have been too dangerous to draw you in. I gave you the opportunity. Thank God,' he crossed himself, 'you refused it. But,' he banged the walking cane against the paving stones, 'I also protected you when I could. Wriothesley hated you. He saw you as a grotesque gargoyle. I heard a story, whether it's true or not I don't know, that Wriothesley had a younger brother, in appearance something like yourself. Cherished and loved by his parents, he died young. They mourned him to the exclusion of their elder son. Wriothesley never forgave or forgot that memory. He wanted you dead. It was he, not me, who discovered your meeting in Whitefriars and dispatched the Council men. Wriothesley certainly proved his hatred for you at Newgate. Balaam hastened to me. I freed you. In the end neither Balaam nor I dared leave the shadows. If you had known the truth, Will, and we were unable to protect you, the likes of Wriothesley would have had you stretched out on the rack, the Scavenger's Daughter in the Tower dungeons.'

'And Surrey?'

'Surrey was his own man, brilliant but wilful. He would never accept being second, bowing to the likes of Seymour and Dudley. Civil war would have raged. Years before he died I begged, I pleaded with him to be moderate in his temper, to ally himself with Seymour and Dudley. He refused. Wriothesley was jubilant at his arrest. He believed it would be only a matter of time before . . .' Paget pointed at the garderobe. 'Surrey tried to escape. You know the rest. Balaam warned him.' He cleared his throat. 'I also did my best to save Norfolk. I argued that to end the old king's reign and mark the accession of his heir with the execution of England's premier duke would be seen as a banquet of blood.'

He rapped the cane against the floor again, peering at me quizzically. 'Ah well, now you are the master, Will. I have been summoned here to refer to you, to account for the past.'

I glanced at Balaam; he nodded imperceptibly.

'One thing only,' I retorted. 'Her Majesty demands the truth about her father's death.'

'That was proclaimed at the time.'

Balaam went over, removed the napkins and filled three goblets with white wine. He served both Paget and myself. The wine was cold and delicious. All three of us sat sipping carefully.

'We are not here to be cozened, flattered or ignored,' Balaam declared. 'Sir William, I have served you well, but there is one secret that is still owed. The Queen is prepared to return you to full office, to grant you as much power and status as you enjoyed before.'

'I submitted myself most humbly to Her Majesty.'

'After Her Majesty raised her banner to which all loyal subjects flocked,' I declared. 'You did not, Sir William. You remained in London with the other rebels. You appended your name, beside that of traitors, on a letter to the Lord Lieutenant of Essex, instructing him to move against his, and your, rightful queen. You submitted because the rebels' cause was lost.'

'I did advise you,' Balaam whispered. 'I did plead . . .'

'And I was threatened,' Paget retorted.

I stared at him. I now accepted why I had to be here. I knew the path we were about to follow.

'You will be confirmed in everything,' I persisted, 'if you tell Her Majesty the truth.'

Paget continued to tap his cane on the ground. A blast of hot air brought us the mixed odours of the Tower, the filthy ooze of the moat below us, smoke from the Tower mint and tanneries. Children laughed and shouted as they played Hob the Lost. The cries of sentries echoed above the shrill screaming from the hog pens where the pigs waited to be slaughtered. A horn brayed. Lurchers barked and horses neighed as a hunting party prepared to leave to chase the hare in Moorfields, north of the old City wall. I stared around that bleak chamber. Did Surrey's ghost walk here? Or was his troubled spirit soothed by the restoration of his family name as well as plans to move his shattered corpse from All Hallows to the Howard mausoleum in St Michael's Church, Framlingham? 'The storms are gone, those clouds dispersed': a line from one of Surrey's last poems echoed through my soul. Paget was lost in his own meditations.

'Oh, you must know,' Balaam glanced quickly at me, 'Somers also heard Dudley's last confession after he had been shriven by the Bishop Heath. Isn't that true, Will?'

Paget glanced up; he smiled crookedly at me.

'Never tell a secret,' he murmured, 'to more than one person. You, Master Balaam, must leave. My surety.' He shrugged. 'I want no other witnesses.'

'So if necessary,' I retorted, 'you can dismiss what I might say in the future as the ravings of a fool.' I drank greedily. 'I assure you, I will tell no one except Her Majesty. I also warn you, sir, I am not so fey-witted as to be unable to distinguish the nettle from the vine. Her Majesty wants the truth, otherwise,' I gestured around, 'this may become more than just your visiting chamber. Master Balaam?'

That man of subtle deceit stood chewing the corner of his lip like a merchant valuing a roll of cloth. He frowned slightly but left the chamber, closing the door quietly behind him. I rose and took my stool closer to Paget so he did not have to raise his voice.

'Let us be brief and succinct. No politicking now.'

'The King our late dead master,' Paget kept his head down, 'did not die on the twenty-eighth of January in the Year of Our Lord 1547, but four days earlier, when Sir Thomas Seymour was sworn of the Council. Now you knew, I knew, we all knew King Henry. What did he boast? There was no man he made that he could not unmake. And there was no head, however noble, he could not make fly. The King destroyed the Howards but he was preparing to clear the board. He had growing suspicions about Dudley and Seymour, their use of the dry stamp, how they were beginning to dominate the Council. He planned to destroy them and us.'

'How?'

'He kept Norfolk alive and comfortable, Gardiner under house arrest. We garnered rumours, whispers that Henry was prepared to indict Queen Katherine for her illicit liaison with Thomas Seymour; even Cranmer was suspect. On the morning of the twenty-second of January,' Paget chose his words carefully, 'you were put under arrest in your chamber. The Council met. Dudley accused Wriothesley of being part of the King's plot to move against him and Seymour.' He picked up his goblet and sipped carefully. 'Wriothesley was truly dangerous,' he gestured with his hand, 'jumping here, jumping there. We believed he was the King's key to unlock the door to a new bloody purge.'

'Of course.' I nodded. 'Wriothesley would know a great deal. He would be the Crown's witness in any treason trial.'

'Naturally Wriothesley denied all this. You see, Will, our king wasn't insane. Oh yes, I know all about Balaam's interpretation of certain paintings, but believe me, Henry had good cause to fear. Seymour and Dudley, together with other members of the Council, were ruefully reflecting on decades of bloody tyranny under Henry. They argued for a commonwealth. A kingdom ruled by a council.'

'And Henry's heirs?'

Paget gazed stonily at me. 'Think, Will. Young Edward, if he had grown to manhood, would have been as bloodthirsty and tyrannical as his father. You know there is a suspicion that Dudley poisoned him?'

I shrugged this off. 'And the two princesses?'

'Ah, that's where I and others proved obdurate. We argued that the kingdom, the people would never accept the total annihilation of Henry's heirs. Now all this is mere speculation, but I believe Wriothesley may have informed Henry.'

'That's why Surrey was removed, wasn't it?'

'Yes, the King thought he was a threat to the young prince, but Dudley and Seymour regarded him as an obstacle to their idea of a commonwealth. God forgive me, I agreed with them.' Paget rose, balancing himself on his walking cane. He stretched, then began to walk up and down. 'The Council was divided into two: those who looked forward to a new king and those who hoped for no king at all. Then there was Henry, determined that no council would ever pose a threat to him and his family. The King was growing stronger. He had recovered from a fever; the burning stages had passed. He began to rant about his treasonous wife and how ill served he was. He expressed deep sorrow over Cromwell's death and regretted the execution of Anne Boleyn, who of course was removed from power because of Seymour's sister. Henry demanded that Wingfield and his Spears be always close by. What he didn't know was that we had bought Wingfield's allegiance.

'We tried to placate the King. I summoned his old comrade Francis Bryant, to no avail. Days passed. Dudley and Seymour were now deeply agitated, Wriothesley even more so. Thomas Seymour was growing increasingly fearful of the consequences of his illicit liaison with the Queen.' Paget breathed in deeply as he hobbled back to his chair. 'Abruptly Henry realised something was wrong. He demanded to see you. Dudley ordered Huicke to feed the King an opiate, the milk of poppy. Huicke had no choice but to agree, though he pointed out that such deep sleeps might invigorate His Majesty.' Paget leaned forward, both hands resting on the walking cane, eyes half closed as he went back down the gallery of the years to those warm, stuffy chambers, littered with all the plunder from Henry's victims, a constant reminder of the King's bloody outbursts.

'The Council continued divided. Dudley and Seymour were fearful that old Norfolk would be released and would be joined by Gardiner. They accused Wriothesley of being party to this. He screamed back about what he had done for both Crown and kingdom, but his savage words did not convince. The younger Seymour joined the shouting; hands fell to daggers. Wriothesley declared he would prove his loyalty and asked if there was man amongst us who would join him.' Paget shook his head. 'Wriothesley and the younger Seymour went into the King's chamber. Huicke was there; the King was fast asleep. They dragged the doctor out, slammed the door shut and locked it from inside. When they came out, Wriothesley, hands clasped together, mournfully pronounced that the King was not sleeping but had quietly slipped away.' Paget wetted his lips. 'Dudley wanted the truth of it. Wriothesley said he had now demonstrated his loyalty to the Council.'

'And the truth?' I asked.

'While Seymour guarded the door, Wriothesley seized

a bolster and placed it over the King's face. Henry became aroused and struggled. Seymour helped Wriothesley even as he whispered how he intended to plunder and ravish Katherine Parr's soft white body. According to Seymour, Wriothesley was giggling like some witless maid. Eventually the King lay quiet. We went into the chamber. Henry lay sprawled, head slightly to one side, eyes all glassy, mouth gaping. At the time no one even dared mention the truth about what had really happened. '

'When was this?'

'Early in the hours of the twenty-fourth of January. After the initial tumult and panic we continued the pretence. Those we could not fully trust, or did not need, remained banished from the royal chambers.'

'Like myself?'

'Like yourself. We simply continued the sham. Huicke, frightened out of his wits, rearranged the corpse as best he could. Somebody mentioned extreme unction, the need for the last rites, so Cranmer was secretly summoned. He viewed the corpse but observed nothing untoward. He performed what rite he could and left immediately. He may have suspected the truth but he could never prove it. Whether he liked it or not, he too was consenting to what had happened. And how could he object? Wriothesley hailed himself as the hero of the hour; his frenetic mood deepened. What could we do? In one way or another we were all his accomplices. To blame Wriothesley and Seymour alone would have been the greatest foolishness. I too was implicated. I urged them to be pragmatic. Henry was dead and we should all unite.'

'Murder!' I interrupted. 'Regicide! Henry the King was murdered and you were an accomplice.'

'We had no choice. Henry would have struck at us all. Think, Will. What if Henry had released Norfolk and Gardiner and made Wriothesley his creature? Wriothesley hated you and the Lady Jane. Even before the King died Wriothesley was dripping poison about you into his ears. Oh yes, Will Somers, if Henry had succeeded, I would have had a better chance at life than you and the Lady Jane.'

I could not contradict that. I closed my eyes and thought of Henry sprawled in that great bed gasping his poppy-drenched dreams. Seymour guarding the door, Wriothesley the assassin closing like a shadow, grasping the bolster and silencing that powerful king once and for all. Now I knew why Wriothesley had hauled me off to Newgate. He was terrified that I knew of his double dealing with the King and might still betray him to the rest.

'Will?'

I opened my eyes.

'I begged them all to unite and I had my way. The King's death would remain secret. Important decisions had to be made. Queen Katherine Parr would be excluded from government but allowed to keep her jewels and lands, even marry Seymour as long as they waited. But Seymour, like Wriothesley, was deeply affected by what he had done. It turned his wits. He insisted on grasping his prize immediately.'

'Did he tell his new wife what he'd done to her late royal husband?'

'I suspect he did. An act of bravado, to show how deeply he loved her. After all, they'd both desired Henry's death. He was the screech owl of their hushed conversations at Greenwich. Whether they were attempting to poison the King remains debatable; the potions and philtres Henry fed himself could have been dangerous. The King certainly misjudged Huicke; he was, first and foremost, the Queen's creature. Strange, isn't it? Huicke was with Katherine when she gave birth to Seymour's child, an act that killed her. In fact when Katherine Parr lay dying, tossing in a fever, she accused Seymour of attempting to murder her. Seymour desperately tried to quieten and soothe her. Why should Katherine think that unless she was dealing with a man, and being tended by a physician, who'd helped murder a king? So why should they baulk at killing her? Both Seymour and Wriothesley grew increasingly frenetic in their behaviour. They had to be silenced; that's why the elder Seymour signed his own brother's death warrant. Balaam took care of Wriothesley. And as for Sir Anthony Denny, Dudley catered for him lest he go to confess and be shriven by Bishop Gardiner.'

'Do you think that good bishop suspects?'

'I don't think so. Gardiner is too absorbed with his

own dreams to restore the power of Rome. Others, however, could have asked questions.'

'Hence your little black book of infamous memory.'

Paget smiled thinly. 'That was the mortar to the bricks of the house I wanted to build. Bribes, estates, titles, sinecures, benefices, gold and silver. No one was over-looked: Huicke, Wendy, Alsop, Roberts, Wingfield, Bryant and others. Once they'd taken the bribe, they were all consenting to what we had done.'

'And you truly believe the King was preparing to destroy you?'

'Us, Will, all of us! He wanted to create a realm where he was both emperor and pope. Read the clas-sics, Will. I can point to many princes who have walked the same path, who strove for the same prize. I also understood Dudley and Seymour's plan, though I tempered it. I wanted to see England being ruled as a commonwealth where there was a king, a monarch, but subject to a council. No more would we accept that one man's will could override Parliament, statute law and even scripture itself. Wriothesley betrayed us. I have no doubt he knew about Seymour's dalliance with the Queen. We simply moved before Henry did.' He rubbed the side of his face. 'That's why Surrey also had to die. In our eyes he was just as dangerous as Henry. Surrey tolerated the King; what chance did we have with a nobleman like that? He believed that his aristocratic blood was the only licence to rule. He would have provoked the wars of a hundred years ago.'

Paget fell silent, turning his head as if half listening to the sounds of the Tower. 'Of course Henry's death did not mark a new beginning. The King was not even in his coffin and my advice was being ignored. Seymour even considered assuming the title of "The Great Lord and Master". Wriothesley, wits already unhinged, was the first to object, claiming he'd been cheated, and so the cracks widened. Young Seymour galloped off to claim his bride. Dudley and Seymour drew apart over failure in Scotland, unrest in the countryside and division over religion. And look at the future. God rest him, Will, but young Edward was a righteous prig who also saw himself as God's will incarnate.'

Paget filled his goblet and offered the jug to me. I shook my head. What these lords intended did not matter now. I was more concerned about why I had been sent here.

'And the King's corpse, Henry the once magnificent prince?'

'Not so magnificent, Will. He died on the twenty-fourth of January but the embalmers were not allowed in till the evening of the thirtieth; six days had elapsed. I visited the corpse myself. I had to go masked, my nose and mouth almost buried in a pomander. The death chamber was crammed with all forms of perfumes and fragrances. The stench was hellish, the corpse even more so; swollen like a balloon so that the belly was bloating to rupture. Corruption and rottenness were seeping from every pore and aperture, be it the eyes, mouth,

337

nose or anus. The embalmers were solemnly sworn to silence and ordered to do what they could. The King's rotting, slime-covered cadaver was washed, cleansed and waxed as swiftly and as expertly as could be done. God knows what was truly buried in that casket under the flagstones at Westminster. We thought the lead coffin and elm casket would contain all the corruption, but the long delay, the rattling of the funeral chariot . . .' Paget shrugged. 'What happened at Syon was inevitable, dismissed as an accident. I was never so grateful to see a corpse buried.'

'Did the King ask to see his family?'

'The Queen, no; the children, yes. Please tell Her Majesty so. Of course we couldn't allow that. Henry might have divulged his suspicions. Princess Mary was astute enough to act. I have no excuses now, no more than the others,' he held up a hand, 'except one. If Henry had lived, I, we and probably you, Will Somers, would have perished. And now we are back at the beginning. A new queen, intent on reversing everything Henry has done over the last twenty years. Some people will resist, some people will die, but you have what you came for. Henry died, smothered in his bed by his own ministers, who feared him more than the devil and wished him gone with that devil. They did so because they suspected Henry was plotting to do the same to them in a more heinous and barbaric way. And that is the truth of it.' Paget shrugged wearily. 'Of course, there is no proof, no witnesses. The official account is well known; it cannot be contradicted,' he smiled, 'except for a court fool and a disgraced minister.' He gestured at me. 'Remember, Will, I warned you. On the day I told you about Cranmer, I wanted to alert you to how, in the coming storm, no one would be safe. How the Princess Mary and her household were watched most closely, as well as what horrors awaited those who fell foul of the King. True,' he winked at me, 'I was being mischievous in establishing where your loyalty lay. In the end I protected you as well as I could. I never sent those council men to Whitefriars; Wriothesley did that, as he tried to break you in Newgate. I repeat, I protected you when I could. I now beg you to return the favour.' Then he was gone.

I heard his footsteps fade and followed him soon after out into the sunshine. Paget was now making his way along one of the gulleys. Balaam was close by, leaning against a wall talking to a vivacious red-haired young lady. She turned and smiled brilliantly at me. I recognised the Princess Elizabeth, garbed in a gown of blue slashed with white, head and hair hidden under a bejewelled gauze veil. She glanced flirtatiously at Balaam and stepped back with a coquettish curtsey. Balaam responded with the most lavish courtly bow. Elizabeth threw her head back, pealing with laughter, then waggled those long white fingers at him, a sign for him to withdraw to where her lady stood some distance away. She watched him go, shading her eyes, then, smiling coyly, walked slowly towards me, hips swaying as she playfully put one foot in front of the other. I know Elizabeth and I admire her, those dark eyes so bright with life and that kissable mouth slightly pouted as if she is always on the verge of bursting into laughter. A born flirt, her appearance masks a sharp, deep intellect, whilst she possesses all the charm and courtesy of a born courtier.

'Why, Master Somers.' She rounded her eyes as she stretched out a hand to be kissed. I did so, and Elizabeth gently brushed my face with her fingers.

'Your Grace?'

'Your Grace wonders why Sir William Paget should be closeted so close with my good friend Will. Why he leaves so humbly when only months ago he was one of the masters of the dance. Now he slinks from the Tower like a beaten dog. Why did he come here?' She smiled and waved her hand airily. 'To this "royal palace" as my good sister calls it, where I reside as her beloved guest.'

'Till better days come, Your Grace.'

'Oh Will, will they come, will they?' She laughed at the pun on my name, then stepped closer, the smile gone, the eyes searching. Oh Lord, save me, I recognised that look, the set of the mouth which reflected the steel in her soul. 'Paget, what did he say?' She leaned even closer. 'My father? His death?'

I glanced to where Balaam flirted with her ladies. 'Your Grace,' I bowed, 'what I know is only for the ears of the Queen.'

'Is it now, Will?' She moved from side to side in a flurry of dress and petticoats; I caught the scent of her heady perfume. 'Will, look at me.' I did so. 'For the ears of the Queen only?'

I nodded.

'So when I am Queen it will be for my ears as well?'

'Of course, Your Grace.'

Elizabeth pecked me on both cheeks. 'There, Will, that's for you and the Lady Jane.' She fluttered her fingers in goodbye, walked away, then turned. 'Oh Will?'

'Yes, Your Grace?'

'Remember . . .'

Will Somers's journal ends here.

The
Ferry Girls

Rosie Archer was born in Gosport, Hampshire, where she still lives. She has had a variety of jobs including waitress, fruit picker, barmaid, shop assistant and market trader selling second-hand books. Rosie is the author of several Second World War sagas set on the south coast, as well as a series of gangster sagas under the name June Hampson.

Also by Rosie Archer

The Munitions Girls
The Canary Girls
The Factory Girls
The Gunpowder and Glory Girls
The Girls from the Local

ROSIE
ARCHER

The
Ferry Girls

Quercus

First published in Great Britain in 2017 by Quercus
This paperback edition published in 2017 by

Quercus Editions Ltd
Carmelite House
50 Victoria Embankment
London EC4Y 0DZ

An Hachette UK company

A CIP catalogue record for this book is available
from the British Library

PB ISBN 978 1 78648 331 7
EBOOK ISBN 978 1 78648 332 4

10 9 8 7 6 5 4 3 2 1

Typeset by CC Book Production
Printed and bound in Great Britain by Clays Ltd, St Ives plc

This one is for Charlie Repp, my grandson.
His IT skills helped when I needed them most.

Chapter One

Vee had never stolen a thing in her life, yet here she was, her hands shaking, fumbling with a large brown envelope, terrified that at any moment the lavatory door might open and she would be discovered, about to thieve from her boss.

But what was the alternative? Stealing was a sin, but better than spending a loathsome weekend in bed in a New Forest hotel with Sammy Chesterton. This was her one chance to keep her virginity and morals intact.

She paused. Bing Crosby's voice seeped from the bar into the disinfectant-swilled ladies' room in Southampton's docklands' Black Cat Club. He was insisting there would be 'Pennies From Heaven'. Vee hoped he was right: pennies would be much more satisfying than the nightly rain of Adolf Hitler's bombs.

Holding her breath and listening until she was satisfied there was no one outside, Vee continued her search, fingers rifling through the cardboard and papers, her eyes flying from one false name to another on the identity cards, ration books, birth certificates and passports that her boss had obtained illegally to sell on for payment in cash or, in her penniless state, sex.

And then she saw them! Her own and her mother's Anglicized names!

Twenty-three-year-old Violetta and May Anne Smith of Honeysuckle Holdings, Leap Lane, Netley. Excitement rose as she pulled out the ration books, medical cards and other documents that would make them legal citizens of the land they had been born in, their beloved England.

Vee's eyes filled with tears. 'Oh!' she murmured. 'How wonderful.'

Now she and her mother would no longer be aliens. The false documents would give them their freedom to live, walk around and shop locally, like any other English person, all of which had been denied to Vee, especially since the start of this awful war with Germany.

Of course, owning and using forged papers was a criminal

offence. Hopefully Vee and her mother would never need to produce them, and as long as no one discovered the truth, they could live and contribute to the war effort by growing food on their smallholding just as Vee's grandparents had done.

Vee fingered the papers, which represented freedom. She wondered how she could explain all this to her mother. May would be appalled to think Vee held herself so cheap that she could agree to Sammy's demands. She knew Vee wanted to remain a virgin until she could give herself freely to the man she truly loved. That man was out there somewhere, waiting to love her. But the loss of her virginity was nothing compared to the possible loss of her mother if they were removed to an internment camp for aliens.

Before Vee was born, her English mother had married a German pilot. He'd been the love of her life. Not for one moment had May thought that, due to the Aliens Restriction Act, marrying a German would take away her and her baby's English birthright and make them Germans.

If the law that imposed a husband's nationality on his wife and children was flouted, serious consequences befell the offender, especially when that citizenship was German.

The British people hated the Germans. This war had come so soon after the bloodbath of the Great War, and now the

Luftwaffe was attacking English airfields, sending at least a thousand aircraft every day. Already Hitler had invaded the Channel Islands. Any hint of German blood, and homes were burned. Friendships disintegrated overnight. Shops were boycotted or, worse, looted and torched.

Vee didn't want a fate like that for her mother and herself. For years they had managed to keep secret her father August Schmidt's marriage to her mother.

Both she and her mother had been born in Netley, near Southampton: why should a government Act decree that they were not British?

Living on a smallholding that provided them with food meant they had so far managed without having to present ration books and other essential documentation. Already the two women made do and mended without tendering clothing coupons, but both Vee and her mother knew that, sooner or later, clarification of their status would be required. They were living in fear.

Two weeks ago, the local post office had been set ablaze, and the elderly Martina and Hartmund Braun, who had served the villagers for ten years, had been severely injured by thugs hurling stones. Villagers who had previously been their customers and friends had shouted obscenities at them as they had been taken away in the back of a lorry.

Vee would never forget the terror on the seventy-year-old woman's face.

She stuffed the papers into her handbag. Now she and her mother could present identification without the fear of being different, of being hated.

A door creaked. Someone was coming! Vee fumbled for the cubicle's bolt, forgetting it was broken. With her back against the door she stared at the package. Where could she hide it?

There was no chance now that she'd be able to replace it beside the till behind the bar. She could hear footsteps and someone singing along with the wireless. Now Frank Sinatra was crooning 'All Or Nothing At All'.

Thinking swiftly, she climbed up on the wooden toilet seat and hauled at the metal cover over the cistern. At first it refused to budge. A spider lurking among the grime swung out but disappeared beneath the metal lid as it lifted. Vee shoved the envelope into the dry space between the cistern and the wall, pushed the lid back into place and stepped down. Whoever was outside the lavatory door was still singing.

Vee ripped a few sheets of shiny San Izal toilet paper from the roll and wiped her hands, then dropped the paper into the lavatory pan. Smoothing her hands down her black skirt, she took a deep breath, picked up her handbag and pulled open the cubicle's door.

Vee saw surprise on Greta's face. The singing had stopped. 'I thought I was alone in here,' the blonde-haired girl said. 'You don't make much noise, do you? I never heard the flush.' She let her hand fall from the cubicle's door.

Vee tried a smile, but it didn't come across the way she wanted. The girl was wearing her usual strong freesia perfume.

Greta frowned. 'You all right? You look a bit peculiar . . .'

Vee sent up a silent prayer of thanks. The girl's words had given her an idea.

'Actually, no, I don't feel too good at all. I think I'll go home. There's no way I could be nice to the punters tonight.'

'The boss won't like it.' Greta took a step away from her.

Vee thought of Sammy Chesterton, the tall, dark-haired gangster, who had taken a fancy to her because, he said, she reminded him of a girl he had once loved and lost. Always dressed in smart suits and with a camel coat slung round his shoulders, he looked exactly what he purported to be, a businessman with sway in politics. He strayed on the wrong side of the law but, with his connections in the police force, had managed to keep his good reputation unsullied and his bad one feared.

'I think Sammy would rather I wasn't here than being sick all over the place,' Vee said.

Greta shrugged. The girls weren't great friends but working together had made them allies.

Oh dear! Not only was Vee now a thief, but she hadn't hesitated to lie. She sighed as she waited for Greta to offer to tell the boss that one of his hostesses wouldn't be putting in an appearance. Greta would normally take any chance to cosy up to Sammy – it was well known that she had designs on him.

'I could let him know . . .'

'Would you?' Vee thrust her arms round a surprised Greta in a hug, then pulled quickly away. She was supposed to be poorly, wasn't she? Not bursting with energy. 'I think it's something I ate,' she said. 'Thank you, you're a good pal.' She held the cubicle door open so Greta could go in, and breathed a sigh of relief when the door had closed.

From inside Greta shouted, 'It'd better be something you ate! I don't want to catch it!'

Vee walked back into the smoke-stale bar.

Small wrought-iron tables and chairs with plush velvet seats faced the stage area where a microphone was set up on the parquet flooring. Red velvet curtains at the sides hid the small dressing rooms and were a backdrop for the striptease shows. The bar area at the side of the huge room had mirrored shelves containing bottles of brightly coloured liquids that purported to be exotic drinks. Vee had never heard a single person ask for one. The clientele, mostly merchant sailors and servicemen, preferred beer or the standard spirits.

A wrinkled, stooped man was sweeping the stage, where pale confetti blew about like tiny butterflies. Mindy's strip act included a snowfall of artificial snow. The punters loved it but it was messy and Donald hated clearing it up. He moaned continually. He'd been with Sammy for years, so it was rumoured, and was one of the few people the boss trusted implicitly.

'All right?' Vee smiled at him.

Donald hadn't been in the bar earlier when the young man had entered the club and handed her the large brown envelope for him to deliver to Sammy. She'd stood it next to the till so he'd see it when he came on duty.

'Me dad was hoping to get paid on delivery,' the thin youth said hesitantly.

'Well, there's only me here and no one's said anything.'

He'd looked at her, then at the package. 'I'll call back later.'

Vee hadn't found out until quite recently that Sammy had many strings to his bow and supplying forged documents was one of them. The idea had fermented in her head until she'd finally plucked up courage to ask him for help. She never would have done if she hadn't overheard him collecting the last of the payments from the new Austrian doorman for his birth certificate. The amount of money Sammy had asked for had been much more than Vee could ever hope to give him.

Later, he'd suggested a few days away in the New Forest in lieu of payment and Vee had agreed. She wanted her mother to feel safe and be able to go on selling her produce. Vee had heard that on the Isle of Man women and men were interned in camps. She couldn't erase from her mind the sight of Martina and Hartmund Braun being loaded on to a lorry.When the forger's lad had left the building, Vee's heart had been pounding and she couldn't resist peeping inside the package.

Then she had snatched it up and taken it to the lavatory. As she did so, she wondered how soon it would be before it was missed. Of course the club would be searched. What if the package was discovered? Sammy would know immediately that her and her mother's papers had gone. Only she could be the culprit and he wouldn't like being made a fool of. His peers would laugh at him. He would have to think up a suitable punishment for her. She shivered. Her voice cracked as she spoke again to Donald:

'I'm in no fit state for either bar work or welcoming punters . . .'

He leant on his broom. 'You do look a bit peaky, girl.' He smiled at her. She hated lying to Donald, who had always been kind to her. He took out a grubby handkerchief and mopped his forehead. 'Leave it with me, love. I'll get your coat.'

She nodded and he lifted the flap in the bar top and shuffled out the back to return moments later with her coat. Vee shrugged herself into it and made for the door, fearing at any moment that she would be called back. One thing seemed to be leading to another: now she had lied to Donald.

Out in the August evening air she nodded to the doorman, then began walking across the park towards the bus station.

Huge cranes towered over the docks, like praying mantis, and she could smell the oily water where the container ships were berthed. Servicemen passed her on their way to the dark streets where the bars and strip clubs waited to entice them in. Sometimes they took no notice of a lone girl walking quickly. At others they called out to her. She ignored them and the smell of alcohol that often followed them.

But the sun was still shining and the flowerbeds along the pathways bloomed with mauve Michaelmas daisies and vibrant red geraniums. They would not be around for long, as people were being asked to dig for victory and all available land was being used to grow vegetables.

Vee, her mother and their few helpers worked backbreaking hours growing vegetables and fruit on their smallholding, so she appreciated the brightness of the flowers. She took a deep breath of the geraniums' scent before she crossed the road and went into the bus station where, once more, the smell of oil and petrol reigned, and rubbish littered the ground.

Sitting on the top deck of the bus, seeing the shops interspersed with the gaps caused by Hitler's relentless bombings along the south coast made her feel sad. So many lost lives and homes demolished. She knew how lucky she was to live where there were no docks or factories for the German bombers to destroy.

The bus wound its way to the leafier countryside outside the city, but Vee couldn't stop thinking of the crime she'd committed. She had stolen from Sammy Chesterton, one of the most feared men in Southampton. And what would he do to her when he came after her, when he found her? Vee had worked at the club for about six months. Before that she'd worked in a bomb factory and enjoyed the camaraderie but had left when one of the men wouldn't stop pestering her, touching her at every available moment as she worked on the line. She was scared walking home – he had begun to follow her and would hang around outside the cottage. She couldn't see him but when she drew the curtains she could feel his presence outside. Vee didn't dare involve the police in case they delved into her history and found out that her name was actually Schmidt. Nor did she want to worry her mother. Walking past the Black Cat Club one day on a shopping expedition, she had noticed the sign requesting a barmaid-hostess and had left the munitions yard. She hadn't seen the man since.

She caught sight of herself reflected in the window of the bus.

Her fair hair was tied back, showing off her deep blue eyes. She knew she owed her looks to her mother but she'd inherited the impulsiveness of her father. There wasn't anyone special in her life at present. She'd been writing to a local lad serving in France in the British Expeditionary Force, but his letters had stopped coming. Then had come the evacuation of Dunkirk . . . Looking back, Vee remembered his letters had been peppered with the name 'Colette', and decided that Colette was probably more than just a friend. She would rather believe he had fallen in love with another girl than perished.

Not having a boyfriend had meant working at the club

with its odd hours wasn't a problem. She knew very well that some men wouldn't have liked her choice of work or the fact that she was driven home, with some of the other girls, in the early hours by one of the male bar staff. At her interview with Sammy she'd been adamant that she wouldn't dance, wouldn't undress and wouldn't go to bed with the punters.

Sometimes she worked behind the bar, serving watered-down overpriced drinks to the men who came into the Black Cat looking for girls. Sometimes she sold cigarettes and cigars to the men sitting at tables watching girls strip. Sometimes, as the cloakroom girl, she took hats and coats from the customers and was often tipped for this service. Vee now realized her reticence had probably drawn Sammy to her.

Her mother hated her working at the club, but never asked too many questions. May knew that living in virtual isolation and working on the land made for a healthy life, but that it wasn't what her daughter needed for fulfilment. Vee needed the companionship of other girls. Working nights meant she could help on the smallholding during the day. She needed to live her life, and her mother trusted her to continue in the honest way she'd been brought up. She had now broken that trust.

The bus lurched on, and Vee stared out of the window,

Rosie Archer

but saw nothing of the countryside's majesty. All she could think of was that she had stolen from Sammy Chesterton. She had welshed on a deal with him and he was not likely to forget it. He would want reparation.

Icy fingers of fear crept over her, not simply for herself but for her mother, who had done nothing to deserve Sammy Chesterton's wrath but would now be in the firing line.

Chapter Two

Jem was chopping wood. The sound of his axe cutting logs to stack against the side of the house for the coming winter rang comfortingly through the trees as Vee walked down the lane from where the bus had dropped her. She opened the wide front gate and pulled it back far enough to step onto the path leading to the front door. The smell of late roses filled the air, but already the blooms had the brown-tipped petals that heralded autumn. She felt sad to know that their colour, perfume and beauty would soon be gone.

'Hello.' Jem waved in greeting, a grin splitting his face. Vee waved back and pushed open the front door, which was never locked. She threw her coat and handbag over the newel post at the bottom of the wide stairs and called to her mother.

May appeared at the top of the stairs, her arms full of

clean bedding. A pregnant grey cat watching Vee from the second stair came down to meet her.

'You're home early . . .' May paused, doubtless noticing Vee's worried expression. She left the pressed sheets on the landing table and continued down the stairs. 'It's not Jem and that blessed newly sharpened axe, is it?'

Vee put her arms around her mother. 'No, he's fine. I need to talk to you.' She could smell the aroma of baking emanating from her mother's skin and wrap-around pinafore. 'Sit down, Mum, while I make a cup of tea.' She bent and patted the cat, which butted her head against her legs. 'Not had your kittens yet?' The animal purred. May sat down at the scrubbed wooden table, a frown creasing her forehead.

Vee shook the kettle, decided there was enough water in it and put it on the stove.

'I think Jem should hear what I have to say.' Going to the door she called his name loudly. 'Otherwise you'll have to explain to him later.' There were no secrets between them.

Vee couldn't remember a time when Jem hadn't walked up daily from the village, where he rented a small terraced house near the church. He employed casual labourers for May when the crops were at their heaviest and needed harvesting. He took it upon himself to look after her cottage, and many times May had offered him a room at Honeysuckle

Holdings, but Jem had always refused, aware of the tittle-tattle his living there with the two women would cause.

He'd begun working for Honeysuckle Holdings about the time that May's mother had died of influenza in the pandemic just after the Great War. To Vee, Jem was like the father she had never known – August Schmidt had been killed shortly before the Great War ended.

As he wiped his boots on the doormat, Vee saw Jem frown as he looked first at May, then back at the axe he'd set down against the kitchen's skirting board. He pulled the door closed behind him. He was tall, with broad shoulders, dressed in corduroy trousers and a cotton shirt. He stopped near May and looked questioningly into her eyes.

'Sit down, Jem,' said Vee. 'I've got something to say that will ultimately concern you – and you, Mum.' Going over to the Aga she picked up the brown earthenware pot and made the tea, careful not to spill any precious leaves. Leaving it to settle, she went to the bottom of the stairs and picked up her handbag. Without another word, she took out the documents and laid them on the table in front of her mother.

May's eyes widened. For a while she sat quite still. Then she picked up the brown ration book bearing the name 'May Smith' and stared at it.

Her voice was soft, almost tearful, as she asked, 'Where did you get this? How?'

Jem had risen protectively and now he stood behind May and whistled through his teeth as his hand reached for an identity card, which he scrutinized.

'These are forged, right?' Vee nodded. 'Must have cost you a pretty penny.' He let out a deep sigh.

'I've done something stupid, and I'm going to have to pay for it.'

At first, May didn't seem to be listening because she said brightly, 'We can be like everyone else now.' Then silence filled the kitchen, until she cried out, 'However did you get hold of them?'

Before Vee could answer, Jem asked, 'Are you sure there's no one who knows you married Gus Schmidt?'

May shook her head. 'No one. The few that were in on the secret are gone now, even my friend Annie who was so kind to me, when . . . when . . .' her voice trailed off into a whisper '. . . Gus and I wed in secret at the register office in Southampton. After Vee arrived, I called myself Smith and, as far as anyone hereabouts knows, I'm Mrs Smith. Schmidt is on my marriage certificate so I've been scared to apply for any papers that might show my husband's surname. And now I'm more petrified after reading in the newspapers of the abuse hurled at anyone with a German-sounding name . . .'

Tears filled May's eyes and she put a hand over her mouth.

Vee spoke: 'I thought when I asked my boss for help I was doing the right thing for you and me, Mum. He does this a lot, providing fake identity papers, passports . . .'

'As well as now having a hold over you.' Jem ran a calloused hand through his grey-blond hair. 'Oh, love, whatever have you done?'

Vee took a deep breath. She'd never meant to cause unhappiness. 'I thought I was getting the best of the bargain when he said, at first, he'd take the money from my wages weekly . . .'

'You'll be paying through the nose for these for the rest of your life.' Jem's words were harsh.

'No, no, I won't. He said afterwards he didn't want any money . . .'

'What does he want?' Jem asked. When she didn't answer straight away, Vee saw sadness in his face. 'Don't tell me, you . . .'

'That's just it.' Vee looked first at her mother then back at Jem. 'I knew I couldn't go through with it.' She wiped her hand across her wet eyes and told them how she had taken the package from the lad at the club and, instead of leaving it behind the till for collection had opened it, stolen their papers, then lodged the envelope in the lavatory cistern. The kitchen became silent again, apart from the ticking of the ancient cuckoo clock above the mantelpiece.

Eventually she said, 'There are many women who'd jump at the chance. Not me. I didn't want to spend two nights in a hotel in the New Forest and have him pawing me.'

'Oh, Vee!' Her mother let the ration book she had been clutching fall to the table.

'He said he didn't want my money, but I honestly believed he'd let me pay him in cash, like the other customers he gets false passports and documents for . . .' She was gabbling on.

Jem's face was like marble as he left May's side and stepped towards Vee, enfolding her in his brawny arms. For such a big man, his voice was now surprisingly gentle. 'He's the one in the wrong, not you, love.'

As he spoke, Vee thought of the many other times he had soothed her as any father would his child. Now, clutched to his chest, she took in his calming smell: the earthiness that came from hard work, and peppermints.

May said softly, 'You'll have to go away.'

Vee broke free from Jem. 'Go where?'

Jem said, 'Your mother's right. You can't stay here – he'll come after you.'

'I can't leave you!' Vee was horrified.

'I don't think you have a choice, Vee,' said Jem. 'Sammy Chesterton's well known for his public acts of kindness when he wants something, but that man's reputation goes before him.' He was now staring at her mother and she could see they were both of one mind.

'But where will I go?'

Jem shook his head. 'Get on a bus or a train before Sammy Chesterton comes looking. This will be his first port of call.'

'I can't leave you to face my problem . . .'

'Vee, you have to go. I'm here with your mother. Even if we had money to offer Sammy Chesterton, out of principle he wouldn't take it, not now. You mustn't worry about us. You have to go, quickly and alone. We can't leave. This is one of the busiest times of the year, coming up to harvest.'

Her mother was nodding. 'You know it's the right thing to do. Unless . . .' She grew thoughtful and turned to Jem. 'What if Vee goes back to Southampton today, sees Sammy Chesterton and appeals to his better nature?'

Jem let out a guffaw of dry laughter. 'What better nature, May? Everyone believes Chesterton was responsible for the man who was hacked to pieces and left in a dustbin a few months back. The gossip was the bloke had been stealing black-market goods from him. My love, that man wants to be thought of as a good businessman, a philanthropist, but the truth is very different. Like the huge party he put on at his club last Easter for the kids of the people who'd been made homeless in the bombing. Then he offered some of his rat-infested properties as emergency housing at extortionate rents, knowing it'll be years before the local council can get around to rebuilding and renovating the places that are still standing. Even if you offered yourself on a plate now, he'd refuse because he'll want you shamed publicly.'

'Don't talk like that.' May sighed and turned to Vee. 'I'll miss you . . . You've not left me before.'

Vee said, 'I'll go tomorrow.' The cat wound herself round her legs as if in sympathy.

'No,' May said. 'You must leave immediately. Jem's right. Sammy Chesterton could come next week or he could arrive tonight. You can't take chances.'

Jem agreed. 'We'll concoct some story, but if he finds you here there's no telling what he might do.' She should go. It would be safer for all of them. Jem wasn't saying they wouldn't stand by any decision she made, but he also knew she would never forgive herself if Sammy Chesterton decided to take out his anger on her mother or the smallholding.

'Just promise me you'll keep in touch,' May said.

Vee nodded miserably. She lifted the knitted cosy on the

teapot and felt its heat. As though reading her mind, her mother said, 'Let's drink this blessed tea before it stews itself to death, then I'll help you pack a few things.'

Jem added, 'She's right, love. Do as your mother says. I'm here to look after her, but I'm no match for Sammy Chesterton.' He patted his pocket, took out his wallet and emptied it on to the table. 'Take what I've got.' Vee dissolved into tears.

Chapter Three

May sat on the old armchair by the fire, her legs tucked beneath her. Her beloved girl had gone. Vee, despite appearing self-possessed, had inherited her own youthful waywardness, which didn't bode well when paired with her father's headstrong determination. She wouldn't cry, she told herself. After all, she'd encouraged Vee to leave, and such was the bond between them that her daughter would let her know where she was. The main thing was that, for now, Vee was out of the clutches of Sammy Chesterton.

The flames flickered and burnt red, yellow. The sweet smell from the apple logs was comforting. May's eyes closed and she thought back to June 1917, when more than a hundred people had been killed and at least four hundred injured during the first daylight German bombing raid over London. She remembered the outrage when a school was hit, killing ten children. In those days there had been no early warning system. The government had been loath to admit in 1914 that war was imminent, in the belief that the news would cause pandemonium among the people. Eventually policemen had cycled about the streets wearing notices of impending attacks.

Later on in 1917, August Schmidt was transferred to the Royal Victoria Hospital at Netley and entered May's life, changing her for ever. After he had been discharged, they had lain on the rag rug in front of this same fire making love, and now she could almost feel his strong arms around her.

His words came back to her as though she, not he, had survived hell, and gave her the comfort she needed . . .

The room was white. There was no pain. A sort of calm seeped through his body. From the bed Gus could see a trim young woman in an ankle-length grey dress with a stiff white apron and neat white square covering her blonde hair as she went about her duties in the ward.

He couldn't move his head, but his eyes took in the cage over his lower left leg. He tried to move the toes on that foot but failed. He tried again. Nothing.

In the dark of the night the pain woke him.

He realized he had been holding his breath and exhaled,

then drew in the antiseptic cleanliness of what he supposed was a hospital ward. In an English hospital. This he could tell by the printed signs hanging from the walls. Silently, he thanked his school near Cologne for teaching him English, though at the time he had thought he would never get to grips with the idiosyncrasies of *gh*, *th*, *ph*.

There was a rasping noise. A crackling sound that didn't seem right, coming from his chest. Relax and breathe, he told himself, but breathing hurt. How had he come to be here? All he could remember was pain and a vague recollection of being bumped along on wheels. He closed his eyes – and saw shells bursting like fireworks. He became agitated. Relax and breathe, he told himself. Relax and breathe. He slept.

Later when he woke he thought she was singing, the blonde girl in the grey ankle-length dress. Then he realized the words had no tune, but were more like lines from a play.

'Don't talk about anything you hear in hospital. Duty before pleasure. Stand when seniors enter, obedience to all seniors. You are but one of many.'

The young woman carefully replaced the cage over his leg and smoothed the thin white blanket tidily across the top of it. She then bent down and emerged upright, holding soiled dressings, thickly clotted with dark red matter. She put them into a bag hanging from her wrist. Her fair hair, which was poking out from the white headdress, was very shiny, cut short. Her face was scrubbed, her eyes blue as a summer sky. To Gus she looked like an angel.

'Don't talk about . . .'

She was repeating the words. 'Is that something you have to remember?' His voice sounded like gravel washed up from the shore. It was a long while since he had spoken to anyone and the sound was foreign to his ears.

He must have startled her because she looked at him, eyes wide.

'It's the VAD's oath,' she said softly. 'And you should sleep.'

He didn't understand.

'VAD?'

'I'm a voluntary nurse. I clear up after the doctors and qualified nurses. We have to remember our place in the order of things in this hospital.'

He tried to smile at her, but his face felt stiff, unyielding.

'Careful,' she added quickly. 'Your scar is healing over nicely. Don't break the stitches.'

What scar? He was conscious of his leg, because now there was a dull ache in it all the time. He also knew he had some internal damage because the pain in his chest was similar to sharp spikes being drawn through his flesh. He tried

Rosie Archer

to lift his arm and managed to run his finger down the side of his cheek where he discovered the beginnings of a beard and tenderness from a raised ridge.

'Leave it alone,' she said.

He let his hand drop. Speaking to her, thinking and moving had worn him out. He closed his eyes and slept.

When he woke again the angel was leaning over him.

Panic set in. Her nearness made him remember how close the enemy aircraft had come to his plane. He had been on reconnaissance. The look of recognition, of kill or be killed, he had seen in the bi-plane's pilot's gaze. The wild noises of the wind and the rat-a-tat-tat of bullets. He remembered machine-gun fire hitting him, the piercing pain. His instrument board had been torn to pieces by a shell. He was going down over Mazingarbe, in France, with the battlefront of Vermelles two kilometres away.

His lower leg was shattered by a bullet. When he touched it, his hand had come away covered with blood. He remembered the descent, more wind, the sound of rushing air and blood dripping from his face, warm and wet.

Half the propeller was gone and his plane was spinning like a child's toy. He had no parachute. There was no room in the tiny cockpit to manoeuvre wearing the bulky object; it was preferable to have a lighter, faster plane. Besides, how could he have deployed it from the burning aircraft that was tumbling towards the earth?

He had watched a Fokker pilot without a parachute, arms and legs flailing like a windmill, hurtling to certain death. Perhaps he had thought choosing to jump was braver than waiting to go down with his machine. Gus was sickened as the man hit the ground. He swore he could hear the thud.

Loos was below.

Memories of that enemy plane, when with the cold wind across his face he had got out his revolver and fired at the enemy pilot. Never would he forget the man's fearful look as their eyes had met.

Despite his leather flying jacket, high leather boots and cap he was so cold.

He didn't bail. Instead, forcing himself to use his fast-failing flying skills he tried to steer the plane.

From the corner of his eye he watched the orange burst of flame, like an exotic sunset, that was his plane, hurtling ever nearer to the French soil. All he could hope for was that he could land before the petrol tank blew.

The ground was coming up fast to meet him. He had no memory of landing.

He had blacked out.

And now he opened his eyes wide. Happiness rushed

through him. He wasn't dead. The vagaries of war had washed him up somewhere in England. His eyes rested on his VAD angel.

'What's your name? Mine is August Schmidt.'

'May,' said his angel, and smiled.

May sighed and gently deposited Cat on the floor. She picked up an apple log from the filled basket, setting it on the fire. Tiny spurts of damp steam puffed out into the room as the log burnt. On the mantelpiece lay the documents that allowed May to stay, to shop, to belong in her own country. The price had been her daughter fleeing from her.

In the mirror she examined her face, her eyes lined at the corners from working outside in the sun. Unlike Vee's, her hair held traces of grey that blended with the blonde. She wasn't beautiful but she'd inspired two men to love her. May said a silent prayer asking God to keep her beloved daughter safe.

The moment May settled back on her chair, Cat jumped determinedly up to settle in the space at her side.

Opening the *Southampton Echo*, May began to read. The RAF had struck back at Germany for the bombs dropped on London. Berlin had taken a hard shelling. She made herself read the distressing news, then turned the page.

The headline spoke of a mystery blaze. A photograph showed a Southampton baker, his hands covering his face. Behind him, in the background, a shop was in flames. The man's anguish was pitiful. Apparently Karl Muller's one crime was to have been born in Germany.

Chapter Four

The train rattled along, the view through the carriage window changing from green fields and farms to the backs of grimy terraced houses with grey washing hanging limply on bowed lines.

Vee wished she hadn't been so hasty, first in asking Sammy Chesterton for help, then in stealing the documentation that had meant so much to her and her mother. How could she have been so stupid?

Neither she nor May was ashamed of her father's nationality – her mother had loved Gus Schmidt with all her heart. But war had changed the way people thought about ordinary German people. It was so unfair. People forgot that love knew no barriers. It was ridiculous for anyone to believe that Vee and May might be traitors simply because her mother had married a man considered an enemy.

Another train passed on the other track, smoke billowing in a cloud alongside, wafting in through the slit of open window. It smelt sharp and acrid. A loud whistle startled her.

'Oh, that made me jump as well!' The elderly woman opposite fanned her wrinkled face with a handkerchief. Vee smiled at her. 'Would you like a sweetie?' The woman proffered a white paper bag of toffees.

'No, thank you.' Vee guessed how precious the sweet ration was to her. She made herself more comfortable, glancing up at her suitcase in the mesh rack above the plush seats.

'At least it was only a train and not another of that dreadful Hitler's bombs. Going to Portsmouth, dear?' The bag of sweeties went back into the woman's capacious handbag. A waft of lavender travelled towards Vee. The sailor sitting next to the old woman grinned at her. Vee thought he looked very young to be fighting for his country. He fingered his round hat with the white band. The train was packed, people squashed together like sardines in tins.

Servicemen squatted on kitbags out in the corridor. Smoke swirled in the air from cigarettes and the floor was awash with dog-ends.

'I . . . I . . . Yes,' Vee finally answered. So that was the train's destination, was it?

Upon reaching the station at Southampton, she had climbed inside the carriage of the first train that had pulled in. She hadn't bought a ticket, for she knew the conductor would supply her with one on whichever train she chose to board. She had no idea where she should go, for there were no relatives she could stay with, and even if there had been she could never have involved them with her problems.

Eventually the carriage door opened and the portly inspector entered.

'Tickets, please.' These were tendered and then he stood looking expectantly at Vee.

'I need to buy one, please.' Her mouth was dry.

'Where to, love?' His dark suit was shiny with constant wear.

Vee must have looked confused. 'Portsmouth?' she said.

He clicked a ticket from the machine hanging at his corpulent waist and handed it to her. 'Single?'

She nodded and paid him. He left the compartment, and Vee gave the woman opposite yet another smile, then closed her eyes. She'd never been to Portsmouth before.

'. . . end of the line.'

Vee awoke to an empty compartment. The disembodied

male voice from the loudspeaker repeated, 'Portsmouth Harbour Station, end of the line.'

Sleepily, Vee gathered her handbag and small case, then stepped out into the corridor. Stationary trains and carriages were all around her. The air smelt of oil and the sea, salty, moist and muddy.

At the office close to the exit she handed the man her ticket and, without a word to or from him, began walking down the steps.

Ships and boats were all around her! The railway station was built on a pier-like structure that streamed out from a main road backed by hotels and shops and ended on iron stilts that jutted into the water, with a sturdy jetty that rose and fell with the tide. Small boats were tied to bollards on the jetty, as was a larger ferry with lifebelts attached all around. She could make out figures on the boat and cyclists pedalling towards it, trying to avoid the foot passengers.

Vee looked at her watch, a birthday present from her mother. It was ten thirty, almost dark, and she had to find lodgings for the night. She hoped they wouldn't be too expensive for she had to make her money last. Tomorrow she must find work and somewhere permanent to stay.

Ahead of her the tide was out and more boats lay on

an expanse of mud, some tied to buoys, some leaning drunkenly in brackish water that looked as dark as the sky.

'Hurry, or we'll miss the last ferry!'

Vee was caught up in a crowd of young people rushing past and found herself following them to a small kiosk.

'One, please.' She opened her purse and bought a return ticket just like the girl in front of her, then hurried with the noisy bunch down the rickety bridge towards the pontoon where the ferry waited, now crammed with people. At one end bicycles were piled together in such a way that she was sure they could never be untangled. There wasn't room to sit so, like some of the other passengers, she stood against the warmth of the large funnel and yawned. She didn't remember ever feeling so tired.

'Are we keeping you up?'

The man stood about six feet tall in his turned-down wellington boots. He wore a dark jumper and laughed, showing even white teeth. Beneath his cap she could see dark curls. She felt the warmth of a blush and was thankful the darkness hid it. Ignoring him, she turned away to stare at a notice tied to a metal pole emerging from a slatted wooden bench where a drunken man lolled – she could smell the beer fumes. She could just make out the words, 'Staff Wanted'.

The drunk rolled, allowing Vee to read more of the notice: 'See the Skipper.'

The comforting heat from the funnel made her yawn again. She wondered what the work would entail and where the skipper might be. She could discern no other information on the notice, which was now hidden by the drunk's bulk. There was no way Vee was going to disturb him. Perhaps she could ask one of the men casting the thick mooring ropes at either end of the craft from the bollards.

Mesmerized, she watched as the boat left the landing stage, churning the seawater into white-topped waves as it arced towards another pontoon, which she could just make out in the distance.

If only it wasn't so dark. What lighting there was consisted mainly of green and red dots on the water among larger moored vessels. The sky suddenly allowed a silvery light to pick out the huge boats she recognized as tankers and dredgers. There also seemed to be some naval boats moored on the Portsmouth side that the small ferry was now leaving behind.

If necessary, she could always come back tomorrow to ask about the job. The main priority was a bed for the night. With a bit of luck she'd arrive on the other side of this stretch of water in time to ask at a café or a public house where she might find accommodation – if they hadn't all closed for the night.

It would be awful if the siren blared, announcing that bombs were imminent, when she had nowhere to go. She shivered, and decided to keep her eyes open for the nearest public air-raid shelter.

She wondered what kind of work would be needed on a ferry. Cleaning? Yes, that was probably it. Vee didn't care what job she took: she needed money for lodgings and food. She watched the port opposite growing bigger and bigger. Soon the ferry would land and she would have arrived at her destination, wherever that might be. She wondered where she would be if she hadn't been swept up with the happy band of travellers, whom she could hear still laughing and chatting on the other side of the boat. Would the opposite direction have taken her into the heart of Portsmouth?

Absentmindedly she watched a man in a thick jumper and boots handling a rope near the boat's exit. A thought occurred, and she made her way towards him, pushing through the crush of people.

'Can you tell me where I can find the skipper?'

He looked her up and down and a smile lit his young, ruddy face. His shock of red hair blew in a breeze that seemed to have sprung up from nowhere.

'Where he should be, Miss. Up on the bridge.' He glanced towards some iron steps back near the funnel and Vee followed his gaze to a man high at the front of the boat, his eyes on the water. Vee nodded her thanks and made her way to the metal ladder.

If the water had been rough, she wouldn't have been able to climb the slippery steps, but keeping a wary eye on her cardboard suitcase, left tucked out of the way of people's feet, she was soon inside a small wooden cabin that was completely open to the elements.

The wind, not really discernible below, was biting at her face and causing her hair to whip into her eyes. She tapped the man on the shoulder. His hands were on the wheel.

'Excuse me!'

'My God!' She'd made him jump. 'What the hell are you doing up here?' He stared at her, then his eyes moved quickly back to the water. 'Don't you know this is out of bounds to passengers?'

Her heart dropped. Never had she expected to be shouted at so fiercely, and by the same man who had accused her of being tired in such a jovial manner when he had caught her yawning.

'I'm sorry,' was all she could manage. The wind was trying to take her words away. Vee pulled her hair back from her face. 'The sign says "See the Skipper", and you're the skipper, aren't you?'

'You could have chosen a better place to see me. What do you want?'

His words were gruff, but the twinkle in his eye showed a sense of humour. The wind, becoming more violent, caused the boat to sway, and she fell against him. 'I'm sorry,' she said, scrambling to regain her composure. 'That notice down on the deck says you need staff.'

For a moment he was silent, as though digesting her words, then he began to laugh. If she wasn't so bewildered she would have thought it was a good sound – a real man's laugh, deep and dry.

'You?' He looked at her quizzically and smiled again. But it was a warm smile.

'I can clean a boat, make tea, scrub a deck.' She knew she was babbling but she didn't care. 'What else would he need a woman for on a boat?'

'You really are desperate for a job, aren't you?' He frowned. 'I thought this was some kind of joke one of my blokes had cooked up.'

Vee was practically shouting to make herself heard above the elements now.

'Look, I need a job and somewhere to stay. I'm a good worker and I'm honest.'

As she uttered the last couple of words she realized she'd just lied to him. She was running away because she hadn't been honest at her last job.

Rain began to fall. Huge wet drops that not only stung her face but were plastering her hair to her head. The man pulled off his cap and stuck it over her hair. He looked down at her – she barely reached his chest. He was staring at her thoughtfully. 'That'll keep your hair dry. It's the best I can do,' he said eventually. 'Now, stand back and let me land this craft.'

Neatly, despite the waves hurling themselves against the pontoon and causing the boat to pitch and toss like a cork, he drew close enough to the wooden jetty for the seaman she had spoken to earlier to throw a rope, encircle a bollard, and haul the vessel against the pontoon. At the other end another man was securing the front.

Only when the boat was steady enough did the young man unclip the chain allowing passengers to safely disembark.

Still standing close to the skipper, Vee watched amazed as the men, once the foot passengers had departed, helped disentangle the bicycles for their rightful owners, who then pushed them up the gangway to disappear into the darkness beyond.

Vee was soaked. She sneezed, then yawned again. The day had been full of surprises, some not so good, and she was hungry, tired and, although she hated to admit it, she was scared. Oh, how she wished she was at home, with her warm cosy bed to climb into.

'Get down in the cabin out of the rain. This is the last ferry for tonight. As soon as I've moored up properly and locked everything away I'll fetch you.'

She looked into his eyes. There were so many questions she wanted to ask but her happiness at hearing him mention a cabin where she would at least be dry overrode everything else. He gave her directions to get to it, then Vee climbed down the ladder, took her suitcase and went down into the bowels of the boat. She sat on a wooden bench in a windowless room that smelt of fags and bodies.

She wondered if Sammy Chesterton had been out to the smallholding. It might be a little too soon as perhaps he hadn't yet discovered that the envelope containing the forged papers was missing.

Before she had left home, Vee had had great difficulty in persuading her mother to hang on to the forged documents. She had put her own into her handbag.

'Even if you never need them, Vee's paid a high price for them and the least you can do is to keep them safe,' advised Jem.

It was warm in the cabin and the floor was littered with rubbish and sweet wrappers. Vee was so tired. How lovely it would be to sit in the armchair in front of the fire with Cat on her lap. Sadness overwhelmed her that she wouldn't see the kittens when they arrived. Already homes had been promised for three and May had decided to keep one. But who knew how many Cat would produce? She was a good mouser and earned her keep. Vee often found her asleep on her bed. She sighed. At present she didn't have a bed.

She smoothed some stray hairs behind one ear and realized she was still wearing the skipper's peaked cap. She took it off, ran her fingers through her hair, put the cap on the bench beside her and closed her eyes. The man with the twinkling eyes would come and find her, if only to claim his cap.

Chapter Five

'Wake up, sleepy-head.'

Vee opened her eyes. For a moment she was unsure of her surroundings and wondered if she was still dreaming. A dark-haired man was shaking her shoulder gently. When he said, 'I think you could do with a cup of tea. Am I right?' she remembered where she was.

She tried a smile. 'My throat feels parched.' The wooden seat seemed welded to her bottom.

'Come on,' he said. 'I'll take you home. We can discuss work there.' He picked up his cap and jammed it on his head.

'I'm not going home with you! I don't know you.' It was as if a light bulb had switched on in her brain. First Sammy Chesterton had wanted to get her into bed and now this stranger wanted to take her to his home. 'What do you think I am?'

'You asked me for a job. Either you want one or you don't. I haven't got time to mess around. There are rooms for workers at my house and my wife will sort one out for you. We can discuss work or . . .' He paused. It was then she saw how tired he was. He rubbed a hand across his chin. '. . . get off this boat and let me go home so I can get some shut-eye.'

She stood up. Without another word, he picked up her case and started towards the doorway. Meekly, Vee followed. When she reached the top of the steps she saw that the rain had stopped. The dark seemed impenetrable and she was glad she wasn't alone. He waited, watching her as she carefully went down the steps, then walked off the boat and onto the pontoon. Because of the blackout he carried a small torch but kept his fingers across its beam so the light shone thinly and only where he needed it. She tried to keep up with him, but his long legs increased the distance between them. At last she cried, 'Wait for me!'

The man stopped, turned and laughed when he saw her struggling to catch up with him in her high heels.

'If you're going to work for me you might think about wearing some proper shoes,' he said. 'Else you'll be in boots all the time.'

When Vee reached his side she took a moment to look about her and catch her breath.

'It's not far now,' he said, striding down a concrete path.

Vee had to step aside – a young woman, looming out of the darkness, nearly knocked into her.

'I'm sorry.' The words came automatically, but the girl didn't answer, just hastened on her way, leaving a waft of cheap perfume.

'Don't worry about Ada,' he said. Vee waited for him to add more, but he said nothing and she carried on walking behind him. Cloud had shut out the moonlight and Vee could feel yet more rain in the air. She made out what she thought was a bus station with several double-deckers silent and empty for the night. There was a ticket office and as they drew close she could make out the boat fares. A board announced, 'Gosport Ferry'. So she was in Gosport. She thought back to the train arriving at Portsmouth Harbour Station, then her journey across the short expanse of water. Just then she heard music coming from what looked like a Nissen hut in darkness across a road. Alongside it, tall, imposing houses faced the water.

'There are no lights in my house,' he said. 'That means my wife's not at home. I don't want you worrying about being there alone with me so I'll take you into the café.' He began to cross the road, slower now so that she could keep up with him.

'Here,' he waved an arm, 'is Beach Street. Known for its boat builders. Tomorrow you'll see the skeletons of small craft and hear the men working on them.' He paused. 'Business is slower than before the war,' he added. 'Take a deep breath.'

Vee breathed in. The smell of wood reminded her of pencil sharpenings.

'I hope that doesn't unsettle you,' he said. He pointed upwards at the windows of one of the tall houses. 'That'll be your room. If you can't stand the smell of wood shavings, you're in trouble!'

Vee didn't speak. The thought of a room with a bed, one she could curl up and sleep in, filled her with relief.

At the Nissen hut he pushed open the door and immediately she was enveloped in light and a fug of fried-food smells that reminded her of how hungry she was. The ever-present cigarette smoke tried to escape out into the road, but the long blackout curtain kept most of it inside.

The skipper stood aside so she could enter. The dance music from the wireless and the brightness of the electric light immediately raised her spirits.

Men and women sat around long tables drinking tea and talking. Some were eating, some laughing and most were smoking. A plump woman in bright overalls, bleached blonde hair piled high on her head, secured with glittery pins and covered with a mesh snood, stood behind the counter.

'Hello, Jack. The usual?' She gave him a warm, welcoming grin. Then a smile came Vee's way.

So, Vee thought, she knew his name now. Jack suited him.

There was a glass container on the counter filled with some kind of pudding on a large plate. It looked greasy and was cut into squares.

'Please, Connie, love, two mugs of tea and two bits of your delectable bread pudding.' He turned to Vee and said, 'Park your bottom there.' He pointed to a seat at an empty table. 'Ever had bread pudding before?' He took off his cap and put it on the table, then ran his fingers through his curly hair and smiled down at her.

Vee shook her head. It didn't look very palatable.

'Connie's bread pudding is the best in Gosport,' he added loudly.

Vee could see the woman was pleased as she poured their tea from a large urn into big white mugs. 'Sit down, Jack, I'll bring it over.' Connie flashed him another wide smile and he took the chair opposite Vee.

'Thank you,' she said, falling on the tea as it was placed in front of her. She eyed the square of pudding that accompanied it with apprehension. Connie stood by the table.

'John Cousins was in here looking for you,' she said.

'He'll catch up with me,' the skipper said. Turning to Vee, 'Now you know my name, Jack Edwards, am I allowed to ask yours?'

'Vee, Violetta Smith.' She forked up a small piece of the pudding. 'Violetta after my grandmother,' she added as she popped it into her mouth and chewed. 'It's lovely,' she gasped, amazed as fruit, sugar and spice flooded her taste buds.

'What did I tell you? The best in Gosport.'

Connie laughed. 'As soon as I can find the mixed fruit to make it, it disappears. We can't always get hold of the ingredients now. Bloody war.' She put a hand on Jack's shoulder and he looked up at her in the way of people who have few secrets between them. The way good friends trust each other, thought Vee.

'I got the baby out the back,' she said quietly. 'Rosie's with her.'

Jack's face clouded and he began to rise but Connie pushed him back into the seat. 'She's fine, asleep. Eat and drink up before you go to her.'

'Where's Madelaine?'

'Gone to see her parents,' she said. 'Didn't want to take the little one in case there was an air raid and she was between public shelters. She knows I got the Morrison in the kitchen.' Connie moved away from the table and made her way back behind the counter, where a small queue had formed.

Already the bread pudding was lining Vee's empty stomach and the strong tea was making her feel better. She wondered who Madelaine was. From the way Connie had spoken of her, Vee decided Connie wasn't enamoured of the woman.

Vee's mother also had a Morrison shelter in their kitchen. The box-like metal contraption held a quilt and pillows, and was just big enough for two or three people when the planes came over, dropping their bombs. Like many others, May had put a sheet of wood across the top and used it as an extra table.

Vee finished eating, then drained her tea. She sat back on the chair and thought how much better she felt. But Jack's demeanour had changed. She thought he seemed preoccupied now, and the light had left him. Whose baby was it? Why was the child out the back?

'If you don't eat anything else until breakfast tomorrow,' he said, 'you won't hurt with that inside you . . . I sometimes wonder why on earth I don't let Connie have a free hand in this place. I suppose I have so much on my mind, I'm scared of changing things.' He wasn't actually talking to her, Vee realized, more voicing his thoughts. There was no need for her to answer him, but she had deduced that the café belonged to him, or was under his management.

He finished his tea, then took a deep breath. 'I'll tell you briefly what I want from you. If you agree, I'll take you next door to my house where not only my wife, child and I live but also Rosie, Connie, and Regine, who works in the ticket office. It's a big old house but there's an empty room overlooking the harbour and the floating bridge . . .'

What on earth was a floating bridge?

Jack answered her unasked question.

'The steam-powered floating bridge takes people and transport across to the point at Portsmouth, and has done since 1840. It can accommodate up to fifty vehicles. At present it's very useful for transporting troops, lorries and munitions. The floating bridge, or car ferry, is nothing to do with me.

'Our ferries transport people to Portsea, near the dockyard, for the princely sum of a penny. We start early, end late, run regularly and don't shut down during the raids.' He stared into her eyes. 'Am I right in thinking you've never been to Gosport before?'

'Never,' she said.

'Well, you've got a lot to learn. But there's no finer folk than true Gosport people. Play straight and they'll do anything for you.'

'But what do you want me to do?' Vee asked. She was mesmerized by his mouth. As he talked the corners seemed to dissolve into upward strokes that made her think he could laugh quite easily if he wasn't being so serious.

'I'm coming to that. The company has lost a few men who decided to join up, even though ferrying is a reserved occupation.'

'What does that mean?'

'It means working on the ferries is a necessary job during this war, so the workers are exempt from joining the forces.' For a moment sadness clouded his face. 'Unfortunately, I can't fight because my heart beats erratically. It also means I've had that blessed notice pinned up there for long enough to know that no one suitable wants a job working on the boats during the war, until you happened along, of course.

'I've had men on their last legs apply, unable to climb the ladder to the wheelhouse. Spotty young lads ready for their call-up, who are no good to me. By the time they were trained they'd be in the services . . . I'm willing to train you up. It'll be hard work, dirty work, and you'll be out in all weathers. You'll probably get some stick from the older ferry men for being a woman in a man's world, but what do you say?'

Vee opened her mouth but that was as far as she got.

Jack didn't give her time to answer: he went on about

the wages, the hours, the room in his house. She noticed he didn't ask where she'd come from or why she'd left.

'Yes,' Vee said.

He slapped his knee. 'Good. I knew you were right when I saw you weren't in the least seasick. No good to me if you're queasy every time you're on the water.'

Vee thought back to the wind, the rain and the heaving of the craft as they'd sailed from Portsmouth.

'No, I wasn't, was I?' She hadn't thought about it at the time and was pleased she could tolerate bad sea conditions.

Just then the thin wail of a baby crying, drowning the music from the wireless, came from the kitchen. 'That's my daughter,' Jack said. Vee saw the pride in his eyes. 'That's my Margaret – we call her Peg. She's only a few weeks old. Got to think about getting her christened soon, keep putting it off.' Vee noted how his voice was soft and his smile reached right to his eyes when he talked about his little girl. 'I'll just go and get her, then take you home and show you your room. Oh, I forgot to ask, you do have your identity papers and ration book, don't you?'

Vee got up from her chair. 'Oh, yes,' she said. 'I have them.'

He stood up, jammed his hat on his head, called good-night to some of the men and women in the room, then

Rosie Archer

disappeared through a door at the back of the counter to reappear moments later with a carry-cot that held the crying child.

'Her mother's gone visiting. I must get my Peg home and changed.'

Vee looked into the carry-cot at the wailing infant. Connie handed her a bag containing an empty bottle and a rolled-up dirty nappy. Vee noted the smell emanating from the little girl. Connie must have tuned into her thoughts for she added, 'Madelaine didn't leave enough stuff for me to make her a feed or to change her again, though I'd have used a dishcloth if Jack hadn't arrived when he did.'

Connie talked of him with warmth, and it was obvious that she was fond of him. Vee wanted to say the baby was lovely, but she thought the screwed-up face and open crying mouth belied that. Yet her motherly instincts rose to the fore.

'Hello, little one,' she murmured. She touched the tiny clenched hand, and immediately the little girl opened her fingers and clutched Vee's finger in a powerful grip. Vee immediately thought of Cat's babies, who would look nothing like pretty little fluffy kittens when they arrived. Living on a smallholding had taught her that newborn animals soon changed and became beautiful. She hoped it would be so with this infant who was surely too small to be without her mother.

Outside the rain was lashing down again and Jack kept close to the walls of the buildings to try to protect Peg. Very soon he stopped, put his shoulder to a door and it opened.

'Put the light on as soon as we're inside,' he said, walking ahead of her. After flicking the electric switch, Vee saw they were in a long passage with doors and stairs leading off it. Ahead Jack had entered a large, comfortable living room-cum-kitchen where a fire was burning low in the grate. Vee relished the warmth after the chill of the rain.

He had put the carry-cot on the table. Miraculously the child had ceased crying. He grinned at Vee.

'Your room is at the top of the stairs at the front. If you open any of the other doors by mistake you'll see they're occupied. Rosie is next to you and Regine is opposite . . . Regine. Don't pay too much attention to her – she has a sharp tongue.' He waved towards a door leading from the room. 'Scullery and garden are through there. Now,' he said, 'you work for me and I expect you to be here in this room at five tomorrow morning. The ferry starts at five thirty. Don't make me late by staying in bed.' He paused. 'I'll expect you to muck in and help in the house – we all do our bit. My wife had a hard birth and is a bit fragile, so Rosie, Regine,

Connie and I help as much as we can. Connie feeds us.' Vee nodded. She was now practically asleep on her feet. Only the strangeness of the situation was keeping her awake. Jack must have seen this for he said, 'Go to bed.'

Vee was only too happy to oblige.

Chapter Six

Sammy Chesterton sat in the layby in his Armstrong Siddeley, smoking. He sighed. Even though the aroma and taste of the expensive cigar soothed him, it didn't stop the memories flooding back that caught at his heartstrings and hurt, like a knife twisting in a wound. He brushed ash off his expensive suit.

The cottage looked the same as it always had: Honeysuckle Holdings, set back a little from the lane with the smallholding and its sheds, fields and greenhouses at the rear. A grey cat, heavily pregnant, walked from the side of the house to flop lazily in the patch of sun on the path.

May had been ten years old when he had first walked her home from school, carrying her books for her, as his father had told him he should. His father was old school, believed in treating women like ladies. Certainly his mother had had his dad wrapped around her little finger, but they'd worshipped each other until that bomb had landed on his village house in 1917. It had happened while Sammy had been away . . .

All these years later his heart still hurt thinking about May.

After college he'd travelled the world, working his way to India, Thailand, Greece, Germany and China, but eventually he'd settled back in Southampton, discovering he could make more money in a place he knew if he kept a finger in a lot of pies.

He imported quality goods made by the Chinese and Thais. Local people were paid a pittance and worked long hours, and he sold their goods at profits he'd never thought possible. Then he had bought his first club, and realized it was easier to slip over to the wrong side of the law, bringing in drink from France rather than buying it from wholesalers in England, his clubs the perfect places to sell it at exorbitant prices. Backhanders to coppers in high places kept everyone happy, most of all him.

He'd even thought about going into politics. Again, cash to councillors made it possible for him to get small changes made in some local laws if they didn't suit him. He'd known early on that he'd never get anywhere with a German name.

At school it hadn't mattered so much. After all, 'Herbert

Lang' was as English-sounding as the next boy's name. His birth certificate told a different story.

Sammy Chesterton was the name of a character in a novel he'd read and admired. So Herbert Lang had become Sammy Chesterton. But his ancestry barred him from the success he wanted. Far too many English Members of Parliament were determined to scour the country of anything or anyone remotely German. The British Nationality and Status of Aliens Act of 1918 contained so many anti-German provisions it was laughable. But Sammy never laughed.

He discovered a brilliant forger who liked being paid for what he was best at, so Sammy put business his way . . . a great deal of business over the years, which was mutually profitable. It allowed peaceful people, who lived and, in some cases, had been born in England to become, albeit illegally, English. It was amazing how many people in high places had skeletons in their closets.

Sammy put a great deal of money into the Nationality of Married Women Bill that had gone before the House of Commons, but even though a Joint Select Committee had been appointed, it had fallen by the wayside, despite the support of at least two hundred MPs.

Sammy reasoned that if the women affected could be given back their own birthright, instead of having to accept their husbands' nationality, their children wouldn't suffer indignity. He firmly believed he could have done much more for his beloved England if his own birthright hadn't been taken from him. Sammy had never suspected that the girl who had worked in his club was the daughter of his childhood sweetheart. May must have married a German lad.

Now the heat rose from his neck and added to the sweat dampening his back. How could he have been so insensitive as to proposition young Vee?

She'd said she had no money and asked if she could pay in instalments. He'd told her she could pay her debt in kind. That a weekend in a hotel in the New Forest would pay for her and her mother's new identities. If only he'd looked closer at the information Vee had given him, he'd have realized her address here in Netley was the home May had been brought up in.

He sighed. Why had he never noticed her resemblance to May? But, then, why should he? He'd driven to this address hoping to catch Vee and instead had spotted May collecting logs from a stack outside the house. His heart had flipped.

When he was a kid, her parents had made him welcome. He remembered apple pie with a latticed pastry top and thick dairy cream, the pie tart and the cream sweet. Fresh strawberries picked in the field, with May at his side. She'd had pigtails then. Sammy drew on his cigar. Best Cuban, hand-rolled. He had money, he had clubs, expensive clothes, things, but objects didn't make a person feel wanted.

He was lonely. Very, very lonely.

Sammy threw his cigar stub out of the window and thought back to that morning when his forger, Tom, had come to the club for his money.

'You're a bit quick off the mark, mate. What's this, cash on delivery?'

Tom had given him a look that would have melted ice. 'C'mon, I need money same as everyone else. Was everything all right?'

He had had nothing in his hands.

'Who did you give the package to?' Sammy was well aware that a few of his employees would like to make a bit more money over and above what he was paying them.

'It weren't me, Boss.'

Sammy looked at Donald. If he said he hadn't been given a package, he believed him. 'It's all right, mate,' he said. He didn't want the old feller's dicky heart playing up.

'My boy brought it in a few days ago.'

Sammy lifted the wooden flap and motioned Tom behind the bar. 'There's the telephone. Get in touch with your lad, ask him who was here.'

Five minutes later it was established that Vee had taken the large brown envelope.

'Search this place from top to bottom,' Sammy growled. 'Likely she won't have stolen stuff that wasn't hers.'

He knew now why she'd left early and it wasn't because she was feeling ill. He hadn't really worried about her absence, thinking she was getting over whatever ailed her, but the little bitch had lied to him, stolen the documents she'd wanted, and made a run for it. Sammy thought quickly. Although there were only a few people in the club who knew what had happened, within hours his peers would be laughing that a chit of a girl had got one over on Sammy Chesterton.

The biggest slap in the face was that she had turned down the offer of a weekend in a hotel with him. He wasn't sure what would be hardest to live down. Women usually flocked to his bed. The bitch had made him look a right fool.

He opened the till and counted out notes, adding a few extra from his wallet to Tom's original price.

'Sorry, Tom,' he said. 'I should know better than to doubt you. No hard feelings?'

Tom shuffled from one foot to the other. There was always honour among thieves. 'None at all, mate,' he said.

Sammy knew they were waiting for him to blow his top,

like he had the other morning when he'd caught one of his drivers with his fingers in the till. Sammy would give money freely if it suited him but if anyone took it without asking . . .

'What are you doing, Al?' He had caught the young man with the till drawer open and banknotes clutched in his hand. He'd tried to return them, but Sammy was beside him and had pinned Al's hand to the counter with one of his own. Like a flash Sammy's fingers went to his breast pocket. His flick knife was out and Al's hand, still holding the notes, was skewered to the bar. Above Al's screams of pain, Sammy said, 'Never steal from the hand that feeds you.' Sammy looked at the young man, the blood, his fractured hand, and at Donald, who had come in to see what all the noise was about.

'Get rid of him, Donald,' he'd said.

The young man hadn't been seen at the club since.

Sammy now looked at Greta, the bar staff and Donald. 'Don't just stand there! Carry on looking for the rest of the documents.' He went to his office, slamming the door after him.

A while later a knock on the door and a small voice asked, 'Boss, are you in there?'

When he opened the door, Greta was standing outside in

the silky siren suit she wore for her dance practice. A turban covered her hair and in her hands was a cobwebbed package.

'I remembered the night Vee said she was poorly, she was in the lavatory for ages. I thought she was being sick . . .'

He took the envelope, shook off the detritus and looked inside.

'Well done, love.' He smiled at her. Running his eyes along the cards and birth certificates, he saw it was as he'd guessed: her and her mother's papers had gone. He threw the package onto his desk. He'd recoup the money he'd already paid out for the forged papers from the punters, but in the meantime he'd think up a suitable punishment for Miss Vee Schmidt.

'Do you want me to get you a drink or something, Boss?'

He looked into Greta's face. She was one of his best girls. She had a look of Betty Grable about her, and her legs weren't bad. A waft of perfume reached him and he treated her to another smile. 'I'll take you out for a meal as a thank-you after the club closes,' he said.

He'd thought the look in her eyes showed eagerness, and she readily agreed. It was another of those nights when he had nothing else to do.

'What a bloody mess,' he said now, taking another cigar and cutting it.

The trouble was, he'd allowed Vee to work at the Black

Cat even though she didn't give out to the punters. After all, some girls were a little shy at first. Stripping came easier when the money rolled in from the men in the audience. The patrons liked the feel of nubile skin. Vee seemed to think he could go on paying her when she wasn't pulling her weight. He'd believed it wouldn't be long before he could entice her to be . . . friendly to his customers. True, she'd stolen from him, but underneath she was a nice girl, a little naive perhaps, but then she was May's daughter.

'What a bloody mess,' he said again.

How could he take May's daughter to task for making him look a fool? But if he did nothing about her theft he'd be a laughing stock, wouldn't he?

He threw the part-smoked cigar out of the open window, started the car and slowly drove back to Southampton and the Black Cat Club.

May had spotted the car in the layby. For a moment she thought the driver looked familiar, but then she laughed at herself. Who did she know with a car as expensive as that?

In her arms she carried logs for the living-room fire. It was really rather warm during the day for a fire but Cat liked to snooze in the corner behind the old chair and at night the cottage became quite cold. May had no doubt that the grey cat would produce her kittens in the house. She smiled to herself. Vee would never forgive her if anything happened to Cat. She wondered which tom had fathered the kittens. Cat had had several suitors. An orange thug with a crooked tooth, a black and white stranger that had hung about, then disappeared, and the black mouser from the barn that didn't really belong to her but that May fed anyway.

Cat had appeared one stormy night when May had been, as usual, sitting in the kitchen trying not to feel sorry for herself that Gus was gone for good. The rain had lashed against the windows and she'd heard the faint scratching on the door and the plaintive miaows. That night she'd let Cat into the house and her heart.

Gus had loved cats. The strays that gathered in the grounds and buildings of the Royal Victoria Hospital at Netley were always in for a petting from him when at last he was able to hobble about on crutches. Sometimes he managed to save them scraps from his meals.

Set on the shores of the river Hamble, the hospital had been built in 1856. Its 2,500 patients were partly looked after by Red Cross volunteers as most of the regular nursing staff were working overseas during the Great War.

May couldn't keep August Schmidt out of her mind. The tall, slim man always seemed to be watching her whenever and wherever she was in the ward. Now he was up on crutches, he wore the thick cotton suit of a detainee with large red dots on the back. The clothing made the prisoners think twice about trying to escape when their injuries had healed. May had known only of one who had escaped. He had reached Waterloo station by clinging to the underside of the train from Southampton before he was captured again.

Most of the Germans, once they had recovered, stayed in the hospital's prison or were sent out to work, returning nightly. Of course, the people living around Netley hated the Germans being treated well at the hospital; they imagined the men were better fed than their own lads at the front. Quite possibly they were correct, thought May.

The hospital was self-contained, with the main wards facing the inner courtyard, the nurses' and doctors' quarters in kit-built units at the rear. As well as the prison, it had its own gasworks, bakery, reservoir, asylum, and even a ballroom to keep the workers happy when time and circumstances permitted.

May and the nurses loved the dances. There was music, of course, and the chance to dress up in clothes that were not their uniform. On those evenings May found it easy to pretend the war didn't exist, especially when she was dancing with a young doctor. That bubble usually burst when the next batch of bloodied, stinking men arrived on a ship from Southampton Water, and moored at the hospital's jetty to be brought in.

'What does VAD mean?' Gus had asked her one day, as she cleared away the detritus one of the doctors had left after cleaning his leg.

'Voluntary Aid Detachment,' she'd replied. 'We're a sort of back-up for the regular nurses.'

'Is that why your clothes are different?'

She'd nodded. 'The hospital needs all the help it can get.' She didn't tell him that some of the regular nurses looked down on the VADs. After all, they had trained for much longer than the volunteers. He'd put his hand on her arm. 'I thought I had died and I was sure you were an angel . . .'

Had those words come from anyone else May would have thought they were taking liberties with her. She knew how badly he'd been injured, so he was trying to tell her how grateful he was to be alive. She'd smiled at him and something inside her had told her he would love her like no one else had ever loved her.

Now May sighed as she picked up the *Evening News* from the table and settled in the armchair to read: young men between the ages of eighteen and forty-one were now obliged to register for military service. Previously many men had volunteered to fight. She read down the list of workers who were exempt. Selfishly, she was happy that Jem was considered too old.

War had taken her first love; she didn't want to lose the second.

Chapter Seven

When Vee awoke to the tinny clatter of the alarm clock she looked around the room in which she had tumbled, unwashed, into bed the night before. Her last memory was of the smiling lips of Jack Edwards.

Last night she'd pulled back the bedclothes, which were clean and sweet-smelling, then wound and set the clock. As soon as she'd closed her eyes, she'd been asleep. Now the morning sun burst into her room as she pulled back the blackout curtains and gasped. Across the road a huge metal monstrosity was half in and half out of the water. Already several delivery vans and cars were parked at either side of the central bridge on the boat-like contraption. People were milling about. Vee opened the window and the smell of the sea greeted her with a torrent of noise. So that was the floating bridge. Along its bow a painted sign proclaimed,

'Brickwood's Sunshine Ale Bright To The Last Drop'. Advertising for a brewery no doubt, she thought. She could also make out the boat's name, *Ceto*. Vee wondered what it meant. People were stepping from the sloping hard on Beach Street on to the weirdly shaped chained craft. Despite the bustle outside she felt calm. Surely Sammy Chesterton wouldn't find her here. Vee put her elbows on the window-sill and took a deep breath of the sunny morning. Not far away, beyond the ticket office, she could see the squat ferry she had travelled on last night. Across the harbour at the Portsmouth side there was another boat. The sea between the two points was filled with craft of all sorts and sizes. Even at this early hour people were working, queuing and laughing, and the greeny-grey sea washed against the sea wall, splashing against the concrete as the movement of the larger ships caused the water to swell.

Vee was pleased with her room. It had a double bed, wardrobe, dressing-table, chair and toe-comfy rag rug, and was very clean and comfortable. There was a basin in the corner and immediately she began a strip-wash, hauling on wide-legged grey trousers and a darker grey lightweight woollen sweater from her suitcase.

She'd slept well last night despite an argument that had been going on downstairs. She had heard a woman's high-pitched voice screaming obscenities and a heavier calming tone. Vee hadn't heard what the couple were quarrelling about, and they had stopped when the baby began crying. Now, tidying the room and emptying her suitcase, Vee took her birth certificates and other papers, for now she had two of everything, and hid the originals, which told the truth, in the space behind the bottom drawer of the dressing-table. She felt they would be safely out of sight there. It ran through her mind that she should perhaps destroy them but somehow that seemed disloyal to her father.

Along with her gas mask, her identity papers had to be carried at all times. But since she had no idea of what her work would entail, she decided to keep her papers in her large purse in her pocket and leave her shoulder bag in her room.

She brushed her hair and pulled it into a ponytail, then took a deep breath and went down the wide stairs to the huge kitchen, following the smell of toast.

A pretty woman with a blonde pageboy hairstyle and a sulky mouth was stirring a cup of tea while she sat at the large table. Her silk dressing-gown gaped open, showing a matching nightdress. Smoke curled from the cigarette she had placed on a saucer.

'So you're the new girl?' she said.

Vee nodded. A dark-haired imp of a girl was toasting bread on a long-handled fork while kneeling in front of the range, which was sending out a fierce heat. She turned to Vee. 'How many bits of toast?'

'Two, please,' said Vee. 'You're Rosie?' She hoped she'd got her name right. She vaguely remembered the names Rosie and Connie from the café the previous evening, and she had already met Connie.

The girl nodded. 'And you are?'

'Vee, Vee Smith. I'm—'

'Oh, we know who you are.' The voice came from a dark-haired young woman who had come in from a door leading into what Vee supposed was the scullery and the back garden. 'You're the girl who's going to be a stand-in for the fellas on our ferries.'

'Well, I—'

'All the decent blokes have been called up.' She set on the table the bag of clothes pegs she'd been carrying. 'What's left are either too young or too old. Jack thought because some of our own men have insisted on going to fight he'd do what the farmers have done with the land girls and train women up.'

Before Vee had a chance to reply, she continued, 'As

long as he doesn't put you in the ticket office with me, I don't care what he does.' She began to move away then said, 'Madelaine sometimes gives me a hand when she gets time off from Peg, don't you, Mads? And that's the way I like it.' She turned to the blonde. 'It's a lovely day. Those nappies I boiled should soon be dry.'

She passed Vee in a cloud of perfume and, with a toss of her dark sleek hair, left the kitchen. Vee heard her going upstairs.

'Here you are.' Rosie held out a plate with two slices of bread toasted to perfection. 'Don't take any notice of Regine. She thinks she's above us all. Put some marge on this before it gets cold. There's strawberry jam if you'd rather.'

Vee gave Rosie a smile and thanked her.

The woman with the pageboy hairstyle asked, 'What's Vee short for?' She took a long drag on her cigarette, blew the smoke high in the air, then stubbed it out in the saucer.

'Violetta – it was my grandmother's name.' Vee began to take in the comfort of the large room: several plump armchairs, a huge table, a wireless on the sideboard and a dresser full of blue and white crockery. A copy of *Tide Times* lay on the table.

'I'm Madelaine, Jack's wife and the mother of that eternally crying child.'

'Hello,' said Vee.

Madelaine blinked her almond-shaped eyes, but didn't smile.

Jack had told Vee he was married, but she would never have thought Madelaine could be his wife. They looked totally unsuited. But that was love for you, she thought. Love made for strange partners. Yet if that was so, why did she feel Jack deserved someone different? She thought of his lips, kissable, smiling . . . Suddenly ashamed of herself, she brushed the thoughts away.

Vee saw that Rosie had poured her a cup of tea and smiled her thanks at her.

'Connie also lives here and she's usually first up in the mornings. She opens the café for the early-bird workers,' Rosie told her. 'I should be there as well by now. Jack said for you to wait until he arrives.'

A few moments later Rosie had gone. Madelaine was reading a newspaper, using her long red fingernails to flick through the pages.

Vee thought about her mother and decided she should let her know where she was. May would be worried sick because she knew Vee's money wouldn't last long. On the other hand, thought Vee, if she told her mother where she was, then decided she didn't want to stay and moved on, May would be even more worried. She decided to get in touch with her as soon as she knew she was truly settled.

'Did you know the government has levied a twenty-four per cent tax on luxuries?'

Vee realized Madelaine was talking to her, reading from the newspaper she was holding. She shook the pages. 'I wonder what they consider luxuries. Some of us might consider them essentials.' She neither waited for nor expected a reply. She didn't move when a cry cut through her voice. 'They've also banned the buying and selling of new cars. How ridiculous!'

Just then Vee heard the front door open and heavy footsteps paused in the hallway. Presently Jack entered the kitchen carrying the grizzling baby. Vee noted he was extremely careful that the little one's head didn't wobble, supporting it with his large hand against his thick navy jumper.

'Morning, everyone,' he said cheerfully.

'Oh, Jack, why not let her sleep?' Madelaine sighed and let the newspaper slide to the floor. She made no move to retrieve it.

'Peg had just opened her eyes, hadn't you, my darling?' Jack said. 'She was telling the world she was awake.' He placed the baby in the carry-cot that lay on a chair. Tiny fists began waving and punching at the air. It occurred to

Vee that the argument she had heard last night might have been between Jack and Madelaine. Possibly he was angry that she'd left the child with Connie for so long. Vee, her toast and tea a memory, got up and went to look at the baby.

'She's got such blue eyes,' she said. 'I wonder if they'll change.' On the smallholding the eye colouring of newborn creatures often changed after a few weeks.

'Isn't she beautiful?' Clearly Jack was smitten with his daughter.

Vee touched a tiny hand and Peg immediately gripped her finger. She gazed down at the baby and something fluttered in her heart.

'Yes,' she said.

Regine clattered down the stairs. 'I'm off,' she said, standing in the doorway with her capacious handbag over her arm. 'See you later, Mads, everyone.'

'Bye,' called Vee, noting she was the only one who acknowledged Regine's leaving.

Madelaine said, 'I wish she wouldn't call me by that ridiculous name.'

Jack walked over to Madelaine and spoke quietly to her, so softly that Vee couldn't hear what he said. Then he turned to her and motioned for her to follow him. 'C'mon, Vee. I'll show you around.'

She glanced at the clock on the mantelpiece. It was a quarter past five. Her first day at work was beginning. Jack already had the front door open.

'I'm going to show you the ropes today,' he said, striding across the road, 'if you'll pardon the pun.' She was almost running to keep up with him, glad she'd put on a pair of flat shoes. 'You're not going to do any work and I'm sending you home when I've shown you enough for you to decide whether you can handle it or not. Then you can take a walk about the town, have a think and let me know tonight if you want to stay. I won't have you doing a specific job, just filling in where I need you to be.'

As they passed the ticket office, she saw Regine sitting on a stool behind a window issuing tickets and taking change. Jack said, 'If you decide to stay I'll get you some boots and black oilskins. If you're helping in the ticket office, you can wear your own clothes. If you work in the café you'll get an overall, same as Connie and Rosie.'

Vee could see a girl standing in the doorway of a cigarette kiosk, holding a large bag close to her side. As Vee passed her, she smelt the perfume she had noticed the evening before. The girl was about twenty, her untidy hair scraped back from her thin face with a clip. Vee was surprised when Jack acknowledged her and went over to her, dipping his hand into his trouser pocket and handing her something that made her smile before he caught up with Vee once more. Had she imagined it or had Jack called the girl 'Ada'?

Two men were busy at the open gate where the ferry was moored against the pontoon. One, who had a shock of dark hair, was clipping tickets as the other waited by the gate, ready to let the passengers on to the boat. Both men, catching sight of Jack, waved and he raised his hand in acknowledgement. Suddenly Vee's attention was taken by the boat's name.

'Why is the ferry called *Galatea*?'

Jack said, 'All the ferries are named after Greek sea goddesses. All craft are "she". *Calliste* is ready on the Portsmouth side, waiting for the bell to ring to announce we're ready for the off. They're steam craft.' He pointed towards the funnel. Vee glanced at it, remembering its comforting warmth from the previous night.

'Such a lot of people,' she said. A heaving crowd was waiting for the gates to swing back, allowing them to board the first ferry of the day. Most were men, some holding on to bicycles, and many carried lunch boxes.

'That's Portsmouth dockyard over there,' he pointed across the expanse of sea, 'and we've got the munitions yard this side. There's a steady exchange of workers backwards and forwards. There's so much Hitler would like to flatten on the south coast. One of the reasons we have so many air raids here.' He smiled down at her. Again she saw the gentle curve of his lips and wondered what it would be like to kiss them. Then she looked away, angry with herself. He was a married man, for goodness' sake! He was talking once more. 'There are other crew members. One's the stoker – we call him the driver. Then there's our rope man, my mate, and the skipper, usually me.' He grinned, lightening her heart again.

'Do you have a second crew?'

'Of course. We can't work seventeen hours a day, even though we work long hours.'

'There's a lot for me to learn.' She didn't want to let Jack down, but she needed the job and the room that went with it.

Already she had decided she would save her money until she had the same amount of cash that Sammy Chesterton charged other people for their forged papers. She'd pay him and be out of his debt. Surely he'd agree to take the money if she offered it to him?

'Who cleans the boats?' Vee remembered that when she'd left the ferry the previous night there was rubbish to be cleared and the decks were filthy.

'The early-morning crew does that,' he said. 'And a lad's paid to haul in the coal and water needed before we start up in the mornings.'

The squat ferry was filling with passengers now. When Jack saw that she had stepped safely on board, he led her towards the engine room. She could see a grey-haired man below stoking the fires.

Jack stopped at the door and put out a hand so Vee couldn't enter.

'All right, Jack?' The man didn't look pleased to see her, even though Vee smiled at him brightly.

'It gets pretty hot down here during the summer,' Jack said, 'but Eddie here keeps these engines running as sweet as a nut.'

Vee saw the brass fittings were polished to within an inch of their lives. Everything gleamed in the engine room.

'Does Eddie work all day and into the night?'

Eddie stared at her as though she'd sprouted three heads. 'No, I don't. The night men clean out the fires ready for me in the mornings. Don't need anyone else in here when I'm on duty, except my lad.'

Beads of sweat were running down Vee's neck, and she saw that Eddie wore a kerchief to soak it up. He was glaring at her. It was painfully obvious he wanted her out of his domain.

'We'll leave you to it, Eddie.' Jack was out of the engine room and climbing up the steps to the main deck. He pointed to *Galatea*'s deck entrance and exit areas. 'There are safety chains to stop passengers falling overboard, and the outside of the boat, as you can see, is festooned with life-buoys. Unfortunately people still go into the water regularly.'

He gestured to a boat waiting on the Portsmouth side of the ferry route. 'There have been ferrymen plying their trade across this stretch of water for many years, and competition between the Portsmouth and Gosport companies was always fierce. The rivalry between the ferrymen couldn't go on so they've joined forces. Families have a bloodline of watermen reaching back to when the very first small boats, wherries, were carrying up to six passengers at a time. Each boat has, as I've already told you, a skipper, mate and, below deck, the driver, plus ticket handlers at the gates and in the kiosks. Extra mates handle the ropes.

'In 1888 an arrangement was made whereby a launch from each company would leave Portsmouth and Gosport simultaneously. This stopped a great deal of the bullying and bumping that the rival boats engaged in and the payment taken for tickets is shared by the companies . . . But we've not been doing so well this side, lately. Takings are down.'

Vee could see how much his work meant to him and how troubled he was about the shortfall in money.

'What about the car ferry?'

He laughed. 'The floating bridge runs on chains and is steam-powered. You won't be expected to work on her. Nor will you have anything to do with the island boats.'

She must have looked confused for he added, 'The Isle of Wight ferries, which can be boarded at Portsmouth Harbour railway station.' She remembered then that the railway tracks and stations were built on metal stilts and iron girders that jutted out into the sea. The sea must be pretty deep at that end of the station, she thought, if the huge Isle of Wight ferries could moor there.

Jack unclipped the metal barrier and jumped off the boat at the opposite end from which he'd boarded, Vee following. Then he turned and pointed to a young man holding on to a length of thick rope, most of which was wound around a bollard on the jetty and another on the ferry.

'Mac ties up. It's an art throwing the rope towards the bollards and pulling in so the boat is close enough for the passengers to jump safely on and off. We don't want to lose anyone down the side.' Vee looked at the red-haired young man. She liked his freckled face, with its easy smile. He waved at her.

'We're a close-knit family of workers. We pull together. Last night you had a taste of how uncomfortable it can be up in the wheelhouse. There's very little escape from the elements. It was suggested we put up shields across the bridge to prevent shrapnel hitting the skippers during the bombing. Not good for visibility. The boats don't stop running during raids.'

Jack turned to her. 'I'm sending you back now. Make up your mind if you want to stay with us or not. Go into the café and get yourself a cuppa – we all eat in there from time to time. It's Connie's place to see we're fed and watered. If you decide to stay she may want you to help her. The café does a good trade, sometimes too much for Connie and Rosie to handle on their own. I'll see you later.' He put on his cap, which until now he'd been carrying, then foraged in his pocket and brought out a key, which he handed to her. 'For the front door,' he said, 'though it's hardly ever locked.'

Vee took it wordlessly and stood watching as Jack hopped back on to the boat and climbed to the wheelhouse. At the front of the vessel another pile of bicycles was in a huge metal tangle that she was sure would take ages to unravel.

She heard a whistle blast and the engine growled fully into life. She watched as the metal gates clanged shut and the ropes were coiled ready for use on the Portsmouth pontoon. Then, as the squat boat moved out into the channel, she saw

Jack wave to her. At last his figure grew too small for Vee to distinguish so she began walking up the jetty towards the Ferry Gardens and the town of Gosport. Suddenly she felt very alone.

Chapter Eight

'I hate peeling potatoes.'

Rosie slipped them into a large saucepan full of cold water on the stove in the kitchen of the Ferry Café.

'It's better to make chips than have no job at all,' said Connie. 'At least in here we're more or less our own boss.'

'True – and who knows? One day we might even make some more money,' agreed Rosie. 'Did you talk to Madelaine about that sandwich idea?'

'She don't want to know about anything that goes on in this café. She said she'll mention it to Jack but I'm not hopeful. Her head's full of that Hugh.' Connie began slicing the potatoes into chips and dropping them into another pan of cold water. 'I ought to talk to Jack but he looks worn out so I don't fancy bothering him. Up all night again with Peg, he was.' Connie sighed. A hairpin struggled free from her piled-up bleached hair and dropped with a ping into the sink. 'Botheration!' she said, putting down the sharp knife, retrieving the hairpin then skewering it back through her curls. 'Let's have a sit-down, while it's quiet.' She glanced at the old station clock on the wall. 'In a while we'll be run off our feet. Let's make the most of this slow period.'

Rosie wiped her hands on a tea-towel and went out into the café area. The wireless was playing dance music and she plonked herself down at a table and crossed her legs at the ankles. It wasn't long before Connie appeared and set down two cups of tea on the Formica table.

'Thanks, I could do with that.' Rosie watched Connie park her ample behind on a chair. 'What d'you think of Vee?'

Connie stirred her tea. 'Seems a nice girl. Jack's taken to her.'

'That's because she's a worker, I can tell.' She sipped her tea and looked at Old Tom sitting against the Nissen hut's wall. He raised a hand in greeting.

'I'll give him a refill in a bit,' Rosie said. The old man had been bombed out a while back and had lost his wife in the blast. He couldn't seem to get over it and spent a lot of time staring into space.

'You could make him a sandwich to go with it,' Connie said. 'Poor bugger.'

Her kindness was one of the many things Rosie liked about Connie.

Connie had taken her under her wing when she'd come into the café enquiring about the 'Waitress Wanted' postcard she'd spotted in the newsagent's window opposite the ferry. She knew she must have looked a sight with her black eye and her face all puffy from crying, but Connie had merely asked her if she'd worked in a café before and, when she said she had, agreed to her starting the next morning.

Rosie had known Mick would still be sleeping off the skinful of beer he'd had the night before and wouldn't even remember he'd knocked her down the stairs, so it was no problem for her to pack up a few bits and pieces – not that she had much – and move into Jack's house. Connie had shown her to a room that looked like a palace.

That night she'd slept like a child. No more fears that her husband would come home drunk and start in on her again. Best thing she'd ever done was leave Mick. It had taken her long enough to pluck up the courage. Since she'd lost the baby, she'd also lost all her confidence, and it was easier to let Mick knock her about than strike out on her own.

She never used to be so downtrodden, but it was her own fault for putting up with his temper. Mind, if he'd shown his nasty side before she'd walked up the aisle to him, a big good-looking Irishman, she'd never have married him. Perhaps it was a blessing that that punch had made her lose the kiddie. God forgive her for thinking that. She was grateful that Connie asked no questions, just let her find her feet in the café and in the house.

It was as if Jack trusted Connie's judgement in hiring her. Since then Rosie had worked consistently for Jack at the Ferry Café and she'd enjoyed every minute of it.

Did she wonder about Mick? Where he was, what he was doing? Maybe he was living with someone else now. Did she care? No! She was glad she was away from his flying fists.

'D'you ever wish you had another job, Connie?'

Connie's eyes narrowed. 'Not really,' she said. 'But I'd like to put a bit of money behind me. Maybe then I could visit my family. I got a grandson I've only ever seen in a photograph. That's why I'd like it if we got this sandwich idea off the ground.'

Rosie saw the dreamy look in her eyes.

'If we had them in packets all ready for the customers it would save a lot of time and trouble. I get so fed up trying to cook and make up sandwiches at the same time. If we could get known for having tasty fillings it could become a decent little earner. Who knows? We might be able to sell ready-prepared sandwiches to some of the shops – Woolworth's, even.'

'Maybe Jack could take on another girl—'

'No, Rosie. It's our idea. I just want him to give the go-ahead. I'd work every night if I had to. We could come up with some interesting fillings! I know there's a war on and there's shortages but . . .'

Connie's voice tailed off. Rosie knew how fond she was of Jack – he was like a son to her.

Connie had a grown-up daughter but she was in Australia. The girl had married young and Connie thought she'd never see her again. Brisbane was a long way from Gosport and Connie needed money to get there. She had photos of her grandson but it wasn't the same as holding a little body in her arms, was it?

Maybe Connie's daughter would visit on a holiday. Still, when the café was busy there wasn't the time to think of what might have been or could be. Now Rosie and Connie went dancing with the servicemen in the Connaught Hall and to the pictures together on their time off – a couple of women from the other ferry crew took over the café duties.

Her thoughts scattered as the door opened and a couple of bus conductresses came in. More and more women were taking over men's jobs while the lads were away fighting.

'Egg and chips twice, please,' said the shorter of the two.

'Only powdered egg,' said Connie, rising from her chair.

'Omelette and chips twice, then.' The girl smiled, taking off her Southdown jacket.

Rosie gathered up her and Connie's cups and got to her feet just as the door opened again and three soldiers entered.

'Roses Of Picardy' came softly from the wireless, accompanying May as she attempted to complete her accounts. She was humming along to the emotional First World War song. After adding up the same column of figures four times and getting a different total each time, she abandoned her morning project.

The music made her think of Gus, and of her time at the hospital and how it hadn't always been doom and gloom.

One evening, she and her friend Annie had been told to help decorate the big hall. They were going to have a dance! Once, dances had been held regularly but now that so many men came back from the battlefields with such horrific wounds they had been abandoned. Ceaseless bombardments in Flanders at the third battle of Ypres and the never-ending rain made it difficult for the men to decide what they feared most, the mud or the German machine-gunners.

'Dying men can't dance,' Annie had said, when Matron

had sent the news around that the hall was to be hung with garlands and bunting, and a band was to be provided, along with a buffet.

'We can't dance without proper music,' Annie complained. 'Matron's idea of a band is bleedin' violins and harps.'

'There are several patients who can play instruments and would be willing in spite of their injuries to join in the fun.'

'All right, May,' said Annie, almost smiling. 'I suppose we can push in the beds of those who want to come from other wards. And it will help with morale.'

Annie Bell was also a local girl, born in Southampton. She'd joined the VADs hoping to see something of the world, but Netley was as far as she'd got. May and Annie shared a hut that had a pot-bellied stove, two single beds with lumpy mattresses, oil lamps, wooden floors with a couple of rag rugs, and a small wardrobe each for their things. A spotted mirror had been nailed to the wooden wall. There was no sanitation or water in the hut, apart from the jugs and bowls for washing that had to be filled and emptied daily, along with their chamber pots. The contents were thrown on to the garden rubbish heap, then the pots swilled out at a nearby outside tap. There was a washing block a short distance away that also contained the lavatories. Meals were taken in the main building.

At first May had found it a miserable existence and wished she could live at home on the smallholding. It seemed so silly to her that her family lived a short walk away from the hospital but she had to live in. Annie's normally chirpy disposition helped ease her longing for her parents.

On precious days off they had hitched lifts to Kingston Market in Southampton and spent their wages on colourful scraps of material that Annie fashioned into curtains and cushion covers, sewn on a Singer machine borrowed from one of the other nurses.

'After working from six this morning I don't really feel like dancing,' Annie moaned. She was pulling a screen in front of a stack of wooden limbs in boxes ready for amputees.

'You will when the time comes.' May was looking forward to it.

'Did they find that patient?'

'Not another escapee, Annie?'

There was a long stretch of grassland and trees between the hospital and the jetty, where the boats docked on Southampton Water to transfer the wounded into the ambulances waiting to carry them to the hospital. Most patients were more than happy to be ferried to the doctors and nurses, or were unaware of what was happening, but occasionally a bright spark would make a run for it, either to abscond from the services or perhaps, if a foreigner knew he would be imprisoned after his recovery, to escape.

Netley, a wooded area whose residents didn't hide their dislike of the enemy at the hospital, made a poor hiding place: the few patients or prisoners who took their chances were soon returned to the fold more than happy to be fed and have their injuries attended to. Later, their distinctive spotted clothing announced to all who they were.

May had laughed at Annie as they sprinkled chalk on the floor in readiness for the dancing, careful not to get any on the musical instruments that had been brought in for the evening's entertainment. VADs weren't always allowed to dance but this was a special occasion, Matron had decreed.

Neither was it deemed appropriate for the nurses, VADs and other staff to wear civilian clothing, so the most they could do to titivate themselves was to put on clean cuffs and headdresses. A few brave nurses wore garden flowers in their hair.

Outsiders had been invited, but since many of the patients came from outside the area or, indeed, the country, there were few civilians.

Finally, after washing away the dirt of the day, May and Annie sauntered over to the ballroom, eager to have drinks poured for them by two porter friends, who were in charge of the bar, which was two tables pushed together. Mismatched glasses stood on them, with a very large container of a greenish punch that looked and tasted as though it had been concocted in the chemistry department.

'I'd like it if you'd dance with me?'

May looked up at the tall, slim man. His fair hair fell across his forehead and he smiled at her. She consented, and the young doctor claimed her again for 'A Bird in a Gilded Cage', but this time he seemed tense and held her too tightly. His face against her cheek was too intimate, and he murmured words she was unable to hear properly. She felt that if she could, she wouldn't like them.

May was glad when he led her back to the chairs Annie had found. But almost before she had time to sit down, the young doctor claimed her again.

May didn't like being grabbed and marched towards the floor. Without a word, he had encircled her waist with his arm and pulled her close. His face was scraping her cheek as he moved sinuously in time to the music the band was playing 'They Didn't Believe Me'. In that moment May knew that that song would always remind her of this man and that she would hate it for ever.

She waited until the music stopped, then pushed her partner away. 'I think that's enough for tonight,' she whispered. Without waiting for him to lead her back to her chair, she made her way through the rest of the dancers and was finally able to flop down beside Annie.

'He's like an octopus,' she muttered, 'and he's none too sweet-smelling.'

'If he's been on duty a long time, what do you expect?'

Annie handed her a glass of water that she drank gratefully. A mixture of cigarette smoke and hot bodies made it warm in the ballroom.

'I think he fancies you,' Annie said, nudging her arm after the doctor had reappeared at the buffet table. May shook her head. Her eyes followed him as he poked around the plates, now depleted of sandwiches and cake – indeed, it looked as though a swarm of locusts had flown in and devoured the lot. Since the majority of men in the hall were unable to walk, one didn't have to be a genius to guess that the staff had eaten most of it.

'There's something creepy about him,' May said, and shivered.

'I'd fancy him.' Annie pouted. May could smell the heavy scent Annie had poured over herself, although wearing perfume was against the rules.

'You'd fancy anything!' May laughed. 'Have you worked with him?'

Annie shook her head. 'No.'

Such was the turnover of staff and patients that it wasn't surprising. It had seemed to May that as soon as she became used to certain doctors' habits in the operating theatre they disappeared, moving abroad to work among the wounded or to London and private practice.

'There is one man in here who really fancies you,' Annie confided.

May stared past her friend towards the German flyer. Her heart began to race. He was standing now, able to use a crutch. The artificial foot he had been fitted with emphasized his height. She hadn't known how tall he was, never having seen him standing before. The scarring to his face was healing well. All evening she had taken sly glances at him, only to find him staring at her.

'I'm going to ask him to dance.'

'Are you sure that's wise?' Annie grabbed at her. 'You've just refused that young doctor! Won't it look a bit obvious if you walk over and ask the enemy to take a turn around the floor?'

May ignored her friend's words. The dance was to promote better feeling between the English patients and the enemy, and she saw no difference in dancing with a German or one of the hospital's staff.

'Dance with me?' May asked. 'Leave your crutch. You can use me as a support.' She felt as though she could drown in his dark eyes.

She waited while he propped the crutch against the wall, then leant on her, his feet together. 'You might regret this,' he whispered.

'Phooey!' The word came out with more determination than she actually felt. May sensed he was leaning heavily on the arm that went around her body. The band started to play 'Roses Of Picardy'. It was natural for him to lead and he did, despite her worry that he might stumble.

May felt her blood warm in her veins. No man's touch had ever made her feel so alive. Suddenly she was glad she and Annie had sprinkled chalk on the makeshift dance floor, though he needed no props to help him with the steps except her. She guessed he must have been practising walking all day yesterday when he had first been fitted with his artificial limb.

May had asked him to dance out of the desire to be close to him – or as close as she could be in a room full of people. She couldn't say why she was drawn to him but she was, as a moth is drawn to a flame.

Across the floor Annie was dancing with a porter. The look Annie gave her told her she should be careful. She could almost hear tongues wagging over her obvious enjoyment at being in the arms of a man who had tried to kill her countrymen.

'I think we should make this our first and last dance.' His breath was warm on her face.

She nodded. 'It doesn't seem right to save your life, then cut you dead, though.'

'We shouldn't be dancing together,' he repeated. 'This get-together is a sham, and everyone knows it, yet we all conspire to pretend friendship.' Much as May loved his clipped accent, she didn't like what he was saying.

'The Hippocratic Oath means doctors try to save lives regardless of creed, colour or nationality.' Her words came out in a rush.

'But this dance is a farce,' he said. 'Don't tell me you can't feel something special between us. I'm sure others can sense it. And they don't like it. They can't bear to see you and me so close together and enjoying ourselves.'

She knew he was speaking the truth. Previous dances that evening had mostly involved everyone. 'The Gay Gordons' had prompted much laughter among staff and patients.

May felt his grip tighten as his step faltered. Then he regained his momentum. A wave of sadness engulfed her. She could tell by the way his body moved with the music that he must have been popular on the dance floor with women in his home town. Hatred flared in her for the evening's organizers. It wasn't a morale booster at all. It was an outward show to the rest of the hospital that both sides could get on together. But that was a lie.

As her eyes left his face she became aware that other dancers had left the floor to stand and watch them. For a second she thought he hadn't noticed the sudden exodus.

They were the only couple dancing.

'Are you all right with this?' His words were soft.

Was she? May had never felt like this about anyone before. Was she falling in love? Was this what love meant, showing others that neither of them cared what they thought?

'Yes,' she breathed.

So he held her tightly and she refused to be intimidated. And they moved together to the sad little song, about a lifelong love surviving beyond death. Then, when the dance ended, he took her arm and led her back to where he had been standing. May knew now that without a crutch he was unable to walk, let alone dance: it was too soon after the amputation. As a nurse she should have known it. He had danced because she had held him. He had endured pain to be close to her. So, with her arm tightly around his waist, she managed to turn a chair round so he could sit down. Afterwards she picked up his crutch from the floor where it had fallen.

He smiled at her, then bent forward and kissed her cheek.

She went back to her seat next to Annie, leaving Gus in his ridiculous blue hospital uniform of scratchy material with the markings on the jacket at the back that reminded her of a scoreboard. As if eventually leaving the hospital for the prison wasn't enough, he had to look like a clown while he was at the hospital.

The band were playing again and May looked at the German – Gus, his name was. Now she saw blood seeping through the thick trouser material. His exertions on the dance floor had reopened his wound. She didn't go to him. To do so would have taken away the last shred of his pride. May knew then three things. One was that he loved her, the other was that she loved him, and the third was that life would not be easy for either of them.

The music on the wireless had faded and the news caught her attention. Four hundred deaths in London alone. The city was taking the brunt of the Blitz. So much destruction and sadness, May thought. One hundred and eighty-five enemy planes shot down in a single day. How foolish she was to have thought the Great War would never be repeated.

May looked at the columns of figures and began to add them up. Daily life went on. She might hear from Vee tomorrow. It would be enough to know that her daughter had work and a place to sleep. She hoped with all her heart that, one day, her daughter would fall for a man and know the true meaning of love, as she, May, had with Vee's father.

Chapter Nine

Jack stood with his hands on the wheel, watching the Portsmouth landing stage grow larger the closer his boat sailed. He waved to the skipper of the boat passing him, on its way to take his place at Gosport. The ferries passed each other continually. On average they ran every fifteen minutes, but they'd do faster turnarounds if it was necessary.

The morning sun was on his face, the rain of yesterday forgotten. He liked Vee. She had said she was ready and willing to try her hand at any job and he believed her. He hoped she'd stay on. He'd tried to frighten the life out of her by taking her below deck to show her how hard Eddie worked, but she didn't seem put off, not even by the heat down there. He didn't tell her Eddie's boy usually worked with him. The lad was back on Monday after a few days off. Vee would never need to work in the engine room. Eddie would shoot her sooner than let her into his domain, which had been in his family for generations.

Jack was still angry that Peg had been left at the café while Madelaine had visited her parents. She should have been back sooner. She shouldn't have let the kiddie scream. Peg had missed her mother and needed changing and feeding. Connie and Rosie had enough to do in that busy place without looking after his baby as well.

The argument instigated by Madelaine shortly after her return in the early hours had been one of the most violent they'd had. She'd asked him for yet more money towards a new outfit for the christening; the sum he had already given her apparently wasn't enough. It had ended with Madelaine turning her back on him, but not before she'd screamed to the whole of Gosport that he was a 'tight-fisted bastard'.

He didn't know how he had kept his temper. Of course he'd wanted to hit her, to shut her mouth against the vile invective that spewed out, but he'd never hit a woman in his life and didn't intend to start with Madelaine. She was volatile, highly strung. If he'd had money to throw away he'd have given it gladly: she filled his eyes with sunshine when he saw her beautifully dressed, but she'd have looked good in a paper bag. The dockyard was ahead with Nelson's flagship, *Victory*, moored nearby. She was a fine sight. The panorama of the ships, the sea and Portsdown Hill in the background always made him gasp with its beauty, as did Madelaine. Never in his wildest imaginings had he thought he would be the one she would settle for.

He'd known her since his schooldays, but they were far apart in backgrounds. Her parents lived in Alverstoke in a large house set back from the sea in Ashburton Road. Like most of the other Gosport lads, with their grimy hands and scruffy clothes, he'd worshipped her from afar. In her teens she had played tennis at the club in Anglesey Road and he often caught a glimpse of her in her whites as he cycled by. Or she'd be sitting beside some flash Harry in the front of a car. Jack had had his fair share of girls as he grew older, when his shoulders had broadened and his lanky frame had filled out. Some of the girls would ride the ferries just to chat to him, as they did now with Mac and Paul, the two good-looking mates. Paul, on the tickets, almost had to fight them off.

At the dances held at the Connaught Hall he'd catch sight of Madelaine and her friend of the moment. She never seemed to have a best friend, but there was always a crowd about her and she'd be glowing with health and vitality, dancing her heart out, blonde ponytail bobbing.

Later she favoured a dark-haired man as a partner, and

then there had been a subtle change in her looks. She lightened her already blonde hair and changed its style to a long pageboy, going from pretty girl to beautiful woman practically overnight.

Then he'd had to pluck up courage to ask her to dance with him and sometimes he didn't manage it. When he got home he cursed himself for being such a weakling.

The same year he helped his parents buy the house where he now lived on Beach Street, he had made it to skipper. His dad, and his dad before him, had been on the boats and Jack never doubted he'd do anything different. The sea was in his blood. After the night when his parents had died visiting a London friend during an air raid, his job was the only thing that had kept him sane.

Now he had a beautiful daughter and a gorgeous wife. Everything in his garden should have been lovely, but it wasn't. Since Peg had come on the scene Madelaine had changed.

Their love affair, if he could call it that, had started one night at the Lee Tower ballroom. Amazingly she'd come over and asked him to dance while the band was playing 'The Breeze And I'.

Girls didn't usually do that: it was considered too forward. Nice girls waited, sitting around the ballrooms, until the lads asked them to dance. Sometimes they danced with each other.

Of course, earlier he'd spotted her dancing with the tall chappie, one of the chinless wonders who were always hanging around her. And why not? With that gorgeous blonde hair, deep blue eyes and a figure to rival Veronica Lake's, all the men watched her. But this time she'd made a beeline for him.

'She's coming over,' his friend said. John Cousins was forever trying to get him out and about to take his mind off his parents' deaths.

'I bet it's you she talks to,' Jack said. But it wasn't.

He was like an idiot when he held her, not knowing how to touch the object of his fantasies, let alone dance with her. He mumbled answers to her questions, trod on her toes and apologized so many times he truly believed she must think him an absolute idiot.

'I need some air,' she'd said.

Before the dance had finished he'd found himself walking along the beach at Lee-on-the-Solent hardly able to believe his luck that at last Madelaine was actually with him.

The night was hot and sticky and she sat on the sand, pulling him down with her. And then she was kissing him. He remembered the sea below them, rushing and drawing back, and he'd thought he'd died and gone to Heaven. He couldn't talk to her – he wanted to, but the words wouldn't form themselves in his mouth. He let his instincts take over.

Her body was tanned from the summer sun; in the moonlight he could see the white lines on her shoulders where her swimsuit had covered her.

Her kisses were gentle at first, then firm enough to bruise his lips. He could smell alcohol on her breath. Then he had felt her fingers at his belt buckle. Her touch made him grow hard, more so because he couldn't believe this was really happening.

His conscience was telling him it wasn't right, but his heart and body were saying he wanted her more than anything else in the whole world. Her breasts were freed from her bra by his fumbling, and her jasmine perfume filled his nostrils.

Faintly, in the background, the music was spilling from the open windows of the ballroom and it seemed to be urging him on to take what she was offering.

She guided him into her and her soft wetness swallowed him whole. He pushed her back on the sand and moved inside her with ease. She rose up to meet him and, with his kisses wild upon her face, he remembered only the sense of infinite motion that followed, until the stars above blurred and fell to earth, and he was falling with them.

Afterwards, she lay in his arms, not speaking. He was delirious with happiness. Then, as his senses returned to him, he said, 'I shouldn't have done that, I'm sorry.' He felt like crying but couldn't understand why. After all, he'd achieved his secret desire, hadn't he?

'Didn't you want me?' Her voice was brittle.

'You know I did,' he replied. He began to cover her nakedness and she finished the task herself. 'You must know I worship you,' he said.

They were both silent until she said, 'Let's get back inside,' and he stood up, held out a hand and pulled her to her feet. Standing beside him in her stockinged feet, she barely came to his shoulder. A great feeling of protectiveness towards her stole over him.

But even then there was a coldness about her, as if she was locked in a cage of ice that he couldn't melt.

As they walked back, he looked at the clock on the front of the tower. He was amazed that in such a short time his whole life seemed to have changed.

In the foyer, she turned to him. 'I'm going to the cloak-room. It's best we don't go in together. I don't want people to look at us and know we got carried away.'

'Of course,' he mumbled. He was well aware that her reputation was at stake. But as he walked away he thought how proud he would have been to take her back to the table he shared with John and his friends and announce to them that they were now a couple.

Briefly he wondered why she didn't feel the same. He thought she probably needed time to tell her friends, to do it in her own way. The Alverstoke set were quite different with their snobbish ways.

He guessed she might not be as happy as he was about what had just taken place between them. He shrugged. He hadn't forced her – in fact, Madelaine had instigated the whole thing. Women weren't like men when they fell in love. In love? Yes, without a doubt he was in love with her. Hadn't he always been in love with Madelaine Carter? And for her to allow him to make love to her showed she reciprocated that feeling . . . didn't it?

'What's the matter, Jack? You look like you lost a quid and found a tanner.' John eyed him thoughtfully. 'Don't think I didn't notice you come back just before Madelaine.'

John was his best friend, had been for years, but sometimes Jack envied him his job as a plain-clothes copper and his wife, Emily, who adored him. It was as if Jack was on the outside looking in. 'So Emily's with her mother?'

'Changing the subject? I'll play along. Her mother isn't well.'

Jack took a mouthful of his flat beer, not really listening to John, while his eyes roved the ballroom. When he saw Madelaine sitting with the tall man, with Brylcreemed hair and a slim moustache, who usually accompanied their little group, he waited for her to glance in his direction. A smile, a look, any acknowledgement would have done. Eventually, he gave up.

To Eric, his other friend, he said, 'I'm going up for another pint before the beer runs out. I know it's a shame to waste this as it's in such short supply, but it's gone flat and lost its guts for standing so long.' It wasn't that he wanted more beer – but he couldn't just sit there after what had happened between him and Madelaine. Making love to her had meant everything to him. He couldn't understand her coldness towards him.

'If you don't want it, give us it here. I don't mind flat beer.' Eric didn't wait for his reply but picked up Jack's glass and glugged back most of what was left in one go. 'Thought you was never coming back after you'd had a dance with that blonde.'

Jack rose from the stool and, still mystified by Madelaine's behaviour, said, 'I'm beginning to wish I never had.' He left the hall and went out to the Gents – he'd get his beer on the way back. Or maybe not. The evening had lost its charm for him and he thought he'd leave.

When he came out she was waiting in the foyer for him.

She was agitated. 'Look, it's difficult. Please say you'll see me again?' He could see it mattered to her by the tense look in her beautiful eyes.

'Madelaine!'

Before he had time to do more than nod, the chinless wonder was calling her name from the ballroom's doorway.

He managed to gather his wits and say, 'You know where you can find me.' Didn't everyone know Jack worked the boats?

And she did find him, on a Sunday two months later when he had the day off and was lounging at home reading the *News of the World*. No one could have been more surprised than he was when, on answering the door, he came face to face with her.

Madelaine wore a blue dress that perfectly matched the colour of her eyes, and while he stood gaping, she said, 'Aren't you going to ask me in?'

The house was a mess and he felt ashamed of the beer bottles left on the table from last night, the overflowing ashtrays and the smell of stale food. Last night he and a couple of mates had lazed around listening to the wireless and putting the world to rights after Pompey had won the football match at Fratton Park.

He was about to apologize for the mess, when he realized he didn't have to be sorry for anything. Madelaine had come to him: she could take him as she found him, a hardworking bloke relaxing in his own home on a Sunday morning. During the past few weeks he'd almost persuaded himself that their coupling hadn't happened.

He was hurt that she'd allowed him to make love to her, then ignored him. That she had shared such an experience with him must mean she had feelings for him, he thought, but since then she'd acted as though he didn't exist. Of course, it was unthinkable for him to visit her parents' house to seek her out. He was a bloke and blokes like him didn't run after posh women like her.

It was all very confusing, yet there she was, standing at his front door and looking beautiful enough to take his breath away. He stepped back, and as she entered she raised herself on tiptoe to give him the briefest kiss on his cheek.

He decided a walk might make it easier for both of them to talk. After all, there must be a reason she had come calling. Two of his lodgers, Regine and Connie, were in their rooms enjoying a lazy Sunday and he didn't particularly want them coming downstairs to find Madelaine in the kitchen.

He saw her eyes take in her surroundings. He was proud

of his home, its size, its proximity to the town centre – and it was worth serious money. He grabbed his jacket.

'We'll go down Beach Street. It's a nice day.'

In Walpole Park they watched the swans on the pond. She still hadn't explained why she'd sought him out and their dialogue was stilted. Unable to stand it any longer he said, 'Look, what happened at Lee-on-the-Solent that night, I can't get my head round—'

Madelaine burst into tears. 'Neither can I. I'd been watching you in the dance hall. I wanted you to make love to me. I'd had quite a bit to drink, and now . . .'

She put a hand to her forehead and turned away from him.

Jack didn't like to see her or any woman cry, so he put his arm around her.

She took a deep breath and turned back, looking into his eyes. 'I'm expecting. My monthly friend hasn't turned up.'

It took him a few moments to grasp what she'd said.

'You mean . . . But it was only the first time . . .'

'It only takes once.' Her words came out jumbled, with more tears.

'Oh, my God,' Jack said. 'This can't be happening.' But he knew with an awful certainty that it was.

Now she clung to him, sobbing. 'I don't know what to

do. I can't tell my mother – she'd kill me. It's all my fault. I was watching you long before I asked you to dance with me. I've waited and waited for you to ask me out, but you never have. I'd had a couple of glasses of port that night and it gave me the courage I needed. I'm so sorry. I just did what I wanted without thinking about the consequences. Now I don't know what to do.' The clouds had hidden the sun, the warmth suddenly going from the morning.

He held her. His mind felt like a hive of bees, buzzing every which way. And then a great calm came over him as he asked, 'Why haven't you come to see me before now? After all, something very special happened between us the night of the dance.'

She stopped crying and blew her nose in the handkerchief he gave her. 'I was ashamed. The more I thought about it the more I realized how it must have seemed to you. Nice girls don't do that sort of thing. And now, and now . . .'

The tears began again.

How could he be angry with her?

'I need to think.' Jack pulled her down onto the grass. He looked into her beautiful face.

'Are you sure you're not just late?' He knew little about women's things but he was aware that their internal clocks sometimes lost or gained time.

'Jack, I know.'

The sun came out, the clouds disappeared and, as the beams began to chase away the chill, he said, 'We could get married.'

Jack now drew the boat up close to the Portsea pontoon and Mac began tying up. He looked at Ada's bag, safe in his wheelhouse. Mac had found it this morning. As skipper, Jack knew he should never have allowed Ada to sleep on the boat, but what else could he do? He couldn't deny her shelter. He'd thought to give her a job in the café but he couldn't afford to let his heart rule his head. His café customers would soon dwindle. There might even be further repercussions.

He sighed. Here he was, doing the job he'd always loved. He had a little girl who had entered the world before she should have done, but was as strong as any baby and was the apple of his eye. He had a decent home and a beautiful wife he'd been married to for less than a year.

Why wasn't he happy?

Chapter Ten

'Buy these two marrers!'

The man held two large juicy vegetable marrows, one in each hand. 'If you don't want to eat 'em both today, save one for tomarrow!'

Vee smiled at his cheeky banter. What she had seen of Gosport town, she liked. Stallholders had set up their wares beneath canvas awnings along the high street in front of the many shops. Already people were looking for market bargains and her senses were assailed by sights, sounds and smells that made her glad to be alive on such a sunny day.

She found the library housed in another Nissen hut – a bomb had flattened the original building – and came away happily from the friendly librarian with a card to be signed by a householder before she could borrow books. She felt sure either Madelaine or Jack would guarantee she was now a local resident.

There was a swimming pool and bath house, a museum, a town hall, two cinemas and a boating lake, plus several cafés and public houses. She felt sure there was much more Gosport had to offer but she'd leave further exploration for another day.

She pulled open the door of a telephone kiosk and emptied her purse for change. All the while she was trembling. Suppose Sammy had already been to the smallholding – suppose he had hurt her mother because Vee had stolen the documents. Her heart was beating fast as she inserted the money and pressed the button. Previously she'd decided she wouldn't phone her mother until she was sure she intended to stay at Gosport. Now she'd made up her mind. Within moments both Vee and her mother were crying, but their tears were happy ones.

'Don't tell me where you are, just if you're all right,' May said.

'I'm not too far away and I'm safe,' Vee reassured her. 'Has Sammy been to the house?' Her heart lifted when her mother said he hadn't and that she wasn't to worry about anything.

'Cat's had three kittens,' May said. 'And they're the spit of her. So we'll never know who the father is.' She'd used her new ration book, she added. She'd been wary at first, but after all the trouble Vee had taken to obtain it she'd felt she should. Vee laughed. She'd definitely have to send Sammy the money as soon as she could.

Feeling happier, Vee walked along Beach Street where the noise from the boatyards practically deafened her. Hulks and skeletons of work in progress vied for space in the yards, though she knew it had been even busier in the days before the war when goods had been easier to obtain. Shortages of materials and foodstuffs meant hungry bellies and loss of jobs. Curls of cut planking and wood shavings blew at her feet and the smell of wood made her think that if she closed her eyes and ears to the noise she could believe she was in a forest. Across the water, the huge car ferry was chugging through the waves, laden with passengers and vehicles, and was about to pull in.

The clanking and scraping were deafening as, simultaneously, the two bridge-like structures were lowered on to the gravelled road. She watched as the gates were opened so the vehicles could drive out. The craft was enormous. Dirty, rust-covered metal railings enclosed the top deck where the owners of the vehicles and other passengers could sit on wooden seats as the vessel clunked its way to Portsmouth.

Vee recognized the girl. As the cars rolled off the ferry she stood at the side of the open gates and spoke only to male drivers alone in their cars. Some ignored her, a few listened politely, but from their expressions others were angry to have her approach them.

The girl was thin and her clothing, a black skirt and red blouse, looked as though it needed a wash, as did she.

She had stopped a van and was asking the driver something that Vee couldn't hear. But she saw the awful man hawk a huge gob of spit right in the girl's face. The vehicle passed Vee.

The stink from its exhaust pipes almost choked her as she ran towards the girl, who was still standing there, almost as if she had deserved to be humiliated. Another car passed before Vee reached her and this time she heard laughter.

'You didn't deserve that!' Vee was angry – angry with the girl for not retaliating and with the van owner for his disgusting action. She pulled the girl round to face her. Tears spilled from her eyes. Vee asked, 'Why did he do it?' Silence.

Then, holding her arm, Vee swung her away from the ferry that was still spilling out cars and pulled her across the road to the pavement.

'What did you say to him that made him do that?'

'I asked him if he wanted a good time!' The words were flung at her. Sharp, precise speech from someone who obviously wasn't a Gosport girl. 'Leave me be!'

She made to walk off, wiping her arm across her face, but Vee grabbed her. The strong smell of violet perfume was sickening.

'What do you mean?'

'Do I have to spell it out?

Vee stared at her. The penny dropped as she remembered how the girls in Sammy's club who were on the game spoke to the men they hoped would give them money to go to bed with them.

'You're a pros–'

'On the game, please,' the girl said, wiping her eyes. 'But not doing too good. There's an annoying woman queering my pitch.'

Vee looked at her. She saw a girl who was down on her luck. 'I didn't realize. I'm sorry. Look, at least let me buy you a cup of tea.'

'And a sandwich?' The girl's dull eyes brightened as Vee mentally added up the money she had left. She nodded. She took the girl's arm again and made to go towards the Ferry Café.

The girl pulled back. 'Not in there. The Dive is better.'

Vee wondered why she didn't want to go into the place where the boatmen congregated but it wasn't her business. She followed the girl across the bus station to the small café on the corner of the marketplace and walked down the steps.

The proprietor nodded a greeting to them. The girl moved through to a table in the bowels of the café, leaving Vee to bring two teas and a sandwich to the table.

'I've got no time for do-gooders. I've not been doing this long. Today was my first go at soliciting. I have nowhere to live, and if it wasn't for your boss letting me creep on to the ferry boat at night after they've shut down, I'd have nowhere to sleep. He lets me stay because I promised him I wouldn't take the punters there, and I keep my promises.'

Then she picked up the sandwich and sank her small white teeth into the tomato and bread as if she hadn't eaten that day. Perhaps she hadn't, thought Vee, who stirred her tea and looked at the girl. Beneath the grime she was quite pretty.

'Let's hope you never sink this low, eh?' the girl snarled, then picked up her cup and drank the contents.

'What's your name?'

'Ada Klein.'

'But that's a . . .'

Ada glared. 'I was born in Sheffield, moved to Kent when I was eight and my mum and dad bought a fish-and-chip shop. They made money, enough to send me to Norland College, where they train nannies. All I ever wanted to do was look after kiddies. Three years' training, and I came here to look after an admiral's children at Alverstoke. The war broke out and I was thrown out of my job.' She took a deep breath. 'Can't have a German looking after a posh Englishman's children, can we?'

'Couldn't you go home?' Vee asked.

'My parents died when the shop was torched one night. We had a flat above it, see? No parents, no home.'

'Surely there's something else you can do.'

'No one will employ me. I'm the enemy. I have no money, so I get by the best I can. At least I can wash in the public lavatories when no one's around, and the other day I found a bottle of scent that someone had left behind. I can't even lie about who I am because the truth is there for anyone to see on all my documents.' Suddenly her voice softened. 'But I've eaten today, thanks to you.'

Vee opened her purse and looked at her remaining money. She took two brown banknotes and slid them across the table. 'A pound. It's not much . . .'

'And I shall take it because it means food to me. But one

day I hope I'll be able to repay you.' Ada stood up and a waft of strong perfume enveloped Vee.

'I really do have qualifications. To attempt what I had to do today I left everything in my bag on the boat. Jack is a good man. He'll look after it for me. I have good references.. One day I'll show you.' And then she was gone, the smell of cheap perfume following her.

Vee sat pondering the cruelties of war until she got up and left. Out in the fresh air, she crossed the road and walked back to her new home. She had liked Ada's honesty. She wanted to talk to her again.

She had no doubt that she would see her again.

At the house, she inserted the key into the lock and heard the baby crying. She went in, and the child's cries drew her towards the pram in the kitchen. Immediately her heart went out to the little scrap who, by the state of her, must have been crying for a while. Her face was red and tears stained her cheeks.

Automatically she picked up Peg, who was wet and smelly. A sudden vision came into her mind of Cat and her three kittens at home, being cared for and fussed over.

'What a to-do then!' Her words were soft, meaningless and meant to soothe the baby, which they did, for Peg snuffled and quietened, staring at Vee with huge eyes. Vee saw a pile of clean nappies on the table. She could change the baby, but it wasn't her place to step in and take over what was essentially Madelaine's job.

Before she had time to decide what to do, the door along the hall opened and someone was striding down the passage from Madelaine and Jack's bedroom.

A tall man with a moustache, his shirt hanging out of his trousers, came in. He coloured when he saw Vee holding Peg. 'What – what are you doing here? No one's due back until this afternoon.'

Vee had no idea who he was but immediately guessed that a half-dressed man coming from Jack's bedroom wasn't quite right.

'I live here,' she said. 'Do you?'

He surprised her then: 'I might as well.' He seemed to have recovered his composure. He looked her up and down. 'And you are?'

'Vee. An extra pair of hands to help wherever it's needed.'

'Well, you've stopped Peg crying. That's very handy.' He ran his fingers through his Brylcreemed hair. Vee decided that the baby was no longer her concern. Her mother had to be within earshot. She began lowering Peg back onto the damp pram bedding. Footsteps behind her suddenly halted. Vee turned to find Madelaine still in the silky dressing-gown of earlier. It looked as if it had been hastily thrown on. Madelaine's eyes met hers.

'I see you two have met.' Jack's wife, in those few words and moments, had tried but failed to persuade Vee that the man's presence was legitimate. 'Hugh, I think you'd better go.'

The baby began to cry again. Madelaine picked her up. There were no soft motherly words as she laid Peg on a chair and began to remove her wet clothes.

'Don't go on my account, Hugh.' Vee walked towards the stairs. She knew her sarcasm wouldn't endear her to her boss's wife but she doubted very much that Madelaine would say anything to Jack. Vee wasn't stupid: she'd come home and walked in on Madelaine and this Hugh who had obviously been in bed together. Perhaps Jack was aware of what was going on. But what kind of man allows his wife to have a lover? The thought entered her mind, then slipped away again. It really wasn't any of her business.

Upstairs in her room Vee sat on the end of her bed. Her heart was racing. Madelaine was seeing that man behind Jack's back. Surely there could be no other reason for him to be coming out of their bedroom half-dressed while Jack was at work.

Her eyes lit on the dressing-table. A corner of her silk

camisole was caught at the side of the bottom drawer. Vee knew immediately that someone had searched through her things. Her fingers felt for and found her original papers. Nothing had been taken, but Vee knew someone had rifled through them. She felt violated. Who would do this? She shivered. She looked at her original birth certificate, at her German name.

From what her mother had told her of her father, he had loved them both. Vee had no reason to feel ashamed of who she was. Were it not for Hitler, she could be as proud of her father's homeland as he had probably been. But that was the problem. She might have a German surname, but she was an Englishwoman. Her first impulse was to repack her few clothes and leave.

And then what? Board another train? Look for another job? The money left in her purse would get her nowhere.

She looked around the comfortable room. Here, she had a bed and a job. Quite what she was to do she wasn't sure, but she could put money by and pay off Sammy Chesterton. That immediately appealed to her.

What of Madelaine and her lover, Hugh? It wasn't any of her business, was it? Except that Jack had shown himself to be a loving father to Peg. He was a good man, of that Vee was sure. And then she realized that if anything happened and Madelaine left Jack, she really would like to be around to help pick up the pieces . . .

It wasn't long before she was pushing open the Nissen hut door of the Ferry Café. The wireless was playing dance music and customers sitting at their tables were digging into plates of food. Rosie was behind the counter, clearly harassed as she wrote down orders and left them on a spike in the hatchway that separated the kitchen from the dining area. Vee saw her wipe her forehead where sweat gathered, as an angry customer complained that his meal had come minus the chips he'd ordered. He was practically shoving the plate beneath Rosie's chin.

'Not only do I have to wait ages but me order's wrong when it turns up.'

Vee saw Rosie's face: she was tired, about to crumble and let fall the tears that Vee could see in her eyes. She remembered Rosie's kindness earlier that morning at breakfast, when she'd made toast for her.

Vee lifted the hatch in the counter and found her way into the kitchen where Connie was turning slices of bacon in a large pan while watching eggs frying and trying to stir a pan of beans all at the same time.

In the chip fryer, the wire basket contained a portion of almost cooked chips that needed lowering into the boiling fat. Vee lowered the basket. The chips sizzled and spat. Vee ran her hands beneath the tap at the sink, grabbed a clean plate from the pile stacked near the hatch and raised the basket, shaking it to get rid of the excess fat. The chips were not quite to her satisfaction, so she lowered it again.

'Thanks,' came the single word from Connie.

A moment or so later, the chips were cooked. Vee was hungry and the sight of them made her mouth water. Picking up the plate she marched out of the kitchen and up to Rosie, who was still apologizing to the man – he wouldn't let her go without a good argument. A small queue had formed.

'Sorry your chips got left off the order. There's a few extra to make up for it.' She gave the man a glorious smile.

'Well,' he said, 'service with a smile.' He turned back to Rosie. 'I'm sorry, love, I've had a bad morning so far.' He picked up the plate and tipped the golden chips over his meal, then gave Rosie a broad wink and went back to his seat at the table, where he began eating noisily.

Rosie stared at Vee, but before she had time to speak an elderly man said, 'Cuppa, please.'

'Egg and chips for one,' another man, in a navy-blue jumper, said, and Vee wrote his order and left it on the spike, which was now empty.

It wasn't until the rush had petered out that Rosie said,

'Thank you. That man was about to make me cry and you saved the day. Usually I can handle the customers but I didn't sleep so well last night and . . . It's obvious you know the café business.'

'I worked in a club and we served meals.'

Vee didn't feel she needed to tell her what else the club had served up.

Connie came to the hatch. 'Thanks, love. I've been telling Jack for ages we need more help but he's got so much on his mind it goes in one ear and out the other. I've been trying to get him to see sense over some changes that would make things easier in here, but will he listen? Will he heck! I was a bit anxious when you tackled our fryer – it can be a bit temperamental, but you showed it who was boss.' She gave Vee a cuddle, enveloping her in the smell of fried food. 'I'll cook you both a meal,' she said, pulling away. She glanced at the wall clock. 'We'll be quiet for a bit now.'

A while later Vee patted her stomach. 'I never realized I was so hungry.' She'd eaten sausage, egg and chips and declared it was the best meal she'd had for a while. Connie, smiling, got up from the table and went behind the counter.

'Well, are you going to stay and work for Jack?' asked Rosie.

Connie brought three teas back, set them on the table, sat

down, took a packet of Woodbines from her pocket and lit up. She blew smoke high into the air and Rosie continued talking.

'We could do with your help here in the café. Though I've got an idea he's going to make you a jill-of-all-trades, train you up in a bit of everything.'

Connie replaced a hairpin that had slipped from her piled-up blonde curls. She was without the net snood she usually wore over her hair. 'If you don't want to stay you must tell him as soon as possible, though. He's a fair bloke to work for and last week he was run off his feet when the other bloke on the ropes had the flu. Oh, he's had plenty of people apply for a job but as soon as they find out they have to graft hard they don't come back the second day. And he won't take on youngsters because they'll get their call-up papers any day. The reliable elderly fellows ain't strong enough. He don't want anyone dying on him, does he?'

Rosie began laughing. 'Cor, you don't talk much, Connie, but when you do, you don't shut up.'

Vee looked at the two women. 'It'll be good to learn how to do different jobs,' she said. 'I might be a woman but I'm fit and strong . . .'

'Just like them land girls,' said Connie. 'Good, that's settled, then. Drink your tea, then go home and make the most of the rest of today. Don't forget to pop your ration book on the mantelpiece. I need it to do a shop for the house.'

Rosie grinned at her.

Vee had so many questions she wanted to ask but, for now, she had a job and a place to stay with people she liked. The sooner she was able to pay off Sammy Chesterton, the better. Being away from Netley had made her see her problems in a different light.

Chapter Eleven

Sammy Chesterton was parked in his usual place on the layby, smoking another cigar and thinking. His car window was wound down and he could hear birdsong. The fresh country air was making him feel better. Word had got out that one of his girls had pulled a fast one over him. He'd been expecting it ever since Vee had disappeared without paying for her new identity.

William Jacobitz, a newsagent from Botley, had spouted that if a girl could get away without paying a debt to Chesterton so could he.

William Jacobitz was finding it extremely difficult to run a business with ten broken fingers.

'You're lucky I'm letting you live. Don't take liberties, mate,' Sammy had told him. So, for now, his reputation was salvaged. But he was racking his brain for a way to catch up with Vee Schmidt, who seemed to have fallen off the face of the earth. He flicked the ash out of the window. What he ought to do was to pay May a visit. But, underneath his sometimes menacing exterior, he was a sentimental bloke and his memories stopped him doing any more than driving to this blessed layby and staring at her house, hoping for a sight of the girl he had once cared for.

He flicked through the *Daily Sketch*. 'Lock 'Em All Up' was today's headline. Of course it referred to the internment camps. The government believed it was easier to herd aliens into camps than allow them to roam at will. But conditions were poor and internees often assaulted. The authorities tried to make sure that those prisoners were fed and housed decently, but it wasn't long before boredom and depression set in.

Sammy thought that if he had his way papers should be provided for any loyal person who needed them, so they could live in peace in England. A simple check would disbar the unwelcome – the rapists, murderers and traffickers. He'd already been doing this for years at a profit. The government was crazy, Sammy thought.

What made ordinary human beings suddenly hate their fellow men simply because their names didn't fit? Why should loyal men lose their jobs because their names weren't

English? Sammy sighed. Perhaps one day a law would be passed to enable a woman to take her husband's name yet keep her own nationality. He himself would be a legal citizen then.

In the meantime he still had a problem to solve. Vee couldn't be allowed to get away with stealing from him. But how could he resolve the matter without hurting May?

He watched as a lorry slowed, then turned into the clearing at the front of May's smallholding. A man appeared from a barn and waved as the driver jumped down from his cab. Sammy heard voices, then May came out and stood on her garden path. Wearing a knee-length skirt and a blouse with her hair tied back, at first glance she looked like Vee. Ah, well, they say the apple doesn't fall far from the tree. He saw boxes of produce and money change hands. With the boxes stacked inside the vehicle, May waved goodbye as, transaction complete, the driver got back into the lorry. The engine started up and he was on his way.

Sammy knew how hard it had been for May and her labourers to work the land, grow and harvest those vegetables, a long, slow process without profits coming in. To the people who bought from her, she was Mrs May Smith. If word got out she'd married a German, her produce would rot in the fields. Her buyers would disappear.

Where was the sense in that, when food was in short supply? No, May deserved her new identity. So did her daughter. Suddenly it had all become so very complicated. He thought about the forthcoming elections. If he could get voted in somehow for Southampton, maybe in time he could get a bill passed so that marriage didn't take away your legal birthright. The fly in the ointment was that changing laws could take years. Probably he was better out of politics. Maybe he could finance another politician, have another shot at getting laws changed to suit his needs. It would certainly give him something else to focus on. Trouble was, he was such a good financier that he had too much time on his hands. If he wasn't at such a loose end, he wouldn't be sitting in this layby, would he?

He was still watching the cottage when May appeared once more. This time she was alone, standing at her front door, her face turned towards his car. For a moment they stared at each other, then May went back inside. Sammy, his heart thumping, started the car and drove off.

It wasn't the first time May had spotted the car in the layby. Who else could it be but Sammy Chesterton? But if that was so, why didn't he come to the house? He reminded her of someone from her past but she couldn't think. . .

May put the kettle on the stove. Jem would leave soon to go home. Of course he'd offered to stay on the premises – she'd had the devil of a time persuading him she could do without the gossip that would cause.

She tipped fresh tea leaves into the pot to mingle with the used ones. Two ounces per week weren't nearly enough, not when you needed tea to keep you going, she thought. May liked being self-sufficient, but there were some items, like tea, that she couldn't grow.

She switched on the wireless just in time to catch the news.

'Ninety-nine German planes were lost while they were bombing Woolwich Arsenal, a power station and the heart of London. Three hundred enemy bombers flanked by fighter planes have decimated the docks, the gasworks and the port. A few hours later there was a repeat attack. Hitler is trying to bring England to her knees.'

Stunned, May made the tea. The south coast was taking the brunt of the beating, which meant Gosport and Portsmouth, with more than their fair share of airfields and armaments yards, were likely to be attacked. May prayed Vee was still safe. She switched off the wireless.

Of course she'd heard the bombing last night as she stood by the window watching the searchlights and explosions fill the sky over Southampton. Out here, in the countryside, she felt relatively safe.

Would the war never end?

May sat down in the comfortable armchair near the fire. A log blazing in the cool evenings made the room homely. A murmur of kitten squeaks cut into her thoughts as Cat left her babies to jump on to her lap.

'Hello, girl,' May said, tickling her beneath her chin, which she knew the animal loved. Cat began to purr. 'Come for a cuddle away from those demanding babies of yours, have you?'

May guessed Cat would soon return to the box behind the sofa. Mothers were all so protective of their babies, she thought, remembering how she herself had felt when Vee was tiny.

Smoothing Cat's soft fur relaxed her. Memories of her work at the hospital came unbidden. Then a memory she didn't particularly want arrived, followed by one she would never forget.

Gus was lying on the floor in the four-bed ward, unconscious and covered in blood. Two of the beds were empty, but one contained an Italian who'd had both legs amputated.

'I was asleep and I heard nothing,' Bruno insisted.

May thought it highly unlikely that he hadn't witnessed the assault on Gus. Annie had rushed into the pharmacy to tell her about it and she had sneaked along to his ward.

The duty doctor said, 'Take Mr Bruno de Pace, bed and all, and put him on Ward Three. Get someone outside this door at all times until I find out what's going on.'

Later, when Gus had come round sufficiently to speak, May was there.

'I was told to stay away from you,' he said to her. 'The young English doctor, home from France and tired of the bloodshed and fighting, advised me to leave you alone. I thought at the time of the dance he might want you for himself. I didn't see why he had the right to advise me of anything and I told him so.'

May sat on the chair at the side of his bed, which she was not allowed to do, poised for flight if a doctor returned. The scar on Gus's face had opened again and fresh dressings obscured part of one eye. The white of the bandage emphasized the dark bruising.

'I was almost asleep when he returned with one of the porters. They stood in this room with the door closed and insulted me in English and in German. The porter had arms like great hams and seemed unable to keep them still while jeering at me and my country. Then the verbal insults weren't enough and they started hitting me as they dragged me from the bed. I tried to prevent them, but they had the upper hand as I was barely able to stand. I couldn't force my legs to move, not without crutches, but I did try to hit back. I felt like a feeble old man.'

May put her hand over his as his fingers clutched at the counterpane. She sensed his anger at being helpless. Gus had no reason to lie about who had hurt him, yet May couldn't understand how a doctor, of all people, would inflict injuries. It didn't make sense.

'But there was something unusual about the young doctor at the dance,' she said. She remembered telling Annie he was creepy. She had had to wait while the regular doctor changed Gus's dressings. She made herself useful by fetching Gus some fresh drinking water, then disposing of the detritus. The room smelt of surgical spirit. Before the doctor left, he had assured Gus that an investigation would take place. 'This is all highly irregular,' he said.

'I do not think they will worry too much about me,' Gus said to May. 'I am the enemy.'

'No, you're wrong. This is a very good hospital. Doctors and nurses do their very best for patients, regardless of where they come from. This was a one-off that will be looked into. It was just a pity it happened to you.'

Gus, upset, was determined to tell May everything he could remember.

'The young doctor swung a right hook that floored me. I could feel blood trickling from my lips. "Fuckin' Jerry," I heard him say, "Stay away from May." While I was on the floor he kicked me in the head. My ear felt as though it was on fire. Again he warned me away from you. Then the kicking began again, this time from the porter.

'"This is for *Lusitania*. My brother was one of the passengers who won't be coming home." He went on kicking me until the doctor pulled him away, finally realizing, I suppose, that he should save lives, not end them. I must have blacked out then. Tell me you didn't go with this young doctor.'

She squeezed his hand. May was aware that the German patients were advised to keep away from the English nurses. Since many of the men were dying when they arrived for treatment, the nurses were naturally compassionate. Sometimes the men formed attachments with them, but when they left the hospital the nurses became wartime memories. May knew all about the resentment among the English for the sinking of the cruiser, though. More than a thousand lives had been lost.

'You weren't personally responsible for the people who drowned on that cruise ship.'

Gus couldn't stop himself. 'I am German. I am the enemy. War is terrible. I can't help how I feel about you, May, but I don't want to cause you trouble . . .' His eyes closed. Gus had fallen asleep.

He remained alone in the small ward, and May found she was making every excuse she could think of to be with him. He told her of his home in Germany, Pulheim. He showed her photographs of his family, who were dead now: the war had killed them too. She told him about her parents, their smallholding.

Every day he grew stronger. The guard at the door was dispensed with. The young doctor seemed to have disappeared. No more was said about the investigation.

Annie said, 'I thought that doctor would be dealt with. This is not a good thing to happen in a hospital. Certainly not in a place like this where everything is so . . . self-contained. Did you have any contact with him after the dance? Has he been bothering you?'

'No,' said May. 'But I don't go out alone at night. Thank God you and I go back to our quarters together.'

She refused to listen for strange night noises. As her one concession to fear, she didn't venture on her own to the washrooms or the lavatories, but instead used the poor facilities in the room.

As Gus grew stronger May took in board games. He couldn't beat her at draughts, so he began to teach her to play chess. They talked of anything and everything. They discussed the war.

'The Americans have entered and are at the French coast,' May told him.

'For more than two years President Woodrow Wilson has been trying to steer a middle course,' Gus answered. 'I fear for my country now.'

'I doubt you'll ever fight again,' said May. 'And your priority is to get well. Well enough to leave the hospital and work. Patients are allowed to work outside the hospital when their health is stable. They're trusted to leave in the mornings and return in the evenings. This is a farming area and many men entered the services, so the prison allows some men to make up the shortfall.'

'I don't think this is possible in Germany. Escape might be on men's minds.'

'The clothing you all have to wear shows you're from the hospital's prison. The hospital can't house men when they're better. Englishmen are sent home or possibly back into the services. Many of your countrymen work in the strawberry fields that this part of Hampshire is famous for.'

'Farmers like this?'

May laughed. 'Since labour is hard to come by, with so many men at the war, the farmers may not be happy to have the enemy working for them, but help is help.'

'I live only for each day so that I can see you.'

His words surprised her, yet she felt as he did. That simple sentence meant everything to her.

Before their conversation she had been reading to him. Supper had come and gone and soon she would help get him ready for sleep. May was still dressed in her hospital clothing but she'd been off duty for some hours, and the regular nurse turned a blind eye to her spending so much time with Gus.

Gus wasn't able to manoeuvre his crutches to use the bath so May fetched water, towels, clean linen and pyjamas.

She began with his arms, soaping from his shoulders to his fingertips. Then his legs, calves first, then thighs. Sometimes they both knew she spent far too long soaping him. She couldn't help herself as she kissed him gently on the lips, loving the feel of his moustache.

He put his arms around her, holding her close.

'You must know how much I want you. Is it all right to tell you?' He let her go and waited for her answer.

May knew that she had fallen in love with him.

She loved the shape of his jaw, his chin, the way his mouth crinkled at the corners, and she ran her hands up his wet body, resting them on his chest. 'It's perfectly all right,' she said.

Before long his arms were around her again and May knew she could wait no longer. If anything was to happen between them it was up to her. The beating he had taken had left Gus unsure. She knew he wasn't worried for himself but was heedful of anything bad happening to her. But May didn't want to wait.

There were few hospital rooms with locks and those were mainly for keeping medicines and important documents safe from prying eyes. Wards were never locked. She left him to put a chair beneath the handle on the door.

May undressed and lay beside him on the small bed while he wiped his body dry. She patted soap from his beautiful face, amazed she'd had the courage to instigate what was about to happen. There was no thought for the consequences: the heat running through her young body needed its outlet. Surely it couldn't be wrong to show the man she loved how much she loved him. 'See what you've done to me?' Her words were soft. 'I've never wanted anyone before you.' She noted how he lay, naked now, his flesh glistening where the towel hadn't dried it. There was a ladder of muscle running from his chest to his waist. His internal injuries had healed, his scars fading more each day. Her fingers moved over his skin. How she had longed to touch him, and now here he was waiting for her touch, her breath, her tongue.

He brushed small kisses on her cheeks, then across her breasts. He reached for her and took her nipple in his mouth. May leant forward to lie on top of him, careful of his amputated limb. She heard herself say all of the things lovers say that sound so silly afterwards, but she couldn't stop herself.

He was slender, taut-limbed, and fine dark hairs glistened on his chest and arms. She knew other things about him: his weight, his height, the touch of his hand, his fingers, the sleepy musky smell of him she'd come to love.

It was unreal and like nothing she could have imagined as he slowly, carefully, drove himself into her. He was practised. He turned her, tumbled her, surprised her with an agility he didn't possess out of bed. It was her first time, and although she had orchestrated the lovemaking, it was every bit as wonderful as she'd hoped it would be.

Afterwards, he said, 'I am your first?'

'Of course,' she said. 'And I must change your sheets or everyone will know you and I have made love.'

She had believed the first time would be painful, but he had loved her, really loved her. Gus had made her a woman. May smiled at him, already gathering her clothes, not speaking but thinking he was her weakness and her strength.

With the chair away from the door she finished his make-shift bath, laughing as he pushed her hand away as she went to wash him. 'No,' he said. 'I want to keep your smell on me, to remember you when you aren't here.'

Chapter Twelve

As May lay in bed, she began to worry about Vee but knew she'd only feel better when she heard from her again and was reassured that she was all right.

Jem had arranged for the pickers to gather the last of the raspberries today – most of the fruit had already gone to local shops. Tomorrow they would start on the runner beans. Freshly picked runners were always tasty. May couldn't remember a time when her life hadn't been governed by the seasons, the vegetables and the fruit on the small-holding. It wasn't a large place, but it was big enough for a good living and she'd spent most of her life working the land . . .

In 1914, after the initial flush of men had volunteered to fight for their country, the government had had to beg others to enlist. May had read the posters requesting women to apply to the nursing profession.

'Have you been told how long it takes to become a fully qualified nurse?' her father asked.

Of course she had. 'I know you don't want me to leave here, Dad, but I feel I must do something for my country.' She'd not left home before.

'Growing food is doing something.'

'I'm going to join the VADs.' He could hardly argue with her. Nevertheless, she had amazed herself by sticking to her convictions.

Sent to London, she felt terribly grown-up sharing a small room and working in a ward at the Charing Cross Hospital with another VAD as her introduction to nursing.

Except that actual nursing didn't come into it: any dirty job automatically went to the VADs. Bedpans to scrub, washing bowls to scour, screens to move, and all the time worrying about being told off because her removable cuffs and white over-sleeves were grubby. She remembered Annie's excitement on being told she was to embark on a hospital ship to help bring home the wounded from France. May was also going on a ship, but only as far as Southampton Water where the Royal Victoria Hospital at Netley needed her assistance. She wasn't even allowed to commute to the hospital daily but was expected to live in. It didn't take May long to find out that the professional nurses weren't happy to work alongside the VADs, so she was relieved when Annie was transferred to the same hospital. The two girls shared one of the huts at the rear of the hospital and May looked forward to the days when she could go home to see her parents. Now, unable to sleep, May went downstairs and lit the gas beneath the kettle.

She sat in her favourite armchair thinking of the time she'd spent at the London hospital. Somehow she'd become the recipient of an 'efficiency' stripe, a scarlet ribbon she was entitled to wear on her sleeve that showed she had reached the high standard required by the London borough during the year she'd spent there.

May often wondered how her life would have been had she not been sent to work on the German ward at the Royal Victoria Hospital.

Stories abounded of how evil Germans were so May was surprised to discover that they were very like their English counterparts, frightened patients who didn't want to die. She was also surprised at the amount of English they spoke.

Three German orderlies helped dress wounds and did everything asked of them by the charge sister, who spoke fluent German, having spent time in Cologne before the war.

Most of the men had horrific wounds and weren't expected

to live long, so Matron had insisted that the window in the ward be left open at the top for their souls to fly to Heaven when they died. May remembered seeing Gus, so still, so broken after he had been unloaded on to the pontoon from the hospital ship, then delivered on a trolley to the ward. She had felt his eyes watching her. Each day she had expected to find his bed empty, his soul claimed by death, but he had survived . . .

She remembered the day in the nurses' canteen when she had heard that an English doctor had been sent to an asylum further down the south coast, and couldn't wait to tell Gus. 'He'd been in France, working constantly with little sleep, watching men die, mostly the British, with shells screaming and bombs dropping. The war had unhinged him. Then his fiancée had ended their engagement, and that tipped him over the edge. His hatred of Germans showed itself when he began operating badly, cutting what wasn't supposed to be cut. His staff, horrified, complained, but with no outward signs of illness, except his erratic work, it was a while before they realized exactly how ill he was. He was sent home to England and was supposed to go to Knowle Hospital but left the ship here at Netley, not as a patient but as a doctor. With little outward sign of instability, he was accepted as the doctor he was.'

'Surely this hospital has records.'

'It's wartime. If a man in a white coat acts like a doctor and speaks like a doctor, who's going to say they don't need his help with a ship full of injured men arriving at the gates?'

Gus sighed.

'You weren't the only patient he assaulted. But it was you dancing with me that upset him. Annie said he carried pictures of a young woman very like myself.'

'But that doesn't explain why that porter—'

'Orderlies, nurses, porters do as they're told. They wouldn't have known he was ill and probably didn't question his strangeness.'

'It might have been better had his past come out before . . .'

'You're lucky to be well. It will be a long while before he recovers from his breakdown. This war has such a lot to answer for.'

'What has happened to the porter?'

'He's been sacked. What he did was unforgivable.'

Gus said, 'Hatred is like a plague of locusts feeding off a field of green shoots.' She watched him. He was obviously thinking about what had happened.

'You might be told officially about all of this,' she said.

'I think not.'

But May knew Gus now understood why the young man

had wanted to hurt him. Perhaps he could forgive. The young doctor had lost everything – his happiness, his job, his mind.

May was woken by a gentle knock on the back door. Before she had time to answer it, Jem came through to the kitchen.

'I knew you were still up,' he said. 'I saw the lights. I had to walk down to make sure you were all right.'

'And why shouldn't I be? I was all right when you left, wasn't I?'

Jem had always had a key to come and go at will. She felt the teapot and decided to make fresh for him. She smiled as she stepped past him.

He put a hand on her arm. The other held a rolled newspaper.

'I had to come down. The car that's been in the layby belongs to Sammy Chesterton. I had a good look at the driver this afternoon and remembered there was an article in the *Echo* about him providing money for a kids' party after their school had been bombed. Luckily, there was no one in the place but while alternative school buildings were being found – he just happened to donate them – the newspaper took pictures.'

He showed May the article.

'We knew he'd come looking for her, Jem.' May tried to sound calm but her heart was pounding. Of course Jem was right. The man in the newspaper pictures and the man in the car were the same person. 'What worries me is that on paper he sounds a nice chap.'

Jem said, 'No man ever made money without standing on a few toes on the way up.'

May stared at him. Jem was always there when she needed him, always had been. There were times when she wished she'd agreed to marry him. She couldn't imagine her life without his solid figure in it. Long ago she'd told herself and him that marrying to change her name wasn't fair on him.

'I wish I could remember where I met him before.'

Jem tucked strands of her hair back behind her ear. 'I couldn't bear it if anything happened to you, May.' He looked at the tea she'd poured for him. 'I'll drink this, then walk back,' he said.

May wondered why she didn't take him up on his many offers to move in with her. After all, he spent most of his time on the smallholding, and Vee looked on him as a father. She knew he cared for them both deeply.

Being outside in all weathers had given her a healthy, if unfashionable, glow, and hard work had roughened her hands but it had kept her supple, too. For a woman in her early fifties May attracted more than her fair share of second glances from the men she met at the markets. Now she smiled at him. 'You won't be leaving this house without a kiss and cuddle, Jem Worthington.'

He put his arms around her and love for him warmed her heart.

'Of course,' he said. 'That's another thing I came back for.'

Vee stepped on board *Eurybia*.

'Goddess of the seas, this ferry,' said Jack, standing on the deck beside her. Vee yawned, tried to hide it, and Jack laughed. 'Yesterday's boat is in for a refit and a quick paint job.' He looked at his watch. 'I'm sorry that you'll do most of your training early in the mornings but with so many passengers crossing to Portsmouth daily, it's the best time for me to bring you up to scratch with what's needed.' He gave her a wide smile. 'I'm glad you've decided to stay around and help.'

'You said the ferries carry on running even through raids?'

'Yes,' he answered. 'Of course.'

That morning, Vee and Jack had left the house together. She'd slept well and eaten a hearty breakfast cooked by Connie. She had even persuaded Jack to sign her library card and looked forward to borrowing books. When he had discovered she liked reading, Jack had shown her a small room in his house near the main bedroom that was lined with books. Some were very old, but there was also a shelf of modern authors, mainly thriller writers.

'You're welcome to take anything you like,' he said. 'Madelaine's not a bookworm like me.' Every day she learnt something new about her employer, Vee thought.

She'd told him she would stay, even though she realized how hard she would have to work. Helping in the Ferry Café had made up her mind for her. She'd liked the camaraderie between Rosie and Connie. If she could work permanently in the café it would be lovely, but Jack had said he wanted someone who could be familiar with most of the work on the ferries, not simply a waitress.

It was a clear, sunny morning and Gosport seemed to be sleeping. Jack stood next to a puddle of rope on the deck near the exit gates of the sturdy launch.

'See how it's coiled? Most important to leave the excess rope like that. Easy to see and hard to fall over. Don't need mishaps on the boat. I'm going to show you the lighterman's hitch, which is Mac's preferred tying-up procedure. This morning you can do a few trips under his watchful eye and tie up the ferry as he likes it done.' He was looking at her as though defying her to disagree. She nodded. He lifted the rope and unwound it until only the loop was around the bollard on the jetty. He handed her the rope.

'I never expected it to be so heavy,' Vee said. She hoped it might begin to feel lighter as she got used to it.

'It's a dry day. Imagine it wet and heavier.' He smiled. If he went on looking at her like that, Vee thought, she could do anything he asked of her. His next words jolted her out of her sudden daydream. 'This is a bight.'

He wrapped the rope twice around the bollard while the boat barely moved, so still was the water. Then he passed the rope under the end, making a loop. 'A bight,' he said again. Then she watched, fascinated, as he passed the end of the bight through the loop, opened it up and brought the entire knot around to encircle the bollard.

'Sometimes known as the backhanded knot. You're going to practise it with Mac this morning until he knows you can tie and untie this vessel.'

'While there's people about?' Inside she was panicking. Suppose she got it wrong? Suppose people started laughing at her? She looked at the rope holding the boat close to the jetty. Jack had made it all look so easy.

'Mac'll be there to guide you.'

She watched his back as he walked away and began

climbing the stairway to the wheelhouse. 'When he's had enough of you I'll expect you up here beside me so I can explain a few things,' he shouted down at her.

Vee watched the people queuing for tickets at the kiosk. While Jack had been showing her how to tie knots, Gosport had woken up.

The boat had been cleaned before she and Jack had stepped aboard. She looked down at her navy blue dungarees, handed to her that morning. They fitted her quite well, considering they were a men's size medium! She wiggled her toes in the new rubber-soled shoes. They looked heavier than they were and were actually quite comfortable, even though they had newspaper pushed tightly into them to make them fit better. And now passengers were on the boat, chattering, laughing, leaning bicycles against the rails. Vee began to panic. She looked down at the rope and hated it.

Then, striding towards the ferry, there was Mac, his red hair bright in the sunshine. She raised a hand in greeting and was relieved when he waved back.

Chapter Thirteen

At six o'clock Vee climbed down the ladder from the wheel-house, leaving Jack and Albert Haytor, his mate, discussing the finer points of her docking and steering of *Eurybia* across the stretch of water from Gosport to Portsmouth.

'How d'you feel?' Mac was lighting a roll-up, drawing on it deeply. She, Mac and Jack were going home and the second crew were taking over.

'Oh, it feels funny standing on firm ground,' she said. Vee didn't think she'd ever been so tired in her whole life. Neither had her hands ever been so sore and calloused.

She was on the pontoon and it was certainly firmer than the bucking, swaying sea she'd been on since that morning.

At one o'clock Jack had taken her to the café for a bite to eat, handing over *Eurybia* to Albert Haytor. Vee had taken the chance to hurry to the library and hand in her request form. The librarian had allowed her to choose two books. She was looking forward to starting Raymond Chandler's *The Big Sleep*. The librarian had also suggested Christopher Morley's *Kitty Foyle*, and Vee could think of nothing more pleasurable than a bath and bed with two books to choose between.

'You'll soon get used to the feel of the sea beneath you. I reckon you did well today.'

Vee didn't agree. She'd been terrified of docking the craft, but she'd listened carefully to all Jack's instructions and he'd never left her side while she was in the wheelhouse.

Standing beside him with his hands on the large wooden wheel she'd listened carefully as he'd said, 'You need to be part manager, part navigator. Here's how you start up. There isn't time for me to take out a boat without passengers so I'm showing you as we go.'

As soon as the boat was untied, he turned the wheel and moved away from the jetty. 'Good eyesight, quick thinking. You can't afford to make mistakes with passengers' lives in your hands. You'll need to understand the sea traffic in the waters here.' He waved expansively, encompassing the boats and ships moored nearby. 'Before you start a shift it's essential you look the boat over to check everything is as it should be. Check the equipment, check the crew are happy.' Then he explained the function of every lever, every handle, every button. She was sure she'd never remember it all.

She watched his strong, tanned hands turn the wheel and the boat passed an Isle of Wight ferry with ease, then turned and made for the distant shore. 'Take the wheel,' he said. To do this Vee had to stand in front of him and put her hands where his were. She could feel his body behind her, which was unsettling in a good way, almost as if he was sending strength into her by his very closeness. 'See the tanker moored ahead?' She nodded, her eyes judging the distance. Surely he would suggest turning the wheel so they could give it a wide berth. 'It's not like a car where you can press the brake and expect to stop. You need to assess the distance so you can clear any obstacles well before you reach them.' He turned the wheel again and the boat swung out into clear, traffic-free sea. 'There's a great deal of movement in these waters. Small craft can pop up from nowhere. You're doing fine.'

A surge of excitement rose within her.

'You need a licence for this. As I'm in charge, you're covered by mine, and it wouldn't be a good idea to put in for a licence until you're absolutely familiar with the boat and the route.' She sighed. 'Don't worry, it'll all work out in the end,' he said. 'No need to rush things. Bit like driving a car. Can you drive?'

'We have a van at home that I use,' she answered.

'That's good.' He sounded as if he genuinely meant it.

She didn't want to start talking about herself in case she let out more information than she should, so she said quickly, 'Everything on this boat seems different from a car.'

He put his hand to her waist and squeezed gently. 'Well, it would be, wouldn't it? This is a boat!' She laughed and his hand dropped away.

Vee could see the Gosport pontoon looming. If she didn't give out too much information about herself, she thought, when Sammy Chesterton came after her, it would be difficult for him to trace her.

'Slow down,' he said.

It seemed to her that nothing happened when she moved the small black handle. The engine pulsated; she pressed down harder.

'Slow down!' He knocked her hands from the wheel and stepped in front of her just as the boat clipped the jetty, then swung out widely. The boat, now in reverse, was pushing against the rubber buoys hanging from the pontoon. The seawater, churned up by the engines, was splashing high into the air and drenching some of the passengers near that side.

Vee was petrified. If he hadn't been so quick-witted, the boat would have rammed right into the jetty.

'I'm so sorry.' She felt like crying but knew that would be self-indulgent.

'I'm sorry,' she said once more.

A voice called out, 'You want to take more water with it, mate!' Everyone was remarkably jolly about the knock.

'Sorry, folks!' shouted Jack, and cheers erupted.

Vee said, 'I'm—'

'If you say "sorry" once more I shall chuck you in. On my first steering lesson I overshot the jetty and landed in the mud. We've all got to start somewhere and there's no harm done.' The corners of his mouth curved up in a smile and she longed to touch it with her fingers or, better still, her lips. Instantly, she was ashamed of herself. Jack was a married man with a family! 'I can guarantee you'll never go fast when you should go slow ever again,' he said kindly. 'I expect you could do with a cuppa now. There's a flask in that cubby-hole beside you. We'll carry on with this later.'

She had left the wheelhouse and spent almost all the rest of her time with Mac and the ropes. But later Jack had called her to him and, determined she wouldn't make the same mistake again, she went on with her tuition.

'I got a lot of funny looks from the passengers,' she remarked.

'It's not usual to see a pretty girl taking on jobs done by men. But because of this war it doesn't matter who tackles a difficult job, only that it gets done.' Jack smiled at her.

Mac was tall and slim with strong shoulders, and she'd noticed the girls giving him the eye all day. Some had boarded the boat and made their way to the rear so they could stand and talk to him while he coiled the ropes and made sure the chains were fastened securely to stop accidents happening. People got too enthusiastic, pushing against the gates in their haste to be among the first off the boat, and were sometimes careless.

She'd been worried Mac might not take to her, but Jack had assured him she wasn't taking over his job, just needed to be able to do it if necessary.

Walking towards the bus station, Mac fell into step beside her. 'Did Jack tell you about the christening?'

'Didn't shut up about it,' she said. 'I feel honoured to be invited on Sunday.'

'Connie's buying a silver bracelet for Peg. We're all putting in money so it'll be a joint gift. D'you want to be included?'

'Oh, yes.' She was glad he'd asked her.

Vee was happy that Jack had invited her to attend St John's

Church on Sunday morning. She'd seen little of Madelaine, and when she had, the woman had looked at her as if a bad smell had arisen beneath her nose. She knew Madelaine felt awkward with her because she had interrupted her when she was with Hugh.

Vee still had some money left, although not much, but Jack had explained she would be paid weekly. She felt it prudent to keep some money back to telephone her mother. She'd discovered there was a phone at the house, but with it being in the hall, she didn't feel as if she could talk to May in case her side of the conversation was overheard. In any case, she would still have wanted to pay Jack for the call.

Anyway, it wasn't her share of the money for the christening gift she was worried about but what to wear. When she'd left the smallholding, her suitcase had contained only the bare essentials, mostly trousers and skirts with sweaters to match. It had seemed pointless filling the case with the silky and glittery clothes that were suitable for the club but useless for everyday wear.

'Vee!' Up ahead she saw Rosie waiting by the ticket office. Vee waved and Rosie began walking towards her through the crowds wandering in the Ferry Gardens.

'See you tomorrow?' Mac said.

Vee had no idea whether or not she'd see him the next day,

but she smiled into his cheerful freckled face and nodded. From their chats during the day she'd learnt that he lived with his mum in Queen's Road and had been on the ferries since leaving school. His dad had been a stoker, and when he had died a few years ago, Mac had taken over his dad's work with Eddie. Eventually Jack had offered him the job 'up top', which he much preferred. He'd already confessed to her that he liked the attention from the girls but rarely took up their offers. He had a regular girlfriend, Vera, and was saving up to get married.

'She'd have my guts for garters if I so much as glanced at another girl,' he said proudly.

Mac walked towards Mumby Road and was soon swallowed by the crowd.

'I saw you get off the boat so thought I'd wait,' said Rosie. 'How did it go today?'

'I don't know.'

Rosie slipped her arm through Vee's.

'I made a few stupid mistakes with the rope, and my aim for the bollards wasn't so good,' Vee confessed, 'but in the end I got the hang of it.' She rubbed her arms. 'I feel worn out.' If she went to bed at that very moment she'd sleep for ever, she thought.

'Did you get to steer the boat?'

Suddenly Vee was reminded of Jack's closeness, the smell of Imperial Leather soap from his morning wash and his natural male muskiness. His kindness and patience with her had paid off and things had begun to make sense. 'Yes, but I don't know that I'd be any good in an emergency,' she said. 'Or that I'd be asked to skipper the boat regularly. There are other skippers with far more experience who wouldn't be happy to find out I was doing their job. But I understand that Jack needs someone who could take over anywhere if need be. So if he thinks I can be that person, I'm happy to take on the work.'

'It's wartime. Us women are taking on all sorts of jobs now.' Rosie threw back her head and laughed. 'I hope he finally lets you work in the café with us. We could do with the extra help.'

Vee nodded. 'It's nice you came to meet me . . .'

Rosie clapped a hand to her head. 'I forgot. I came to ask you if you wanted to come to the pictures with us some time. Me and Connie.'

Vee's tiredness lifted. She almost felt she could cry with happiness at being asked to join them. Rosie must have taken the pause in her answering to mean she didn't want to go.

'It's George Formby this week. He's not much to look at, but he certainly makes us laugh. *Come On George*, the picture's called.'

Vee threw her arms around Rosie. 'Oh, I'd love to come,' she said, almost knocking Rosie off her feet. In her head she was adding up whether there would be enough money left after she'd put some towards Peg's christening present. If she was careful, there would be.

Together they walked towards the house. Vee knew it didn't matter what she wore to the pictures because it was dark in the cinema. But Sunday was a different matter and it was important to her that Jack saw she'd made an effort. Madelaine always looked so smart – even in her nightwear she was glamorous.

'What are you wearing on Sunday?' The words popped out of her mouth.

'I bought some lace in the market and sewed it on the cuffs of my navy blue dress. I made a matching collar too. It's a nice dress but had got a bit tired. How about you?' asked Rosie.

'That's just it. I only have a few clothes with me . . . '

Rosie stopped walking, turned and looked Vee up and down thoughtfully.

'Have a lend of my strawberry pink dress with the box pleats.' A frown appeared in her forehead. 'You're taller than me, but we're about the same size.'

'I didn't ask you that question because I expected you to lend me something.'

Rosie squeezed her arm. 'I'm offering because you can't go in slacks or a skirt. Perhaps you don't like pink.'

Her face had fallen and Vee felt sure she'd hurt the girl's feelings. 'Oh, I do!'

'That's all right, then.' Rosie grinned at her and Vee knew she was forgiven. She was becoming accepted by the girls who ran the Ferry Café and didn't feel so lonely any more.

Jack was already at the house when the girls arrived. Peg was crying and he was clearly worn out trying to pacify her.

'She doesn't seem to want that, does she?'

The baby was screaming now and Vee's heart went out to the tiny soul.

'Give her here. You get on with making her a bottle, it's possible she's hungry.' Vee took the little one and sat in the armchair. Jack had told her he had changed Peg's nappy, so Vee knew she wasn't crying because she was wet and uncomfortable. 'It must be time for her feed?'

She didn't ask where Madelaine was. At times she seemed to have forgotten she had a baby to look after.

'I'll put the kettle on,' said Rosie.

Vee turned Peg on to her stomach and began rubbing her back with firm circular motions. Presently the little girl gave a couple of deep sobs. Then, breathing evenly, she fell asleep over Vee's knees.

'Where did you learn that trick?' Jack stood with the bottle of milk in his hand, watching her intently.

'I was brought up on a smallholding. We don't have any animals now, but we did when I was growing up and my mum used to cuddle and soothe the small animals when they'd been scared by a fox. She said she used to do it to me – guaranteed to shut me up!'

'It works,' he said, smiling at her. 'Thank you. You say you don't have animals now?'

'No, just a few acres to farm. Tomatoes, beans, strawberries, that kind of thing. My mum has a few helpers. When I was younger I couldn't wait to leave, but now I'm beginning to think it wasn't such a hard life after all.' Vee realized she was talking too much. The trouble was that Jack was easy to talk to and listened to her. 'Anyway, where's your wife? She can't be far away – I'm sure she wouldn't leave this little scrap for long.'

A shadow fell across Jack's face. 'No. She can't be far away.'

Just then Rosie clattered over with the tea tray and the steaming teapot.

'That looks good,' said Vee. Rosie poured the tea, Jack sat on a chair at the table, and Vee sipped from her cup, careful not to drip any on baby Peg, who was still sprawled contentedly across her lap. She could hear Connie singing upstairs in the bathroom and, for a while, she felt every bit as relaxed as the sleeping child.

'I'm going to have a bath,' Rosie said. 'I'm off out later.'

'I think I'd like a soak after you,' Vee said. 'If that's all right?'

'Oh, I'm sorry,' Jack said. 'I didn't know you were going out. Better pass that bundle of joy over to me. You did really well today, Vee. One or two moments when I thought you might not clear traffic in the harbour . . .'

'Rosie's asked me to go to the pictures, but it's not tonight. I think I'd like to go to bed and read. Anyway,' she began to laugh, 'it's a wonder you weren't scared half to death. I saw your knuckles go white as we passed that oil tanker.' Jack coughed and looked down at the floor. Once or twice Vee had terrified herself, misjudging the distances between craft. But when that had happened Jack had quickly taken over the wheel. She'd been glad that he was at her side as she knew he wouldn't let any harm come to the boat, herself or the paying customers.

They heard footsteps click-clacking along the hallway and Madelaine burst into the kitchen.

'This is a cosy little scene.'

Vee guiltily handed the sleeping child to Jack, who was

already on his feet. He slipped past his wife with a grim 'Hello, Madelaine,' and out along the hallway to their room. Vee got up and tried a smile at Madelaine, who was still glaring at her.

'Do you want a cuppa? There's tea in the pot,' Rosie asked Madelaine, but all she received was a stony look.

Vee went upstairs and Rosie followed. On the stairs Vee turned to Rosie and pulled a face. It was quite obvious a storm was brewing between Jack and Madelaine and Vee wanted no part of it.

Ada pulled her coat over herself and closed her eyes. The gentle bobbing of the boat usually lulled her to sleep quickly, despite the lack of pillows and mattress. But tonight the cold was seeping into her bones.

She was hungry, and that was also keeping her awake. She still had money left from the notes that girl, Vee, had given her. Who knew when she could persuade the market stall-holders to allow her to help erect their stalls? The cash they gave her wasn't much, but if she was careful she could make her money last.

Ada sighed. Her hair was still wet. In the public toilets near the bus station she'd attempted to wash it after finding a sliver of soap on the porcelain sink. She'd taken off her petticoat and used it as a towel. Now she glanced at the off-white garment hanging to dry over the wooden bench on the other side of the cabin.

She felt as though she was caught in a trap. She was German and therefore the enemy. No one would employ her in a proper job. 'Bloody Germans, they want shooting!' How many times had she heard that said?

It wasn't her fault that Hitler was at war with everyone. He might be ruling Germany, but it didn't mean she or her countrymen agreed with his way of running their country. The man was deranged, everyone knew that. The trouble was that the English thought the ordinary people were like him. German families were going hungry too, and the constant bombing made life difficult for everyone.

She thought about Vee, who had bought her food and a cup of tea in the Dive. She'd had no problems getting a job. Unlike Ada she had her identity papers. Nevertheless, she was a kind person. She must have known some trouble in her life to enable her to empathize with Ada.

Fancy her being taken on as a ferry-girl-of-all-trades by Jack Edwards! He was a good man. If it wasn't for his kindness, Ada would be sleeping out in the open or in some doorway.

She heard the splatter of rain on the cabin's roof and

the wind, which caused the boat to rock more violently against the dock's buoys. What would happen to her when the winter got a proper hold on Gosport? She doubted very much that the war would be over by Christmas.

If only she was still living with her parents in their home above the chip shop. But they were dead and gone. Or even with those darling children in Alverstoke.

It had been such a wrench leaving little Hannah and George. That was the trouble with being a nanny: you got so fond of the kiddies. But of course her employer couldn't keep her on once he knew she was the enemy.

Her qualifications from Norland College were of the highest standard. She should have known her job in Alverstoke was too good to last. Hitler wanted to rule the world and all the hatred of the Great War had been dragged up again.

'I'm sorry, Ada, but I have to let you go.' She'd had no idea it would be so difficult to find another job – any job.

Ada shivered. Torrential rain was now hitting the boat. Her stomach grumbled with hunger, and the stench of the cigarette butts on the floor was making her insides churn.

She wondered what the time was. At four the lad who cleaned the boat would arrive. That was her signal to be on her way. He would be mopping the decks and hauling fuel aboard. She had a lot to be thankful for. Jack was worth a hundred of that stuck-up bitch he'd married. She'd heard the gossip that Madelaine with her cut-glass accent, her cheating, didn't care a fig about that lovely little girl.

A tear, like a chip of ice, fell down her cheek. If she had a nice man like Jack Edwards, she'd never mess him about. Wouldn't it be wonderful if she could meet an older man who would fall in love with her? She'd love him back so much. More tears fell. She had as much chance of that as there was of the war ending before Christmas.

Chapter Fourteen

Rosie shook some lurid mauve bath crystals into the water. They sank like stones, turning the regulation five inches of water to a salty-smelling pink. The crystals had come from the market and were better than nothing – but, oh, how she longed to be able to soak in something expensive, something that smelt like the picture on the bottle. Maybe after the war was over things would return to normal.

Not that she'd ever been able to buy expensive toiletries. There had been no money left for fripperies after Mick had come back from the pub.

Rosie shook her hair free of the muslin snood she wore in the café to stop hairs falling into the food. Long-lashed eyes stared back at her. Lipstick had settled into the creases around her mouth. Tiny lines had formed that showed how hard her life had been before she had come to live in Beach Street. She leant closer to the mirror and rubbed away some of the Miami red colour. Her knuckle on the second finger of her right hand was pronounced and stuck up at an angle. It didn't hurt now, but it had when Mick had thrown the teapot at her and she'd put up her hand to deflect the boiling tea from her face. Instead a shard had cut the tendon to that finger. It had healed, and the scar on her palm was now a thin white line. Luckily, she had full use of her hand.

She smiled, and now her face was transformed. A wide, white-toothed grin showed her that she was still pretty. Her eyes travelled down her naked body, liking its slimness, the length of her legs, the firmness of her breasts. Maybe one day a customer might come into the café and be the answer to her prayers. A good man, who respected women. A man who would love her. In return she would love him and never leave. They would have babies together, a boy, then a girl . . .

'Will you be long?'

Vee's voice cut into Rosie's thoughts.

'No,' she yelled back, and stepped into the salty water.

At least Mick would never hurt her again. Not now, not after Jack had sorted him out. Her mind went back to that day in the café . . .

*

'There's a bloke sitting over near the door who keeps staring at the hatch.'

Connie dumped a large pile of greasy plates on the draining-board and began to separate the cutlery. Then she slipped the plates into the hot water in the sink. Rosie tackled them. It was late afternoon and reasonably quiet in the café.

Rosie didn't speak, so Connie continued, 'He's got dark curly hair and broad shoulders, looks Irish . . .'

'How can anyone look Irish?'

'Deep blue eyes and something about . . .'

Rosie felt the hairs on the back of her neck jump to attention. Her hands came out of the water. 'Did he speak?'

'No, he just keeps staring at the hatch. He's not in uniform. Got a dark jacket on, bit like a navvy.'

Her words had the desired effect and Rosie had moved, wiping her hands on a tea-towel, to the doorway and stood rigidly while attempting to peep round it.

'Bugger!'

'Oi! I don't want that language in my café.'

'But it's Mick. What's he doing here?'

Rosie scuttled back to the sink and plunged her hands once more into the water. 'If I stay in here, maybe he'll go away.'

'You can't stay in here all the time. I need you to do jobs out there!'

Connie had a point there, thought Rosie. She looked at her fearfully. 'But you don't understand . . .'

'I understand that that's your old man but he won't get near you while I'm here. We have to serve the punters, Rosie.'

'You don't know what he's like.'

'He's a bloke.'

Noise from the café took over. Rosie was scraping dried egg off a plate. She was shivering with fear.

'I got to serve,' said Connie, and went through the door. 'Egg and chips three times, three teas, bread and marge.'

Rosie heard the sound of the till's drawer pinging. The scraps of paper containing the orders grew on the spike. She was well aware she should be taking orders, or out in the café collecting dirty plates and cups. It wasn't fair to leave it all to Connie. Rosie moved to the door and took another peep.

Jack had come in now. He was sitting at his usual table. He looked as though all the worries in the world rested on his shoulders. Rosie's heart went out to him. He had a miserable life and a bitch for a wife.

He called to Connie, who was trying to do several jobs at once while pinning up the front of her hair that had come loose from its snood.

'Can you do me a fry-up?' He had dropped a newspaper, folded, on to the table. 'And a cuppa?'

Connie yelled back, 'Yes, but with scrambled egg?'

He grinned. He was easy to please, was Jack. He nodded and poked around in his pocket for his handkerchief. Rosie dared to look out into the café.

Mick was staring at her. A dark curl lay low over his forehead and his eyes, like forest bluebells, seemed to bore into her. Using his hands flat on the table as a support, he attempted to rise. He was unsteady on his feet. Was he ill?

No. He had been drinking. Now he was upright, but swaying. It was a wonder Connie hadn't smelt the booze on him when she'd served him. She was spot on about things like that.

The queue had dwindled and Connie came back. She didn't look happy. Mick was making a beeline for the kitchen. Rosie grabbed the frying pan. Her heart was bumping against her ribs. Then he was filling the doorway.

He looked at her over Connie's head.

'Thought you could sneak out on me, did you?'

Rosie could smell the staleness of him in the small spotless kitchen. His clothes were crumpled, as if he'd slept in them.

'Keep away from me, Mick.' Her voice was a whisper.

'You didn't think I'd find you, did you?' He put a hand on the doorframe to steady himself.

'Get out of my kitchen.' Connie's voice was calm.

With one hand he pushed Connie aside as he stepped towards Rosie.

'If you thought I'd let my wife bugger off, you got another think coming. A marriage licence means I bought you. I own you . . . like a dog.' The last seemed to have been an afterthought. He laughed. 'Get your stuff. You're coming home with me.'

Rosie's eyes filled with tears as she looked at his big clenched fists. She was waiting for the inevitable punch. She gripped the pan more tightly and from somewhere deep inside her a small voice spoke:

'No!' Rosie seemed to grow in stature. The voice spoke again, louder: 'I'm not coming with you, not now, not ever.'

'You fuckin' dare to defy me?' Mick's face was a black mask of anger. He lunged forward. Connie jumped between the pair, deflecting the punch that landed in mid-air, just as the frying-pan caught Mick on the shoulder. The big Irishman staggered back against the sink as a hand curved in a fist landed on his jaw.

'Get the fuck out of my place!'

Jack's voice was loud and cold. Mick put a hand to his face. Jack, in his shirtsleeves, stood in front of him, the muscles in his arms bulging. His eyes were on Mick as he said, 'No one messes with my girls. Get out now while you're still able.'

Mick seemed to shrivel as he slunk past Jack and out through the kitchen door. Rosie fell into Connie's arms. Jack followed Mick out into the café and the customers' heavy silence. Through the hatch Connie and Rosie watched Mick open the door and leave without a backward glance.

Jack practically fell onto his chair. He picked up his newspaper and shook out the *Evening News* to its broadsheet size. People began chatting again.

In the kitchen Connie said to Rosie, 'He won't come back.'

'I hope not,' whispered Rosie. She smiled damply at Connie, then began to put cut potatoes into the hot fat.

Connie left the kitchen and went to Jack. She stood over him at the small table and asked, 'You all right?'

Rosie watched from the hatch while she spread margarine on slices of bread.

She heard Jack say, 'I can't stand men who talk to women with their fists. I've noticed him hanging around and guessed he was looking for Rosie.'

Connie put a hand on his arm. 'She had the guts to tell him she wasn't going back, didn't she?'

He grinned at her, then asked, 'Where's my tea?'

*

It was the car ferry that woke Vee the next morning. The clanking of chains, the whistling of the men cleaning the decks and laughter as people shared early-morning jokes.

Last night's argument had seemed to go on for hours. It wasn't Jack's deep voice that resonated through the dark so much as Madelaine's high-pitched screaming. Vee thought their bedroom must be directly beneath hers. It had finally stopped when she'd heard Jack leave the room with the baby, who had joined in, crying. Vee wondered where the love was in that marriage.

She thought of her mother and Jem, who wasn't exactly her husband but had been around for as long as Vee could remember. She'd thought Jem was her daddy when she was a little girl because he'd always been there for her.

Later she'd learnt that the handsome man with the moustache in the photograph on the living-room mantelpiece was her father, but she had grown up hearing her mother and Jem apologize to each other after mishaps. She'd seen them kiss and make up after silly disagreements. She'd also witnessed Jem's warmth towards her mother and his face lighting up when she entered the room. She'd smiled at the wild flowers he'd set in jam-jars as small gifts for May. She'd often wondered as a little girl why Jem couldn't be her daddy if the real one was dead.

Jem lived in a small house in the village. He spent all his time at the smallholding, but went home each night. Sometimes Vee was scared that he wouldn't be there in the mornings when she woke.

Now that she was older she understood, which wasn't to say she agreed with how her mother lived her life, but it was her choice, wasn't it? And Jem went along with the arrangement, even if he wasn't happy. Sometimes she wondered if her mother's way of looking at love had affected her own past love affairs. There had been Ben, a librarian, who was serious and caring but not adventurous enough for her, then Alan, who had insisted on caring too much. George had been older and quite moneyed. He'd been married before and couldn't understand why Vee said she wouldn't sleep with any man until she knew she loved him.

Perhaps it *was* her mother's fault. Vee wanted desperately to feel what her real parents had had: a love that could surmount anything. And, she thought, in their own way May and Jem had that sort of love.

Jack intrigued her.

She was drawn to him but he couldn't make a move on her, even supposing he wanted to. He was out of bounds. He had a child, an unhappy marriage, yet she'd had those feelings yesterday when they were close together on the boat. And today he'd decided she was ready for another shot behind the wheel of the ferry, with himself close at hand.

'You can't let the mistake you made put you off. Later you'll be proud of the progress you've made.' His words went round and round in her head. He was her boss, so what else could she do but get on with the job he wanted her to do?

Later, her stomach tied in knots, Vee had stood beside him in the wheelhouse and answered his questions on what she had learnt yesterday.

It was exciting to know that one flick of her wrist could turn the vessel any way she liked, but as she'd stood with both hands in the position he had shown her to guide the boat, all she'd wanted to do was to please him.

Today the water was choppy, with a stiff breeze blowing, and she was glad of the navy blue jumper Jack had handed her before they'd left the house.

'That's good. You're thinking ahead,' he said, as she turned the wheel to make space for a small sailing dinghy to pass safely.

The sun was high overhead, the wind cool on her cheeks, but she was well wrapped up against the cold that the approaching winter was bringing to Gosport.

Seagulls swooped and cried, and a large group of children

from a local school was on board. Vee had heard the teachers talking about the proposed visit to the Isle of Wight to look for fossils. The big white ferry left from the landing stage near the harbour railway station. The children were excited, but Vee kept her eyes on Portsmouth and the craft in the water surrounding the ferry.

She didn't hear the splash but she heard Jack shout, 'That little devil's gone over.'

Then the comforting body giving her the courage to steer the craft was gone. She was alone! She saw his peaked hat had been thrown to the deck of the wheelhouse. She picked it up and put it into a cubby-hole.

Voices were raised, and she heard what she thought was the sound of heavy lifebelts hitting the water – they sounded like the belly-flops people did in the swimming pool. Vee thought quickly. She decided against putting the boat into reverse. Surely the sudden churning of the water could pull the child beneath it. She let the vessel cruise ahead and when she thought she was well away from the place when the child had fallen into the water, she turned back, having made sure that there was enough room for the boat to make a wide arc. Her heart was throwing itself against her ribs. She was terrified. But she'd decided to try to move close to whoever had jumped into the freezing sea to rescue the child so that others could pull them out. The yelling and shouting from the passengers was tremendous.

'Get another lifebelt! He's gone under!' The other children, who were obviously very frightened, were screaming. Vee was aware that the boat was listing to one side as most of the passengers peered into the choppy sea.

Still trying to keep the boat stationary, although the current was moving it towards a tanker, Vee glanced at what was going on. She saw Mac at the deck's rail pulling on a rope attached to a lifebelt. A young boy was inside it, wriggling, and Jack held on to him as he swam towards the ferry.

Even though the child was inside the belt, he was small enough to slip out if Jack let go of him.

Jack reached the side of the boat, legs kicking wildly. Vee saw that his feet were bare. When he grabbed another rope, cheers rose as Mac hauled the lifebelt up. It cleared the water as Jack pushed the boy high so that Mac could reach out for him.

The boy flopped on to the deck and Mac began rubbing his legs, then his arms. Jack looked weary as he climbed aboard but he fell to his knees and turned the little boy on to his back.

Then he took a deep breath and blew into the child's mouth while intermittently massaging his chest. Suddenly the lad threw up. Jack sat back on his heels and laughed. The crowd, who had been silent, erupted with claps and cheers.

A couple of blankets arrived and the boy was wrapped up. A man was now shaking Jack's hand, and a young woman was kneeling with the patient, who was coughing and crying at the same time. Vee supposed they were teachers.

Jack stood up and used a blanket to dry himself. A man handed him his own jacket. It was too tight for him but Jack shook his hand gratefully. As Jack, still carrying the blanket, moved through the passengers to handshakes and shouts of 'Well done', Vee shoved the lever to 'Ahead' and the boat ploughed forward.

When Jack, wet-haired, barefoot and red-faced with cold, reached the wheelhouse Vee was heading towards the Portsmouth jetty. She could feel him shivering as he stood behind her. 'You did well,' he said. She didn't turn but was aware of him as a man, and suddenly it mattered very much that he'd said those words to her.

Vee didn't ask if the boy would be all right. The child was young and strong, and she could see him below her, surrounded by his schoolfriends. He seemed fully recovered from his ordeal, enjoying the chatter among his mates. He'd be the centre of attention for a long while, she thought, even on the boat going across to the island. That was if the teachers didn't insist on calling for an ambulance.

Down on the deck, Mac and another ferryman, whose name Vee didn't know, were using mops to swab up the water in case someone slipped.

'I think you've done that before,' Vee said to Jack.

He put his hand on the wheel. It wasn't touching hers but she could feel the heat of him on her skin. She wanted to hold on to that feeling and to him. He'd just saved a boy's life and was now behaving as if nothing had happened! She studied his fingers, splayed yet firm, his grip secure on the wooden wheel. And she wanted to lean back so that she could feel his body firm against hers. But she didn't. Instead she reminded herself that he had a wife. But his breath was warm on her neck as he said, 'A ferry hazard. I hope you can swim. Maybe a lifesaving course would be a good idea. That's if you intend to stay on. What the heck have you done with my cap?'

She pulled it from the cubby-hole, handed it to him, and he jammed it on to his wet hair. She laughed. 'You lost your boots as well,' she said.

'Mac's looking in the cupboard for another pair to fit me,' he said. 'I had to shake them off, else the weight of them would have taken me down to the depths. Still, the boy's all right. That's the main thing.'

The pontoon was ahead. Vee manoeuvred the craft so that, unlike yesterday when she'd nearly hit the jetty, she slowed easily, reversing so that the boat glided in. Mac gave her a thumbs-up as his rope slid easily over the jetty's bollard.

Chapter Fifteen

Rosie had been right. George Formby had made Vee laugh until tears filled her eyes. That had been the main feature at the Forum, with the B picture a crime story starring Ida Lupino, whom Vee thought terribly glamorous. Pathé News had shown scenes of bloodshed amid the war-torn fields of France, later softened by a Mickey Mouse cartoon.

When the film rolled round to where they'd come in, they left the picture house and walked back through the town. Connie and Rosie decided to have a drink in the Royal Arms, a pub along Stoke Road. Through the open doors they could see the bar was full of British sailors in their navy bell-bottoms, and the smell of beer and cigarettes wafted out to them, enticing them in.

Vee left them and began the short walk home on her own. Being out on the water all day was tiring, and she'd been responsible for the passengers' lives while Jack was saving the child. She didn't remember being so weary when she'd been working in the fields in the sun on the smallholding.

Coming off the Gosport ferry, Jack had been congratulated many times and someone had even taken a photo of him. Vee hoped it hadn't included her. They'd had to make the return journey to Gosport so the other team of ferrymen could take over, and Vee guessed the phone wires had been red-hot with news of the rescue. Before they reached the ticket office he said to her, 'I can't stand this. I'll see you later.' He'd handed her the blanket and disappeared. Without him she was nobody so, with a wave to Ada, who was standing near the Dive café, she had made her way home alone. She thought Jack was admirable not to want the limelight. Vee didn't need it either, but that was because she didn't want anyone to discover her whereabouts.

Vee jumped when she switched on the light and saw Jack sitting alone in the house.

'Jesus, you made me jump!' She thought how tired he looked. The fire had burnt low and the house was quiet. She could smell drink on him.

'Just thinking,' he said. 'Sorry, I didn't mean to alarm you. Earlier a reporter came to chat about the boy who fell in the water. He said it was newsworthy, and I told him it happened more often than people realized. But it didn't always end so well. The bloke had brought a bottle of Scotch with him.' He ran his hand through his hair.

'Everyone on the boat thought you were brilliant. Do you know what happened to the boy?'

'Apparently the ambulance took him to hospital. He was yelling and crying because he'd been looking forward to the school trip and insisted he didn't want to be left behind. A teacher went with him, promising that if his parents and the hospital said he could, they'd catch up with the others the next day.'

Vee asked if he'd like some tea. He shook his head. 'I'm not drunk, if that's what you're thinking. I've just got a lot on my mind. You didn't see my wife out anywhere, did you?'

'No, but I wasn't looking. Is Peg . . .?'

'The little one's fast asleep.' He gave her a small smile. 'Sorry about the unpleasantness between my wife and myself. I get so angry when I find she's left Peg alone.'

Vee wanted to say that perhaps Madelaine had had some good reason for it, but even animals protected their young. Madelaine seemed totally devoid of maternal instincts.

Jack was talking again.

'Look, Vee, even though it's unlikely you'll need to set foot in there I'd planned on taking you down to the engine room again tomorrow so you can get to know how it all works, but I'm going . . .'

Vee was aware she'd allowed her face to show her lack of enthusiasm.

'No, no! It won't be necessary for you to shovel the coal!'

'Thank goodness for that,' she said.

'I want you to understand how the engines run, though. Eddie wouldn't let you touch a thing down there. Vince, his boy, is usually with him and will be his natural successor, I'm pleased to say. The other crew respect them . . .' Her confusion must have shown on her face. 'Eddie's brother is a stoker. It runs in the family, see? When my crew and I have finished for the day, the other crew take over, as you know, but the stoker is one of Eddie's family.'

'So I won't be going down into the engine room to work?' On the smallholding she had had to get on with loads of filthy and heavy jobs, but that didn't mean she liked doing them.

He shook his head. 'I'm putting you in the ticket kiosk with Regine. The Portsmouth side have been complaining that ticket sales are down.'

So far Regine was the only person in the house who seemed unfriendly towards her. Or was Vee being silly and imagining things?

'I don't want you to spy,' he continued. 'Just watch her.'

Did he mean for her to check Regine was taking the right amount of money for the tickets?

'You'll be watching what goes on, from the sale of a ticket in the kiosk to its clip before the passenger boards the boat, then the handing back on the return. We don't date tickets. Portsmouth agrees that people who cross on the ferry usually come back. The passenger hangs on to the ticket for the return journey. It is then clipped and collected for disposal. If the ticket has been clipped more than once, the passenger is trying to pull a fast one. If I ever need you to punch tickets I must know you understand how the procedure works, okay?'

Vee nodded. 'So the person at the gate punching tickets on the Gosport side travels over on the boat and does the same job on the Portsmouth side?'

Jack nodded.

'Is there a ticket office on the Portsmouth side?'

Again he nodded. 'Have you forgotten you must have bought a ticket to come over on my boat?'

She nodded, and he carried on: 'The number of passengers should tally with the ticket sales. But something's not quite right . . .'

So tomorrow she'd be in the ticket office? At least he

didn't intend for her to stoke the boilers and for that she was grateful. She stifled a yawn, closing her eyes.

When she opened them he was looking at her intently.

'Sorry I've kept you up.' He gave her a beautiful smile. 'Goodnight. See you in the morning.'

'Madelaine will come back eventually. She always does, I believe.'

'You're right, but I'll wait up all the same.'

Vee climbed the stairs. In the bathroom she washed, then picked up her toothbrush, ready to clean her teeth, but there was no paste. Her pink tin of Gibbs wasn't where she had left it. She opened the bathroom cabinet and saw that it had been put on the shelf. As she picked it up, thinking someone must have borrowed it, which she didn't mind, she noticed a packet pushed behind a bottle of hydrogen peroxide. Vee took it out and found it contained powder. The writing on the packet said it was bleach. She realized immediately that the peroxide and the powder were what Madelaine used to keep her hair that gorgeous pale yellow blonde. Vee smiled to herself. She wasn't a natural blonde then. She looked at her own fair hair. Perhaps she should make a bit more of herself. She put the bottle and powder back.

She was asleep as soon as her head touched the pillow.

*

The bang woke her .

'Vee! Get down here!'

Her first instinct was to burrow beneath the warm bed-clothes but when Jack's voice came again, sharp and clear, her senses took over. It was an air raid.

Vee slipped from the covers and grabbed her coat, slinging it over her nightgown. Her sleepy brain began to function properly and she grasped her documents and purse, stuffed them into her handbag, then ran for the door as another huge bang shook the house, sending slivers of plaster dropping down into the room like snow.

'Vee!'

This time she shouted back, 'Coming.'

Despite the thick walls of the old house the noise of the many planes droning overhead was clear. Fear gripped her. The night raids had fallen across Southampton, aimed at the docks, the ships. At Netley the bombs that fell were likely discharged to make the aircraft lighter on their way home to Germany. Here, as in Southampton, the targets were the dockyard, the factories, the boat builders, the armaments yards – and at any moment she could be blown to smithereens.

'Grab those flasks!' Jack shouted as, clutching his daughter, he made for the back door. Vee saw he had a bag over his shoulder containing the baby's cotton nappies and clothing.

He stopped near the carrycot and put his precious charge inside, covering her with a blanket.

Vee hesitated. Was she meant to follow him?

'There's a shelter in the garden.'

With both flasks in her arms she managed to open the back door, allowing Jack to pass ahead of her. Vee had had no cause to go into the garden in her short time at the house other than to use the lavatory that was just outside the back door. It wasn't her favourite place, with its newspaper squares on a string and fat black spiders sitting on the walls ready to pounce. She much preferred the bathroom upstairs.

Vee followed him, watchful of where he was treading.

'There are steps down. Be careful.'

The Anderson shelter was practically buried in the soil. Jack elbowed open the door and Vee felt the dampness envelop her. He must have read her thoughts, for he whispered, 'We'll soon get it warm. Sit there for a while.' He passed the child to her waiting arms after she'd put the flasks down. It was pitch black. She held the baby close, smelling her talcum-powder freshness. She'd lowered herself gently to what she thought was a kitchen chair and thought it best to let him do whatever was needed to make them and the shelter secure.

Through the open door, she could see searchlights flashing

and hear the returning ground fire. She smelt smoke, something acrid burning. The noise was horrific. It felt to Vee as if the whole earth was moving each time a crash announced that a target had been hit.

Thoughts of her mother, the smallholding and Cat, furry and warm, surrounded by tiny kittens, filled her head and she wanted to cry. But it was Peg who whimpered and Vee lowered her face to her and whispered, 'It'll be all right, my love, I'm here.'

What with the rescue of the little boy earlier and now this, it had been a hell of a day and night, she thought.

Then the door was closed and absolute darkness reigned. Until she heard the strike of a match, which flared, then an oil lamp flickered. 'There, that's better. I'll light the fire as well . . .'

'Won't the fumes . . .' She trailed off. Now it was brighter inside the shelter, Vee could see what looked like a greenhouse heater.

'No, it's quite safe.'

She saw then that there were bunks one above the other at the end of the metal shelter and seating against the walls. No privacy at all in the very small space, but with the warmth from the stove it was becoming cosy. There was a box against the bottom bunk and Jack must have noticed her staring at it.

'There's clean, dry bedding in there. Can't leave stuff out – it would get damp and go mouldy. I dug this Anderson deep into the soil for safety's sake.' He paused. 'I realized too late that the deeper I dug, the more water could seep in. Did you have a shelter at home?' While waiting for her answer he moved the carrycot onto a bunk.

Vee nodded. 'A Morrison. In the kitchen.' He was now making up the little bed for Peg. She watched his hands, sure and nimble. Neither of them spoke as he took the child from her and put her into the cot, covering her lightly with the blanket.

Jack sighed. 'Now, do you want a cup of tea?'

She must have looked questioning.

'The flasks. One's the baby's milk, the other's tea.'

She smiled at him and nodded.

He busied himself with cups. 'There's one in the café.'

He was still thinking of the shelters.

'A Morrison,' he added.

Vee remembered Connie had said she'd put Peg in the shelter.

'Named after Herbert Morrison.'

He passed her a steaming mug, 'Clever clogs,' he said with a grin.

Just then a huge bang shook the shelter and Vee almost

dropped the mug. The tea splashed over her hand, hot enough to make her gasp but not to harm. He handed her his handkerchief and she mopped her skin. 'I take it you've not been in any heavy raids.'

Vee shook her head. He was looking at her intently.

She knew that at any moment he was going to ask her about herself and she wouldn't be able to lie to him. But it was too soon for her to explain about Sammy Chesterton, the forged papers, her guilt. She was still trying to impress Jack: she needed her work, a place to live, wages. She would tell him, but later, in her own time.

Then Fate smiled kindly on Vee as a voice cried above the noise outside, 'Let me in! It's awful out here.'

Jack moved towards the door and pulled the blackout curtain across so no light would be visible outside. He opened the door and the girl almost fell into the shelter.

Regine regained her dignity as Jack closed it behind her.

'I guessed someone would be in here, and I couldn't bear to stay alone in the house.'

'Are you all right?' Vee asked quietly, then put her finger to her lips and moved her head towards the still sleeping child.

Regine laughed, showing small white teeth.

'Amazing, isn't it, that babies can sleep through almost anything except human voices?' She took off her coat and undid the knot tying her headscarf beneath her chin. 'Where is everyone?'

She put her coat and scarf on the seat beside her and looked at them expectantly. She had brought in with her the stink of cordite and the scent of flowery perfume.

'I was hoping you could tell me that,' Jack said.

Vee sipped her still warm tea.

'If you mean your wife, she's round her mother's house. She said something about trying to persuade her to come to Peg's christening. Any more tea in that flask?'

Jack passed it to her with a white enamel mug. 'Why didn't she tell me?'

'Probably because you'd have expected her to take the baby.'

Jack sighed. 'I simply wish she'd discuss things with me first. Then I could make arrangements.'

Regine, carefully pouring hot tea, said, 'Don't go on at me!' She glared at him, then looked towards the cot on the bottom bunk. 'Baby seems okay to me.'

For a moment there was relative silence apart from the *thwump, thwump* of bombs falling. Vee finished her tea and put down her cup.

'I wonder how long . . .'

'Who knows?' Regine answered her question before Vee

had uttered it. 'We could be out of here in a while or stuck here until morning.'

'Vee's helping you out tomorrow,' Jack said. His voice was cold and sharp.

Regine frowned. 'I don't need any help. There's hardly room for me in that office.' She added, 'Congrats for saving that little boy. Everyone was talking about it. I think a few people actually bought tickets just to gawp at you, not realizing you weren't skippering the boat and had already left. Look, I really don't need any help.'

'That's as may be, but I want Vee to get a grasp of what goes on in every aspect of the business.'

The frown deepened on Regine's face and she ran her slim fingers through her dark hair. 'Fair enough,' she said. She put her empty mug on the floor of the shelter.

Only it wasn't, thought Vee. Not fair enough with Regine at all. She watched as the girl pulled her coat around herself, then closed her eyes. After a while Vee, too, dozed in the warmth of the small room. When she looked at Jack, he was watching her. He smiled, then closed his eyes.

When Vee woke daylight was streaming through her window and the clanking of the car ferry had broken into her dream, like a metal monster on the rampage.

The alarm was just about to scream so she put out her hand to still it. She had a vague memory of climbing the stairs to her bedroom after the all-clear had sounded, with no idea of what time it had been, except it was still dark. She remembered lying in bed listening to the argument floating indistinctly upwards from downstairs.

Madelaine had either returned late, or had been inside the house while they'd hidden in the shelter from the bombing.

It was the start of a new day. One she wasn't looking forward to because she would be spending her time with Regine.

Chapter Sixteen

May felt the sun on her face and cherished its warmth, then bent forward to the straw-covered earth. Her fingers were red with the sweet juice of the strawberries she was picking from their hiding places beneath green leaves. The scent of the fruit mingled with that of the rich earth.

The second picking was almost at an end. She was alone in the field that, weeks ago, had held throngs of people, filling wicker baskets for her to pack into containers and send to market. There was something infinitely peaceful about being alone, at one with the earth and sun.

She glanced towards the wooden shack. On the shelves inside, out of the sun's heat, were the fruits of her labours from early this morning. In June, queues of pickers had been waiting for their baskets to be weighed and added to their totals. It was piecework, so they were paid by the amount of fruit they picked. A summer job, strawberry picking, tried and tested over the years. The same people worked in her strawberry fields as had for her father when she was a girl. Travellers pitched up year after year, their wagons pulled by horses, and gathered in the field set aside for them.

This was the last of the fruit before the strawberry runners were transplanted by the few regular workers she and Jem kept on through the winter. The last strawberries always seemed to May to be the sweetest. In the past Vee had picked with her and it had been peaceful, mother and daughter sharing precious time together. Some of the luscious fruit would go to the village shops first thing in the morning, but mostly it would stay with May to be bottled, made into jam or eaten as it was, fat, red and delicious. Above her a skylark was hovering.

Last night Vee had telephoned.

Her daughter was well, she said, happy, and learning new skills. She wouldn't tell May exactly where she was living. May knew she should feel easier about her welfare. Vee had asked whether Sammy Chesterton had spoken to her, and May had told her truthfully that he hadn't. She hadn't mentioned that he came to the house some days and sat in the layby in his car. Of course she felt uneasy about his presence because he had a bad reputation, but the less Vee had to worry about, the better, she thought. Besides, he did no harm. Merely sat and watched. It was as though he was making his mind up about something.

May told her about the kittens. Three tiny bundles of fur and fluff now eager to explore away from their box and their mother's care. They loved paper bags and bits of string. May told Vee how the most adventurous of the three had had to have a long piece of string carefully pulled from his mouth before it choked him. Cat had her work cut out rounding them up. Vee had laughed, which assured May she really was all right, so she had put the phone down feeling happier than she had in ages.

Gus had loved being out in the strawberry fields.

When he was no longer confined to his bed and able to move about freely with the other prisoners, he was encouraged to work for his keep. The fact that the hospital was deep in the countryside meant farming, although some men were sent to work in the boatyards at the mouth of the Hamble river. The prisoners had become a welcome, if peculiar, sight in their distinctive suits, as they toiled in the fields or on the banks of the river . . .

May's father had taken much persuading before he agreed to take on several men. Eventually he concluded that help from the Germans was far better than no help at all. He was allowed two Germans and one Italian. They arrived by truck at seven o'clock in the mornings and were picked up at six in the evenings.

Manfred was blond, a giant of a man, gentle with animals and softly spoken.

Bruno, the Italian, from a village outside Rome, had expert knowledge of horses, and Gus had somehow wheedled his way in, becoming the third man to work for May's family. Of course, Joe, May's father, knew nothing of the burgeoning love affair between his daughter and Gus.

'They are exemplary workers,' he admitted, but all the same he instructed the rest of his team to stay away from them, unless it was absolutely necessary. Joe had applied for land girls and had been a little put out to discover he had to accept the foreign workers or go without.

Sometimes May thought she had spent more time with Gus when he was near death's door than now when he worked for her father. It had become increasingly difficult to steal time to be with him, so they savoured the sweetness of the precious moments they spent together. She knew she must never allow her parents to find out that she was in love with him.

'If it wasn't for the time I can steal away before curfew at nine, I'd never be able to see you,' he would grumble.

Their favourite place to meet was the hospital's church-yard, where she would fly into his arms. It wasn't always to make love.

The sick and wounded were emerging daily now from the boats that tied up in Southampton Water, the extent of the men's injuries appalling. The train, too, brought in casualties. Her dark memories gave May nightmares and she needed to offload each day's happenings on someone besides Annie. Gus was there for her.

'We took in twenty-nine very severe cases today from the train. Most of the men hadn't a hope of surviving. Some had trench foot so bad we had to cut off their socks and parts of their feet fell off too. Poor men, clotted with blood, frightened, with only dirty bandages holding their bodies together. I unwound a man's filthy bandage on his arm to find the bandage was keeping it on . . .'

Gus would hold her, let her talk, and she knew he was remembering when he had first woken at the hospital and had no idea whether he was alive or dead.

There was no way she could keep such hellish daily events inside her. She had been told to wash the occupant of bed fourteen who complained his arm hurt and pulled back the coverings to discover he had no arm. When she went to feed the man in bed three, most of his face had been shot away.

Talking to Gus kept her sane. A nurse who held everything bottled inside her had run screaming from the operating theatre. May never saw her again. But then the young doctor – she never had discovered his name – who had harmed Gus had been driven mad by the carnage he'd witnessed. 'I am so glad to have you,' Gus would say, after she had talked herself hoarse. And they would make love hurriedly, fearful it might be the last time, for neither knew if the other would still be there the next day. She might be sent to another hospital, he to a prison camp. Now that many thousands of prisoners were being brought to England, camps had been set up for them alongside those for the internees. Hampshire's Gosport and Frimley were the camps nearest to Southampton, but that didn't mean Gus, if he was moved from Netley, would be sent to either. May knew that any day she might discover Gus had been sent away and it was quite possible that she would never see him again.

Gus had told her of his childhood in Pulheim. He had been born in a street not far from the abbey and had gone to a good school where he had been taught English. As a boy, he couldn't wait to join the Jagdstaffel, the air arm of the Imperial German Army. His parents had been killed in a train crash and he had no siblings. He had loved a girl named Hildegarde, who hadn't returned his love, so flying had become his life and he had ended up in reconnaissance.

'I think because of my foot it is unlikely I will fly again. If I ever get home to Germany it will be a desk job.' His one fear was of being parted from May.

May had told him of her upbringing in the country outside Southampton, the village school, the strictness of her father, who nevertheless had allowed her to enter the Summer Princess competition, which she had won.

At carnival time, surrounded by flowers, wearing an ankle-length frilly white dress, with the two runners-up beside her, May had trundled along the streets of Netley on a hay wagon pulled by two Shire horses.

As soon as she left school she had worked on the small-holding until, grudgingly, her father accepted she wanted to nurse. She had expected to travel abroad, but so far it hadn't happened.

May found hatred towards the enemy didn't end at the hospital gates.

One day she had time off and was at home in the large, comfortable kitchen. Through the window she watched the three prisoners sitting on logs eating the breakfast her mother had cooked.

'I don't see why we can't all eat together,' she said. Her

father often suggested they set up the big table outside on a fine day so the English field workers could have a meal with the family.

'I'll not sit at a table with my enemies,' her father snapped. 'They get fed well enough, here and at the Queen Victoria. There are men fighting in trenches to save this country who would gladly eat half of what those men are getting. It doesn't matter where they eat.'

When it was wet the men were fed in the barn.

May wondered why her father didn't think of the prisoners as men who had been pressured by their countries to do as they were told.

Regine unlocked the door to the ticket kiosk and ushered Vee inside.

'I've no idea why he wants you to understand about selling a boat ticket. It's not as if I won't be here to carry on.' She put her handbag on the counter, then filled the cash drawer with the float. It was always taken home at the end of each shift so that those who took over started from scratch.

'The tickets are kept here.' Regine showed her a large roll of yellow tickets that had to be torn off according to the number purchased. 'They're all returns. Portsmouth and Gosport know that if a person travels one way they'll come back.' She pointed to a high stool. 'Sit here, opposite the glass window. Take the money first and give change if necessary, then offer the tickets. Don't give them before you've taken the money in case they run off without paying. I'm going to stand here and watch you give the correct change.'

Regine locked the door behind them.

'Don't make it easy for thieves,' she said.

She had spoken to Vee as if she were a five-year-old. Nevertheless Vee sat on a stool beside her to await their first customer.

It seemed to Vee that the tickets were sold in waves. Noisy people queued and were served. Then there was a lull when she was able to gather her thoughts. Regine must have been reading her mind because she said, 'It's the buses. People get off a bus and come for a ticket. When there aren't any buses due in, it's quieter.'

'How many people cross in a day?'

'About the most is twenty-two thousand on a Saturday when Portsmouth Football Club is playing at home.'

'Gosh!' Vee couldn't help herself.

'Course, it's not like that every day.' Vee saw Regine smile, her teeth showing white in the dully lit room. Even though they were enclosed in the small square building, the heavy smell of seaweed and mud pervaded. 'Some people will come simply to ask questions about times of boats.' Regine put a manicured hand on a large dog-eared book at the side of the counter. 'This contains information about our own ferries. If they want to know about the floating bridge, Isle of Wight ferries or the boat trips around the harbour, send them to the tobacconist across the road, who deals with bookings. We just sell tickets.'

Vee nodded. Of all the jobs she'd attempted so far she thought this was the most boring. Earlier her mind had wandered and one customer had nearly received change for a pound when she'd handed over a ten-shilling note. Luckily Vee had spotted her mistake before she pushed a brown note through the hatch into the woman's eager hands.

'At the end of the shift, the number of tickets sold must tally with the amount of money taken,' Regine snapped.

Since that episode Vee had kept a sharp eye on her change. She had also refused two foreign coins. 'Sometimes it's a genuine mistake, sometimes not,' Regine said.

'Would you like a cup of tea?'

Vee could have killed for one. 'How—'

'We can bring in a flask,' Regine took one from her voluminous handbag, 'which the Ferry Café girls fill at no charge.' She glanced at the clock on the wall. 'Usually by now someone's been over to collect it, so if you're sure you can manage I'll take it across the road.'

'I can manage,' said Vee, actually rather proud that she was about to be trusted to work on her own.

Once Regine wasn't breathing down her neck, Vee found she could smile and chat to the customers while dealing with the tickets and change. She could see why Regine resented her intrusion in the ticket kiosk. Now that she was alone she felt as if she owned the place.

All too soon Vee had to unlock the door and let in Regine, who carried the flask beneath her arm and a plate covered with a tea-towel in her hand.

'Rock cakes. Too bad if you don't like them.' She put the plate down, then the flask, and fumbled beneath the counter for two cups. 'These are clean,' she said. 'You carry on while I sort this out. I tore them off a strip in the café for forgetting about us, but they said they'd been extra busy.'

Vee was beginning to think she'd been mistaken about Regine and that she wasn't as prickly as she'd first thought.

Regine said, 'Get that down you. I'll take over while you have a break.'

Vee moved away from the window and stood up. Her legs felt stiff after sitting down for so long. She saw the rock cakes were cut in half and spread with marge, and eyed them hungrily as she lifted her cup to her lips.

Regine was now on the stool Vee had occupied and was about to serve a man who had asked for two tickets.

Instead of tearing them from the roll they had been using, she turned away, took two loose unmarked tickets from her large handbag and gave them to the man, after taking his money and putting it in a jar near the till drawer.

All the breath seemed to leave Vee's body.

Regine said, 'Of course you won't say a word about me reusing tickets. If you do, imagine how you'll feel when everyone knows you're a fuckin' German.'

Chapter Seventeen

Jack stirred his tea. It was just as he liked it, dark and thick enough to stand a spoon in.

'Anything to eat, Jack?' Connie's cheery face appeared before him.

'Not now, maybe later,' he said. He watched as her tidy, plump figure wound its way through the packed tables towards the kitchen. He realized he hadn't thanked her for her concern. She was a good sort, was Connie. His crew were hand-picked and, in the main, he was happy with them. There were two he wasn't too keen on, but as long as they did their jobs properly that was all that mattered.

Like Paul. He was a ticket clipper. Oh, the bloke was sociable enough but not the type to have a laugh with. Sometimes you needed a laugh, he thought.

He drank some tea. He hoped everything would go

according to plan on Sunday. Christening in the afternoon, then back to the café for tea to celebrate. He smiled to himself. He'd heard some of the girls talking about the clothes they would wear. He was glad they wanted to look their best for his daughter's special day.

'So you're not opening on Sunday?'

Jack looked up and caught the bus driver's eye. He shook his head.

'You must be raking it in to be able to take a day off.'

Jack laughed. He didn't want to get into a heated discussion about why Sunday was to be special for his baby and his workers, despite the ferry takings being down. Until he'd sorted out why the money was trickling away, he'd have to keep his fears to himself. The trouble was, there weren't any discrepancies in the takings, not in the amount of ticket sales for the boat fares. Regine showed him the takings and tickets sold, which tallied. People just weren't travelling as much from the Gosport side. Mel, from Portsmouth, couldn't understand it: there were more passengers coming over to Gosport than ever before.

He shook his head. He was tired.

Madelaine had had a go at him last night because he'd gone to her parents' house to hand them the invitation to St John's Church and the do afterwards.

As soon as he'd knocked on the front door of the detached house in Alverstoke he knew he'd made a mistake.

'Not often we see you here.' Madeleine's father, who was ex-navy, was clearly unsure as to whether he should invite him in! Jack had seen the hesitation in his eyes, and if the rain hadn't decided to fall heavily at that moment, they would have conducted their business on the doorstep.

'We have a visitor, Ellen.'

Clearly Madelaine's mother expected anyone but him, because her smile froze when she saw him.

He gave them the invitation, said a few words and left.

There were no promises to 'see you on Sunday'.

Jack doubted Madeleine's father would attend the christening, although her mother might. All this hatred was because he had made their daughter pregnant. As he was Peg's father, that must be why they weren't interested in the little girl.

Of course, Madelaine had had to be married off, and quickly. An unmarried pregnant daughter would have sent her father's reputation tumbling.

Jack swallowed some more of his tea, then sighed. A moment of madness on the beach and look at him now, unwanted son-in-law and unwanted husband. The reason for their dislike? He wasn't good enough for Madelaine. They had insisted, after the immediate shock, on spending a small fortune on the wedding, and Thorngate Hall had been full of people Jack had never met before and never wanted to see again.

He was amazed that Madelaine had decided she wanted to live with him at his parents' house. Later, he worked out that there was usually a steady stream of babysitters present, so she was able to visit her parents unencumbered. He thought that, like him, they would have relished every moment they could spend with Peg, but apparently not. Perhaps he adored his child too much.

'I've brought you over some more tea. That must be stone cold by now.'

Connie's words made him smile.

'Thanks,' he said. His gaze automatically went towards the door as it opened and his smile widened as he saw Vee enter, bearing a flask, plate and cups.

He waved as she made to join the small queue that had formed at the counter.

'Give us them,' said Connie, going over and taking Vee's crockery. 'Sit down with the boss, cheer him up. I'll bring these back in a minute.'

*

The last thing Vee wanted was to sit down and talk to Jack.

The first night she had spent in Jack's house someone had been through her stuff. Now she knew without a doubt that that someone had been Regine. Funnily enough, she didn't blame the girl for seizing the moment but she hated her own stupidity in not getting rid of the documents. After all, she didn't need her old papers when she had the new forged ones, did she? Why, oh why hadn't she disposed of them?

After Regine's outburst Vee had merely stood staring at her, unable to speak, until at last she could no longer stand the torment. With Regine's cruel laughter burning her ears, she had picked up the empty cups and plates and walked out of the kiosk. She needed to think.

Of course she could say nothing of Regine selling unused tickets. How the unused tickets had come to be in Regine's possession she had no idea, but the girl now had a hold over her. Regine could tell Jack of Vee's parentage. Without a doubt Vee would be sacked and then what would she do? Jack would know she had lied to him by omission, and if there was one person she really wanted to be completely honest with, it was him.

So far the work had been hard but not unpleasant. Vee

had made a couple of friends. And Jack? There was definitely a softer side to him, which he didn't show to everyone, and she wanted to find out more.

Then Vee realized that Regine's threat cut both ways. If Regine told anyone of her Germanic parentage, Vee would point out that the girl was stealing from Jack. Regine's fraud was the reason that Jack's takings were down.

Throughout her life her mother had brought her up not to lie, not to steal, and to be a good person. Why, then, was she ignoring May's training? She felt tears reach her eyes and she had to work hard to blink them away. All these lies were for her own self-preservation. But they weren't making her happy, were they?

'I see Regine has you doing the tea run.'

Vee tried a smile, decided it worked, and sat down on the chair next to Jack. The wireless was playing music from *The Wizard of Oz*. When the film came to the local picture-house she would ask Rosie to go with her.

'Did you sleep well after all the bombing last night?' Without waiting for her to answer, Jack added, 'Gosport copped a few bombs. Not as bad as London – the news reckons four hundred people died last night. Bloody Germans.'

'I hope our boys gave as good as we got,' she said. Surely,

she thought, some German people must think like her and wish Hitler dead.

'Apparently we shot down nearly two hundred planes.'

'Such a waste of human life,' Vee said. He was looking at her strangely, but Connie was at the table again. Her flowery perfume reminded Vee of the scent her mother wore. A wave of homesickness overwhelmed her. 'A good cuppa works wonders, Connie.'

'Have you worked out the best way to sell tickets? Not hard, is it?' As usual, he looked tired, Vee thought. Was it because of the crying baby, or did Peg cry because she was woken by her parents arguing? Or was it the pressure of his work?

'No, it's simple,' she answered. All the while she was wondering how Regine was working the racket. And how she could stop her stealing from one of the best bosses Vee had ever worked for.

'If you've cracked the mystery of selling tickets, you can do something else tomorrow, Miss Smith.'

'I'd like that,' she replied. Though she wished he hadn't reminded her of her name. Smith, Schmidt – why did life have to be so complicated?

Jack put a hand across the table and rested it on her arm. A tingle akin to an electric shock ran through her.

'Regine isn't one of my favourite workers, but she gets the job done.' He looked down at the Formica table.

'She certainly does,' admitted Vee. And to her own advantage, she thought. But she kept her mouth closed.

'Here we are. Something to keep you going until it's time to knock off work.' Connie was hovering.

She slipped two clean mugs and a refilled flask on to the table, followed by two plates of cheese and onion sandwiches.

Vee's mouth watered. She hadn't eaten a decent piece of cheese for ages, certainly not since leaving home. Again she felt the tears rise. How could people be so nice to her when she was such an awful person?

'That's so kind of you, Connie,' she said in a small voice, as the older woman smiled at her, then left to return to the busy counter. On her way she picked up empty cups and plates to deliver to the kitchen.

'Tomorrow you can clip the tickets,' Jack said. 'How do you feel about that?'

'I don't mind what I do as long as I'm useful,' she said.

'If you weren't useful, you wouldn't be working for me.' He looked at his hand, which was still on her arm, and hastily moved it away, as though he had just noticed he was taking a liberty. 'Sorry,' he mumbled.

As the heat left her skin, Vee felt sad. She knew then she

would have to find a way to end Regine's thieving, even if it meant that Jack discovered her papers were forged. He was too nice a man to be taken for a fool. Vee didn't know how she was going to do it, but she would.

She was glad she hadn't lost her temper with Regine when the girl had blatantly admitted she was stealing ticket money. She would go back to her now and see what she could find out, without making her questioning too obvious. 'So,' she said softly, 'tomorrow I'll be outside again?'

Jack nodded. 'I gave you wet-weather gear?'

'You did, and a warm sweater,' Vee said.

She got up to leave the table, managing to carry everything.

She thought of the heavy black jacket and trousers. Until it actually rained, she decided, she would take the water-proofs but not wear the cumbersome things. It would be nice to see Mac again. That reminded her of something else: she hadn't given Connie anything towards the christening present. She put everything back on the table and, wishing Jack wasn't watching her every move, walked over to the counter, called for Connie and gave her the requisite amount for the gift, taking the money from her purse in her back pocket. Then, with the sandwich plates clutched to her once again, she went towards the Nissen hut's door.

'Wish everyone was as honest as you, Vee,' called Connie.

Vee felt even worse.

She was just about to open the door when Jack called, 'Vee, you've forgotten the flask.' He was coming towards her with a smile on his face.

Chapter Eighteen

Vee banged on the door of the kiosk with her elbow and Regine let her in.

'Thought I'd seen the last of you,' the girl sneered.

Vee set down the flask. 'Oh? Why's that, then?'

Regine ignored her to attend to a customer with a ticket from her handbag. Vee noted the girl really was surprised by her return. The glass jar near the till was practically full of pennies. Vee could see why Regine carried a large handbag: it held a multitude of things other women didn't carry with them.

Again the pennies dropped into the jar as the customer took the tickets offered.

Vee poured the tea. Regine was now watching her suspiciously. 'I'm not splitting the proceeds with you,' she snapped.

'Why would I want you to do that?' Vee shoved a sandwich along the counter towards her. 'Just don't expect me to steal for you.' She began to eat. 'This cheese is delicious,' she said. Regine shot her a curious look as she took a bite.

'Are you going to the christening?' Vee moved Regine's tea towards her.

'I think most people have been invited.'

'What? Even the dark-haired bloke with a moustache who's always hanging around Jack's wife?'

'Hugh's an old friend of Madelaine's.'

'Very friendly, if you ask me.'

'Nobody did. Look, if you knew how difficult it was for that girl to settle in this dump after Alverstoke, you'd have a bit more sympathy for her.'

'That's just it, Regine. I can only judge what I've seen with my own eyes . . . '

'Jack's no angel . . .'

'I've heard the rows.'

'She came from money and has no idea how to look after a kid.'

'That's easy to see. She palms Peg off on anyone who'll have her.' There was silence. It was almost as if Regine was assessing the situation before she spoke again. In near silence she served several customers. Then she sat back on the stool. 'They had to get married, Jack and Madelaine. You know what they say, "Marry in haste, repent at leisure."'

'They must have loved each other or Peg wouldn't be here.'

Regine glared at her, then turned towards the ticket window. It was too late, though: Vee had noticed the hesitation, the drawn breath before Regine took the customer's money. There was more information to be had, but the moment had passed. Vee had got Regine talking but it was as if she had suddenly realized what was happening and the time for sharing had come to an end. More about Jack and Madelaine's marriage was ready to rise to the surface and Vee intended to find out what it was.

It was dusk when the customers thinned. Regine began counting the money in her jar. Then she changed it into more manageable notes and put them into her handbag.

Vee watched in silence as she counted the money in the wooden drawer of the till and marked it down in a cashbook that she put back beneath the counter. She also noted the number of tickets sold from the roll, making sure they matched with the money that was now in a blue bank bag. The roll of unused tickets in the bag, along with the money, was destined for Jack.

'It's six. Time for the next shift.' A knock on the door. Regine snapped, 'Bring our mugs and plates.'

Shoving herself past Vee, she checked it was the usual night girl, let her in and pushed Vee out into the fresh air.

'All right, Sal?' Regine greeted the girl.

'Oi! Are we gonna have to wait all night for our tickets?'

'Just changing staff,' shouted the girl, the door closing on her.

Vee was surprised by how cold it was. A wind had risen off the sea.

'I hate the autumn,' said Regine. 'I suppose tonight we'll be treated to more bombing. See you tomorrow?'

'No,' said Vee. 'Jack wants me somewhere else.'

Regine stopped walking and looked at her. 'Can't say I'm sorry,' she said. Then she grinned. 'Don't forget our little secret.'

Back in her room, Regine again counted the money she'd stolen. Soon she'd have enough to leave Gosport. She was fed up with living in this filthy place where drunks spilt out of the town's many pubs and spewed on the pavements.

She glanced at her bedside clock. Her own mother would now be propping up the bar in the Robin Hood at the end of Mayfield Road. That was where she spent her days and nights, cadging drinks from any feller who'd put his hand in his pocket for her.

She smoothed back her dark silky hair. Regine had thanked her lucky stars when Jack had offered her the job in the ticket office. It meant she never needed to return to the house in Old Road and no longer had to put up with the men who came into her bedroom when her drunken mother was asleep.

Sometimes, if she was lucky, one might stammer an apology that he'd opened the wrong door. Most times they'd hover over her, looking down at her, especially when she had been a child in a scrappy nightdress. Some had sat on the side of her bed wanting to 'talk' to her.

She'd taken to pulling the dressing-table in front of the door. Her mother had told her she was 'imagining things'. But the probing fingers and dirty hands had been real enough.

She'd been fourteen when she'd escaped. Got a job working as a barmaid in the Point of No Return in the high street. Her big breasts and curvy body made it easy to lie about her age, until she could no longer put off her boss, Mervyn: he had asked for her National Insurance card, which of course she couldn't produce as she was below the age of sixteen and thus shouldn't have been working.

She was sacked. She moved out of the pub and into a friend's house and began working in Woolworths, telling the same lie: 'Hasn't my previous employer sent my cards on yet?'

Spending her wages on going to the pictures, Regine fell in love with America.

She'd sit in the dark, smoky atmosphere watching the Hollywood sign, the mountains, the men in their flash suits, the cars. Even the water sprinklers and the brownstone houses of crowded New York fascinated her and she longed to be a part of that fabled land. It cost a lot of money to visit America, but Regine was determined that once she set foot on American soil she would never come back. She'd live in Hollywood, maybe get into pictures. To make her dream a reality she began to save her money.

She had never visited her mother since the day she'd walked out, and if she saw her in Gosport, she crossed the road to avoid her.

When Regine was sixteen and legally able to work, she met Paul who worked on the ferries. He was besotted with her. When Jack gave her the job in the ticket office it didn't take her long to come up with her plan. She managed to keep Paul sweet so he would collect clean tickets for her, which she then sold on. The funds in her post-office savings book were growing nicely. Paul didn't know he would be ditched as soon as she had enough money for her fresh start, and things had gone very nicely for her until Jack had realized they were losing money. It didn't make sense to him that Portsmouth was raking in higher profits than Gosport.

Regine studied her finely arched eyebrows in the dressing-table mirror. She knew she was pretty and she was going to make the most of her looks and figure. She would never end up like her mother, a slut living on men's handouts. She looked at the amount in her savings book. Tomorrow she could add more money to it. Her reflection smiled back at her.

In the bathroom, Vee finished cleaning her teeth and put her toothbrush back into the glass. The air was still hot and steamy. Five inches of water wasn't much to bathe in, but when it was scalding it seemed to wash away the cares of the day. She would finish drying her hair in her bedroom, pin it up, then put on her button-through dress before she went along to the Ferry Café for something to eat.

Maybe she could help out in the kitchen for a while before coming back for an early night. It wasn't part of her job and she certainly wouldn't be paid for her services, but what was the alternative? Go to bed with a book? Listen to the wireless? It really was too chilly to go out for a walk. Besides, the Germans sent bombers over practically nightly, so it wouldn't be long before she ended up in the shelter. Anyway, she rather liked the jolly atmosphere in the café.

Back in her room Vee knelt in front of the gas fire and shook out her hair. She had brought up the *Evening News*, and began to read.

She turned the page and there was a photograph of a fire in the high street. So many fires caused by the bombing. She was about to move on when she saw the name of the fish shop's owner, Karl Baum. The man was pressing two small children to his side. Apparently his wife had gone back into the burning shop to find the family dog. The newspaper said he had begged her not to go, but when his back was turned, unable to stand the little girl's fears for the dog, his wife had disappeared.

And so it goes on, Vee thought. Not a bomb blast, a mysterious fire. Her heart went out to the children. Not only had they lost their mother, but the two little girls were on the receiving end of the country's hatred of anything or anyone German. Again she berated herself for not destroying her original papers.

The brush flew through her now almost dry hair. Vee thought about Regine. If by some remarkable chance Sammy

Chesterton discovered her whereabouts, Regine wouldn't keep the bargain she had made. She would be the first to point the finger at Vee.

She decided she would telephone home before she went along to the café to eat. She needed to make sure her mother was safe. And tomorrow she would keep her eyes open: surely Regine had an accomplice. If she worked every day in the kiosk, how did she get hold of the unclipped tickets?

She nimbly plaited her hair and fastened the end with a piece of wool. Then she picked up the newspaper, intending to return it to the kitchen table for someone else to read. Her eyes lit on a short piece about 2,500 potentially dangerous aliens, interned in Britain, who would be taken to Canada and housed in camps.

So that was where men like Karl Baum would eventually end up, was it? It stood to reason that internment camps in Britain could hold only so many 'dangerous aliens': men like Karl Baum, who had worked in England for many years, raising a family, only to have their businesses burnt down in front of them because their names weren't right. A wave of disgust rose inside her.

One word from Regine about her parentage could mean her mother's smallholding being torched. She had to find out who else was involved in defrauding Jack, before

Regine grew bored with keeping the secret of Vee's false papers. She was about to get up when she decided to read the entire newspaper article about the aliens. It stated that those men had the chance of their status being reclassified as interned refugees, friendly aliens, with a view to being offered Canadian citizenship.

Was there light at the end of the tunnel?

Canada was trying to show the rest of the world that if you had the wrong name you didn't necessarily mean any harm to your chosen country.

How long would it be before England realized that making an Englishwoman take her husband's nationality on marriage was wrong? Vee's mother and father had married, believing that giving their child a name was the right thing to do, to show the world that Vee wasn't a bastard. Now, with a German name, Vee and her mother, like so many others, lived in fear of being classed as aliens.

She sighed. If it hadn't been for the war she wouldn't have needed the ration books and other documents that denied her true parentage. Well, one thing was for sure: she would destroy the original documents – now, tonight. Her ration book in the name of Smith was lined up neatly downstairs on the mantelpiece with all the others, ready for Connie to use when she was shopping.

So, dressed warmly, Vee decided she'd telephone her mother, get rid of the old documents, then eat in the café. She'd have a reasonably early night and her next job tomorrow as a ferry girl.

When she opened the drawer to take out her documents, they were gone.

Chapter Nineteen

Inside the church the air was filled with the smell of flowers that brightened the stark interior. Vee looked at the board on the stone pillar announcing the hymns to be sung and opened her hymnbook at the first. A rumble of thunder broke the relative silence. The weather forecast had promised a wet day.

St John's was Church of England, and although Vee had never been a regular churchgoer, her mother had made sure she adhered to the Commandments. Now, standing in the solemn peace of the beautiful old building, she knew she had broken at least one. Vee was mortified.

'That's Madelaine's mother.' Rosie nodded towards a woman in the front pew, who was alone, wearing a navy outfit and a white hat. Rosie's cheery voice had interrupted Vee's thoughts.

'No father?'

Rosie shook her head. 'She doesn't look like she wants to be here either, does she?'

'Sssh!' Connie looked very pretty in her grey woollen dress. She stood at the end of the aisle, ready to go forward when required: Jack had asked her to be a godmother to Peg. Vee knew she was both excited at being asked and terrified she would do something wrong. The other godmother was a woman Vee hadn't seen before.

'Who's she?' Vee now asked Rosie.

'That's Emily Cousins. Her husband, John, is a detective based at Gosport's South Street police station. John is going to be Peg's godfather. I saw him talking to Jack earlier. They've been mates since school.'

Vee liked the look of John. Tall, fair, and dressed in a dark suit, he had a commanding presence. He'd walked up the aisle and now stood next to Madelaine, who was in a pale blue costume with padded shoulders. She was carrying a navy handbag and it was Jack who held the sleeping child. Vee noticed a silver bangle on the child's chubby wrist.

'Look at Peg! She's wearing the bangle. And I've never seen Jack so smart,' she whispered. The required group was ready for the service to begin and Connie walked forward and joined them.

The vicar, in cassock and surplice, began to speak and the congregation quietened. And so the service began.

Vee was happy with the way her two friends had dressed her. The strawberry-coloured dress had required very little alteration and Connie had lent her a hat that had a pink flower on the band and was practically the same colour as her dress.

Jack looked over at her and smiled. Vee felt the familiar jolt of electricity pass through her as their eyes met. She didn't want to look away, but she did. It was Peg's big day and Jack was so handsome. Vee had a sudden vision of herself standing next to him as he gazed down at her with love in his eyes.

She apologized to God for the thought. Jack was a married man with a child. So many times lately Vee had ignored her mother's warnings about how she should behave that she was certainly not about to throw herself at Jack, no matter how she felt about him.

And how did she feel? She wanted to make him happy. She felt sure he had been miserable for a long time.

'They make a nice couple,' Rosie whispered. 'But look who's at the back of the church. Her fancy man, and he looks angry.'

Sure enough, Hugh was staring at Madelaine as though

he could have killed her. He swayed as he adjusted his hat, and Vee wondered if he had been drinking. She glanced at Madelaine, but her face gave nothing away.

The vicar was saying a prayer and had yet to touch Peg's head with the holy water.

The church was packed. Vee saw many of her fellow workers from the boats standing in the pews. That told of the loyalty Jack instilled in his workforce, she thought. There were many male faces she couldn't put names to and she guessed that even the Portsmouth watermen had come out of respect for him.

Vee followed Jack's gaze, which rested on Hugh. Something inside her told Vee that the man hadn't been invited. Jack's face was as black as the thunder roaring overhead. Thunder that wasn't anything to do with the inclement weather, but was the dull, heavy noise of enemy planes.

The congregation, white-faced and shuffling in their pews, were definitely uneasy.

'I baptize this child Margaret Eleanor—'

'Saunders!' shouted Hugh from the rear of the church, just as the water trickled over the unsuspecting baby's forehead. His voice had drowned Jack's surname. 'She's my child, not yours!'

Gasps rose. Hugh was pushing past the guests, his hat

askew, and Vee saw that he was unsteady on his feet. He stumbled, swore, and she realized he was indeed drunk. As he reached the aisle he fell.

'No, Hugh, not now!' shouted Madelaine. She left Jack and ran towards him. Jack clutched Peg so tightly that either that or the shock of the wetness on her forehead caused her to cry out just as the siren announced a raid.

Even through its wail, Jack's voice could be heard: 'You bastard! I'll kill you!'

'Please leave the church in an orderly manner,' advised the vicar. His voice was brittle yet as calm as possible under the circumstances and his hand went to Jack to still him.

Madelaine was now pushing her way back through the tide of people eager to leave the church for the safety of a shelter. 'You go if you want. My daughter stays with me.' Vee heard the coldness in Jack's voice, which, despite the noise, was loud enough for everyone to hear. From the back of the church Hugh, trying to rise, was knocked off his feet again by the crowd of people heeding the siren's call to get to safety.

'C'mon,' said Rosie, tugging at Vee's arm. 'It's starting again.'

And then the first bomb fell.

Vee fell to her knees, pulling Rosie down with her beneath

the pew. The church shook and slivers of plaster and dust rained down from the exposed beams. Ornaments and sconces fell from the whitewashed walls. Brightly polished brasses tumbled from the long table below the stained-glass window depicting the Crucifixion.

A second crash, this time even closer, caused the roof trusses to move.

'We must get out of here,' yelled Rosie. All around them people were rushing towards the rear of the church, where there was a crush of bodies trying to escape.

Grabbing Rosie's hand, Vee moved along the pew and escaped into the side aisle.

Smoke was making it difficult to see inside the already dim interior, but it wasn't so dark that Vee didn't see Madelaine move back towards Hugh, who was miraculously already at the exit.

It was then Rosie shouted, 'Connie's hurt!'

Jack looked as though he was in difficulties. He was holding the crying child, yet trying to drag Connie away from the pulpit, part of which had split and toppled from its elevated plinth. It now lay across Connie and blood was coming from her shoulder and neck.

'Come with me!' shouted Vee, dodging around the front row of pews. She dropped Rosie's hand to take the baby from Jack. At first he was reluctant to let Peg go, until Vee shouted, 'Help Connie,' and grabbed the child. Then Jack heaved the pulpit off Connie and dragged her clear just as the stained-glass window caved in.

Glass fell like a multi-coloured hailstorm. The strange creaking noises that Vee could hear were of the lead breaking away from the ages-old glass, as fire raged from a burning room behind the altar.

Vee moved as quickly as she could up the side aisle, seeing people lying on the floor with blood oozing from cuts. She wanted to help but her first responsibility was to the now crying baby in her arms.

Rosie was holding Connie's good hand. Connie's other arm hung loosely over Jack's shoulder, bumping against his back. The church was filled with smoke that stung Vee's throat and eyes. She had pulled Peg's long dress up and over her head, partly for protection from the smoking wooden slivers dropping from the rafters and partly to keep the child breathing freely, for acrid smoke now filled the holy building. She reached the open doorway and, gasping, almost fell outside on to the wet pavement and into Emily Cousins's arms.

'Thank God the baby's safe.' The young woman led Vee across the road and into the Queen Charlotte pub.

Vee was suddenly enveloped in the warmth of the bar and was led to a chair. She sank on to it gratefully.

Aircraft screamed overhead. Vee hugged Peg to her breast and was instantly comforted by the feeling of safety that surrounded her.

'So near, yet so far,' said Emily. 'Give Peg to me.'

Reluctantly Vee handed her to Emily and was rewarded with a mug of tea thrust into her hands by John Cousins. 'Thank God so many of the congregation's accounted for.'

'Where's Peg's mother?' For some reason she couldn't utter the woman's name.

Bits of white dust clung to John's Brylcreemed hair and thick eyebrows. He put a hand to her shoulder. 'She got out all right.'

'Put some music on,' came a disembodied voice. A moment later the noise of the enemy aircraft was diluted by big-band sounds.

Vee felt the strength returning to her brain and body. She moved her feet and arms, realizing she was still in one piece and thankful for it. 'Where's Connie?'

Emily said, 'She looked worse than she was. We're lucky that one of the pub's regulars is a doctor, so he's sorting her out now.'

Vee glanced around the bar and saw Mac with a small

plump girl. His intended, she thought. Regine was near the bar with Paul.

'Shouldn't we be in a shelter?'

John waved her question away. 'Andersons and Morrisons are fine, and so are the communal ones if they're near enough, but a lot of people take their chance and stay just where they are. We're better in here than out there. Remember, lightning doesn't strike the same place twice.' He gave a smile that made it easy to see how he had won a pretty wife like Emily. 'Who'd have thought a pub would be safer than a church?'

His answer lightened Vee's heart. She finished her tea. Through the curtained window she could see the church, flames leaping from its rear where the altar was. Rain was pelting across the sky and for once Vee blessed it. She couldn't see Jack and didn't want to ask where he was, even though she longed to know. She peered around the pub again, and then she saw him.

He was sitting near the fire with his head in his hands and appeared to be in a world of his own.

John said, 'If you want to go and talk to him, I'll come along, but I wouldn't advise it. He loves that kiddie. To find out she's not his, on what should have been one of his happiest days, is not good. Not good at all.'

Somehow it didn't seem wrong to be talking to John about Jack and his marriage. John was his friend, after all.

'Did he know about that man and Madelaine?'

'He had his suspicions. Not about his child, though, I'm sure.'

'I can't just sit here while he's in pain.'

'Well, don't worry about Peg. She's in safe hands with my Emily.'

Vee stood up. She wove her way between tables and chairs to stand in front of Jack, who looked up at her. His eyes were red-rimmed.

'I saw you with Peg,' he said. 'I don't know how to thank . . . I couldn't bear it if you've come to gloat . . .' His words tailed off.

'I'm not gloating and neither is anyone else. You should know people aren't good at saying how they feel about things that don't concern them.'

'I'm a laughing stock . . .'

'You're sitting here on your own repelling people, daring them to come and talk. Don't you think you ought to take a deep breath and show these good people what you're made of?'

'What d'you mean?'

'You won't be the first man whose wife has pretended a

kiddie belongs to him when it doesn't. There's going to be a few men coming home from the war to find out their dates of leave don't coincide with a child's conception. Are you going to take it out on Peg?'

'No! Don't be stupid!'

'Steady,' said John. 'Vee's only trying to make you see a bit of sense.'

She put out a hand and laid it on his arm. 'Peg is still the child she was first thing this morning. You're the one loving her, getting up to see to her at night . . .'

His eyes were boring into hers.

For the first time, she noticed his jacket was missing a sleeve and his arm was scratched. There was also a cut on his chin.

'You're right! If that streak of piss thinks he's going to step in and take her he's got another think coming.'

'That's it,' said John. 'Possession is nine-tenths of the law. Peg's here with you, as she should be. Make sure it stays that way.'

Just then Emily came over with Peg in her arms. 'This little tinker has made a right mess of her nappy. Don't suppose there's a bag anywhere with her clean stuff in?'

Just then another bomb fell close by, and the bar shuddered. The noise from outside killed the chatter, and glasses shattered as they slid from the tables.

'That's another too close for comfort.' John, Emily, Jack and Vee crouched on the floor. Jack put out his arms and Emily handed over Peg.

'She stinks.' Vee wrinkled her nose.

Jack looked down at the baby. 'Let's ask the manager's wife if she's got a spare towel to clean you up, shall we?'

Emily smiled at Vee, who grinned back at her. He might not have been the child's biological father, if what Hugh had shouted was correct, but Jack wasn't about to let his daughter go without a struggle.

Emily said, 'I've already asked her to make up a bottle of orange or something and luckily she's got some of her grandson's baby stuff here.'

'Well done,' said John. 'Look, mate,' he turned to Jack, 'Madelaine and her fancy man aren't here in the pub. I've done a head count. Most of the christening guests are accounted for . . . One way and another—'

'Casualties?' Jack broke in. Vee watched as Emily made her way to the bar where the landlady was filling small glasses with whisky tots. She left what she was doing and went out the back through a curtain at the rear of the bar.

'Your Connie's shoulder looks worse than it is.' John gave a knowing smile. 'Poor woman fainted when the doc shoved the dislocation back.' Vee winced. 'Panic causes lots of problems.'

Jack whispered, 'It's over now between me and Madelaine, John.' He gave an enormous sigh. 'I've tried for a long time to get things on an even keel between us, but now I know it would never have worked out. I've had my suspicions for a long time. I think she had that Hugh at my house. I've often smelt hair cream on the pillows . . .'

'Stop it!' John shook a finger at Jack. 'What's the point in torturing yourself?'

Just then Emily returned and Vee saw she had managed to carry four glasses of whisky, a nappy and a baby's bottle of warm milk.

'Well done, lass,' said John, taking the glasses from her and handing them round. 'Let's drink to a new beginning.'

'I'll second that,' said Jack, leaving his empty glass on a table while he fed Peg.

Chapter Twenty

May dropped the corner of the curtain. She had been spying on the car parked in the layby opposite her cottage.

'I'm going out to ask him what he's up to,' she said to Jem. There was determination in her voice.

'Do you really think that's a good idea?' He folded the *Evening News* and put it down on the small table. The saucepans on the stove were bubbling. On the scrubbed dinner table was a freshly baked pie, made with vegetables and no meat, the crust a glorious golden brown.

'I can't go on wondering what he's hoping to achieve by sitting out there, can I?'

'I'm here to look after you,' Jem said gruffly.

'I know that.' May went over to him and put her hand on his shoulder. 'But I have to ask him what he wants.'

She heard Jem sigh. 'You want me to come?'

'Keep an eye on the dinner. I'll be all right.'

Collecting her coat from the hooks near the door, May went out into the sharp air of the early evening. In a little while it would be dark. Since Vee had left, the summer had disappeared. May wondered if her daughter would ever come home again.

As she neared the car he started up the engine. May banged on the window. Up close he was just an ordinary man, good-looking in an over-the-hill way but nevertheless just a man, and May decided she wasn't scared of him, no matter what Jem or the newspapers implied.

'Stop the car,' she demanded. Amazingly, after looking at her closely, he did. 'I'd like you to come inside. It's too cold to talk out here.' Then she turned and walked back across the road, her heart drumming, giving him time to follow.

She heard the sound of the car door opening, then closing, and pretty soon he caught her up. In silence they walked towards the house together. May thought of the man's villainous reputation. Perhaps she was being extremely silly, inviting him into her home. Suppose he turned on her, hurt her? She swept those thoughts away. Jem was in the house, perhaps deflated that she hadn't allowed him to accompany her, but no doubt he was watching every step she was taking.

'Come on in.' She pushed open the oak door and stepped

into the warmth of the kitchen. Sammy Chesterton followed. 'Hang your coat up there.' She waved towards the pegs where she was draping her coat. So far he hadn't spoken a word.

May went over to the stove, checked the vegetables and, after replacing the lids, said, 'We're just about to eat. Would you like to join us?' He looked about the room and nodded at Jem, who returned the greeting but didn't speak.

A soft miaow made her look down. One of the kittens, a kitten no longer, was at her feet. May quickly scooped a potato from the pan on the stove, mashed it with meaty-smelling thick gravy in a saucer and set it down where the cats' water bowl was. The little cat began lapping, quickly joined by her mother. May smiled again.

She turned, saw the surprise on Sammy's face and almost burst out laughing.

'You don't like cats?' She didn't give him time to answer. 'I do know you're keeping an eye on me. If it's in case my daughter comes back . . .'

'I – I—'

'It's all right,' May said. She walked towards the table, moved a place setting further along, then took out cutlery and proceeded to lay a place for him. 'The only way to sort this is to talk things through, and that won't happen with you sitting in the layby, will it?'

Jem rose from the comfortable chair and pulled out a kitchen chair for him. 'Better do as she wants, mate. She can be a Tartar if you cross her.' Jem, May knew, understood that she needed to get to the bottom of things so he was willing to do whatever she wanted to help her.

May moved the pie to the centre of the table.

'No meat, I'm afraid, and I don't want to kill another of my chickens. It's Polly's turn for the pot, but I've had her since a chick and she'll be a bit stringy now. Besides, I'd rather see her scrabbling about in the yard.'

Sammy sank down on to the chair, still with the look of surprise on his face.

May drained the vegetables and Jem set the dishes on the table when she'd filled them.

She knew the smell of the cooked dinner was enticing, especially the gravy that Jem put in the centre of the table. It was in the white gravy boat her mother had used.

The three of them sat, food steaming, and May said, 'I'm not waiting on anyone. Serve yourselves.'

Jem spooned potatoes on to his plate.

Sammy Chesterton looked up as May said, 'I know my daughter stole from you but she's been sending me money. I've been able to make up the shortfall and after dinner I'll give it to you. It's almost the original sum you asked for, before you decided to get her to spend a couple of nights with you in a hotel.'

Jem coughed and Sammy went bright red.

May was suddenly aware he wasn't used to women saying exactly what they thought. She shrugged. She'd been her own boss too long to mince words.

'There's no point in beating about the bush. That's why you've been keeping an eye on my house, isn't it? Take some of the sprouts. They're the first of the season and so sweet.' She pushed the dish towards him. 'For goodness' sake, don't be scared to dig into the pie.' Jem passed it to him.

'Didn't you ever wonder why my Vee kept to the menial jobs instead of dancing about half naked?'

Jem looked at her pleadingly. 'May—'

She interrupted him and went on: 'Vee's not been with a man. Not in the biblical sense. What you wanted of her went against everything she's been brought up to believe is right.'

Sammy said quickly, 'Yet she stole from me. Asking me to provide false documents is a crime.'

She stared at him. 'But don't you agree that what's happening here to people whose only crime is to have the wrong name is worse?' He stared at her. She could see in his eyes that he agreed. 'Eat up,' she said. 'Your food'll get cold.'

Amazingly, Sammy put a forkful into his mouth. May

watched as he closed his eyes and chewed. She guessed he didn't eat too many home-cooked meals. Of course she was aware he sold overpriced meals in his club, but she was willing to bet they weren't cooked half as well as this.

'Look, Bertie . . .'

Jem put down his knife and stared at Sammy, who had gone as white as a sheet.

'Bertie?' He echoed May's voice.

'Jem.' She turned to him. His mouth was hanging open. Quickly she leant across and touched his chin. He closed his mouth but still stared at her. 'This man used to be one of my greatest friends. He was very young at the time and his name, Herbert Lang, means he's also of German lineage. Just like I am now. At school it didn't matter a jot, did it? Or if it did, we weren't aware of it.'

'If I'd known Vee was your daughter I would never have suggested . . .' Sammy was blustering.

'Of course not. And, for the same reason you've put your original name behind you, Vee wanted to protect me.'

She could see Sammy wasn't sure what to say next, so she said kindly, 'Eat up, the pair of you. There's apple crumble for afters.'

To May Sammy seemed relieved that everything was out in the open. Jem nodded at her. His plate was almost empty and he gave a big sigh of contentment. She knew later she'd have to explain how it had suddenly dawned on her why the man sitting in his car in the layby looked familiar. And also that because he knew who she was and obviously still cared about that long-ago friendship, his threats to her daughter had remained just that, threats that hadn't been fulfilled.

Sammy pushed his empty plate away. 'Thank you, May. That was one of the best meals I've had in a while. I don't have to ask how you are after all these years. I can see. I've listened to everything you've said and I agree wholeheartedly, but I've a position to keep up. Vee stole from me. I've been laughed at because I've not done anything about it. Accepting payment in cash is all right but it's not enough. Of course, you can do something to help.' He looked at her expectantly. 'It isn't in my own interests to give out that I'm part German, and there's an awful lot of us about, May. More than you'd think. Germans who love England and have to lie to live here. Suppose I make you pay, because Vee did what she did partly for you? In a small way and only if you agree.'

'I'm not coming away with you for a weekend in the New Forest!' May laughed. 'You were always my friend, not a lad I fancied.'

'That's not what I had in mind.' He grinned at Jem.

'Though you're a fine woman, May.' He made a face at Jem to dissipate the man's sudden jealousy and show he meant no harm. 'Would you give me a box of fresh vegetables every week? I'll collect them. Even pay for them, if you want. The meals in my Southampton club would certainly improve . . .'

'I can do that,' May said. She'd digested his strange request. After all, wasn't it fair she should help her daughter pay for the forged papers? Vee had been thinking not just of herself but of them both. 'You'd have to take pot luck, though. I send to market weekly, but this time of year it's mainly greens. It's too late for salad stuff and fruit.'

'That would be fine. Are you all right with that, Jem?'

Jem nodded. 'It seems little enough . . .'

'When people see how the problem's been resolved they'll either think I'm an idiot or that I'm a good man for forgiving my childhood friend. Either is fine by me.'

'Do people have to know May's business?' Jem asked.

'Things have a nasty habit of coming out. Gossip is, a girl employee stole from me. How, what, isn't public knowledge. Nor need it be. If I personally collect on a Friday afternoon or early evening, can I invite myself to a meal again?'

'It'd be nice to chat over old times,' said May.

'I could bring a bottle of whisky, Jem.'

'That'd be all right, I guess,' Jem said.

May glanced at Jem. She saw that he, too, had realized the man was lonely. For May to invite him for a meal was a small price to pay for Vee stealing from him. 'Good. Glad that's settled. Bertie, you're welcome to my home any time.' May got up and walked over to the stove. She picked up a home-made oven glove. She'd been right all along, she thought. The big man wasn't so big after all, but he was in need of friends. Money doesn't make for happiness and if she could spend a little time every week talking over how their lives had changed since childhood, it might not be such a bad thing. She smiled at Jem but he was grinning at Sammy. They were two men cut from the same cloth, she thought.

She'd certainly have a lot to tell Vee when she next phoned. 'Anyone for apple crumble?' May asked.

Chapter Twenty-one

'I suppose she'll be able to say she was the last child christened in St John's Church before it was bombed.'

An uneasy breakfast was taking place in the kitchen at Jack's house. Both Vee and Emily glared at Rosie.

'Bad taste?'

'Extremely, Rosie,' said Emily. She and John had stayed the night. When Madelaine had failed to come home, Emily hadn't wanted to leave Peg, and John had had a few drinks with Jack, sitting in the darkened kitchen until they'd fallen asleep. Both men had now left for work, slightly the worse for wear.

'Wonder where Madelaine spent the night?' Rosie mused.

Vee had slept fitfully. 'Where d'you think?' she said.

'Who are you talking about?' The click-clack of heels announced Regine, already made up with bright lipstick and her hair just so. She went to the teapot, pulled up the cosy and felt the side. Vee watched her take a cup from the dresser and pour herself some tea.

'Madelaine didn't come home,' Emily said.

'Why would she? It's all out in the open now about her and Hugh, so you don't have to be a genius to know she'd be with him,' Regine said. She examined her red nails.

'Did Jack ever suspect . . .?'

'Shut up, Rosie,' said Emily.

Vee had heard Emily offer to take care of Peg until Jack made other plans, or Peg's mother came home.

Connie, who liked to have the little one in her carrycot in the café with her, had offered but couldn't yet use her arm properly. Her shoulder still hurt after the dislocation. Vee, too, had offered but Jack had told her he still wanted her to shadow Paul with ticket-punching, for today at any rate. 'I didn't hire you as a babyminder!'

Knowing he was under a great deal of strain, she'd held her tongue. She wondered if she should confess to walking in on Madelaine and Hugh that day but decided against it. That would be like throwing fat on the fire.

'According to John, Jack had guessed he wasn't the love of Madelaine's life, but he always hoped the affair would blow itself out,' Emily said, folding Peg's white cotton night-dresses that she'd draped over the fender to air overnight.

Regine said loftily, 'I don't want to speak out of turn but it nearly broke Madelaine's heart when Hugh married.'

Vee and Emily stood transfixed.

Happy she had their attention, Regine carried on: 'Hugh is married with two little girls. His wife has money. He strings Madelaine along with lie after lie. He'd leave his wife when the children were older, so he said. Madelaine married Jack to give a name to Hugh's baby. She thought she could get away with it, still see Hugh.

'Until yesterday, Hugh had never acknowledged the poor little mite in there.'

Rosie tutted.

'The reason it came out yesterday, like it did, was because Madelaine was going to tell Judith – that's Hugh's wife – everything unless he owned up to fathering her baby. She knew there'd be a rumpus but thought she'd get her man. Hugh likes money too much though, and the status it gives him, if you ask me. At times I felt so sorry for Madelaine.'

'Don't see why,' Vee said. 'I don't think she's a nice person. She doesn't care a jot about Peg.' She put down the slice of toast she was eating.

'She couldn't help falling in love with Hugh. She told me she met him at a party when she was very young. He turned her head.' Regine was relishing being the centre of attention.

'So she married Jack, believing him to be the best bet moneywise if she couldn't have Hugh? That's awful.' Vee looked at her plate. She'd lost her appetite.

Regine said, 'She couldn't be an unmarried mother, could she?'

'That's still a dirty trick,' said Vee. 'Jack loves that kiddie.'

'Welcome to the big world, little girl,' said Regine.

Vee glared at her. 'And so he could still have Madelaine, Hugh shouts out to all and sundry, telling Jack that Peg belongs to him?'

'I suppose he was hoping it wouldn't get back to his wife. After all, none of his posh set was at the church.'

'Except Madelaine's mother. I mean, it was a foregone conclusion her father wouldn't attend the christening. He thinks Jack's common. I expect Hugh was surprised to see her mother in the church.'

Vee put her head in her hands. 'Maybe he didn't notice she was there. Poor Jack. What a terrible business.'

'It'll be worse if we don't get to work,' Rosie said. 'And it's raining, so you'll need wet-weather gear.'

Vee groaned.

'I'm going to be here all day with Peg if anyone feels like coming and sharing a cuppa with me—' said Emily.

'So you're not working with me today?' Regine broke in, glaring at Vee. 'You won't need wet-weather gear in the ticket office.'

'No, I'm not.' Vee shook her head.

'See you all later, then.' Regine pulled her mackintosh from the back of the chair and Vee watched her walk down the hallway towards the front door, her high heels clattering on the hard surface.

'I'm off as well,' said Rosie. As she passed Vee, she said, 'If I was you I'd stay away from Regine. She's trouble. Think about it. She's just been saying awful things about Madelaine, yet she's supposed to be her friend.'

'Thanks for the tip,' said Vee.

'I expect you're beginning to feel as though you've landed in a nest of vipers,' said Emily. She looked at her wristwatch. 'You've time for another cup of tea?'

It was quiet in the warm kitchen now that the others had gone and Vee had about fifteen minutes before she needed to get to the ferry for the first boat of the day. She watched Emily top up the pot.

'He thinks a lot of you, you know,' Emily said.

'Who?'

'Jack.'

Vee stared at her. 'Did he say so?' Her heart had begun to thump alarmingly.

'Not to me, but he told John.'

'Oh, well, I like him too, but he's got a lot of problems and I'm not sure I'm strong enough to take them on as well.'

'If you care enough, you can.' Emily stirred the pot, then poured the tea. 'I've known Jack a long time. Madelaine has shaken his faith in women. He feels he can't trust us.'

'We're not all like his wife.' Vee thought about Emily's words. It would be wonderful if Jack did think of her as more than an employee. She could understand that he would need to take his time before he could love again.

'If you want him, Vee, you'll have to show him he can trust you. And it's not going to happen overnight. How about Peg? Are you willing to take her on as well?'

'Peg's a lovely little kid. It's about time she was shown some decent mothering.'

'I'm glad you think like that, because Jack won't give her up. They come as a pair.'

'But at the moment there's three of them. Jack's married to Madelaine. If he left her, I'd go with him like a shot. But he wouldn't do that. It's not in his nature, is it?' She was hoping Emily would say otherwise. When she didn't,

Vee saw that the situation was hopeless. She couldn't get involved in a divorce. The scandal would open up her own life to examination. She hadn't told Jack the truth about her parentage. Besides, how could she bring such shame on her mother?

'Anyway, apart from being friendly, giving me a job when I needed one and a place to stay, he's not shown the slightest interest in me . . .'

'Would you prefer a married man to be all over you? Would you think much of him if he sailed quite happily from his wife to you?'

'Of course not!' She'd heard the old saying that 'if a married man strays from his wife to you, he won't hesitate to stray to someone else'. Jack wasn't like that.

'Well, perhaps I'm speaking out of turn, but I'm telling you what my husband thinks.' She laughed. 'And my John doesn't mince his words. As I've already said, they've known each other for years.'

The clock on the mantelpiece chimed a quarter past the hour and Vee pushed her cup aside. 'I'd better get going,' she said. Outside the rain was hitting the windows with force.

She hauled on the heavy wet-weather trousers over her grey slacks and stuck her arms into the shiny black coat.

'Smells all new and funny,' she said, grabbing the sou'wester and stuffing it into her pocket with her purse.

'If Peg was older you'd probably frighten the life out of her dressed like that,' Emily observed.

At that the baby's cry shattered the relative peace of the early morning.

Vee called, 'Good morning little girl!' into the room where Peg was, opened the front door, grinned over her shoulder at Emily, and then she was gone, running past the car ferry.

She saw Ada walking up from the boats clutching her bag.

Since their first meeting she'd had several cups of tea with the girl, who was older than Vee had first thought. It had been hard persuading her to take gifts of warm clothing, the skirts Vee had no use for now that slacks were her more usual form of workwear. Harder still for her to accept food and sometimes money. She didn't ask Ada how she was surviving, but she was definitely in better shape now than when Vee had first met her.

Vee's forged papers enabled her to work, but Ada wasn't so lucky. She waved and Ada waved back.

Vee ran past the queue of people buying the first ferry tickets of the day and down to the wire mesh gates that separated the boat from the pontoon. She could feel Jack's eyes on her, so she looked up through the rain that was coming down like spears and waved. His face split into a grin and he raised his hand in welcome from the open wheelhouse.

Moving through the sea of people, with their early-morning smells of perfume, soap and sleep, she took her place next to Paul. The purring of the ferry's engine as the boat bobbed against the jetty and the smell from the funnel made the boat a haven for those passengers who could find a place in the downstairs cabin. Those who couldn't would make for the funnel, to stand around its warmth. Though the smell of her new waterproofs wasn't good, at least Vee was dry. Except for her feet. The rain had run down the shiny surface of her coat and trousers to puddle in her shoes.

Paul grinned at her with large white teeth. His hand went to his pocket and he pulled out a pair of clippers.

'You do the people your side and I'll do this. Just one punch. If you make a mistake and clip twice, the ticket will be invalid for the return journey.'

She nodded. The clippers were heavy, a bit unwieldy, but she'd soon get used to them. They were like a pair of scissors that, instead of cutting, made a hole.

The piercing whistle blew from the Portsmouth side, there

was a sudden lull in the noise of chattering people and Mac
pulled back the heavy gate. He gave her a huge wink, then
went towards the rope, ready to unwind it from the bollard.
The people surged forward, tickets in their hands.

Chapter Twenty-two

May poured the strong tea into two cups. She decided to leave Jem out because, with his long legs sprawled in front of him, his hands over his stomach, she thought he'd rather continue sleeping than be woken to drink another cup of tea.

There had been a moment earlier in the evening when she'd thought the two men might come to blows.

'So you think it's all right to force a girl to go to bed with you in payment for something you've done for her?' Jem had asked Sammy.

May wished he'd leave the subject alone, but sometimes he was like a dog with a bone.

'In my line of business the women sometimes see that as the only possible form of payment.'

She had seen Jem bristle with indignation. But her glare

had been enough for him to drop the subject. They were, after all, different men from different backgrounds.

She was happy with the way things had gone tonight. Both men lounging in the armchairs in front of the fire looked contented. She'd fed them well. Damn the war and the lack of food, she'd made a tasty meal they'd all enjoyed – it was certainly true that the way to a man's heart was through his stomach. She'd achieved deliverance for Vee from Sammy Chesterton's wrath by agreeing to provide vegetables for the foreseeable future to be collected each Friday. She smiled to herself. It was a fair bargain. Of course he'd kept the money Vee had sent. He was a businessman, after all. And Friday evenings had become something to look forward to. Especially tonight, when Sammy had arrived with a huge joint of beef!

Actually these evenings were more than a fair trade. It was a ridiculous way to settle things, and if the poor man hadn't had such a crush on her when she was a girl, it would never have worked so well to her advantage. Sammy Chesterton, alias Herbert Lang, might have travelled the world, and now owned clubs that made him money, but he needed a family, and May was quite happy to include him in hers.

Nevertheless she had seen the way he looked at her sometimes. She certainly wasn't in the first flush of youth, but she believed the word that best described her might be 'comely'. She had no intention of his visits ever amounting to anything. If – when – she decided she wanted to settle with a man, he would be Jem. That was how she felt now, and the future could look after itself.

'So you married him?'

May looked at Sammy, for it was he who had spoken, bringing her out of her reverie.

'The German?' he prodded.

'I did,' said May. 'As soon as I announced I was pregnant, Gus, with the aid of my friend Annie, worked out a way we could marry.'

'Surely that presented problems?'

'Actually, it didn't. Finding clothes for Gus did!'

Jem's eyes were closed and she could see his chest rising and falling with the even breaths that signified he was deeply asleep. He'd arrived at five that morning and was cleaning out the chicken run when she'd stepped outside with a mug of tea for him. She smiled fondly.

'You have to explain yourself,' Sammy said..

'When I discovered I was pregnant I had no idea how I'd be able to tell my parents without an almighty row, which would be even worse because Gus worked here.'

May told him how she and Gus had met and fallen in love.

'No doubt your father would have been extremely hurt at what he would have seen as your betrayal.'

'He hadn't wanted me to leave this place, and when I did, I'd got myself pregnant. I felt as though I'd let my dad down, but I just wanted to be with Gus every moment I could, so I didn't think about anything else.'

'Surely he couldn't simply say to the authorities at the hospital that he wanted to marry you and they'd let him.'

May frowned. 'Of course not. I discovered where Southampton register office was and found I needed to present documentation in the form of birth certificates and passports, before they would give me a diary date for three weeks hence. They were wonderfully helpful, maybe because there was a war on. Gus had no papers. Actually, that wasn't true. He had a wallet that had survived his plane crash. But his identification had been taken from him and was now locked in an office at the hospital, where all identity papers that survived their owners' demise or hospital stay were kept.

'Annie had access to this room. She made Gus promise to allow her to return his passport to his wallet if she borrowed it for the registrar.

'In due course, along with my birth certificate, I had a single paper sheet folded in eight with a cardboard cover – Gus's details and his photograph. The passport was charred but legible and amazingly presented no problems at Southampton's register office.

'It was decided Gus would come to the smallholding as usual and we would go on the bus to Southampton. Everything went according to plan, except for the distinctive hospital clothes Gus was forced to wear. He could move about fairly freely as long as he wasn't late for curfew. The prison authorities had begun to trust him. At the smallholding he was under the jurisdiction of my father. As long as Dad thought Gus was working there wasn't a problem.

'I begged a few hours off and met Gus with some of my father's clothing.' May began to laugh. 'My dad's trousers were very short in the leg even though Gus pulled the turn-ups down. But we had to ignore all that. I had on the ankle-length dress I had worn at the village carnival. It was made of white lace, you see, and still fitted me. Annie made me a coronet of flowers and I felt beautiful. At least I wasn't going to become an unmarried mother and heap further shame on my family. We had discussed the future. Gus was determined to marry me and I decided that being wed to a German was infinitely better than becoming an unmarried mother. How naive we were.'

May got up, went to the corner cupboard and took out a shoebox. She flicked through a Bible. Nestling inside was a faded white rose, which, even though it was flattened, was still strangely beautiful.

'I had two white roses,' she said. 'Gus kept one. I don't know what happened to his, though.' She couldn't help herself, and a tear rolled down her cheek.

For a while she stood with the faded flower in her fingers. Then Sammy took it from her, put it back in the Bible and replaced it in the box.

'Surely you couldn't live together, you and Gus.'

May shook her head. She seemed more composed now. 'No. I was surprised that everything in Southampton had gone without a hitch. Lots of young couples were getting married – it was the war, you see. Neither of us needed permission as we were over the age of consent. It was all so easy.'

'I would have thought, being away from Netley, Gus would have made a run for it.'

'You don't know how it was between us. He wanted us to be together. Besides, where would we have gone? Our situation at that time was the best one for us to be in, with him having relative freedom and me as his wife. He hadn't shamed me by giving me a child out of wedlock.

'When we got back here, Gus had to get on with his work. Bruno and Manfred had covered for him while he was away. My friend Annie returned Gus's passport. She'd wanted to come with us but it wasn't possible so we called in two people off the street as witnesses. I managed to replace my dad's clothes and went back to work at Netley Hospital. It became like any other day, except that I had a marriage certificate, proof I was married to the man I loved.'

He nodded.

'It wasn't the wedding my parents wanted for me, I knew that, but I was selfish in those days. I also knew that as soon as the baby began to show the whole story would come out, not to all and sundry but certainly to my parents.'

'But Gus's part in it was deceitful, as was yours . . .' Sammy finished his tea.

The sound of the cup being replaced on the saucer must have woken Jem, for he yawned, stretched, and gave May a sleepy smile. She nodded towards the teapot and he mouthed, 'Yes.'

'We were in love, it was wartime, and if I'd suggested to Gus that we fly to the moon he would have done it to make me happy. He wanted to be my husband for the child's sake. I got my comeuppance later.'

'We've all done things in the past that have hurt other people,' said Sammy. 'Does Vee know all this?'

'You're very inquisitive,' said Jem.

'It's a very unusual story,' said Sammy.

May nodded. 'Quite so. I think because I acted in such an outrageous way I wanted something better for Vee. We don't have secrets, not ones that really matter, and I've tried so hard to bring her up knowing right from wrong. That moment when she stole from you was out of character, but I was the one who persuaded her to run away.' She had taken the lid off the teapot. 'This is stewed. I'll make some more.' Then she bit her lip. 'I was wrong. You have no idea how much I miss her.'

'You can tell her to come home now,' Jem said. He rose from the table, stretched, and took the teapot to the sink to rinse it out. Then he went to the kettle, shook it to make sure it held enough water, and lit the gas.

May felt the tears rise so close to the surface that she fumbled in the pocket of her skirt for a handkerchief, but Sammy beat her to it and handed her a snowy white square.

'I don't know where she is. She telephones . . .'

'We must find her, then.' Sammy patted her arm. 'We must put her mind at rest, and yours.' He looked at Jem for assurance.

May nodded. 'It's not good when you can't be proud of who you are. I loved Gus so much and yet now I'm ashamed . . .'

'Don't forget I, too, have to pretend to be someone I'm not, just like thousands of other people.'

'Will it end?' May asked. She watched Jem busying himself at the stove, then went to the fire and put on another log. The smell of the wood as the flames licked beneath it was comforting. 'I never realized I was taking on Gus's nationality when I married him.'

'Change is inevitable.' Jem's voice was calm and clear. 'There are rumours of the open-door policy that Canada hopes for. If you live in a country for five years you can apply to become a national. I don't know why in our country each person can't be treated as an individual. Do you want to hear of another ridiculous thing that's happening?'

'Ridiculous or funny, please.' She dabbed her eyes. 'I hate talking about my past. Sometimes it makes me so sad . . .' She smiled. 'Go on, tell me.'

'People of German origin, not already interned, are being forbidden to live along our coastline as they might be spies and could possibly use torches to enable the enemy to land on our shores.'

'That's propaganda leading to hysteria,' said Sammy. 'How silly.'

'How about the banning of German composers like

Beethoven and Bach from community music?' offered Jem.

'Apparently we mustn't be influenced by them.'

May started to laugh.

'There's one more,' said Jem.

'Go on,' said Sammy.

'I believe German measles is now called liberty measles!'

Chapter Twenty-three

Vee stood at the front rail of the boat. The back of her neck was wet, her hair hung in rat's tails and her feet were freezing. Across the water the majestic floating bridge puffed and clanged, the waves spilling to either side as it cut through the sea. Passengers stood on its decks near vehicles that shone with the never-ending rain.

'That's a magnificent sight,' Paul said. He lounged against the wooden seat that for once was empty: very few passengers liked to stand on top of the boat in the rain, preferring instead to squeeze up together in the smoky cabin below deck.

'How long have they been running?' Vee asked.

'*Alexandra* replaced *Victoria* around 1864. But don't quote me on that,' he said.

She thought of the noise that sometimes woke her in her

room overlooking the landing stage at Gosport. 'Have you always done this job?' she asked.

'No, but I started quite a while ago. Then I met Regine and we became friends. I was a builder's labourer before that.'

Vee was surprised. 'Are you and she . . . ?'

'I'd like to think so, but she's after bigger fish than me.' He smiled at her. 'But you never know. I might be able to win her.' They'd travelled backwards and forwards across the strip of water between Gosport and Portsmouth all morning. Vee was cold, hungry and fed up with clipping tickets.

The different jobs she'd tackled so far had given her a better understanding of how the ferries ran. It was hard work, but she'd never felt so fit or well.

'When we've done the return journey why don't you go to the café, get yourself warmed up?' Paul said.

A vision of the warm Nissen hut, a cup of tea and possibly a sandwich suddenly seemed very appealing.

'I'm supposed to stay with you until the other lot takes over,' she said. She was fearful of upsetting Jack, who was preoccupied over the weekend's events.

Ahead loomed the Portsmouth landing stage – she could just about see it through the sheet of rain. Automatically her head turned towards the wheelhouse. Jack had left the boat a couple of hours ago. One moment he'd been there and the next he'd been replaced by a man of about fifty with a full beard, who reminded Vee of the sailor on the Player's Navy Cut cigarette packets. 'I'd ask Jack but he's not here, and I don't know him.' She waved towards the man with his hand on the wheel, staring straight ahead towards the jetty.

'That's Si. He won't mind. Another couple of hours and our shift's finished for the day anyway. Wait a bit.' Vee watched as Paul caught Si's attention by doing arm movements that ended with him pointing to her, then miming drinking a cup of tea. Si nodded back furiously. 'There! Told you it'd be fine, didn't I?'

'That's given me something to look forward to,' she said, thinking how nice it would be to be warm and dry again. A seagull landed on the rail. Up close it looked huge and menacing. It turned its head towards her and cawed loudly, making her jump before it flew off to join its mates.

'Every seagull contains the soul of a dead mariner.'

Vee was about to come back to him with a quick retort but realized he was serious. Perhaps that was what he believed and, if so, who was she to say otherwise?

She watched as Mac skilfully threw the rope and pulled the ferry towards the jetty. On the landing stage, despite the rain, people were queuing to board. Colourful umbrellas jostled, lending a little brightness to the dull day. When the boat was secured, and only then, the chains came down so the passengers could leave. They hastened up one side of the gangway towards the railway station and the buses into the heart of Portsmouth.

Eventually the ferry was empty and the gates to board the boat were opened so the flood of wet people could trail in, stepping aboard from the wooden jetty. Vee was standing beside Paul and no passenger was allowed on without a ticket.

'I'll be glad when the shift's over,' said Paul, but his voice was almost drowned in the noise of people eager to get out of the worst of the rain. With their tickets in wet fingers they surged forward, and Vee began the chore of clipping and collecting them.

Her line of passengers dwindled before Paul's, the passengers no doubt thinking that Paul as the regular ferryman would allow them on the boat quicker than the girl who was unsure of herself. Vee was watching him when he took a ticket and, without clipping it, put it into his cavernous pocket. She wiped the rain from her face, left him to deal with the stragglers and stood back on board.

The whole operation of a boat coming in and completing

a turnaround was swift so that one left every fifteen minutes from either landing stage.

'I'll put these boots back,' called Vee, making her way through the disgruntled crowd to the cupboard to replace them and change into her own shoes, which were still soggy from earlier.

Sitting on the bench and pulling off her wet boots, as the boat bucked and slid over the waves, took most of her concentration. It was still windy and the rain was coming down harder.

Nevertheless, the memory of Paul putting the ticket into his pocket played on her mind. The clipped return tickets were passed to Regine at the end of the shift and should in theory add up to the number of tickets sold, but because passengers didn't always return the same day there were minor discrepancies. What nagged at Vee was that Paul had pocketed an unclipped ticket.

A clean unclipped ticket returned to Regine could be used and paid for again. She'd not noticed Paul pocket tickets before . . . Because the tickets handed to him were wet! He only wanted dry clean ones!

Her body felt heavy as she trudged up the Gosport gangway towards the Ferry Gardens. At the kiosk, warm and snug inside, she could see Regine doing her job. And that was when the penny dropped.

Vee remembered Regine handing out tickets from her bag and making no bones about the fact that money from those tickets went into her jar. They had been sold and not punched. Passengers kept their return tickets safe so they were always in pristine condition. How many really noticed that they were supposed to have them clipped? If a ticket was shown and you were waved through in the stream of people, the clean ticket could be presented at the gate for the return journey. If it wasn't clipped it could be reused. A penny a ticket. It didn't sound a great deal of money, but when Portsmouth Football Club played at home and upwards of twenty-two thousand people travelled across the water to watch the match, the pickings would be very good indeed.

Vee's heart lifted: she'd discovered the answer to Jack's problem about the takings being down. Then it dropped. Hadn't Regine said that if Vee breathed a word about it, she would tell Jack that she had forged papers? She would tell anyone who would listen that Vee Smith was Vee Schmidt.

Vee would be back where she started. Running away from her heritage. Oh, she could run – she'd done it once, she could do it again – but leave Jack?

Vee felt as if all the air had been knocked out of her.

Part of her wanted so much to help the man she cared for. But once he found out she hadn't been honest with him, she would be just another person who had lied to him.

The dance music from the wireless enveloped her, along with the fug of cigarette smoke, as soon as she pushed open the café's door.

A few people were sitting at tables and Vee could almost taste the pleasure a cup of tea would bring her.

Rosie saw her first and called her to the counter. 'Look at the state of you! You're wet through and you look frozen!'

Vee gave her a half-hearted smile. 'At least I'll get warm in here. How's Connie?'

Evidently hearing her name, Connie poked her head out from the hatch. Her blonde hair, covered with the snood, made her look quite glamorous. 'I'm fine,' she called. 'Arm aches a bit but I'm one of the lucky ones. Doctor's put it in a sling and I'm to try not to use it.' Her voice dropped to a whisper: 'Go and talk to Jack. I'm worried about him. Got baby-minding problems. Emily's mother's been hurt, fell down some stairs. I don't think Emily's going to want to take the little one along to see her, do you?'

After divesting herself of her waterproofs and hanging them on the wooden pegs near the door, Vee walked across to the table where Jack was sitting, looking disconsolately through what appeared to be invoices.

Connie and Rosie seemed almost like substitute mothers to Peg but it wasn't an ideal situation, especially if Connie had been advised not to use her arm too much. But if Emily had to look after her mother and Madelaine didn't return soon, how would Jack cope?

'How are you?' Her voice was soft but loud enough to rouse him from his miserable reverie.

'I thought you were punching tickets.'

For a moment she'd forgotten she was supposed to be on the boat with Paul.

'They took pity on me because the weather's awful.' She expected him to come back at her with some retort but he didn't.

'How did you like the work?'

'It was one of the most boring jobs I've ever had to do.'

His whole face seemed to light up as he said, 'I guess at least you're honest.'

Just then Rosie arrived with two mugs of tea and Vee pounced on hers. 'I need that to warm me up,' she said, watching as Rosie found a space for the other mug among the papers on the table.

'I'm trying to make sense of the accounts,' he said.

'Thought I'd look at this lot before I go back to the house to take over from Emily. I suppose you've heard about her mother?' He must have guessed Rosie had told her.

'I take it Madelaine's not returned yet?'

He took a swig of tea, then shook his head. When he'd put his mug down he said, 'I'm babyminding this afternoon.'

'I could look after Peg. I'd like to.'

His voice became hard. 'I told you before, I didn't take you on as a babyminder.'

She smiled. 'No, honestly, I'd like—'

'Don't you understand what "No" means?'

His glare made Vee's stomach turn to mush.

'I'm sorry,' she said quietly. She looked down at the table. Jack began sweeping the papers into a pile.

Vee thought of the accounts she and her mother needed to keep up to date for tax purposes and for billing to customers. She was every bit as competent as her mother. Maybe she'd ask Jack if he'd like her to take over some of the office work. Not now, though. She'd already said enough to make him angry.

Then he said, 'I've involved enough people in my marriage . . .'

'It's not your fault.'

'Peg needs her mother.' He folded the papers and dropped

them into a brown carrier bag. Then the chair scraped as he pushed it back, stood up, took his coat from the back of the chair and put it on. Vee watched as he walked to the door, which swung shut behind him.

Rosie returned to the table for the empty crockery. 'I told you he doesn't know what he's doing.' She sighed, twisted a length of her hair behind her ear, then said, 'We've got some vegetable soup that I think would do you good.'

'I'd like that.' A gust of wind hit the side of the hut with force and rain began rattling down again. 'I could help you after I've eaten . . .'

'Go home. If this bad weather continues, the ferry will stop running. Already our customers have been few and far between – we might even close early. Take the chance to catch up on some sleep. Or you could come with us to the Connaught? There's a dance on later.'

'Surely if the ferries run through air raids they won't shut down because of the weather?'

'Oh yes they will. Safety of the passengers is paramount.'

Rosie left her, and returned second later with a steaming bowl.

Vee toyed with her spoon. She might like to go back to the house, maybe have a bath and sleep for a while. Going dancing, she wasn't so sure about.

The vegetable soup made her mouth water. Rosie had put a great doorstep of crusty bread on the side of her plate.

'That looks and smells delicious. Tell me, has Jack's wife ever been gone this long before?'

Rosie shook her head. 'Not to my knowledge, but she might be scared to come back. Who knows what happened after she caught up with that Hugh last Sunday? She dotes on him. Maybe the two of them have gone away together.'

'What – and leave her daughter?'

'She's not the motherly type, is she? She knows Jack won't let anything happen to Peg.' Rosie paused, then said quietly, 'I don't know what that Hugh has, apart from looking like Zachary Scott . . .'

Vee must have looked confused.

'Zachary Scott is going to be a big star. There was a bit about him in *Photoplay*.'

Vee had forgotten how much of a film fan Rosie was but she was reminded when Rosie said, 'The latest issue's on my bed. You can read it if you want.'

Connie shouted for Rosie, and Vee was left to eat her soup.

It was still raining when Vee walked out of the café holding her waterproof coat over her head to keep off the worst of the weather. It was quiet when she entered the house. The fire was burning and Peg's terry-towelling nappies were steaming gently over the fireguard. The kitchen was tidy, no dirty washing-up on the wooden draining-board.

Vee left her wet-weather gear in the shed, propped over an empty box. Relishing the peace and quiet, she went upstairs and ran a bath.

On Rosie's bed was the copy of *Photoplay* with a picture of Joan Crawford on the front and Vee took it to her room. She went to the window and stared across at the space where the car ferry drew in. There was no queue of vehicles waiting to cross the water. The rain was hitting her window so hard she was fearful it might break. But common sense told her the tape stuck on the glass would stop it falling inwards. She looked longingly at her bed and the magazine, then went to have her bath.

Chapter Twenty-four

May felt Jem's hand on her shoulder as she waved goodbye to Sammy, then closed the door on the man who had previously fed fear into her and her daughter.

'Whoever would have thought that sitting down and talking through problems could make them practically disappear?' she said.

He turned her around to face him. 'It's when people can't share their thoughts and talk about them that difficulties arise.'

May didn't move away. 'And you, are you all right with him calling here weekly?'

'You are your own woman. You always have been. But winter isn't the best time of the year to provide vegetables.'

'Sammy won't care about the produce.' She frowned. 'Seems funny thinking of him as Sammy when I knew him as Herbert. Can't you see how lonely he is?' She walked over to the table and collected up the dirty crockery. When she glanced at Jem, she saw he was still standing by the door. She replaced the plates and went back to him.

'Don't tell me that after all this time you're jealous?'

The blush rose up his neck into his face. He turned his head away.

She said, 'After all we've meant to each other, you can't possibly think . . .'

'You're a very desirable woman, May.'

She took his hand and looked at it. At the calluses and the hard skin that had come from working on her smallholding.

'And you are a wonderful man, Jem. I'd never hurt you.'

She thought of the times they had made love. Though never once had Jem stayed overnight for fear of her name being sullied.

'Vee was a baby when I came looking for work. I loved you the moment I saw you. You told me enough times that you'd never marry again, and that Gus was the only man you could ever give your heart to. I never minded being second to a dead man.'

May held on to him and pushed him towards the sofa. She sat down with him. 'You and I don't talk much nowadays, either.'

'I always thought that was because we've said all that had to be said to each other.'

'Well, that's where you're wrong. If it hadn't been for you, Vee and I couldn't have survived after Mum and Dad died of influenza.' Her mind went back to the terrible pandemic that had swept the world at the latter end of the Great War.

She thought back to when, instead of nursing men from the forces, she'd turned the large bedroom into a nursing section where only she was allowed to go. For days she'd bathed and cooled the feverish bodies of both her parents. Even so, when flu was known to be on the smallholding some of the hired staff had refused to work, even while wearing the cotton masks people were advised to wear to ward off the germs.

'I only did what most people would have done.'

'No, you did more. You also cared for Vee.'

She smiled, remembering how he had taken the pram out into the fields and at times had wheeled the child home with him to the village so May could spend more time in the sick room and away from Vee, in case she became infected.

Before Gus died she had stopped nursing at Netley Hospital. Her father had never accepted Gus, not even when he was told Gus was the baby's father, but his feelings had thawed towards his daughter. He had allowed her to come home for the birth. What else could she have done? There was nowhere she could go. Her VAD life was over.

But the price she paid was never to admit to anyone that she'd gone behind her father's back and married a German.

No one could have foreseen what would happen to Gus.

May would sometimes take out her memories and examine them. She hadn't been with Gus when the end came. But she had known the man she loved so well that she could imagine everything.

Gus felt he had a friend in Annie. The notes she carried back and forth between him and May gave him something to live for, as did the coming child. May's father had banned him from the smallholding.

One Saturday night, Annie found him in the small cell-like room he shared with another prisoner.

'May's gone into labour,' she said. 'Tomorrow you'll have a son or daughter.'

He let the news sink in, then asked, 'Why aren't you with her? Surely she needs you.'

'Because I'm like you. This place dictates all my movements. Her mother's there, so don't worry.'

But he did worry. How could he not? All night he tossed

and turned in the bed in the hated room with the locked door, waiting for the new day so he could at least be out in the fresh air working, hoping Annie would come so she could take another letter to May.

'You're being irrational. Childbirth's normal. At least let me get some sleep.' His cellmate, who was older and a father, understood his worries but tossed them aside.

'I should be with her. I want to be with her.'

'Women in childbirth don't need men cluttering up the place,' the man said. 'Try to rest.'

His May was having his child.

Many times he had wished they hadn't been overcome with lust and love. He should have tried to spare her the indignity of becoming pregnant. Because of him she had lost her job and was on bad terms with her family.

After queuing for breakfast, the long line of prisoners in their distinctive suits set about their duties. As he wasn't allowed to go to the smallholding any more, he now worked in the hospital gardens.

But he had to see May. His desire to go to her became unbearable.

'Where are you going?' the armed guard barked. Gus had thrown down the hoe he was using.

He didn't answer. He guessed the guard would think he

was going to relieve himself in the bushes. As long as Gus didn't leave the grounds, he could do as he liked. But he continued walking towards the furthest corner of the park-like area where the gate led on to the road.

'Nothing matters except that I have to be with May.' His words were swept away in the breeze as he walked determinedly along.

Men were watching now.

'Turn around and come back.'

Gus ignored the guard, walking like someone possessed. Nothing mattered except his May.

Gus could feel the cold wind blowing off Southampton Water. It was like a caress.

'Stop!'

Still he walked.

'Come back, you fool!' That was his roommate.

The first shot hit the gate, splintering the wood as Gus put up his hand to draw back the bolt. He flinched.

The sudden pain in his back was excruciating as the second shot hit him and felled him to his knees.

May's features filled his eyes as the darkness descended.

Vee was twenty-four hours old before May was informed that Gus was dead.

*

It was thought the soldiers had brought the flu home from the trenches where disease of all kinds was rife. But it was indiscriminate with its victims. May found out much later that five hundred million people worldwide had been affected by it and fifty million had died.

Life ended in less than a day for her father. He felt shivery in the morning, had a sore throat, and his skin changed colour to a fiery purple. Before midnight he was choking on globules of scarlet jelly-like blood. May had seen it before with the men she nursed. Her mother lasted almost a week.

May remembered screaming at Jem because he wouldn't let her see her baby after her mother had breathed her last. Afterwards she praised him for his unfailing care. Had she been with her child she could so easily have passed on the virus.

'I always felt Vee was like my own daughter,' he said later. 'I didn't want to lose her.'

May kicked off her slippers and leaned against Jem. She could hear his heart beating. She ran her hands over his shirt. 'Your body is still beautiful.'

She wanted to have him always in her life. And now she could. It had taken the loss of Vee to show her how fleeting happiness was. It should be grabbed with both hands.

Jem pushed her down into the softness of the sofa and began brushing her cheeks and neck with kisses.

'I want you,' he said. 'Is it all right?'

'It's more than all right.'

He removed part of her clothing, then drove himself into her, slowly, slowly. May found once more she was saying all the silly things that come to mind when making love. But it seemed right. Everything was so perfect, so amazing, so unreal, and he waited for her.

The next morning she was awake before Jem. It had rained in the night, and she could smell the freshness through the open window. Birds were singing. Cat looked up from her place at the end of the bed and blinked lazily.

May was surprised he was still with her, for she had expected him to disappear in the night. It was so nice waking up beside him. His mouth was slightly open, his lips curved in a smile. She always loved to kiss the corners of his mouth. He had grown stubble during the night. She couldn't help herself – she leant over him and kissed his lips.

His eyes opened and he ran a hand over her nakedness, stopping when he reached her bottom. He gave it a small friendly slap.

'Don't look at me,' May said.

'But I want to look, to touch you. Or have you changed your mind about what we said last night?'

May realized she'd been hiding from happiness all these years, forgetting how it felt to give in.

'I wouldn't agree to marry you before because I wanted to be loyal to Gus, no matter how hard it was, and when you first asked me I thought if I agreed you'd think it was to make my life easier, to have a new name, not because I really loved you. Mind you, I'm not sure you'll be allowed to marry an alien! It's taken me all this time to see what a fool I've been. I've said I'll marry you and I will.'

Chapter Twenty-five

The siren cut into her sleep. Like a person drugged, Vee hauled herself from her bed and threw on her coat. Downstairs she found a hive of activity. Regine was making up flasks, yawning as she did so. Jack, hair tousled, was getting in her way making up bottles of milk for the baby, and Peg was screaming in the downstairs bedroom. Vee looked at the clock: it was two thirty.

'Butter that bread,' demanded Regine, and Vee immediately got on with scraping margarine on to a loaf that had already been cut into slices.

Vee saw a tin of corned beef upended on a saucer. 'This the filling?'

'Don't turn your nose up. There's many won't have even that,' snapped Regine. Vee felt as though she'd been cut down a peg or two.

Already they could hear the sound of planes droning overhead.

'That's the trouble. We never have enough time to get anything done.' Jack put a basket containing Peg's parapher-nalia on the table, then found room in it for four bottles. He moved swiftly to the bottom of the stairs and yelled, 'Rosie! Connie!'

He disappeared, coming back moments later to push a wet child into Vee's wide open arms and take over slicing the corned beef.

Vee loved the milky smell of Peg, who was now exam-ining her face, poking tiny hands into her eyes. Vee kissed her tear-wet cheek. 'It's all right,' she said. 'Nasty planes woke us all up.' Then, 'I expect those two went to the Connaught after all. There was a dance there tonight.'

'But it's been pouring with rain practically all day,' Jack said.

'They wouldn't be dancing in the rain, silly,' came Regine's voice. 'And all the more reason to get out for a bit of enjoy-ment. They've probably stopped over with a friend.'

'So it's just us three for the shelter, then?' Jack said, put-ting the sandwiches into a bag and settling it in with Peg's stuff. 'This is full now.'

'We ought to make up some food and leave it in the

shelter in case it's needed,' Regine said. Then, 'Where's my handbag?'

'I prefer to eat something fresh, thank you very much,' said Jack. 'And food that the rats haven't had a go at first. All ready?'

'Almost,' said Vee. She passed Regine her big handbag, noting that the girl never went anywhere without it. She had changed Peg's nappy and transferred the wet one to a bucket of water mixed with Milton. Regine grabbed her coat, threw it over her shoulders and made for the back door. Vee was a few paces behind her and saw her take a small torch from the shelf. Jack returned to the front door and turned off the electricity.

The house was plunged into darkness but the stench of cordite had already seeped in from outside and Vee could see quite clearly the back path down to the shelter – the sky was bright with searchlights, and over Portsmouth it was orange, tinged with smoke, which told her that the city, just across the narrow stretch of water, was getting a beating. The returning ground fire was no match for the enemy planes. The noise of the aircraft was interspersed by huge bangs as shells exploded, sending up sparkles of fire.

'Hurry!' shouted Jack from close behind her. She pulled the child closer and followed Regine, head down, watching the path so she wouldn't trip.

'Jesus, it stinks down here.' Regine was at the air-raid shelter, pulling at the latch to open the door.

'The place gets damp. And I wish I could make sure of keeping rats out,' Jack said.

Vee followed the small light that disappeared as Regine shone it inside.

'Careful,' shouted Regine. 'Something's on the floor.'

The scream that followed was unearthly.

Vee saw a small animal scuttle into the darkness. Something smelt bad, like meat gone off, she thought. She clutched Peg even tighter. The door of the shelter banged shut as she and Jack followed Regine inside. The oil lamp was lit.

Flies flew like tiny Spitfires in the confined space. With one hand covering Peg's face for safety, Vee looked down at the body of Madelaine. Regine's screaming was hurting her ears.

'Shut up!' Jack threw down the bag he was carrying and everything spilt across the floor. He shook Regine with both hands as though she was a rag doll. 'Stop screaming!'

Vee tried to move further into the shelter, away from the smell and the flies. The sudden silence hurt as Regine quietened, then fell against the chair and slid to the floor, moaning softly.

'We've got to get help,' Jack said.

Vee, shocked, began to shiver. 'She's dead, isn't she? We can't stay in here with her.'

'Best get back to the house.' He fell to his knees and touched Madelaine's grey face. He stared at her, then seemed to shake himself back to normal. Vee saw Madelaine's hair was matted with dried blood. Her eyes were open as if she was looking for something she couldn't find. 'Yes, get back to the house,' Jack snapped. 'There's many people never leave their own fireside when a raid comes.' Then he rose and said to Vee, 'Are you all right?'

She nodded, then gestured at Regine. 'She's not.' She glanced back to Jack and their eyes met and held.

'I need to telephone for help – the police first.' He gathered up Peg's things, then handed Vee the bag. 'Can you take this as well as Peg?'

Vee nodded.

'We've got to get out of here. Take a chance.' He opened the door so Vee could step into the night. The smell of cordite and burning was a welcome relief after the stench of death. She looked back at the couple still in the shelter.

'C'mon.' Jack put his hands beneath Regine's arms and pulled her upright, while Vee waited on the path, taking deep breaths and willing Regine to gather her wits enough to walk back to the house.

Then she heard the shelter door close and felt Regine slip an arm through hers, the one that was clutching Peg so tightly. 'All right, Regine?' Vee asked.

'Let's get indoors,' the girl said, and they began walking carefully back up the path. 'Those flies . . .' She shuddered, and Vee knew she didn't expect an answer.

Vee took Peg through to the main bedroom and put the baby into her cot against the wall. The noise coming in from outside wasn't so bad, but the searchlights lit the front bedroom, despite the heavy blackout curtains.

'You'll soon be in Dreamland,' she said, and covered the little girl with a knitted blanket. The light came on outside the room – Jack had switched the utilities back on. Her eyes moved around the bedroom. No pictures on the walls, no photos in frames. It was quite Spartan, unfinished, as if no one cared about the decorations. She saw Jack's suit thrown over a chair, the hanger on the floor. Madelaine's silky dressing-gown was hanging from the hook on the back of the door. Impulsively she picked up Jack's suit, shook it out and hung it straight on the hanger before opening the wardrobe.

Madelaine's clothes were in there, alongside Jack's shirts. The wardrobe was full, so it didn't look as though Madelaine had intended to run away. She noticed her hands were shaking. Madelaine was dead. She heard Jack on the telephone. She couldn't catch what he was saying but his voice was brisk and business-like.

She looked again at Peg, whose eyelids were fluttering as children's do when they're being overtaken by sleep, so she felt it was safe to leave her. There was a small table lamp next to the unmade double bed so Vee switched it on, glad it wasn't too bright. She remembered when she was a little girl how she'd hated waking in the dark. She didn't want Peg to become scared of shadows, like she had been.

She pulled the door to and went out into the hall. Jack was staring at the telephone. His shoulders were slumped. He had his back to her. He put his hand to his forehead and sighed. Vee was sure he didn't know she was there. After a little while she saw his shoulders rise, then fall. He was crying, and her heart went out to him.

He didn't turn towards her but said, 'It had got so I hated her. But I never would have wished anything like this to happen.' He wiped his hand across his face. 'The police will be here as soon as possible, but it mightn't be until the raid's over.'

'What do you think happened to her, Jack?'

Vee thought it was possible she had gone down to the shelter, slipped perhaps and hit her head. The body had obviously been in the shelter for a couple of days – the smell and the flies proved that.

'I think someone hurt her.' She saw his throat rise and fall as he swallowed his emotion.

A huge bang made the house shake. Flakes of ceiling plaster drifted down and Vee fell against Jack. She scrambled back, standing upright once more as someone shrieked outside on the street. The bell of a fire engine cut into the sounds of thumps and crashes. Vee heard water splashing.

'Incendiaries,' he explained. 'They scare me when I'm out on the boat.'

He took a deep breath. 'Look, I'm going to ask a big favour. I don't know what's going to happen when the police get here, but there's every possibility I'll be asked to go down to the station in South Street. I'm going to phone the other crew in case I'm not back for my shift. They'll find someone to cover for me. The girls in the house can work as usual, if that's possible. I know they'll not let me down. It's Peg.'

'I begged before to look after her. It'll be no bother—'

'There's something else. I'm going to give you my keys. To the house, the safe . . .'

'Why?' Vee thought he'd trust one of the others more than her.

He sighed. 'Someone's stealing from me. There's

something going on and until I find out who is behind it, everyone's under suspicion, except you.' He took her arm. 'It was going on before you arrived. Find someone to help with Peg so you can carry on working different shifts and keep your eyes open for me.'

'Anyone would think you expected to be gone ages. You'll only be in for questioning and they might not even want you down the police station for that. It's your wife lying out there, remember. You'll be home in a few hours.'

'I have to be realistic, Vee. I'm the obvious suspect. Of course it might have been an accident, and I sincerely hope her death was accidental. But I have to make sure every eventuality is covered and the ferries must keep running. You know all about writing the log and you said you were used to paperwork . . .'

'The others aren't going to like me taking over. And I'm not sure I feel capable.'

'The others, if they want to keep their jobs, will back you up, and maybe I haven't said it but I reckon you're more than capable of standing in for me.'

The kitchen door opened and Regine stood in the doorway. 'I've got to keep myself occupied – I'm going mad. Do you want tea?'

She looked as if she'd been crying.

'That's a good idea,' Jack said, going over to her and putting his hand on her shoulder. 'I know how friendly you and Madelaine were. Did she contact you during the last few days?'

Regine shook her head.

'I believe you,' Jack said.

Regine turned away but he touched her arm and said, 'I did care about her. No matter what she might have confided to you.' She shook him off and walked towards the stove. She picked up the kettle, went to the sink to fill it, then put it on the hob. She lit the gas and orange and blue flames crawled up from the kettle's base. 'Vee's going to be in charge if I'm kept at the police station.'

'Why?' Regine whirled round.

'Something's going on here – oh, I'm not saying you're involved, but I know Vee has nothing to hide.'

'You sure about that?' The words hurtled from her mouth.

'Regine!'

It had the desired effect. Vee meant only to stop her telling Jack she was working on forged papers. If her secret was revealed she'd have no compunction about telling Jack she was sure Regine was stealing from him. But this wasn't the right moment for the ticket fraud to be revealed. Vee needed more proof. Regine and her accomplice could deny everything. How could she prove what she knew to be the truth?

Regine drew a deep breath and Vee sighed with relief. The moment had passed. Jack hadn't realized anything was amiss except cattiness at his decision to put Vee in charge.

Moaning Minnie, the all-clear siren, began her mournful wail as the kettle boiled. Regine glared at Vee, then stalked off to put a small spoonful of tea onto the used leaves.

'So, you're all right with my decision?' Jack said.

Regine said, 'I have to be. Thank God the raid's over. The other two will comply. You're acting as though you expect to be found guilty. The poor cow's body has only just been discovered. What if her death's an accident?'

No one answered her, because a man's voice, accompanied by loud knocking on the front door, shouted, 'Police! Open up!'

Chapter Twenty-six

Vee was upset that her name had appeared not only in the local *Evening News* but also in the *Southampton Echo*. The press had decided a body being discovered in the air-raid shelter of the ferryman who'd saved a little boy's life recently was more than newsworthy.

The papers had praised the ferry's 'other skipper'. Vee suspected the bottle of whisky no doubt given to him by the reporter loosened Jack's tongue. He had no reason to suppose she might not be pleased at receiving approval.

Peg didn't like it that her daddy wasn't around and grizzled constantly that first evening. As he had feared, Jack had been taken in for questioning.

'You'll have to sleep in their room,' Regine said. She gave a wicked smile.

'I don't think so,' said Vee, who could think of nothing

worse than sleeping in a bed where not only the dead woman had slept but also Jack. Since she didn't want to start moving furniture about and she was convinced Jack would shortly return, she made up the carrycot, put Peg into it and took the little girl upstairs with her. Peg seemed to like the sound of the voices and the wireless floating up the stairs and, to Vee's delight, promptly fell asleep.

Madelaine's body had been taken away. Luckily there was a back way into the garden near the shelter so it hadn't come through the house. The police said they would arrange for a post mortem, and Rosie and Connie arrived home in the thick of all the questioning.

One by one the girls were taken into the scullery to speak privately with a policeman.

'I was Madelaine's friend,' began Regine, before anyone asked her a single question. She was bundled into the scullery but her loud voice betrayed her: they all heard her tell of the christening and Jack's outburst.

'She'll have him hanged, drawn and quartered, will that girl,' said Connie, who shed a tear as Jack was taken away.

Eventually the police left and the women sat around discussing the night's happenings. No one shed a tear for Madelaine.

Even though Vee doubted she would sleep, she eventually

went to bed. The baby's snuffling somehow comforted her and she dozed.

She was first up in the morning and had bathed and fed Peg when Connie stumbled downstairs, closely followed by Rosie.

'If you're in charge, there's a couple of changes we'd like to make in the café.'

They made her sit down, then got on with the breakfast chores, all the while telling her of what they'd decided. Vee blessed Rosie and Connie that first morning for their forced cheerfulness because it certainly lightened her mood.

'Don't go expecting me to agree to things you wouldn't ask Jack about,' she said. 'He'll be back shortly, and I'll get it in the neck for agreeing to your demands.'

'We want to start a takeaway service for sandwiches.' Connie grinned at her. 'Customers eat food on the premises and sometimes ask if we can pack up a sandwich for later. We do, but we both think if we advertised, word of mouth, we could do a roaring trade. And having some sandwiches already made up would save us time.'

'Where will the extra food come from? There's a war on, you know, which means the café can only sell what can be bought.'

'We can order differently. Use more salad stuff, ideal

in sandwiches. Corned beef tastes better with lettuce, tomatoes.'

'It's too cold. The season's over for that kind of stuff.'

'Tinned beetroot, shredded cabbage, onions, pickles . . .' Connie had jumped in with stock they already had in abundance.

Vee thought quickly. 'If you're so set on this, why hasn't Jack given it the go-ahead? What's in it for you?'

'A percentage,' Connie said. Vee frowned. 'When we came up with the idea, Jack said to talk it over with Madelaine. But she didn't want to know.'

'Why?'

'She didn't care about making money for Jack, only about meeting up with Hugh.'

Rosie put her hand over her mouth. 'I shouldn't have said that. That's speaking ill of the dead.'

'You should if it's true. I hope when that copper took you into the kitchen to talk to you in private you told him everything you know?' Vee could see from Rosie's face where her loyalty lay. 'Look, if you want to do this, go ahead, but if the profit goes down instead of up, that's it, finished.' Their eyes told her they would make it work. She guessed they'd put their hearts and souls into the idea.

As both of them trudged towards the front passage, she

heard Rosie say softly, 'See? I told you she'd listen and I know we'll make a profit.'

'You'd better,' called Vee. 'I'm going through the books today.'

Connie laughed and blew her a kiss before the door closed behind them.

Vee berated herself. Jack had been out of the house just five minutes and she was changing the way things were done. When he'd told her to look after his business, he probably hadn't expected her to agree to Connie and Rosie's scheme.

'Regine!' Vee shouted up the stairs. 'You'll be late if you don't hurry.'

A short while later the girl came downstairs.

'Jack not back yet?' Dark rings circled her eyes. Vee guessed she'd been crying.

'Not yet,' Vee answered. 'There's tea in the pot and I'll toast you some bread, if you like.'

'I'm not hungry,' Regine said.

If Regine had found it so easy to talk about Jack's shortcomings, would she disclose that Vee had forged papers? Since no one had confronted her yet, Vee was able to breathe as the front door closed on Regine, leaving her and Peg alone in the house.

One of the first things she had to do was make sure Jack's job was covered.

'The ferries must keep running,' Jack had said. A phone call made sure that was so. Si was sincere in his agreement to help Jack all he could until his return.

'When they find someone dead like that, the culprit is nearly always someone who knew the victim well. It's normal to take the husband or boyfriend in for questioning,' he said. 'But I know Jack wouldn't have harmed a hair of her head.'

As Vee poured a last cup of tea for herself, deciding to make a list of what needed to be tackled first, Peg woke up and this time Vee couldn't settle her.

The rain hit the windows with force. One of her priorities had to be finding a good babyminder. Peg's cheeks were pink and she was hot. She'd have to take the child out in the rain – there was no way she could leave her on her own, even if she was completely well.

Peg let out a great howl and Vee picked her up. Her tiny body was rigid. Surely she couldn't be ill.

The announcer on the wireless was discussing the Germans' raid on Coventry last night. So it hadn't only been along the south coast that the bombers had done their worst. She gasped. At least a thousand people had died.

As Vee drank her tea, she wondered how her mother was. She hadn't telephoned her for a while.

Walking up and down the warm kitchen, trying to soothe the fractious child, Vee knew she ought to let May know she was safe and well. She worried constantly that Sammy Chesterton would find her and had now sent her mother almost enough money to cover the normal price he charged for forgeries. She was surprised the time had passed so quickly while she'd been living in Gosport. Each week she bought little, just necessities for herself, but what if the money wasn't enough? What if he had decided interest was due? Soon it would be Christmas.

Thinking of the festive season, she realized this would be the first year she wouldn't be involved in cutting down the mistletoe and bunching it, ready for market. It was one of the jobs she loved helping with.

There was an old apple orchard behind the house where the trees were now too old to bear good fruit but still supported *Viscum album* or mistletoe.

For many years her grandfather had supplied mistletoe for Tenbury's yearly festival, as did some other local smallholdings and farms. As a girl Vee had sat in the barn, making up holly and mistletoe wreaths that Jem sold at market. She missed the smallholding and her mother. Vee shook herself.

This little scrap of a baby in her arms now had no mother, so it was up to her to make sure she didn't suffer because her father wasn't there at present.

Peg refused her bottle and instead grizzled continuously.

Perhaps a visit to the doctor, or at least the duty nurse, was necessary.

When Vee finally had the child ready to leave the house, Peg was sick, and she had to start all over again washing and dressing her. Now convinced Peg was ill, she set off with the pram towards the doctor's surgery.

The streets were full of rubbish, broken slates, bricks and rubble from the previous night's bombing. Vee walked carefully with the pram, fearing she might buckle the wheels as she pushed it over the uneven ground. As she passed Walpole Park she spied Ada sitting hunched in the rain on one of the wooden seats.

Ada rose and came towards her. 'Sorry to hear all about the troubles Jack's having. Oh, don't worry, nobody believes he did it. Have you time for a cup of tea?'

'I can't – I need to get to the surgery. This little madam's been sick – she's ever so hot and I'm worried.'

Ada looked into the pram. 'How long has she had those bright spots on her cheeks?'

'I didn't notice them before this morning but she's done nothing but grizzle and she's hot, sickly . . .'

'Have you tried rubbing her gums with a cold spoon?'

What on earth was Ada on about? It was only these past few days that Connie had suggested Peg could possibly be started on different foods besides milk. She couldn't eat with a spoon!

Ada laughed and fell into step beside her. 'The cold spoon will soothe her hot gums. Or a piece of clean material soaked in cold water – let her chew on it.'

'But she's been sick!'

'She's teething,' said Ada. 'Lean over the pram and see if you can look into her mouth. I daren't touch her – my hands aren't clean enough.'

'Well, it's easy enough with her screaming like this, isn't it?' They both stared into the baby's gaping mouth.

Vee saw two tiny white pinpricks in her bottom jaw and her top gums were red and inflamed. Peg was crying real tears. 'Ada, how clever! And Peg, you're such a brilliant baby! Your daddy will be pleased!'

For a little while Vee had forgotten that Jack was still at the police station. Now it all came back to her. If she went round to South Street, would they let her see him? Everything looked so black at present . . . Perhaps if she could have a chat with him, tell him about Peg and her new teeth, it would cheer him up. She sighed.

Ada said, 'They must realize surely that Jack loved the woman. There was no way he would have harmed her.'

Vee knew Jack wouldn't hit a woman. She didn't know how she knew but she did.

'Ada, I've such a lot to do today, but now you've told me what to do for Peg, I must go home. If you'd like to come with me, I'll make us tea and get you something to eat.'

Ada stared at her. 'I'm not a charity case, Vee.'

Vee was taken aback. 'Have you never thought I might just like chatting to you?'

Ada squeezed her arm. 'Sorry,' she said. 'I get prickly because people look down on me. I feel so ashamed of myself. I think that man spitting at me was the last straw. I haven't been back to that pitch near the car ferry and I haven't sold myself for money. What you gave me eventually ran out, but I manage to earn a few coppers on market days helping pack up the stalls, and if I'm there early in the mornings, *very* early,' she added, 'I help the stallholders set up. A hot cuppa and a sandwich can sort me out for the day. I've been getting by . . . No one's asked my name. I just get called, "Oi, you!"'

Vee put her arm through Ada's. She'd already turned the

pram round. 'I'm really pleased to hear that,' she said. 'You're too honest a person to sell your body.' And then it dawned on her that it was possible her troubles could be over if she asked Ada to look after Peg. Then she could get on with the other things she should be doing for Jack. There was the paperwork, wages . . .

As soon as she got home, Vee put the kettle on. She was disappointed Jack still hadn't got back. Within minutes, Ada had washed her hands and was busy with Peg, somehow stopping the little girl's crying. Vee noticed Ada carried the bag with her in which Jack had said she kept the certificates that showed she was a qualified children's nurse. She decided to take a chance.

'How would you feel about looking after Peg permanently?'

She was astounded by Ada's clipped reply. 'I can't . . . Look at me. I have nothing, not even an English name.'

Vee wasn't going to suggest the obvious, that the girl had something that mattered more: on paper she was extremely qualified to look after Peg. Vee trusted her. She wasn't going to ask to look at her documentation. 'You can have a room in this house and your keep. The wages will be minimal at first but, if you trust me as I'm going to trust you, I think we'll work well together.' Vee smiled at Peg, who was now tracing Ada's cheek with her tiny fingers.

Vee knew she'd won Ada over when she said, 'I can show you awards I've won, but Jack knows I'm the enemy.'

'Let me worry about that,' Vee said. 'Is it a deal?'

Ada started crying with happiness and Peg copied her.

After they'd had their tea Vee took Ada upstairs and showed her a room at the back of the house.

'I'll prepare the bed and clean up – I don't think Madelaine liked housework. Then I'm going to make a stew. I expect Jack, when he eventually comes in, will be starving. I think he'd rather eat here than in the café where people will stare at him. If you want a bath, there's plenty of hot water but don't forget five inches is the limit. There's a spare toothbrush in the bathroom cabinet.'

She thought that later she would ask Ada to help her take the baby's cot upstairs.

Before she began searching for fresh bedding, Vee went into her own room and looked out some more of her clothes, not that she'd got many. She found a skirt and a jumper. Luckily they had the same shoe size so she was able to put aside a pretty pair that she knew she'd never wear again. On the ferries she wore clothes for comfort.

Vee was humming along to the wireless. The dance music was making her feel so much better. Peg was fast asleep in her pram outside the front door in the fresh air beneath the shelter of the porch roof where it was dry, and she had also discovered clean sheets and blankets in the airing cupboard downstairs.

Vee put the clothes for Ada on the floor outside the bathroom and called through the door that she'd be making up her bed.

She was surprised when Ada opened the door, a towel around her, and said, 'I've found bleach and peroxide in the cabinet. Could I use some on my hair?'

'I believe they belonged to Madelaine,' Vee said. 'You might as well.'

Ada spotted the clothes on the floor.

'I'm never going to be able to thank you enough, am I?'

Vee saw the fresh tears in her eyes. 'I've a strong feeling that you'd do exactly the same for me,' she said. It was then she saw the bruises on Ada's lower neck.

Ada tried to cover them as soon as she saw Vee's eyes go towards the dark blue marks. There were bruise bracelets around her wrists too.

'It's not easy living on the streets,' Ada confessed. 'Some blokes came down to the ferry, thought I was fair game . . . They held me down.' For a moment there was silence, a long awkward silence that spoke volumes.

Vee said eventually, 'You're safe here with me.' And so that Ada wouldn't see her cry she went quickly downstairs to start making a meal. She knew that without her forged papers, rape could easily have happened to her too.

Chapter Twenty-seven

Clean nappies were drying over the fireguard and a stew was bubbling on the stove when Ada came down to the kitchen to dry her hair in front of the fire. She was wearing Vee's clothes, and when she took the towel off her head, Vee gasped.

'You look . . . lovely,' she whispered.

Ada knelt on the rag rug and began brushing out her hair. The more it dried, the brighter it became.

'Thank you,' Ada said. 'I'm never going to forget what you've done for me.'

Vee wondered momentarily if she'd taken too much on her shoulders in the relatively short time that Jack had left her in charge. After all, Ada had no papers and Jack was well aware of it. What would he say to Vee giving her the job of looking after his daughter? As for herself, she rued the day she'd asked Sammy Chesterton for help and hated herself for becoming not only a thief but a liar. Oh, well, she thought. She'd worry about that later. There was no turning back now.

'I've been doing as you suggested, giving Peg something cool to chew on,' Vee said.

'Did it work?'

Vee waved towards the hallway. When the rain had come down hard, she'd brought in the pram. Ada jumped up and went to look. Vee heard her saying baby things to the little girl, who was awake, happy and making noises at the toys strung across the front of the pram.

'She's still chewing on it,' Ada called.

Peeved because the happy film music had been interrupted for the news, Vee heard the announcer say, 'There will be four ounces of sugar and two ounces of tea extra for everyone at Christmas,' but they were to go easy on milk because there were more shortages. Vee was grateful when the stirring songs took up where they'd left off.

'That raid last night was bad,' said Ada. Her newly touched-up blonde hair was hanging in a curtain round her face. Vee thought she must have been scared on the boat as the bombs rained down and more so when the men had invaded it.

She wondered whether she should ask Ada if she intended

to pursue the matter with the police, then decided against it. Ada wouldn't want the police involved: she was an alien. She didn't mention that. Instead she said, thinking of Madelaine's body in the air-raid shelter, 'I can't use the Anderson ever again. But I believe Jack's got a Morrison here somewhere. There's certainly one in the café.'

Just then there was the sound of a key in the door and footsteps in the hall. She heard Jack's voice as he spoke nonsense to Peg in a cheerful voice. As he stepped into the kitchen her heart missed a beat.

His eyes met hers. 'Hello,' he said. 'I bet you thought I wasn't ever coming home again.' She shook her head, went over and kissed his cheek. Jack didn't push her away. Instead he smiled.

'That's a nice welcome,' he said, his eyes holding hers.

'Hello,' said John Cousins, as he entered the room behind Jack. 'And who's this?' Both men took off their wet coats and Jack draped them over the end of the fireguard that was free of babywear.

John was staring at Ada.

'I'm Peg's nanny, Ada,' she said.

Vee was surprised that she showed no sign of unease as she put out her hand for John to shake.

Introductions over, Jack said, 'Do you have papers?' Vee

wasn't sure whether he was asking Ada if she had a ration book and medical card or whether she had qualifications, but Ada went to the sideboard, took out her brown bag, pulled from it a large envelope and showed him several certificates.

'I'll put the kettle on,' Vee said, and turned her back on the two men and Ada. This was a ridiculous state of affairs, she thought, as she lit the gas beneath the kettle. Having a bath and bleaching her hair hadn't disguised Ada that much! Whatever was Jack playing at?

Then it dawned on Vee that John had no idea who Ada was. Jack was doing all the talking before his friend started wondering about 'the new nanny'.

'How's Emily's mother?' she asked John.

John grinned at her, the new nanny forgotten. 'Emily's fed up because her mother's a very demanding woman and Emily can't do anything right.'

Jack chipped in, laughing, 'I only met her once, but that was enough!'

John grinned at him. 'The old girl must keep off her feet for a while so I'm eating in the canteen.' He pulled a face. Vee took it to mean the food in the police canteen wasn't too tasty.

'I've got just the thing to warm you on a horrible day like

this. A dish of stew? Not much meat, but there's freshly baked crusty bread to go with it, and I put potatoes to cook in the bottom of the oven.'

Jack was gazing at her. She wasn't sure what she could see in his eyes – gratitude? Then he winked at her and she knew it was going to be all right. Not only was Ada welcome in his home, but he'd told no out-and-out lie to his best friend, John. Plus she and Jack now shared a secret. A feeling of contentment spread through her.

It didn't take long to put out cutlery and dishes and set chairs around the table.

As they ate they talked, the good hearty smell of the food and the warmth in the kitchen promoting conversation between them.

'I was hoping to come and visit you,' Vee said.

'Thank God I wasn't at the police station any longer,' Jack said. He turned to John. 'Will you be needing me any more?'

'Not now her fancy man's confessed . . .'

Vee's eyes shot across the table to Jack's face. 'Apparently he reckons they had a row and she fell. It was his fault, he says,' continued John.

Vee could tell there was something he wasn't saying. 'Don't you believe him?'

'There's a few discrepancies.'

'You think he's covering for someone else?' Ada chipped in.

'Look, I shouldn't be talking about an ongoing case.' John turned towards Jack. 'She was your wife, mate.'

'I shouldn't speak ill of the dead, but she'd not really been a wife to me for a while . . .'

'But I'd stake my job on it that you didn't kill her.' John was adamant.

'I hope you go on feeling that way,' Jack said.

John poured the remainder of his tea down his throat. 'Look, I've got to get back.' His chair scraped against the floor as he pushed back from the table and rose. 'That was a good, filling meal, Vee, thanks.' His plate was scraped clean. It was always gratifying to see a man appreciate his food, she thought.

Jack got up and handed his friend his now dry coat.

'Don't come to the door, I can see myself out,' John said.

'Say hello to Emily for me,' said Vee.

Ada began removing the dirty dishes and started on the washing-up. She had her hands in the sink when Jack returned from the front door.

Vee's heart was pounding as he came into the kitchen. What was he going to say to her? Would he be very angry that she'd made him an accomplice to her crime of giving an alien work?

She was still sitting at the table. His face was inscrutable, but he looked shattered. She guessed they hadn't allowed him to sleep while he was being questioned. While it was true that he and John were friends, he would have been treated like any other person they had taken in for questioning about a murder. But, wait, wasn't she jumping the gun? Was it really murder? And when had Hugh confessed? What was the story behind that?

As he entered the room, Jack stopped and stared at her. 'So, now I have two possible detainees under my roof!'

Chapter Twenty-eight

'You can handle everything here for a couple of days, can't you, Donald?'

'Wouldn't be the first time you've left the Black Cat in my hands, would it?' The old man was sorting out the change in the till. 'Got a bit of fluff you want to take away?'

'If I was anything like the bad boss I'm supposed to be, I should punch your nose for that remark, you crusty old bugger.' Sammy Chesterton put down the glass from which he'd just swallowed the last of his single malt whisky and smiled.

'You do that and I won't be in any fit state to look after nuffink!' Donald slid the till drawer shut, listened for the ping, then finished his own drink.

Sammy Chesterton nodded amiably and, his coat slung

over his shoulders, walked out of the club into the fresh Southampton air.

It wasn't often he regretted anything, but he felt bad that May didn't know where her daughter was. The stupid debt had been paid in full and May and Jem had shown him nothing but kindness. Every time he stepped inside Honeysuckle Holdings he was made to feel like one of her family, fed like royalty, and now that bloody man of hers had him doing chores about the place, like he was some hired hand.

Last week when he'd arrived with a nice bit of gammon, expecting to play a few hands of whist after the meal, Jem had told him, 'We've got a little job to do first. The back bedroom of this place has a rotten window. I've made one up and done most of the preparation but I need someone with a bit of savvy to hold on to the thing while I fit it. Half an hour and it'll be finished.'

What could he do? He'd stood on a ladder out in the freezing cold while Jem had knocked out the rotten window frame in one piece. Of course Jem'd been inside the house, fannying about, while he'd stood on the ladder in his cashmere coat, then pushed the window in so Matey could put in the glass and putty it. Naturally all the crap fell outwards, over him and his nice warm coat.

Still, the grateful look on May's face had made up for his discomfort.

'I've been scared to open that window for ages,' she'd said.

No wonder he'd fallen asleep in the armchair after dinner. Never did get to play whist!

He'd reached his car now, inserted the key and climbed inside. He smiled, remembering he hadn't woken until much later, and when he had he'd found May had covered him with a blanket. Not only that but her damn cat had been sleeping on his cashmere coat and made a nest in it. Hairs all over it!

He put the *Southampton Echo* on the seat next to him and started the engine of his Armstrong Siddeley.

It wouldn't take long to get down to Gosport and, thanks to the skipper who'd jumped into the Solent and rescued the boy, he knew where he could find Vee. And wouldn't May be happy to see her daughter again! It really was the least he could do for her.

There was a great deal of bomb damage in Southampton, with gaps in the rows of houses, like missing teeth in an old man's mouth. Bit like Donald's, he thought.

There was a lot of farmland between Southampton and Fareham but it wasn't long before he was on the main road from Fareham going down towards Gosport ferry.

Bloody Hitler had had a right go at the place. Parts of the main road were like an obstacle course where buildings had caved in. Whole walls had been taken out, leaving the spectacle of half an upstairs room complete with an iron bed ready to fall to the rubble below. There had been a raid last night and he wondered how many unsuspecting people had copped it. Mind you, it wasn't only the bombs that were knocking people off. One day that young bloke was being praised on the news for saving a kiddie, the next his wife was found dead in a shelter! Don't seem fair, really, Sammy thought.

He'd done a bit of phoning around and discovered Vee lived with several other ferry girls in the house owned by Jack Edwards. For her to have saved up to pay him for her ration book and papers she must have worked all hours without spending anything on herself, poor kid. Still, he'd make it right now.

When he reached the ferry, he'd park up, then watch a while. He was looking forward to surprising her.

'You said two?'

Vee stared at Jack and awaited his reply, not that she didn't guess what had happened. But she couldn't help herself: 'Did Regine tell you?'

'No, but she left some papers of yours around where I'd find them.'

Suddenly she wanted to tell him about the ticket fraud. But she kept her mouth tightly closed. She had no proof to show him and it would look as if she was trying to get her own back on the girl.

Ada folded the tea-towel over the fireguard. 'That's the quickest I've ever been sacked from a job,' she said. Her face showed her misery.

'Wait a minute,' Jack said. 'If I didn't want you here I'd have given you away to my mate, the copper. You'd probably have been on your way to a camp by now, wouldn't you?'

'So you're all right with me looking after Peg?' Ada frowned, unsure of herself and his expected answer.

'Of course I'm not, but I'm willing to take a chance if you are.' Vee watched as Ada drew a huge sigh of relief.

'I know how hard you've been trying to make money legally, Ada. I need someone to look after my daughter and you're qualified. The last thing she needs is more upsets, and there'll be plenty of those in this house in the next few months.'

'You won't regret it,' Ada said.

'I hope not.' He turned to Vee. 'She cleans up well. I take it you had a hand in that?'

Before she could answer a small cry came from the pram in the hall. Ada grabbed the cardigan Vee had given her earlier. 'I'll take Peg for a walk.'

Vee listened as the front door opened and she heard the pram's wheels bump down the step and onto the pavement. Jack didn't say anything until the door clicked shut.

'If Regine let you know I was working on forged papers, why didn't you say something to me?'

'What difference would it make whether I sacked you a couple of days after you arrived or much later?'

'It's me who should be asking you that.'

'Ask yourself why I took you on.'

'You needed help, the notice on the boat said.'

'And you didn't ask yourself why it was you I took on?' Jack needed a shave and he looked so tired she wondered how he could cope with everything.

Vee shook her head. 'Why?'

'Something happened when I saw you asleep in the cabin.' He looked sheepish. 'But what could I do? Say, "I really fancy you and I'm married and sleeping with my wife so come and live in my house"?'

It was a long while before either of them spoke. A piece of coal sparked from the fire in the range and landed on the brick surround, then fizzled out.

Quietly Vee said, 'So I've been learning to do jobs on the ferries that I might never need to do?'

'No, that part is real enough. If I lose my regular staff because they want to join the forces, I need reliable people I can depend on to take over their jobs.'

That answer didn't satisfy Vee.

'Never once have you ever admitted you even liked me.'

'Would you have liked a married man making a pass at you?'

Vee hung her head. 'Probably not. But why didn't you sack me when you found out I'm not legal?'

'You're no more a spy than I'm Winston Churchill. I'd like to think I'm a decent enough judge of a person's character.' He was staring at her intently. 'If I could take all the shit my wife was dishing out to me, I could wait until you were ready to tell me the truth. In fact, now is the ideal time for you to explain yourself.'

Vee looked at his beautiful mouth with the corners curved in a smile. 'Shall I make another cuppa? It's quite a story.'

'You have tea if you want. I'm having a proper drink.' He went over to the sideboard, opened the door and took out a bottle of beer. Then he sat on the sofa and patted the seat for her to sit next to him.

'Before you speak, let me ask one question. I have to

work tonight. I've already had too much time off. Will you come with me? We can talk more up in the wheelhouse. But for now I promise I won't kiss you until you've told me everything about your past and then I'll only kiss you if you want me to.'

When she'd finished telling him her story, he set down the empty beer bottle and picked up her hand. His eyes seemed to bore into her soul. He didn't speak, just leant forward and kissed her.

Those lips were everything Vee had thought they'd be, when they came down firmly on hers, sending shivers of delight along her spine. As he broke away he said, 'All this time I've been too scared and ashamed of what you'd think of me to do any more than talk to you. Even that taxed my mental strength at times. Do you know what it means to a man to have a woman beside him who not only cares about him but is willing to risk her life working alongside him?'

'Oh, Jack,' she said. 'I wish you'd been brave enough to do this before.'

'It wasn't right. The timing was all wrong – and I'm not even sure I'm doing the proper thing now. I don't want to take advantage . . .'

She heard the key in the door that heralded Ada's return. Vee sprang away from him, but as she stood up she said,

'You're breaking the law by not informing the authorities you have two aliens in your house.'

'Hellooo!' called Ada. 'We're back. A little girl is hungry.'

Jack rose and gripped her wrist. 'Let me worry about that. I know two wrongs don't make a right, but because the government has lost its head, many people have been forced to do things they never expected to have to do to survive. I have to speak out, Vee. You are the girl of my dreams and I won't let you go without a struggle. I'm not in the right situation yet to prove it to you,' he put his face close to hers, 'but I will, love.' His lips brushed her cheek.

Ada pushed open the kitchen door. She had Peg in her arms and moved towards Vee. 'Take her for a moment, Vee. I need to get my coat off.'

Vee saw she'd worn her old coat over the clean clothes she'd given her. It smelt musty. Ada had no doubt slept rough in it. She determined to get her another as soon as she could. The less Ada reminded people of her origins, the safer she would be.

But before Vee could take Peg, Jack stepped forward. Vee was surprised to see the little girl, small as she was, give him an open-mouthed smile. He was talking to her about her 'toofy pegs', and Vee smiled.

Jack took Peg upstairs with him. He was going to have

a bath and shave, he confided, to get rid of the smell of South Street's police station. Peg could have a swim with her daddy at the same time. He went upstairs carrying her and her yellow toy duck.

Vee was on cloud nine as she lit the gas beneath the kettle. Now her secret was out in the open with Jack, the relief was tremendous. Jack had made it easy for her to answer his questions about her past and had contributed information about his life with Madelaine. Never had she felt so comfortable talking to anyone as she had with him. She felt as if she had known him all her life.

The caress of Jack's mouth was still on her lips and cheek as she stirred the large pan with the remainder of the stew she'd made earlier. Neither she, Ada nor Jack had eaten in the café today, but there was plenty of food here should they want a snack later.

The other three girls came home, but Regine went out again quickly. She was going to the pictures with Paul, but before she left she asked what had transpired between the police and Jack. She seemed surprised that Hugh had voluntarily walked into the police station and given himself up.

'He's not the violent kind,' was all she said.

'Everyone has secrets,' said Vee sharply. She didn't divulge that Jack had told her he knew she was an alien. Regine didn't waste breath on talking to Ada. She accepted her as Peg's new nanny. It was quite obvious that she neither knew nor recognized the other girl. Connie did, though.

As Vee put a shovelful of coal on the fire, Connie said, 'Everyone deserves a second chance. Don't let that bitch Regine spoil anything. She's like a viper in our midst.'

Then she told Vee how successful the takeaway sandwiches had been.

'Does he know?'

Vee realized she was asking if Jack had agreed to their new venture.

She was ready for that. 'He said if you lose him money he'll skin you both alive!'

Connie looked petrified.

Vee laughed. 'It's all right. Jack couldn't very well put me in charge then moan about any changes I made, could he?'

The older woman sighed. 'Every time I tried to talk to Madelaine about anything to do with the café she bit my head off. I hope you stay around for a long time. Jack's much easier to be with now you're here.' Suddenly Connie put her arms around Vee. 'You saw what a gent he was in rescuing me from the church in that air raid. If it hadn't been for Jack I might not be around to tell the tale. He saved me, despite that rogue Hugh shouting about his affair with

Madelaine. Jack's a good bloke.' She let her arms drop. 'I'm not stupid. I've known for a while that he cares for you. Please stay around and make him happy.' Connie paused. 'This business with Madelaine's not over yet, not by a long chalk. Poor Jack's likely to go through a lot of trouble before it's cleared up. Me and Rosie'll be there for him. I hope you will be too. Tell you what . . .' Connie rescued a hairpin that had come adrift '. . . why don't you come with me and Rosie this evening? There's a gangster film on at the Criterion.'

Vee said, 'I've already promised Jack I'll work with him tonight. We've come to a bit of an understanding.' She didn't want to tell Connie everything that had gone on between them, but she knew she could confide in her. 'You don't need to worry. I'll stand by him as well, Connie.'

Connie gave her a heartfelt smile. 'That's good to hear, Vee. But you take care tonight. It's clear, and I wouldn't be a bit surprised if there was another raid. Them Germans are buggers!' She looked at Ada. 'If you'll pardon my French!'

Chapter Twenty-nine

'It's been a while now since I've heard from Vee. I do hope everything's all right.'

'Knowing what you women are like, I guess you want her to help with the wedding.' Jem took off his work boots, went over to May, who was peeling potatoes at the sink, put his arms around her waist and snuggled his face into the back of her neck. 'That's only natural, my love.' He breathed in deeply. 'You smell delicious,' he said. 'Vee hasn't stopped phoning, has she? It's just been a while since you last heard her voice.'

'I suppose so,' she said, turning in his arms and kissing him full on the mouth. 'I think it's a good idea getting a special licence. At least when I do hear from her, we can be married as soon as she gets home.'

'She'll be thrilled to know she doesn't have to stay away

now everything's all right with Bertie Lang – whoops, Sammy Chesterton. I still think, though, that you should have told her he's been visiting us.'

'And if I had, she'd have thought he was out to cause trouble . . .'

Jem sighed. 'Who'd have thought a leopard can change its spots? That man's not half as bad as I thought he was.'

'We all make mistakes,' May said. 'My biggest mistake was taking you for granted all these years.'

'It's water under the bridge,' he said. 'I love you, May.'

Sammy left the car on a piece of waste ground in North Street and walked to the Central Café, which seemed the wrong name, he thought, especially as the place was on a corner. Who knew why people named things the way they did?

It was dingy inside but the tea was good and strong, thick enough for the spoon to stand up in, and it went down well. A Frank Sinatra song was blaring from the wireless. He struck up a conversation with the owner, Bert, and found out the ferry changed its crew of workers at six. The smell of bacon frying made him feel hungry, so he ate a bacon sandwich while sitting at the greasy counter and asked a few questions.

It didn't take him long to discover that Bert was no blabbermouth and would only talk of inconsequential matters.

'Don't see many women skippering a boat,' Sammy muttered, loud enough for Bert to hear. He'd already spread out the *Echo* so it looked as if he was reading the piece about the schoolboy being saved.

'P'raps we're a bit more adventurous here,' Bert said, 'than where you come from.'

Sammy knew it wasn't his accent that had told the man he was new in town – Southampton was only just up the road. His expensive clothes set him apart from the café's usual customers.

'Anyway, the women are doing all sorts now there's a war on.'

Sammy pushed his mug forward for more tea and looked around at the noisy layabouts lounging at the tables. He guessed they'd soon get their call-up papers, and be replaced by another set of youngsters pretending to be big shots.

Sammy wanted to ask if Bert knew where the girl lived. But Bert wasn't forthcoming. The one bit of information he provided was the time at which the crew changed.

Well, he'd have to go down and hang about the ferry to find out if Vee was on duty. He'd rather have been civilized and knocked at the house where she lodged, which could have resulted in a one-to-one confrontation. But it wasn't to be, so he'd have to catch her as she left the boat, if she was working. It was after nine and Bert said the ferry shut down around ten thirty. He'd have a wander around Gosport until then, he decided.

The siren started wailing as he walked past Lloyds Bank.

The main road was empty so he couldn't follow anyone to a shelter and he had no idea where the public ones were. He had two choices: carry on walking towards the ferry or go into a pub.

He wondered if the ferries stopped running during an air raid. If so, and Vee was on duty, she might go home early and then when he got to the boats he wouldn't see her. Bugger it, he'd carry on down to the water – he hadn't come this far to miss her. And if she wasn't working, maybe one of the boatmen might know where she lived.

The noise of the planes grew louder and Sammy stood in a shop doorway to watch the spectacle. Searchlights filled the sky, darting hither and thither in an effort to catch the enemy in their beams. Ack-ack fire started up from the ground forces and then the sky was lit like a huge firework display as bombs dropped from the planes to fall on Portsmouth. The night sky changed colour from black to orange as a hit was scored in what Sammy knew was the city's dockyard.

Carefully he ran down the high street, dodging from shop doorway to shop doorway. Rubble left from the previous bombing raid was piled on what remained of the pavements. He guessed the road needed to be cleared frequently for ambulances and buses. Life had to go on.

The noise was tremendous. The smell of cordite and burning filled the air, and dust stung his eyes. He paused near an alley to lean against the wall.

Suddenly he felt the wall move, heard a rumble and jumped straight out into the street again. Behind him the chimney crashed into the space he'd just vacated. The dust cloud enveloped him and he dropped to his knees. With his arms about his head he waited for something to fall on him, but after a short while he realized his luck was holding and stood up. There was noise all around him but the pounding of his heart was the loudest.

Just ahead he could see the ferry ticket office so he picked his way through the rubble to stand next to the locked door. Sammy wiped a hand across his face. Somehow he'd lost his trilby.

'We gonna make this the last trip, Skip?'

Mac had shouted up to Jack and was waiting below on the deck for his answer. Four passengers had got on to the ferry at Portsmouth. Jack glanced at his watch and shouted back, 'Yes, let's get off.'

Vee, wearing her waterproofs to keep out the cold, huddled against the wheel and stared at the huge fire burning in the dockyard.

'I wish you'd go down into the cabin,' Jack said. 'I've only just found you and I don't want you hurt.' He started the boat's engine. The passengers had gone into the cabin.

'I wouldn't like to think of you up here on your own,' Vee said. 'Anyway, it won't be long and we'll be back on the Gosport side.'

On an impulse Jack removed his peaked cap and jammed it on Vee's head.

'Aye, aye, Captain,' he said, and saluted her smartly.

The siren had started wailing as the boat docked.

Almost immediately, the sky was filled with bombers unleashing their loads. The noise of their engines and the thuds as those shells found targets was terrifying. Vee wasn't just scared, she was petrified. Never before had she been outside during a raid and at that moment she would have given anything to be inside a shelter.

The boat left the jetty, swinging out past moored craft on its journey back to Gosport. The water looked as if golden raindrops flew above the waves . . . It was shrapnel burning as it fell from the skies, hissing as it hit the water.

Below her, Mac had coiled the ropes and was standing with his back against the funnel, using it to protect him, as best as it could, from the falling fire.

She snuggled against Jack. On the way over they'd barely stopped talking. She was glad that he felt able to offload his worries on to her shoulders. He'd praised her for finding a good nanny for his daughter, and when she'd handed him back his keys, he said, 'It's not just the business I'd trust you with, but my daughter and my life, Vee.'

'I love you.' It was the first time she'd ever said those words to any man. 'And I'd like it better if we were out of the line of fire. The bombs won't stop coming.'

'Old Hitler's really giving it to us tonight.' He looked down at her, making her feel safe as, facing the sea, she leant into him.

Vee didn't see the burning shrapnel that fell against his head, face and neck until he'd given a strangled cry and slid to the floor of the wheelhouse.

It had scorched his skin, searing into his flesh, leaving it like melted candle wax before sliding down to burn on the wooden planks. The stench of singed clothing alerted her, along with his cries, and she knew she had to get rid of the burning metal before it started a fire. Had she not been wearing Jack's stout cap, scraps of the molten metal would have fallen into her hair or on to her skin.

No one was at the wheel. She glanced ahead and was relieved the boat was in open water. The shrapnel was too large for Vee to kick over the side and into the sea and she stopped herself trying – its fiery heat could hurt her.

Jack had let the wheel spin and now Vee grabbed at it. Holding it steady with one hand, she felt for the flask in the cubby-hole to use as a lever to poke the hot metal inch by inch until it fell over the side and into the water where it could do no more harm.

'Oh, Jack . . .' Her voice was hoarse, the dust in the air choking her as she threw the flask aside and tried to keep the boat steady. She managed to give a reverse signal to the engine so the boat slowed sufficiently for her to kneel and gauge Jack's injuries. The side of his head was a mess and he was unconscious, lying still and quiet. She was briefly glad he was out of it. She grabbed the wheel once more and set off for the Gosport shore.

There was no time to think, just to act. She wanted to kneel at Jack's side to watch over him – he was badly hurt and bleeding – but she daren't let go of the wheel. Obstacles in the shape of other boats in the channel appeared without warning in front of her, looming straight up in the unreal light.

'Mac!' Vee screamed. By some twist of fate he heard her voice and came running. To her it seemed that they were the only three people on the craft.

When Mac's head appeared as he climbed the ladder Vee could have kissed him.

'Jack's hurt. Take the wheel.'

Now Vee dropped to her knees. Jack was out cold. His face was charred and his neck was bleeding. Some of his hair had frizzled away. She breathed a sigh of relief that the blood didn't seem to be gushing from an artery but was dribbling from a huge wound near his ear. She blessed the bright lights searching for the overhead planes that were still droning above them. She wanted to clasp Jack to her, cradle him in her arms, but she knew she had to leave him lying on the deck while she and Mac docked the ferry.

It needed both of them to berth it. There seemed no end to the noise of fighting aircraft above her. An enemy plane was hit by ground machine-gun fire and Vee watched as it spiralled, whining, into the sea on the Portsmouth side.

'No one'll get out of that alive,' said Mac. Then he asked, 'How is he?'

'Bad,' said Vee. 'He needs the hospital. Oh, Mac,' she said, gazing up into his freckled face, 'I'm so glad you're here.' She took off her waterproof jacket and laid it over the man she loved.

The all-clear rang out as Mac was tying up the boat. Paul had disappeared when the passengers alighted on the pontoon. Vee couldn't blame him – he probably hadn't known what had occurred if he was in the cabin with them. But she was angry that he hadn't been around during the raid or shouted goodnight.

Vee was loath to move Jack, but he couldn't stay where he was. 'We need an ambulance!'

Mac waved his arm towards the jetty where people were moving again, now the bombers had passed over the town. 'It'll take ages. Probably some bad town hits to attend.'

Vee saw a man walking swiftly down the wooden pontoon. He stepped through the open exit gate and aboard the boat.

'Who on earth is that?'

But the moment the words left her mouth she recognized him.

'This is private property, mate, and there's no more trips across the harbour tonight,' Mac shouted, obviously thinking the man was a passenger.

Vee got to her feet and climbed down the ladder. She ran to Sammy Chesterton.

'I've paid in full! You got nothing on me!'

He was smiling! She couldn't believe the look on his face – he was pleased to see her!

'It's all right, Vee. I'm here for May, your mother.'

For a moment she didn't understand what he was saying. What had he to do with May?

'Why? What's wrong with her?'

'Nothing. She's marrying Jem and needs you home.' Her gasp was loud. Her cry, louder.

'Whatever's the matter?'

She had fallen against him, and the jumbled words coming from her mouth barely made sense even to her. 'Jack needs taking to hospital, now!' she finally said clearly. 'Fast.'

'Where is he?' Sammy pushed her away from him and stared into her face. His frown and silence told her he understood.

'On the boat. He's badly hurt.'

Sammy got no further than the bottom of the ladder.

'Go for transport, mate, it's fuckin' serious!' Mac shouted down to him.

Chapter Thirty

Sammy Chesterton sat beside Vee and Mac in the waiting room at the War Memorial Hospital. His warmth was comforting in the room's sterile whiteness.

There had been pandemonium in the place when Sammy had drawn up in his car and run into the foyer. Apparently Gosport had taken another severe beating from the evening raid. But within moments Jack was on a trolley being whisked away, leaving the three of them stunned, until they were offered tea and shown where to wait.

'I took Jack's keys,' said Mac. 'You've got a front-door key. I know how worried you are, so if it's all right with you, I'll arrange for the relief crew to be on hand tomorrow. Then you can stay here as long as you need to.'

'Bless you,' said Vee, now sipping her tea. She looked at Sammy. 'He'll be all right, won't he?'

'Well, he's in the best place,' Mac answered for him. 'Tell you what, I never realized what a bloody big bugger he was until we had to carry him from the boat to your motor, mate.'

Vee looked down at Sammy's cashmere coat. He'd been wearing it when he helped to carry Jack. The dark brown stains on the camel looked ugly, even more so as she knew it was Jack's blood. Sammy had eventually put it around her shoulders when he saw she was shivering with cold.

As if on cue, he said, 'I don't know what it is with your family. That's the second expensive coat you lot have ruined in less than a few weeks. I messed up the other one helping to put in a window at your mum's place. I reckon I'm going to have to order these coats by the dozen!'

Vee couldn't help a smile touching her lips. While they'd been waiting, Sammy had told her of all the happenings at home that her mother had barely had time to talk about when Vee telephoned her. From her initial fear at first setting eyes on Sammy on the pontoon, Vee now knew he wanted only to help her. She broke her silence to tell him and Mac more than she'd ever let on to her mother about her life in Gosport.

'So, you see, I'm terrified there'll be repercussions on Jack for allowing an alien to work for him.'

'We're a close-knit community on the boats, Vee,' Mac said. 'Do you think anyone would ever believe or suspect you might be a bleedin' spy?' He laughed. 'You've risked your life for Jack,' he added.

Vee didn't mention that Ada had no papers.

'I've put a lot of money into our government trying to sort out the discrepancies in the citizenship laws,' said Sammy. 'Canada is pushing ahead with naturalization reforms. It's my opinion there'll be a breakthrough before long.'

'But until then people live in fear of a knock on the door or a flaming torch being thrown through their windows!' Vee was passionate. She put down her cup with a loud bang on the small table.

'You can't blame the English for hating everything German,' Sammy said. 'Two wars are proving they've every right.'

'But it's not Germany as such, surely. It's that Hitler.' Mac was angry, his ruddy face even redder than usual. 'The sooner we beat him the better.'

'We can all agree with that,' said Sammy.

A family came to sit in the waiting room and Vee saw in Sammy's eyes that their conversation must end. The parents and two small boys looked very glum and their faces were marked by tears.

'Mac, if you want to get off home, I know you've got a lot to do sorting out the ferry. I can take Vee back to wherever she's living, then come round, telephone or whatever to let you know what's happening to Jack.' He'd barely got those words out when a nurse rustled alongside them.

'Mr Edwards is stable now. I can allow one of you to see him for a few moments.' She walked away, and Vee jumped up to follow her down the winding corridors.

'Is he going to be all right?'

The nurse, in blue and white, said, 'I can't tell you anything at the moment. Someone will talk to you before you leave. I take it you're a relative?' Vee nodded. She'd have said she was Mary Christmas if they allowed her just a peep at Jack.

Vee drew in a sharp breath. She wasn't prepared for the machine dripping blood into his body or the tiny part of his face that could be seen between the bandages covering his head and neck.

There was a chair beside the bed in the tiny room. She sat down, then searched for his hand and held it. It was cold, clammy even. She willed some of the heat from her own body to enter his, all the while knowing it was futile. 'Can you feel me loving you?' Vee murmured.

The door behind her closed and a doctor stood with notes

pinned to a clipboard that he scrutinized carefully. 'You are Mrs Edwards?'

'We live together.' It was easier than more lies, and she let the doctor make of that what he would. Besides, it was true.

Vee was surprised when he sat on the edge of the bed. 'Mr Edwards is lucky to be with us. He's had transfusions. We've got that under control, but there's not a lot we can do here at the War Memorial for the burns to his face and neck. He's pumped full of stuff to help him sleep and tomorrow we're sending him to a special burns unit that can deal with this better than we can.'

'Where?'

He consulted the notes, then looked at her kindly. 'The Queen Victoria Hospital at East Grinstead. There's a plastic surgery and burns unit there that has been pioneering the way for intensive burns and disfigurements.'

Vee was silent while she took this in. 'Is it very far? Will I be able to visit?'

'It's some thirty miles from London so, yes, I see no reason why you can't visit him.'

'Can I go with him?'

He adjusted his spectacles. 'That won't be possible, but I can give you a number to ring tomorrow. I suggest you go home now and try to rest. He's full of painkillers and it's highly unlikely he'll wake before tomorrow.'

Vee rose from the chair as a scribbled note was handed to her. She folded it carefully and put it into the pocket of Sammy's coat, which she was still wearing. Tears rose to her eyes as she looked down at Jack lying so still. Unsure where to kiss him because of the bandages, she reached again for his hand and squeezed it. But she felt no answering pressure.

Mac had decided to wait to see Vee for news of Jack so Sammy dropped him at his home before taking Vee back to the house. The roads were strewn with bricks and detritus from bombed buildings and Vee saw ARP men and helpers digging in the rubble to find loved ones and possessions. The Women's Institute were helping people recover from shock with hot tea and blankets. It was amazing, Vee thought, how everyone rallied round in emergencies.

Her head was full of Jack's suffering when Sammy pulled up outside the house.

'What's *that*?' He was looking at the car ferry moored for the night.

Vee explained, then asked if he'd like to stay at the house, which was in darkness. She knew he shouldn't drive back to Southampton – he was exhausted.

Once in the warm kitchen, she found that someone had thoughtfully banked up the fire, so she made tea. Vee was glad Sammy had stayed as she wanted advice and had decided he was the best person to offer it.

The house was silent. Vee suddenly realized that no one except herself knew about Jack. Regine, Rosie and Connie would have gone to bed after the raid, as on any normal night, and Ada was no doubt fast asleep with Peg in her cot beside her.

As she lit the gas she said, 'I need to talk to you about what's been going on here. So far, you've gathered I'm in love with Jack, but it's difficult . . .'

He listened as it all poured from her: Madelaine's death, Jack's time at the police station, his friendship with John, who was the detective now handling the case, and Regine and Paul's fraud with the ferry tickets.

'I'm sorry I stole from you. It was an isolated incident and one I've regretted. I've been terrified to tell my mother exactly where I was because I thought you'd come looking for me.'

'I might have done, had I not had such a warm welcome from your mother.' He told her that he and May had known each other at school. 'May deserves happiness with Jem

– he's a good bloke.' He grinned at her and stretched his legs out straight in front of him. 'He seems to think with her taking his name in marriage everything else goes away, but I'm not so sure. Will you and Jack tie the knot?'

Vee sighed. 'It's too soon after Madelaine's death. The murderer has to be brought to justice. There's a question mark hanging over the confession the police have had, and I'd like Mum to meet Jack and accept him, but that won't be until he's out of hospital.'

'What's not to accept? From what you've said, Jack's a decent bloke.'

'Yes, he is.' She took the tray with teapot and cups over to the fire and set them on the small table.

She told him about Peg and how she'd love to have a hand in bringing up the little girl. 'Could you imagine her on the smallholding cramming strawberries into her mouth on a hot sunny day in June?' They smiled at the thought. Vee knew her mother would adore the little girl.

'You do understand that it'll be a long haul before Jack is able to leave hospital? When he does, have you thought how you'll cope with . . . with . . .'

'He's not going to be the same. I do realize that.' Vee pushed a full cup towards Sammy.

'I've heard that the hospital at East Grinstead makes sure

its patients can integrate with society again, especially when heavy scarring might remain.'

'I don't love him for his looks. I love him for the person he is.' She was adamant.

'Jack's going to need all the love he can get,' Sammy said. 'But it will be how he feels about himself that matters most. Some people get very depressed.'

Vee looked into Sammy's eyes. She wondered why she had never given him the chance to listen to her before. Maybe if she'd told him straight out she didn't intend to sleep with him, or indeed anyone, until she had a ring on her finger, there was every possibility they could have come to some other arrangement over payment for the forged documents. On an impulse she asked, 'Do you provide many forged papers?' She drank some tea, relishing the renewed strength it gave her.

He gave her a knowing smile and tapped the side of his nose. 'You have no idea how many upper-class people have a German skeleton rattling in their closet and don't want anyone to find out . . .'

'Really?'

'Yes, really. And a few revered cabinet ministers need a change in the law before their true identities are forth-coming. These men love England . . .'

'Really?' said Vee again.

'That's all I'm saying on the matter,' said Sammy, 'but I've got an idea what to do about the missing ticket money.'

'What? Please tell me! It would be wonderful if I could sort that out for Jack.'

'Let me sleep on it.'

Vee left Sammy drinking his tea and went into Jack's room where she was delighted to discover someone had changed the bed linen. It looked tidy, different. She noticed a suitcase on the floor in the corner and guessed someone had packed up Madelaine's clothing. On opening the wardrobe door, she saw only Jack's clothes hanging there.

She dragged Sammy into the bedroom. 'No sofa for you. This is Jack's room. Sleep tight.' She turned to go, then looked round shyly at him. 'I'm really happy for Mum and Jem,' she said, 'and so glad you came to find me.'

Chapter Thirty-one

'Does that mean you're in charge again, Vee?' Connie was wiping her eyes after being told about Jack being sent to the burns unit. She was eager to know who to go to with any problems now she'd been assured Jack wasn't going to die.

The kitchen smelt of toast and was warm and cosy. Peg was sitting in her high chair with a cushion at her back to stop her sliding. She had a bowl of mush in front of her and was using the spoon to bang on the table top. A lump of wet rusk was stuck in her hair.

Vee had already decided that one person had to make sure everything carried on in an orderly fashion, both in the house and at work. 'I will be, if that's all right with you lot.'

Nods of assent came from Ada, Rosie and Connie, but Regine said, 'You take too much on yourself. You've only been working here five minutes.'

'Until we hear differently from Jack I'll carry on as I did when he'd been taken in for questioning by the police. Tonight we'll discuss this further, all right?'

Sammy had gone out; he'd said he needed some fresh air and wouldn't be too long.

She thought if she got them all together later they could put forward any queries. In the meantime she'd follow up on Jack's progress, make arrangements to visit him and, with help from Mac and the other crew, sort out a new strategy for work.

'I don't have a skipper's certificate of competence to steer the ferry legally,' she said to Ada, when the girls had all gone to work and she was left with Ada and Peg. 'If Jack's likely to be in hospital some time I'll need to make an arrangement with the bank to pay the wages . . .'

Mac had popped in first thing and told her the other crew were ready to work whatever hours were needed to keep the ferries running. Vee was happy about this and, through him, had arranged a meeting with Si. If everything went according to plan, Sammy's plan, they were going to be not only minus Jack but Regine and Paul as well.

'Thank God Jack made me do a stint working at all aspects of the job,' Vee said. 'If Regine goes, I'll step into the breach selling tickets, and maybe Si can come up with a replacement for Paul.'

She had just begun cleaning up Peg so Ada could eat some breakfast in peace when Sammy knocked on the street door. Ada let him in. It hadn't escaped Vee's notice that Ada was tongue-tied whenever she tried to speak to Sammy.

'Whew, it's cold out there,' said Sammy, putting his hands to the fire's warmth. He took off his coat and threw it over the back of a chair.

'Well?' began Vee. 'Tell us what happened.'

'I finally got to see John Cousins and he's agreed to come round tonight.'

Vee frowned. 'I know Regine's going to implicate me . . .'

'That's a foregone conclusion. But if that detective is any good, and if he believes Jack to be as straight a man as he thinks he is, all you do is look surprised and say she's lying.'

'But what if he wants to check my papers?'

'Let him. I've been selling forgeries for long enough to know that my mate supplies the real deal. Why, there's a few in Westminster knows that . . .'

Vee felt better. She looked at Ada, busy making tea for Sammy. Already Peg's eyes were drooping. She lifted her from the high chair, kissed the soft spot on her head and handed her to Ada. She loved the baby's milky, talcum-powder smell. In such a short time Peg had made her way deep into Vee's heart.

'I'll take her out for a walk. She'll sleep better in the fresh air,' said Ada. 'Save me a cuppa. Oh, I wish we had some bourbon biscuits to go with the tea. They're my favourites and I haven't seen one for ages.'

'You're not the only one,' said Vee. 'I'll phone and find out how Jack is.'

'And as you won't be needing me until tonight I'll drive back to Netley and put your mother in the picture,' Sammy said. 'I'm sure she's been worrying long enough.'

Vee spent part of the day going through Jack's books and bringing his paperwork up to date. She was astonished by how much work she could get through when someone else was looking after Peg. In the afternoon, though, she told Ada to take some time off because she missed being with the little girl.

'Sammy is coming back tonight, isn't he?' Ada asked.

'I think you've got a twinkle in your eye for him,' Vee said jokingly. But no one was more surprised than her when Ada coloured.

'You have!' Vee giggled. She laid Peg on her lap and began to change her wet nappy. Halfway through she sat back and watched Peg kicking. 'Who's a clever little Peg, then?'

'Just because I asked about him doesn't mean anything,' Ada said.

'Then why has your face gone even more cherry-coloured?'

'He doesn't act like he's an older man, and he certainly doesn't look old.'

'That's because he's well off.'

Vee was surprised to see tears in Ada's eyes.

'Then he definitely won't want to have anything to do with me. I've got bugger-all.' Ada turned to Peg. 'Sorry for swearing, my love.'

'If he didn't have any money, would you still fancy him?'

'Yes. I like older men. Young ones are only interested in getting drunk and showing off.'

Vee thought about Jack. He wasn't old, but he wasn't like that. Then again, she'd hardly been around him long enough to find out what his bad points were, had she? She thought for a bit. 'I think if you really love someone you take the good with the bad, don't you? But I do agree that older men are generally more settled.'

'I look at him and he makes me want to cuddle him. I don't believe he's settled at all. Why hasn't he married?'

'From what I gathered at the Black Cat, he's travelled, done a lot of stuff on his own, but that doesn't mean he hasn't had a lot of women. When I worked at that club he only had to snap his fingers and the girls came running.'

'I think he's lonely.'

'Don't talk daft! There was this girl in the club who used to go out with him. Greta, her name was. She was quite fond of him. He used to buy her things . . .' Vee stood Peg up on her feet.

'See what I mean?' Ada said. 'He bought Greta's affection. Blokes who do that can't believe women could love them for themselves.' Ada took the wet nappy, went to the tap, rinsed it and dropped it into the bucket beneath the sink. 'And don't think I fancy him because I'm hoping he can get me forged papers. I've got this far on my own during the war and I'll get on with the rest of it!'

'All right,' said Vee. 'I believe you. But you can't rush love, can you?' She looked at the clock above the mantelpiece. 'I don't know about you but I'm hungry again. Worrying about Jack doesn't make me feel any better. Shall we go round to the café and get something hot to eat? We can see how their sandwich venture's going, can't we?'

When Vee and Ada walked in with Peg, it was as if the customers had never seen a baby before. Wide-eyed, little Peg was taking it all in as fingers and faces came from all directions. 'Isn't she a little beauty?' A Glenn Miller song was playing on the wireless and people were crowding around Vee, asking about Jack. It hadn't taken long for the jungle drums to beat in Gosport and Jack was well liked.

Connie dished up Vee's favourite egg and chips with thick doorsteps of crusty bread. Vee was becoming tired of people congratulating her on bringing in the boat. She hated being in the limelight, so when Peg gave a wail as yet another bus conductress filled the pram with her face, Vee said, 'I've had enough, I'm off.'

'You only popped in to see if our sandwich idea was going well.' Connie grinned at her. The poor woman's face was sweaty and her hair had tumbled down from its curly topknot.

Vee had already noted the paper bags on the counter with the contents scrawled on them and she'd seen them fast disappearing. She made a mental note to see if she could buy some bags from the wholesaler with see-through sides to show the tasty fillings to their best advantage. Paper was difficult to get hold of, but she thought she might be lucky.

'Wait till we bring home the takings. I think you'll be very surprised,' Connie said. 'And very pleased.' Then she asked, 'When are you going to see Jack?'

'Do you want more tea before you go?' Rosie interrupted.

Vee shook her head.

'Tomorrow. He's awake and he's expecting me.' The tingle started in her toes and worked its way through her at the expectation of seeing Jack. A phone call earlier to the War

Memorial had confirmed he was stable and could have visitors once he'd settled in at the Queen Victoria.

'I expect you miss him,' said Rosie. 'Well, we all do.' She was trying to pacify Peg, who had got fed up and was bawling.

As Ada wiped her plate with a piece of bread, mopping up the egg, she said, 'Peg'll be having nightmares about all these people poking her. We should take her home.'

'Thank God someone's on the same wavelength as me,' said Vee, looking at the wall clock. It wouldn't be long before Sammy came back to Gosport with news from her mother.

When Vee and Ada reached the house, Regine was in the bath.

Vee knocked softly on the bathroom door. 'Don't forget we're having a chat about the future tonight.'

'I hadn't forgotten,' came the clipped reply. 'There's one or two things I'm not happy about.'

Me too, thought Vee.

Later, John arrived with a constable in uniform. Vee wasn't expecting that. He caught up with her in the hallway.

'I have to go to East Grinstead tomorrow, so if you're planning to visit him, I can give you a lift. It'll save you bothering with trains and buses.'

'Does he know you're going?'

'Yes, it's police business. I've been assured by the surgeon he'll be up and about, getting used to the place. After all, there's nothing wrong with his legs, they said. They plan on operating over the weekend. Then the fun begins.' He made a sympathetic face at her.

'I'd love to come with you,' Vee said. She liked John. He was a kind, understanding man. It was easy to see why he and Jack had been friends for so long.

Shortly afterwards Sammy knocked at the door and came in, carrying a large bag in which there was a huge cake. He handed it to Vee.

She stared at his smart camel coat. 'Is that new?'

He nodded. 'I wonder how long this one will last . . . Your mother made the cake this morning for the next meeting of her Women's Institute. When I said I was coming back to you she made me bring it. Said she expected you were getting skinny without her cooking.'

'Wish I had a mother like that,' said Ada.

'I wish I had someone to make me cakes,' said Sammy. Vee saw him look at Ada as though he hadn't noticed her before but liked what he was seeing now.

Ada put Peg to bed and it wasn't long before Regine appeared, all pink from her bath. Vee could smell the fragrance of her bath salts. She'd put her hair in pin curls and had tied a chiffon scarf around her head. As soon as she came into the kitchen and saw the constable she blushed. Vee knew she hated to be caught without her make-up.

'Why didn't you tell me we had visitors?' She put her handbag down at her feet. She stared at John. 'Any movement on Madelaine's death?'

'Actually, there is,' he said. 'The post mortem shows she hit her head when she fell. That was what killed her. But there was skin beneath her fingernails and bruising to her body so it looks as if she had a fight with someone shortly beforehand.'

The room went silent. It was as if each of the people in that kitchen was in a world of their own, thought Vee. To break the silence she got up and went to the stove to make tea. While she was doing that, she listened to the conversations going on around her. John and Sammy seemed to have a lot to say to each other but their voices were indistinct. Regine had stood a small hand mirror in front of the sugar bowl and was attempting to put on mascara with the little blue brush she kept in her handbag. Vee thought her mother would have had a heart attack if she'd done that. May said putting on make-up should be private, never done in public.

She made the tea in the big earthenware teapot, then put it

in the centre of the table along with milk in a jug. After she'd produced a large knife and laid it on top of the cake, she set down a tray of crockery. Looking at the cake, she sighed. In her mind's eye, she could see May getting everything ready in their kitchen for baking. She imagined the smell while the cake was in the oven, filling the room. She missed her mother so much and gulped back a tear.

Then she sat at the table between Sammy and Ada, facing Regine.

'Have you got Hugh in the cells?' Vee asked, rising quickly again, like a jack-in-the-box. She pulled out a tall stool and beckoned the uniformed policeman to sit, but he refused. She shrugged. John caught her eye and frowned. Vee realized the constable was there on duty, ready to be a witness to anything that might occur, not as a guest.

John said, 'We've let him go.'

There were several intakes of breath.

'I thought he confessed?' Vee said.

'So he did, but he did it to protect his wife.' John drummed his fingers on the table. He was wearing cufflinks that glittered. His shirt was very white against his well-cut dark suit.

'Are you allowed to tell us this?' Sammy queried.

Vee was mulling over his words.

'The press were in attendance. It'll be on the evening news tomorrow,' said John, 'so why not?'

'Come on, then.' Regine seemed very interested. She spat on her brush and ran it along the cake of black mascara. 'Tell us everything.'

'Apparently the scene in the church at the christening was relayed to Hugh's wife, Eleanor. The poor woman was at the end of her tether. If you remember, when the church caught that bomb we all ran for the pub. Madelaine and Hugh disappeared, and Mrs Carter, Madelaine's mother, went telling tales. Eleanor had stood by that bounder knowing he was seeing Madelaine and hoping the affair would fizzle out because they have two little girls. She knew nothing of Peg.'

'Jack always said Madelaine's mother was a cow,' Rosie said.

'Well, Jack was right,' Connie said. She started pouring tea for everyone, then sliced the cake and set pieces on small plates. Its rich smell filled the room.

John added, 'Finding out that Peg was her husband's child sent his wife over the edge. She came into Gosport looking for Madelaine, who had come back alone to this house feeling sorry for herself. When she answered the door, no doubt expecting to see Hugh, and instead found Eleanor

377

screaming at her, she went out the back and down to the air-raid shelter. She didn't want anyone else returning to the house and witnessing the row. The upshot of it all was that they argued, fought, and Madelaine was knocked down, hitting her head.'

'And her body was just left there?' Vee could hardly believe it. She took a bite of her mother's cake. It was every bit as delicious as she'd known it would be. She caught Sammy's eye and his wink told her he found it delicious too.

'Apparently so,' John said. 'You have to remember Hugh's wife was in a right state. She went home and tried to act normal, believe it or not.'

Vee could hardly believe it. 'And we stumbled on Madelaine's body when the next raid began.'

'What I don't understand is why Hugh confessed.' Connie was trying to pin up her wayward hair, without much success.

'Hugh probably did the only honourable thing he's ever done in his life. After he found out Madelaine was dead, he came down to the station and told us he'd hit her and killed her. He made up a story about her flying at him because he'd called out in church that Peg belonged to him. Apparently Madelaine had been on at him to admit to being Peg's father and she wanted him to take her away from Gosport, away from Jack. Of course, without his wife's money the bloke was stony broke.' John paused to drink some of his tea. 'But that's love for you.'

Again there was silence. Vee knew each person was contemplating what had happened.

'So how come his wife's in custody? Your mum makes scrummy cakes,' said Rosie.

'The post mortem showed Hugh was lying. He couldn't have hit Madelaine and killed her. It had to have been a fall on a sharp item, like the top of that garden heater in the shelter.' John motioned to Vee that he'd like more tea. She nodded as he added, 'Hugh's wife broke down and confessed. She still loves him, you see, despite everything. She was grateful he cared enough for her to try to take the rap. She's a mess, poor woman.' He sighed.

'How will the judge deal with her?' Connie asked.

Vee could see she was distraught that Eleanor had been forced to take things into her own hands to stop her husband's affair.

'The judge and jury will take everything into consideration. There are also Hugh's two girls to consider.' He peered at his watch, then at the faces around the table. 'I think we'd better get on with what's next on the agenda.' He picked up his cup and drank the tea. Then he got up and walked round to Regine, who stared at him in amazement as he took the eye make-up brush from her fingers.

'I presume you were going to bed, so why doll yourself up?'

Regine obviously thought the detective was flirting with her, for she said coquettishly, 'Well, I never know who I might meet in my dreams.'

Rosie laughed and Connie smiled, but John said, very seriously, 'You'll not be meeting many men where you're going. I'm arresting you for stealing from the Gosport Ferry Company.'

Regine's face was a picture.

The uniformed policeman was now standing at Regine's side too. He removed handcuffs from his pocket, but John said, 'I think she'll come quietly, without any need for those bracelets.'

He'd hardly got the words out when Regine stood up and yelled, 'You can't prove a thing! If you want a real villain, try taking her down the station! She's a German!' She pointed at Vee, who closed her eyes at the invective now being hurled at her.

After a while she composed herself and stood up.

'I am not a spy,' she said calmly. 'You're trying to deflect the blame.'

'On second thoughts, cuff her,' said John. 'Can you come with me now, Vee?'

Vee's heart was racing. Surely he didn't believe Regine's words. She breathed a sigh of relief when John added quickly, 'We'll need a statement, Vee. We'll also pick up her accomplice.'

'I'm coming with you,' said Sammy. Rosie and Connie were speechless.

'You don't have to,' Vee said, hoping against hope that Sammy would take no notice of her. She needed him by her side.

'I think I do,' Sammy said, rising. 'The rest of you will be all right, yes?'

Connie found her voice. 'Well I never!'

Ada said kindly, 'You ought to let Regine get dressed – she can't go out in her nightwear.'

It was gone midnight when a police car dropped Sammy and Vee outside the house. Inside, no one had gone to bed because they were worried about Vee and wanted to know what was going on.

'Regine's been charged,' said Vee, practically collapsing on to a chair at the table after taking off her coat.

'Rosie, kettle,' commanded Connie, and fresh tea was made.

'We'll be out of leaves at this rate and gasping by the time the government gives us the extra for Christmas,' said Vee.

'Oh, I forgot,' said Sammy, and took from his new cashmere coat's deep pockets three packets of Brooke Bond Green Dividend tea with the orange stamps on the packets. 'Meant to hand that to you when I arrived earlier but I didn't want that detective bloke thinking I was breaking the law,' he said. He hung his coat on the back of the door.

Connie pounced on the tea.

He delved into his other pocket and brought out a large blue sugar bag, 'Look in there, Ada.'

She needed no second bidding and gave a little scream when she saw what was inside. Then she came to Sammy and threw her arms around his neck.

'You are bloody lovely.' She kissed his cheek, and Sammy actually blushed.

Ada bit into a bourbon biscuit and gave a sigh of ecstasy. 'You remembered,' she said, through crumbs.

'You told me they're your favourites,' Sammy reminded her.

Vee caught Ada's eye and winked.

Then she told them what had gone on at the police station: she'd signed a statement saying she'd seen Regine taking clean used tickets from her bag and putting the money for them in a jar in the ticket office.

'Regine told them straight out that she was in partnership with Paul, who saved the tickets he'd previously not clipped. She didn't want to be charged without them knowing all about him,' she said. 'She really is a horrible person.'

'Did they just take your word for it that when you'd been working with her she'd reused the tickets?' Rosie asked.

'Ah!' said Sammy. 'All along she was denying everything, saying there was no proof and that Vee was lying. But the silly girl slipped up. A policewoman came in and took her into another room where she was searched. When her handbag was opened, there was a load of unused tickets inside it!'

Chapter Thirty-two

Jack sat in the rose garden, trying to read Nathanael West's *The Day of the Locust*. It had been on his reading list for a while, but now he had it in his hands he couldn't concentrate on the words. They kept running into one another. He put it down on the seat beside him. Anyway, he wanted to move the bandage away from one of his eyes so the damned white material wasn't obscuring his vision. He had been told by a young nurse that he must not on any account touch his face or neck.

He'd had no idea where he was when he woke in a single room. And then he'd kept falling asleep again until a pretty young nurse popped her head around the door and told him he'd been brought there from Gosport's War Memorial Hospital. She'd given him an injection and he'd slept some more.

He felt no pain. He'd been drinking tea through a straw when a well-built tall doctor had practically filled all the space in his room and explained that they were going to operate as soon as they'd assessed him.

God knew what they were pumping into him, but every time he thought about the ferry and began to wonder what was going on, his thoughts faded into nothingness and he slept.

'Do you remember what happened?' the doctor had asked, catching him awake one morning. Jack had looked at the tall man in a white coat with a stethoscope around his neck. 'I had my hands on the wheel and then nothing.'

Vee's face wouldn't go away. He remembered the worry in her eyes. Instead he thought about Peg and her tiny new teeth, which brought a smile to his heart. Ada seemed the perfect person to look after Peg, but he honestly didn't know how such a little thing had stolen his heart as she had. How could she not be his daughter? He was the one who got up in the night and held her rigid little body when she screamed so that gradually the tears stopped and her little arms and legs relaxed again. Jack was crying. He wanted to hold his daughter now, *his* daughter.

It was all such a bloody mess. Vee's face floated before him again. He'd tried not to fall for her, he really had. She was bright and funny and she got on with things. She never knew he'd watched her with Peg, her arms around the little girl and his Peg leaning into her, safe and relaxed. Babies know a lot. Peg knew she was safe with Vee. Oh, she'd known she wasn't safe with her mother. That was why she'd cried all the time, and you couldn't blame her for it. In a way he was glad Madelaine was gone. He shouldn't wish harm on anyone – but why had his wife taken out her unhappiness on a baby? Madelaine had deceived him and he had been a bloody fool. And look at him now. He had nothing to give Vee. He'd never be able to bring himself to touch her, however much he desired her. He was going to be grotesque. 'You might need another operation,' he'd been told. He was a mess, his life was a mess. There was only one thing he could do and he was going to do it.

And now his head fell to his chest and he slept again.

'You've got visitors.' His shoulder was being shaken gently, and Jack opened his eyes to see Vee sitting on the bench by his side. The nurse made to move away, adding, 'Better your other friend comes in later. Too much too soon and all that.'

So John was here. Good. He had a great deal he wanted to discuss with him, but meanwhile it was better to get it all out in the open.

'These gardens are lovely.'

God, he loved the sound of her voice.

He nodded as best he could. There were so many dressings that he thought when they were taken away his head might fall off. Good. There was still no pain. The sleep had reinforced his decision. It was for her own good.

He looked down at the blue and white candlewick dressing-gown beneath which were white pyjamas, washed and bleached so many times he wondered what their original colour had been. Then his eyes found hers. She wasn't smiling. It was almost as if she knew what he was going to say. This lovely girl needed so much more than he could ever give her.

Vee leant in towards him and found his hand. Her touch was like a million fireflies lighting his body, his heart, his brain. He didn't want to, but for her sake he had to do this.

'I've been a fool.' His voice didn't sound as if it belonged to him. A frown had appeared on Vee's beautiful forehead. He swallowed. 'I've got to let you go.'

She hadn't moved! She hadn't spoken! Perhaps Vee hadn't heard him. 'It's got to stop, now, before I hurt you any more.'

Dear God this was killing him. His guts were twisted into knots. He pulled his hand away from hers, roughly, so that her hand remained palm upwards, her fingers splayed open.

And then he watched as those fingers curled inwards and her hand moved from him to the seat of the wooden bench. Using her arm as a lever, she pushed herself upright and, without even a second glance at him, walked across the grass towards the hospital building. He saw her shoulders move. He thought she might be crying.

But he had done it. He had given her back her life.

'That was quick.' John put down the magazine he'd been thumbing through. He longed for the magazines of before the war when there had been oodles to read and pictures galore. The paper shortage had put paid to decent reading matter.

Vee's high heels stopped clacking on the tiles as she slumped down next to him. He hadn't been a copper all these years not to know immediately when something was wrong, very wrong. Mind, you, the girl hadn't been chatty on the way up in the car. He wondered if it was because she expected him to come out with the words 'forged papers'? Didn't have to be a genius for him to see she was scared of something, so he'd made it his business to look into Sammy Chesterton and all his legal and illegal dealings. A few phone calls, a few words here and there, and he'd discovered her heritage was sound as a bell. Vee was just another person caught up in the country's red tape, which was slowly strangling honest, decent people. And Sammy Chesterton? As long as the bloke kept his nose clean around this area, what he got up to in Southampton was nothing to do with John. Besides, he admired the chap. Sammy Chesterton had built an empire from nothing.

'You'd better go in now.' Vee's voice was hardly more than a whisper. Her face was swollen from crying.

'He's upset you. How?'

She shook her head. 'Please leave me. I don't want you to see me . . .'

But she did cry again.

It was an automatic gesture to pull her to his side for comfort and to put his arm around her shoulders. He let her sob into his jacket. After a while the sobbing turned to sniffs, a few hiccups.

'He's given you your marching orders, hasn't he?'

She looked through a curtain of hair. 'Did you know?'

'Of course not! You're the best thing that's happened to him . . .' He felt in his pocket, pulled out a crumpled handkerchief and gave it to her. It wasn't clean. What could he expect with his missus living at Lee-on-the Solent looking after her mother when she should be in Gosport looking after him? Vee didn't seem to mind though, and wiped her eyes, leaving trails of black mascara on the white cotton. He got up, leaving her sitting and sniffing, and walked along the corridor to where a nurse stood marking a clipboard.

'Excuse me, my friend, the lady around the corner,' he waved an arm expansively, 'badly needs a cup of tea. Could you sort her out?'

Expecting a put-down he was surprised and pleased when she said, 'Show me?'

Together they walked back to where Vee was sitting in exactly the same position as before. The young nurse quickly assessed the situation. 'Stay there, I'll get tea.'

John said to Vee, 'You really do love him, don't you?' He didn't wait for an answer but strode back down the corridor, through the front door, down the steps and out into the gardens.

When John reached his friend, his first thought was that he looked like a snowman with his head and neck swaddled in white bandages. He could see one eye and that eye was shedding the tears that had made his dressings damp.

'Do you realize what you've done?' There was no need to explain what he was on about as they both knew John had come from Vee.

'I did it for her.'

'You did fuck-all for her! That woman saved your life,

saved your home-life, and if it wasn't for her, I wouldn't have two thieves in the cells who've been bleeding you dry!'

John could see the amazement on his friend's face. Before Jack had a chance to ask any questions he waded in again: 'You didn't give her time to tell you anything, just discarded her like an empty fag packet. Try talking! Try finding out she brought that bloody ferry in through fallin' shrapnel and got you to hospital. Try talking about how she's been running around like a blue-arsed fly doing your job for you.' He poked Jack with his fingers. 'Try asking yourself what you've got that makes a woman like that do what she's done for you. She's worth a thousand bloody Madelaines. What's wrong with you?'

Jack was breathing quickly. 'I didn't know . . .'

'Of course you didn't because all you're thinking about is yourself!' Before Jack had a chance to say anything, John added, 'So, you'll be scarred. So bloody what? There's young pilots coming home much worse off than you – legless, armless, blind. This war's taken men's lives and all you can do is sit here and whine, "I did it for her sake"?' He barely stopped for breath before he added, 'Ask yourself why that girl's already taken so much shit from you and the answer is *she loves you.*'

He began to walk away, then glanced back. 'I came to tell you most of what you've just heard. I've had enough, mate. We'll talk again later, all right?' He continued to stalk across the grass.

'Tell Vee I'm sorry . . .'

John stopped. He turned. 'You tell her.'

When he reached Vee she was still sitting alone, but he could see a young lad pushing a squeaking tea trolley towards them down the corridor. It was moving unevenly and it was then he noticed the lad had only one arm. He caught up with him.

'Got one for me? I could do with a cuppa,' he said.

The boy halted.

On the trolley there was a mixture of used and unused mugs, a big sugar bowl and a metal jug that John supposed contained milk. In the sugar bowl there was a spoon, covered with tea and brown sugar.

'Like that, is it?' The lad picked up the large brown pot and poured tea carefully into a clean mug. He was slow but methodical. 'I can feel the anger coming off you in waves,' he said. 'Help yourself to milk – sorry all the biscuits are gone. Gotta be quick at them. Load of gannets, this lot is.'

John said, 'Why can't some people see the woods? Is it because the trees are in the way?'

The boy grinned. 'Tell me about it. Some people are simply blind to everything. This place opened my eyes. You want sugar with that?'

'If you go without sugar for long enough, you don't want it any more.'

'That could be said of a lot of things.' The lad shrugged his shoulder and the empty sleeve flapped. 'I'm getting a prosthesis next week. Wish me luck.'

John said, 'Ever thought you're already one of the lucky ones?'

'A hundred times a day, mate, a hundred times a day.' And the trolley trundled off down the corridor, squeaking as it went.

John sipped his tea and thought about what he'd done.

He'd let rip at his friend when none of it was his business. But it was obvious Jack knew nothing of how he'd come to be at the hospital. Probably since then he'd been too doped up to think straight. But he was one selfish bastard if he thought by letting Vee go he was doing the right thing for her. He'd known Jack for a long time and the best thing that ever happened to him was that girl breezing into his life.

He'd never have expected in a thousand years that the silly bugger would send her packing. Never.

John had driven up today to let Jack know the result of

the inquest on his wife. Now the body could be released for burial. It was up to Jack what he wanted to do about a funeral. That bounder Hugh seemed to have gone to ground. John had sent a uniform round to tell him to come and collect his missus as she'd be released on bail pending doctors' reports, but a neighbour reckoned he was in Cornwall with his kiddies. John hoped he'd take more notice of them than he had of little Peg.

He'd been in touch with the other ferry crew, only to be told by Simon Chandler that 'Young Vee has it all in hand.' And that grumpy old bugger didn't take to many people but seemed full of praise for her. He drank the rest of his tea and left the mug on a marble sconce that held a display of twigs and berries. Someone would discover it next to the ashtray full of butts.

Should he go back out into the gardens and talk to Jack? As soon as that thought entered his head, the anger returned. No, he'd take the poor girl home. Let her decide what she wanted to do. There was a house full of women to look after her back in Gosport. It was at times like this, too, that he needed his Emily at home. Still, only another couple of weeks and her mother would be on her feet again.

John began walking down the long empty corridor to find Vee, his leather shoes tapping loudly on the black and white tiles. It was already dark outside now the days were short and it was so near Christmas. It was cold too – he could see condensation rising on the windows. He wouldn't mind betting the staff had this place looking really homely at Christmas. He'd made enquiries about the Queen Victoria Hospital and Jack couldn't have been in a better place.

John rounded the corner. He stopped in amazement. A warm feeling began moving from his heart throughout his body. What had he said to Jack? Tell Vee yourself? Well, he was doing more than talking to her now.

He'd never seen a woman put one foot out in the air behind her when some bloke was kissing her. Vee was snuggled against Jack and there wasn't room to put a bleedin' pin between them.

Chapter Thirty-three

1946

'Taste, Nanny, taste.' May allowed five-year-old Peg to jam another ruby red strawberry against her mouth, which was already running with juice.

'Yum-yum,' she said, then put her arms around the little girl and turned her in a neat somersault so that she shrieked with pure joy.

'You'll make her sick, Mum, after all those strawberries she's eaten.' Vee, sitting in the shade, fanned her face with the local newspaper. It was hot, one of the hottest days ever, surely.

'Didn't do you any harm, did it?' said May. The little girl, tired now, lay across May's knees and she was rubbing her back in a circular motion.

'She'll be asleep soon,' said Vee, gazing around the field at the rows of strawberry plants at the end of their season. The sky was a deep blue above the green of the plants and the trees surrounding the field, and the air smelt of strawberries and earth, a wonderful combination. In the shade beneath a deckchair, Cat lay asleep, her head on her paws.

'Are you going to wake him?'

May nodded towards Vee's husband, sprawled in a deck-chair fast asleep.

Vee looked at Jack, at his puckered neck and cheek, which were tanned like the rest of him. She rose with difficulty from her own deckchair, picked up the large handkerchief from the table and placed it over the side of his face where the scar was to keep the sun off it.

Even now, after all this time, his skin was too thin to take much sun. On the boat he wore roll-neck sweaters and his hat shaded his face. Every time she remembered the fateful night when she had almost lost him she shuddered with fear, and now was no exception. Jack didn't wake: he snorted, then continued sleeping. Vee smiled at the man she loved.

'No, I'll let him sleep. Not often he gets the chance to relax.' She yawned. 'The sun's so strong today.'

'Isn't it lovely?' May said. Then she sniffed. 'It's about time my husband came back with that teapot. Why do men take longer to do things than we do?'

'I heard a car earlier. I wouldn't mind betting you have a visitor and you know what it's like when Jem and Sammy get yacking. Anyway, it's nice sitting out here with you. Jack needed a break for a few days and where better to come than the country?' From the house they could hear faint music from the wireless, the Merry Macs singing 'Sentimental Journey'.

'I wish you'd take things easier, my girl. The pair of you work so hard.' Vee noted her mother had gone into parent mode, but she didn't mind: it showed how much she cared about her, about all of them.

'What better than to have a husband who loves his work? And you have to admit working alongside him I get to see more of the man I love than most wives.'

May sniffed. 'Are you still in the ticket office most days?'

'Yes,' Vee said. 'I like it. Anyway, it won't be for much longer.' She liked passing the time of day with the customers while she handed them their ferry tickets.

'I hope not.'

Vee smiled at her mother. She felt healthier now than she'd ever done. She picked at a mark on her arm, realized it was a freckle, then said, 'Sammy's coming round to let us know whether he's managed to persuade the Hamble

Boatyard that Connie's sandwiches are better than the food they've been buying in from Southampton.'

'I hope you mean "persuade" and not "threaten"!'

'Oh, Mum, you know Connie's made a big success of selling sandwiches to factories. Since the war ended, life's been on the up for us all.'

'I know, love, and no one's happier for you all than I am. Connie's visit to Australia to see her new granddaughter did her the world of good, and I never thought Rosie would turn out to be quite the businesswoman and driving a van.' She began to laugh. 'Remember those driving lessons Jem started giving her? She frightened the life out of him. He said he'd rather pay for her to have professional ones than ever get in a car with her again!'

'I remember how white he was climbing out of that vehicle. He couldn't walk straight and he was sick on the grass verge!'

A voice behind them shook them both from their laughter. 'Tea's up.'

The two newcomers, both in shirtsleeves, stood each with a tray. Jem had a folded card table beneath his arm and was trying hard to let neither the tray nor the table slip. Sammy's tray was bursting with sandwiches and cakes, and Jem's held the big brown teapot, milk, sugar, cups and saucers.

'Ooh,' said Vee. 'Is that your chocolate cake?'

May said, 'Don't go filling up Peg with it. It's too rich and it'll make her sick. Just give her a little bit.'

All the noise had woken Jack, who opened one eye, took in the situation and winked at Vee. She winked back and he gave her a beautiful smile, then said, 'C'mon, Sammy, pour out the tea. I like being waited on!'

'You lazy git!' Sammy took aim at his outstretched leg with the toe of his polished shoe.

'Stop that!' May's voice rang out and Peg woke with a snuffle.

'Oh, darling, did nasty Nanny shout and wake you up?' Vee was laughing as she leant forward as far as she could and slid the little girl from May's lap to her own.

Peg snuggled down again but after a second or two she struggled up and said sleepily, 'There's chocolate cake.'

'Take this, May.' Jem managed to pass his tray to his wife. 'I'm not putting it down on the ground. There's ants the size of cows waiting to pounce on the food.'

May said, 'Don't exaggerate, dear. You'll scare Peg.'

As soon as the tray had left his hands, Jem shook out the card table and secured its feet. Promptly, Sammy put down the tray of food and May rose, set down Jem's tray and began to pour tea.

'How did it go with the sandwiches?' Jack leaned forward and brushed his hand through his dark curls. The handkerchief slid to the ground and he picked it up, smiling at Vee, knowing she'd covered his scar from the sun.

'Sweet as a nut, mate. The only problem is they want them by seven thirty in the mornings . . .'

Jack frowned. 'I don't think that's possible. Those two girls are run off their feet at that time.'

'Hold your horses,' Sammy broke in. 'I was talking to Mac and he said his younger brother's home from the war.'

'Poor bugger's disabled.'

'He lost an arm, Jack, not his head!' Sammy's voice rose. 'He can drive. That's what he was doing in France in the Tank Regiment. Give the poor bloke a chance.'

'That's you told off,' Vee said. 'I'm willing to bet he could make himself useful in other ways.'

'Fair enough. I'll have a word,' said Jack.

'I want cake!' The little voice cut through the sounds of chatter, birdsong and rustling leaves.

'I want cake *please*,' said May, handing Peg a small piece on a plate. Peg reached for the cake and left May holding the plate. She tutted and Vee laughed.

'Say thank you to Nanny,' she admonished the child, and through a mouthful of cake, Peg said, 'Fank you, Nanny.'

She swallowed quickly, then mumbled, 'I like you better than my other nanny.'

Sammy said, 'So Madelaine's parents do visit?'

'Not often, but it's fair that Peg knows she has other family members.' Jack bit into his cake. 'This is scrumptious,' he said to May, then turned back to Sammy. 'What have you done with Ada?'

'She's spending my money.' Sammy licked his lips. 'Don't suppose I could have another bit of that cake?'

'No, you can't. Leave some for Ada, Greedy Guts. Have a sandwich instead,' said May.

Sammy made a face and raised his eyes heavenwards.

'What's Ada buying?' Vee wanted to know what her friend was up to. Sammy was very fond of her, but Vee hoped he wasn't going to steal Ada away until Peg went to school and she could find someone else to take over in the ticket office. She was going to be a stay-at-home mother.

'I sent her to buy some champagne that's better than the stuff I sell in my clubs,' he told her.

'What are we celebrating?' May asked.

'Hand over that newspaper,' said Sammy. Jack picked it up and threw it at him. He caught it neatly. 'I bet not one of you noticed this piece.'

'Haven't had chance to read it yet' and 'I've been too busy

for papers' came thick and fast. Sammy waved them all to be quiet and began to read from the middle pages. As he held it up, Vee saw that the front page was all about the milkmen's strike for higher wages.

'"Canada is introducing her own citizenship laws dealing with British subjects.

'"A conference decided each country should decide for itself, in its own way, what classes of persons were its own citizens. Each country would accept the citizens of every other Commonwealth country."

'Canada has led the way forward,' he said, looking up from the article in the newspaper. 'When we won the war and kicked Hitler into touch it opened all kinds of possibilities in changing laws that can only be better for everyone.'

'Does "classes of persons" mean each woman as well as men?' May was apprehensive.

'Let me read on and you'll get a better picture,' said Sammy.

'"Change in the law. 1946. No female British subject loses her nationality on marrying. Similarly, an alien marrying a British husband will not be deemed a British subject by marriage alone, but her naturalization will be made easier."'There was silence while each of them digested the information.

'So, no one will be able to point a finger at a woman who

marries a German and call her a German because she'll keep her British status?' asked May.

'Exactly,' said Sammy.

May began to cry, but between the sobs, she said 'Why, oh, why couldn't this have happened sooner? All the heartache, all the tears, the subterfuge, the burning of homes, the hatred . . .'

She turned from the card table and, oblivious of the newspaper crackling between their bodies, threw her arms around Sammy. 'You helped with this, you gave money to politicians to help . . .'

'May, May.' Sammy was stroking her hair. 'We all in our own way helped bring this about. Each of us has a story to tell of the inhumanity of man to man. But we didn't give up. Our boys fought and died in a war to prevent Hitler taking over Britain. We'll never be trodden down. But if it takes the powers that be a little longer to implement laws to keep our country strong, so be it. We're all only fallible human beings.'

May was still sniffing. Vee knew she was remembering Gus. At that moment Jem moved forward and took his wife in his arms.

Across the field a cloud of dust heralded the arrival of Sammy's car.

May glanced up. 'Can't that girl walk anywhere? Why

does she have to drive so fast?' She dabbed at her eyes. Vee knew her sharp words tried to mask the exhilaration she was feeling at the wonderful news. Good news that they all felt and were about to celebrate with champagne.

Vee reached for Jack's hand.

'I hope she'll go into the house and pick up some glasses,' said May. 'If not she can blooming well go back and get them.' She glared at Vee.

Vee felt Jack's hand stroke her distended abdomen. He whispered close to her ear, so close she felt the warmth of his breath, 'Say "Yes, Mum."'

'Yes, Mum,' she said.

She smiled fondly at her husband, the father of her forth-coming child.

Acknowledgements

To write this book I relied on journals borrowed from the wonderful staff at Gosport Museum and the Discovery Centre at Gosport. I took the liberty of modifying details, facts and events to suit my story. I am a writer of fiction, not fact. The characters – except for the main character, the ferry – bear no resemblance to any living persons.

I have travelled on the ferry boats all my life. Long may they continue to run.